There was a world-encompassing *blap!* and Roger was standing alone on a sheet of glass that stretched in every direction, shimmering confusingly along a band where the horizon ought to be. Uh-oh, Roger thought; I'm back at the Ultimate Locus. Not far away, a single object rested on the glass. Roger recognized it: it was the brand-new Schwinn he'd wished up that time, smashed by the impact as it had fallen from the sky at his command. No matter—what use would he have for a forty-foot bicycle, anyway?

"I have to be more careful this time," he cautioned himself. He raised his voice to call, "Car!" then added, "Parked by the bike, in perfect running order, with gas in the tank."

Without so much as a *whoosh!* of displaced air, the normal-sized '31 Model A-400 appeared, its convertible sedan styling as snappy as the day Edsel okayed it. Roger went over, looked inside at the shiny new fake leather upholstery in a fine shade of blue to match the shiny Washington Blue paint job. He got in, set the spark and gas, pulled out the choke, pushed the starter button with his toe; paused, switched on the ignition, and tried again. The little four-banger came to life with a contented "I think I can, I think I can."

Roger scanned the stretch of glass ahead for a hint as to which way he should go, saw something over *that* way and drove toward it. When he got close, he saw that it was *another* sixty-foot bicycle, smashed just like the other one. He turned to look back. There was no wrecked bicycle behind him.

"Oh, no," he groaned. "Back in the trap!"

BACK TO THE TIME TRAP

KEITH LAUMER

BAEN BOOKS

BACK TO THE TIME TRAP

Copyright © 1992 by Keith Laumer

A Baen Books Original

Baen Publishing Enterprises
P.O. Box 1403
Riverdale, N.Y. 10471

ISBN: 0-671-72127-5

Cover art by Dean Morrissey

First printing, July 1992

Distributed by
SIMON & SCHUSTER
1230 Avenue of the Americas
New York, N.Y. 10020

Printed in the United States of America

PROLOGUE

Roger Tyson was in his living room, sitting in a grossly overstuffed chair in a pink-and-yellow floral design, which, he realized, would appear grotesque to anyone who didn't know how much Sears had charged him for it. Q'nell came in from the kitchen with a plate of hot-from-the-oven tollhouse cookies and a glass of cold milk.

Roger looked up at his beautiful bride, whom he never called "Nellie," and admired for the zillionth time her perfect profile, her slender neck, and the soul-stirring curve of her right breast. Stifling the impulse to reach out and caress that organ, he picked up a cookie instead.

"This is the life, Nellie," he murmured, and pulled her down into his lap. *Prosser on Torts* fell to the floor with a forlorn *thump!*

"Stop it, silly," Q'nell ordered without conviction.

Just then the phone rang. Roger ignored it, but Q'nell picked it up. She listened with a puzzled expression and said hesitantly, "Yes, it is, but—" She recoiled slightly from the instrument in her hand.

"It's a Mr. Ucker," she told Roger, who put up a hand like a traffic cop.

"I'm not here!" he barked. "Besides, it *couldn't* be! That was all a delirium-dream, remember?"

Q'nell put the phone in his hand, patted his cheek, and went back into the kitchen, casting an anxious glance back at him.

"Never mind how I am!" Roger yelled into the phone, "And I am definitely NOT 'your boy'! And I don't care what dire calamity is about to befall the world! Solve it without my help!"

Roger's eye was caught by a quick movement over behind the home entertainment center, over seven hundred bucks at Simon's, on the blink, and not even paid for yet. His ire intensified. "Q'nell!" he yelled. "Bugs! As big as rats!"

Q'nell came back in, her expression one of mild curiosity.

"T'son," she said softly. "What—"

"Over there!" Roger barked. "Behind the telly! A huge black bettle! Don't you even know how to keep this place clean? If there were no food scraps lying around, bugs wouldn't be attracted!" He realized he was motormouthing and shut up abruptly.

"It's six P.M.!" he said suddenly, then changed his tone to a wheedling one: "Let's watch *Daphne's Dilemma.*" Without awaiting her agreement as she sat beside him, he used his new remote to switch on the TV. The screen flickered and brightened, showing a reddish, rutabaga-like entity with head-tentacles and sharp-pointed limbs like metallic crab-legs. Roger switched off and threw the control unit from him. Q'nell exclaimed and went after it. "Roger," she said reproachfully, using the name she employed only when seriously displeased with her mate's behavior.

"All right! All right!" Tyson groaned. "You see? He's already starting to ruin everything!"

"Oh! My casserole!" Q'nell exclaimed and headed for the kitchen.

"Didn't you see him?" Roger yelled after her.

Her pert features poked around the door. "See whom, dear?" she cooed.

"The Rhox!" Roger barked. "Instead of Daphne, we got the Rhox!"

"What rocks, Roger?"

"*The* Rhox!" Roger snapped. "That Oob fellow! Don't tell me you've forgotten!"

"Roger," Q'nell said reproachfully, coming back to sit beside him again and take his hand in hers. "Didn't we agree that was a delirium induced by the shock of the accident?"

"Sure," Roger agreed, "but we know we were lying!" He took her shapely chin in his hand and turned her face so that he could look into her eyes.

"The Trans-Temporal Bore," he said distinctly, "Culture One, and the null engine, and that damned love-nest contract with R'heet!"

"Roger, we agreed we'd never mention all that again."

"Right!" Roger gobbled. "But I *have* to. Didn't you see him on the TV just then?"

"Whom? Rheet?"

"No! Oob!" Roger corrected. "We agreed not to talk about him, but when I see him right here in our living room . . . ! And there was the phone call before that! It was UKR, warning me, or whatever; wanted me to volunteer for some kind of suicide mission!"

"Why, don't you do it, T'son."

"Don't worry!" Roger said fervently. "Do you think I'm crazy?"

She patted his hand. "Let's not go into that again, dear," she urged softly, looking concernedly into his eyes.

"Watch! I'll show you!" He retrieved the remote tuner and switched it on. The distraught face of a pretty young woman appeared, registering disquiet, or perhaps a bad smell.

"Don't be so upset, Daphne," Q'nell suggested. "Fenwick is coming back; he was only delayed by a flat tire."

"To Perdition with Fenwick!" Roger yelled. "The trouble with TV is they all just look like nice-looking young folks who came to Hollywood to see if maybe they could make it on the tube. Take Fenwick, there; he doesn't look like a brain surgeon—he looks like a TV actor!"

"I see what you mean, Roger," his bride agreed. "But is it worth getting all upset about?"

"It is if it means, wrecking my home!"

"Silly boy. It's only a soap opera. Fenwick is moving on Daphne, not me."

"That's not what I mean. I *saw* him! Just a second ago, right on the screen!"

"Certainly you did. That was just a flashback, so we'd know about the flat tire."

"I don't mean that! I mean that Rhox!"

"Oh, you mean that desert background in the Auburn ad. Lovely! They shoot all those ads in Arizona, I read in the *TV Guide*."

"What do you mean, 'Auburn ad'?" Roger demanded. "Auburn folded back in the Depression!"

"No, I mean Auburn-Cord-Deusenberg," Q'nell amplified. "The big car company."

"That's what *I* mean, too!" Roger cut her off. "There hasn't been an Auburn ad since 1933."

"Don't be silly, Roger," Q'nell urged. "They didn't even *have* TV in 1933!"

"Of course not!" Roger answered. "That's my point!"

"Why, didn't you like the lovely desert scenery?" Q'nell wondered. "I always thought you wanted to go there someday."

"I mean Oob!" Roger corrected. "With UKR phoning me, and Oob popping up on the tube, I feel like we're right back in the Time Trap!"

"But, Roger," Q'nell pointed out. "We *aren't*; we're right here at home, perfectly safe and happy. And your cookies are getting cold. You know you like them while the chocolate chips are still melted."

Roger grabbed one and stuffed it back. "Umm, delicious," he murmured. Q'nell kissed him. The phone rang again.

"Don't answer it!" Roger ordered, and resumed what he was doing.

"Roger, not right here in the living room," Q'nell objected mildly. She picked up the phone.

"Oh, yes, Mary," she said, nodding. "Tomorrow will be fine. About three, then?" She hung up. Roger grabbed the phone:

"UKR?" he yelled into it. "Leave me alone, dammit! I'm *not* going!"

Q'nell took the phone and cradled it again. "You weren't invited," she reported. "It's strictly a hen party."

"Look!" Roger blurted. "He's back!" He pointed to the screen, where Oob, his usual robust magenta darkened to a dull beet-red, was waving his tentacles wildly.

"Tyson!" he called. "Help! In the name of the Builder, help me! They're overwhelming the Control Center! Just come over here, I beg you!" His color faded to a sickly off-white. "Farewell!" he croaked. "I'm done for, Tyson! Perhaps if you act in time, you can still avert—" A shiny blue-black beetle-like creature obtruded between Oob and the camera. Roger just had time to glimpse rows of shredding-hooks on its momentarily exposed underside before it fell on Oob and his voice trailed off in an agonized wail as the creature began to devour him alive.

"Hold it! That's different!" Roger blurted, and rushed to the TV, where, behind the embattled Rhox, Daphne was now holding a match to the corner of a document, watching it begin to blacken and curl. "We have to stop it!" Roger groaned.

"Roger!" Q'nell interceded. "It's only the fake will she had Ben make up to fool Winslow into revealing himself! It's all right! Do sit down! You're spoiling the whole segment!"

"I'm not talking about that dopey soap," Roger retorted. "Didn't you see Oob just then, when he practically filled the screen—and that blue cockroach that was eating him?"

"I don't know what you mean," she said concernedly. "Do sit down, T'son, and tell me what you're talking about!"

"I'm talking about the damned Museum, or filing

system, or laboratory slides, or whatever!" Roger replied in a tightly controlled tone. "I know we agreed to forget the Trans-Temporal Bore and Culture One and all that, but nobody can really just *forget* something! And here it is back! Oob and UKR within five minutes of each other! They're trying to reinvolve us!"

"Why," Q'nell asked reasonably, "would anyone want to involve us, of all people, in such nonsense?"

"It's not nonsense!" Roger yelled, then, "I'm sorry, dear, I didn't mean to shout at you."

The TV burped and flashed spectral colors, then cleared to show a crisp, 3-D image of a lumpy shape like a potato, only dull red, with a wide, lipless mouth, a single enormous eye, and multiple appendages.

Roger stared. "But it's turned off!" he stated in a tone of astonishment, and pushed the OFF button again. There was no change, except that Oob extended a limb like a stainless-steel crab leg—out a good six inches beyond the glass surface of the screen, Roger realized wildly. The pincers-tipped member groped over the control knobs. The image brightened. Roger advanced, reached out and switched channels to UHF. Oob dwindled away for a moment, then reappeared, more vivid than before.

"Thank you, my boy," he said in his familiar gluey voice.

"What are you doing here?" Roger demanded, as Q'nell grasped his arm and tugged gently.

"If you'll just come and lie down awhile," she suggested.

He shook her hand off and whirled to face her. "Can't you *see* him?" he demanded. "It's Oob! You remember Oob! He was the rutabaga on the Yamaha who was chasing you the night we met!"

"That was part of the delirium, Roger," she chided. "We agreed—"

"I don't give a damn what we agreed!" Roger barked in a strangled voice as he attempted to suppress his fury at her imperturbability. He felt a touch from behind, and spun to face Oob, the Rhox, standing on pointed limbs not two feet away, while Daphne chattered on the screen behind him.

"There's no point in fighting it, lad," Oob told him sternly. "She can't see me: I'm in tight focus. There are imbalances in the Cosmic All which only you, due to your accumulation of Y-energies during your transit of the Bore, can remedy. Just come along quietly."

"Never!" Roger yelled, at which Oob sidled deftly past him to confront Q'nell. She smiled sweetly, Roger saw in the instant before he launched himself at the monster's back. Oob fended him off with a complicated thrust of ropy tentacles. Q'nell screamed.

"That's more like it!" Roger clutched her. "I know you didn't see as much as I did of Oob the last time, but anybody can see he's not somebody you'd want climbing out of your practically-new sixty-five-dollar Atwater Kent!" He released the sobbing girl and grabbed two of Oob's muscular tentacles; not without effort, he tied them in a square knot. Oob responded by turning a pale pink and uttering a despairing wail.

"How did you know?" he sobbed. "That sneaky UKR must have tipped you off that intertwining my prime manipulator with my tertiary stabilator-limb would inhibit the function of my stasis-node!"

"He did indeed!" Roger confirmed, wondering what the Rhox was talking about. "Now," he went on, maintaining the bluff, "if you'll just go back where you came from—"

"But how can I, with my node paralyzed?" Oob demanded. "If I should attempt to override—"

The doorbell *clang!*ed in the same instant that Oob ceased to be present. Roger was groping empty space, as Q'nell sank, sobbing, to the (truly hideous, Roger noted absently) floral-patterned carpet. He sprang to her as she sat up, looking dazed but unhurt.

"The door!" she said, and got to her feet. "Roger, *do* see who's there! It's probably poor Mary, wondering where I've gotten to."

Roger obediently went along the short hall and opened the fake old-English oak door, to admit an elderly gentleman of distinguished appearance, clad in a fur-collared overcoat. Behind him a vast and lovely Cadillac phaeton stood at the curb, a liveried driver at the wheel.

"Holy Moses!" the stranger said. "Roger! You haven't changed a bit! Not a bit, by golly. I'd have known you anywhere!" He seized Roger's limp hand and pumped it vigorously.

"Have we met?" Roger mumbled. "Come in, sir, come in."

The newcomer stepped inside, sniffed, looked down the hall and turned a puzzled expression on Roger.

"Why?" he demanded. "Why do you live here in *this* dump—I mean in such modest surroundings? You, the most amazing psychic of all time—and generous, too, no doubt about that! You could be living like a king—like me!" He caught a glimpse of Q'nell as she came along the brown-papered entry-hall.

"Ah, my dear!" he bleated. "You, too, look just as you did the last time I saw you, there in the trench at St. Mihiel! So charming! But I still don't understand! You're *him*, and he's you, and yet you're not! But I only came to express my gratitude, whoever each of you are, or is, or whatever!

"After the war," the old fellow went on, "I was able to trace you by the billfold you dropped, you know; I wanted to return it, and to find out why, in Heaven's name, a beautiful young woman was wandering about on the battlefield!" He paused. "You can imagine my amazement when I found that the owner of the wallet was actually a *man*, just as the name 'Roger Tyson' suggested. But anyway, here you *both* are, and so am I! I acted on your tips, of course, my dear, and got out of Consolidated Wagon and Buggy just in time. I tell you, they were dropping like flies all along the Street that black October day! But not Charles S. Shlumph, nosirree! I had mine! I weathered the Depression, and when World War Two started up, I was able to endow a Hopeless Alcoholic Unit in honor of Ron, and, yes, Ludwig, too! After all, we all shared the same hardships, so why cut him out just because he happened to be on the losing side, eh? After all, my own great-grandfather came from Pomerania! Got through that one OK too, thanks to my aircraft stocks, and I've been looking for you ever since, to thank you!"

"Just who—" Roger started, then looked surprised as a ghostly Mazda lamp of one hundred watts appeared above his head.

"Charlie Shlumph! In the trench!" he blurted. "There was this German with the terrible 'yokes,' and the Englishman, and an American—you! I almost recognize you now! I told you about the future! Warned you about the Crash, and then—"

"Then you turned sideways and disappeared," Charlie supplied. "We hunted for you, explored the trench half a mile in each direction, and not a trace of you did we find! Not even a footprint! That's why I determined to find you and have you explain that whole bizarre incident. Ron didn't survive the war, poor boy, and Ludwig was all caught up in Herman Göring's World Peace Movement, so thereafter . . . anyway, please explain."

"It was like this," Roger replied. "At that particular moment, Q'nell and I had temporarily exchanged bodies, so while it was me there in the trench, I looked like I was her. OK so far?"

"No!" Charlie stated with feeling. "Go on!"

"Well, we finally got that straightened out, and met UKR in person, and got Oob quieted down, and arrived at the Terminal Locus, and found out from the Builder all about the Bore."

"Bored?" Charlie queried. "By no means, kiddo! I don't claim to understand, but who said I have to understand? My net worth, thanks entirely to your tip, is just a bit over ten billions, and—"

" 'Ten billions'?" Roger gasped. "You mean dollars?"

"I don't mean Burmese *kyats*!" Charlie confirmed. "Anything you wish that money can accomplish is yours!" He beamed, his smile fading as his gaze drifted past the Tysons to the room behind them. He edged back, looking horrified.

"It's the Thing!" he squeaked. "The Nightmare Thing! I first caught a glimpse of it back in the trenches; since then it's pursued me in nightmares, and a few times I thought I caught a glimpse of it in a crowd, or across the street—but it's *here! Now!* Right in your living room! I'm going mad!"

Roger caught his arm. "No, you're not crazy," he soothed. "That's just Oob."

"It's . . . coming this way!" Charlie gasped and pulled free of Roger's grip. He blundered toward the door.

"I'll go for help," he croaked.

Behind Roger, Oob spoke up. "Kindly calm your friend, T'son," it urged reasonably. "I'm here to warn you—"

"Threats!" Charlie yelled. "It's uttering dire threats! Shoot it!"

"There is a clear distinction between the denotations of the forms 'threaten' and 'warn,' " Oob pointed out didactically. "Even in *your* simple language. Pray don't waste time shooting me: I'm truly weary of the bother of replacing these simple third-order extrusions every time you people destroy one. It's quite pointless, you know. Aren't you interested in what it is about which I've come to warn you?"

Roger whirled to face the grotesque creature, at the same time drawing Q'nell to his side. "Go ahead," he snapped. "Whatever it is, you have no right to burst in here in that silly fashion, crawling out of the TV and scaring my wife to death!"

"I simply moved my Aperture into congruity with the glass surface," Oob explained patiently, "in order to avoid upsetting you."

"Sure!" Roger retorted hotly. "We see rutabagas climbing out of the middle of *Daphne* every day!"

"Kindly desist from referring to my extrusion as a 'rutabaga,' " Oob requested testily. "The relationship is remote."

"So what's this big warning?" Roger demanded. Q'nell hugged his arm.

"The Bore has been broached at many points," Oob

told them solemnly. "By an alien life-form introduced, accidentally, I suppose, by those infernal meddlers of Culture One again. I should have sterilized that place as soon as I saw it."

"That's a terrible thing to say!" Q'nell burst out. "Even though there *are* some pretty ridiculous people there, it *is* a very highly evolved society, with many commendable traits! Are you sure it was old R'heet and his I-team who—?"

"It hardly matters, my dear," Oob told her. "The salient point is, the Bore is seriously compromised. You know what that means!" He displayed a gnawed-looking tentacle. "The monsters tried to eat me alive," he added.

"Yes, I saw." Roger felt, and looked, horrified. "You don't mean . . . ?"

"Precisely," Oob confirmed, almost smugly, and withdrew.

"That's probably what UKR was trying to tell me," Roger lamented. He turned back toward the garishly papered, carpeted, and slipcovered living room, Q'nell beside him, Charlie trailing.

"Say, Misternmiz Tyson," the veteran said to their backs, "I guess you're wondering what it is I came to see you about—" He broke off short as a probing, jointed, metallic limb poked from the TV screen.

"Say, that's a funny place to have a winder!" he exclaimed.

Roger went over to the tube and said, "Shoo!" and Oob's leg was withdrawn.

Charlie came over and looked at the black screen. "What is it, Tyson?" he inquired. "Got all them knobs on it. What's it for? Some kinda radio?"

"Sort of," Roger agreed. "Only with a picture, too."

"A picture o' what?" Charlie demanded.

"A moving picture; in color," Roger amplified.

Charlie showed his gums in a wintry smile. "OK, Roger, forget I ast. No need to go smarting off."

"I'm *not* 'smarting off,' you damned old fool!" he yelled. "If you weren't so ignorant—"

Q'nell touched his arm and he fell silent. Q'nell smiled at Charlie. "He's upset," she explained. "Do forgive him."

"Sure, honey, no offense," Charlie mumbled. "I just come by to . . ."

Roger noticed a stray buckle evidently torn from Oob's complicated harness; he picked it up and tossed it through the portal. Charlie goggled.

"Oh, a garbage disposer!" he declared, and tossed a crumpled Luckies package after the button; it bounced off the glass, and Charlie recovered it. "Ain't as easy as it looked," he complained.

Roger switched the set on, and at once Daphne's tormented features appeared, reciting a speech of welcome to her mother who, having been reported dead, had reappeared suddenly.

"I get it!" Charlie cried, "Garbage in, garbage out!" Absently, he pulled over an ottoman and sat down, his eyes fixed on the screen. He frowned. "But what good's *that*?" he demanded.

Roger grabbed up the telephone and dialed the office of the sheriff. There was no answer. He put a protective arm around Q'nell.

"There's no telling when that damned Rhox will pop out of there again," he griped. "We have to *do* something! I think I'll go down to Withers' Hardware and ask Chuck to send a man out to repair it!"

"But, T'son," Q'nell objected, "it's not broken; it's just that Oob has aligned his Aperture with the screen!"

"Didn't you hear him?" Roger barked. "The Bore is compromised 'at many places'! We'll have camels in the park, wild Indians charging up Main Street, and extinct critters lurking in the hedges!" he predicted wildly. "We *have* to do what we can!" He went to the front door and stepped out, carefully not slamming the door. "Women!" he snorted. "Offering you cookies while the continuum falls apart!" He got into the car and headed down the street.

CHAPTER ONE

Bob Armstrong got out of bed and into the shower. As the hot water sluiced away the gummy veil of drowsiness, he glanced out the small window he had installed in the shower cubicle to allow him to look at his garden while he bathed. He looked, he stared, he goggled. A wall of deep-blue ice loomed half a mile away, and a group of rather bedraggled deer, reindeer, or caribou—you know, the ones with the clumsy-looking antlers and big feet—were grazing half-heartedly on the sparse lichen growing on the rock precisely where his rose bed ought to be. The garage was gone, an arm of ice extending out from the glacier having pushed it aside.

Bob got it together after a full minute and dashed for the phone, punching in the sheriff's number.

"Zzzz, pop, zzz. *I'm* sawry, that number is *nawt* in service," a canned voice told him.

"Certainly it is, you damned fool!" he yelled back. "That's the sheriff's office!" The recording said it again. Bob slammed the phone down, knocking the little capsule-shaped light bulb out of it. He stalked to the bedroom window and yanked the curtain aside. Where the expanse of more or less neat suburban houses had covered the gentle slope, a lumpy snowfield stretched unbroken to the wall of ice, bits of roof and siding poking from it.

"The hothouse effect!" Bob protested. "Where is it? We're not supposed to have an ice age, we're supposed to drown when sea level rises because the ice caps have melted, because of the CO^2 has built up, because ..." He ran out of "becauses" and went back in and turned off the shower and dried himself on a big, fluffy towel, then got dressed in the shirt and slacks he always wore for his foursome on Saturdays.

At the door, he paused. The air was definitely nippy. He reached in the closet and pulled out the heavy jacket he used in the winter when he went out to bring in firewood. He felt foolish pulling it on in midsummer, but when he stepped outside, he was glad he had done so. It was *cold* out here! And—

"No," he corrected himself, "There *isn't* a mastodon grazing on Fred Meyer's lawn! Couldn't be!" He backed inside, grabbed up the phone on the hall table, the one he hardly ever used, and tried the sheriff again. Busy signal: *gawp! gawp! gawp!* He dropped it and stepped outside again.

To his left, he saw a dense stand of large, and clearly old, spruce, where yesterday. Austin Street had run past. He slammed the door behind him and stalked off into the snow, not looking toward Meyer's lawn. "Damned government, messing with the climate!" he reassured himself. Looking back, he saw that his house was the only undamaged one in sight, the drift of lumpy ice and snow being pushed by the glacier having forced the others off their foundations. Shocking! Even as he watched, the heaped glacial debris heaved and the moraine advanced another twenty feet. It was almost touching his back porch now.

By late afternoon, after he had tramped through the three-inch snow layer, all unmarked by other footprints, he noted uneasily, to visit the city cop-house, the sheriff's office and the Storm, or state troopers station, finding all three deserted, he decided to try Henessey's; there were always a few fellows there, to talk to.

Henessey's was a large former harness store converted into a big, cheerful saloon the year before Prohibition. It was open, but deserted. Only Paddy, the cat, was there, rubbing against Bob's shins in greeting. Bob called, but there was no reply. Suddenly acutely lonely, he tried the pay phone. It told him in a tone of reproach, that the number listed for the mayor's office was "*nawt* in service!" He punched "O" for operator and got nothing. Back in the street, he heard a dull rumbling sound, punctuated by louder *crash!es*, coming from the north. He walked toward the sound. At an intersection, he looked over that way and saw another lobe of the glacier, this one closer, already moving into the downtown area. He watched the six-story Gazette tower shake, shedding ornamentation, then fold wearily in the middle and drop with surprising suddenness out of sight in a cloud of dust.

Bob went to the nearest car parked at the curb; the driver's door opened when he tried the handle. Feeling a little guilty, he hot-wired the ignition, checked the gas gauge, and pulled out into the snow-covered street. No other traffic moved. Then he saw someone ahead and accelerated toward him. It was a young fellow in a black jacket; he had run from a store into the middle of the street. Two others joined him, then more, until a dozen or so youths occupied the middle of the intersection. Each seemed to have a bag of some sort in his hands, and each had emerged from a different store. Looters!

On impulse, Bob braked, pulled to the curb in front of Withers' Hardware. The lock was broken; he could see the splintered wood of the jamb from the car. He hurried inside, feeling guilty, and bent over the display of hunting weapons in a glass-topped case. He picked up the Remington ten-gauge he had long coveted. He found a small duffel bag and filled it with fat, heavy boxes of ammunition, paused at the counter to put three twenties and a ten under the pad the cash register was sitting on, and hurried back to his stolen car. The gang was closer, talking loudly to each other. He saw they were headed for a new pickup parked in front of Dick's Cut Rate Liquors.

As he drove slowly toward them, they spread out in a ragged line across the street and made gestures in his direction; then one ran to the nearest car, a heavy late-model Lincoln, and pulled it out crossways into the street, thus effectively blocking the way.

Bob edged to the left to go behind it, and the line broke and rushed him. One grinning lad smashed his windshield with his bag of loot, the glass shards just missing Bob's eyes. Bob braked hard, then gunned it, sending the attacker sliding off. He made it past the back bumper of the Lincoln.

The rest of the thugs were close now; he accelerated and two of the unwashed teenagers had to leap to avoid being hit. In the mirror he saw them pause to direct poisonous looks after him; then a fusilade began, as the scum threw objects from their grab bags, which bounced off the car. One made a solid hit on the side window, inches from Bob's jaw, but the glass held; then he was past. He drove off, and the yells receded behind him.

Around a corner, he pulled into a parking lot to load his shotgun. As he finished, the Lincoln pulled up beside him on the passenger side; the jolly boys piled out, fanning out in a semicircle around the car. Most of them were wearing fur jackets designed as ladies' wear, with TIGER crudely painted on their backs in blue. One or two had pistols, which they handled awkwardly.

They stood and peered uncertainly in at Bob until he got out of the car and looked over the top at them. They began to edge closer, and he reached inside and brought out the Remington and laid it across the top of the car. The boy under his sights was a burly, red-haired degenerate, with LUMP painted over his pocket. He raised his hands as if to ward off a slap and began babbling.

"Please, Mister, I didn't do nothing. . . . Me and my friends here, we need help!"

"You're lucky," Bob told the momentarily nonplussed

group. "I'm Big Jake Gronek; eleven homicides—and I'm going to give you a break because you didn't know that. Now scram! I'll only shoot the last one in sight. Now!" He cocked the weapon. They ran in all directions, shoving each other aside to reach cover first. When the last of them had disappeared down an alley, unshot, Bob released a breath and clicked on the safety, tossed the piece inside the car, and got in. Good thing they didn't know he was really just a draftsman.

He was sitting behind the wheel, considering his next move, when a cop car came around the corner and parked across from him. A fat cop got out. Bob rolled down the window and called cheerfully:

"Top o' the morning to ye, Ossifer!"

The cop replied with a scowl and allowed his hand to rest on the flap of the holster at his hip.

"Watcher doing here, Mister?" the representative of Law and Order barked, all set to stimulate his gonads with an exercise of petty authority. "This here area has been evacuated," he told Bob in a domineering tone. "What's yer name?"

"Fred Hiesenwhacker, sir," Bob said timidly.

"Well, Fred," the cop drawled. "Looks like you got a little explaining to do." He glanced inside the car, saw the shotgun, and recoiled.

"Now, just don't go getting excited!" he urged.

"I'm perfectly calm, Ossifer," Bob reassured the anxious beadle.

"Now, I was just asting, sir, you unnerstan'," the cop explained. "What you're doing here, sir, if you don't mind my asting? Town's been evacuated, you know. The ice—well, I guess you know all about that, same's me."

"Not quite," Bob corrected. "Tell me about it."

The cop removed his cap, ran a finger around the sweatband and replaced it on his lumpy head. "Sweating—in this here cold snap," he commented. "But the ice—seems like it's got something to do with the nucular tests in the atmosphere the Realigned Underdeveloped Nations' Tribunal has been running in the North Pacific.

They say—the scientist fellers say—RUNT blowed a few cubic miles o' coral dust up there, and cut down on the sunlight, or like that. The ice cap started to grow and now it's all the way down here to Brantville. Been moving ever'body out to the relocation camps. How's come you're still here?"

"I'm a scoutmaster," Bob told the curious cop. "Looking after the troop, you know; the little rascals dodged me, though. I saw some of them go up the alley there. Better see to it they're cared for."

"Absolutely!" the cop agreed. "Pore little kids running around here, loose, nobody to see they get their lunch and everything. See you around, Scoutmaster." He set off toward the alley mouth. Bob sighed and had just decided to rest his eyes for a moment when he saw something move at the limit of his peripheral vision. He looked again. A squat, bulbous *something* with tentacles, moving swiftly on crab-like legs that clattered softly on the greasy blacktop, was busy at a rank of garbage cans. Bob squeezed his eyes shut and opened them suddenly, as if to catch himself off guard. The monstrous shape was still there.

"Must be hungry," Bob hypothesized. "Looking for something to eat." Against his will, he started up, backed, and swung the car around to come up alongside the rummaging monstrosity. It turned a single large and baleful eye on him, dropped the garbage-can lid with a dreadful clatter and darted in close to Bob's open window.

"Say, Tyson," it said, alarmingly.

Bob stared at the foot-wide mouth which had opened where a fellow would expect the ribs to be. "Name's not 'Tyson,' " he grunted.

"Oh, of course," Oob concurred. "All you fellows look alike to me. Just wait here a moment and I'll get right back to you. This is disastrous!" he added. "I'd no idea—" He fled.

Just then, Bob noticed the sound of a car. The street gang! He looked around wildy, and saw a normally dusty year-old Chevy four-door turn in at the lot and pull over beside his car. Roger Tyson, his eyes fixed on the stranger, got out.

"Hi!" he called. "You haven't seen anything of a rutabaga, have you?"

"He was just here!" Bob blurted. "He had all these legs and tentacles and things! He seemed upset about something. He'll be right back."

"You're taking it calmly," Roger observed. "Aren't you curious as to who or what he was?"

"Nope," Bob replied cheerfully. "I'm more concerned about *that*." He pointed. Roger's eyes casually followed in the indicated direction; he gazed at the fissured, chalk-white mountain just over on Third for a full minute before its significance dawned on him.

"Come on," he said to Bob. "I think Oob came this way; we've got to find him and—"

"Who's 'Kube'?" Bob wanted to know. "Slow down, pal, things are going a little too fast for me! Where *is* everybody? Some cop came along and told me RUNT has been doing dirty nuclear tests or something, loaded up the atmosphere with dust, and—"

"Nonsense!" Tyson cut him off. "It's all the fault of—well, I don't exactly know who's fault it is, but there are these holes in the Trans-Temporal Bore, see? And somehow the Pleistocene has gotten superimposed on Now, or vice versa, and—"

"All I caught was something about a 'tempermental bore,'" Bob interrupted. "That ice is headed this way, and if something isn't done, by next year it will cover the place where Brantville used to be!"

"Sure, sure, I know all that," Roger answered the excited fellow. "A cop, you say? Where'd he go?"

"Down the alley," Bob supplied. "The same one the Tigers went down. Probably done for. Didn't hear any gunfire."

"Tiger?" Roger echoed. "Odd; another anomaly. This is getting serious. Gunfire?" he reacted belatedly. "What gunfire?"

"Didn't hear any," Bob repeated.

"Then what are we talking about?" Roger demanded.

"Talking about the glacier sprang up overnight," Bob told him disgustedly. "You got a mind like a grasshopper, pal," he carped.

"I'm sure you mentioned gunfire!" Roger insisted. His eyes went past Bob to the shotgun in the car seat. "What was that about tigers?" he demanded.

"Not *Panthera tigris*," Bob explained. "A street gang."

"Who'd you shoot?" Roger demanded.

"Who, me?" Bob said in a tone of wonderment. "*You* hear any gunfire?"

"There you go again about gunfire," Roger complained. "We've got trouble enough without starting any irresponsible shooting!"

"Never fired it," Bob stated, his eyes following Roger's to the Remington. "Nice weapon," he grunted. "We might need it yet," he added.

"I tried to phone the cop-house," Roger told Bob. "All of 'em. No answer. They're probably out chalking tires."

"That, or posing for TV cameras showing how they help little kids cross the street," Bob agreed glumly. "Where are they when you *need* one?"

"They know better than to stick their nose in if there's real trouble," Roger reminded him. "Mess around with actual lawbreakers, a fellow could get hurt."

"Let's try the bank," Bob suggested. "They couldn't move out so fast; have all that cash and papers to move." The First National was at the center of the block, an incongruous Roman Revival facade between painted cast-iron fronts from the 1880s. Roger and Bob went up and through the big glass doors—and stopped short. They were back outside, looking across a broad plaza lined with unfamiliar buildings. The great ice-cliff was not in sight.

As Roger and Bob went back down the marble steps of the First National, they heard a sound from just around the corner.

"A sort of metallic scraping," Roger tried to explain to Bob, who was nodding. Both men had halted to stare toward the source of the noise. It came again, louder. Then a shiny blue-black rod appeared from behind the brick building on the corner, six feet above the pavement. It twitched, waved around aimlessly. Another appeared, then a large pointed object of the same glossy midnight-blue poked out hesitantly.

"That reminds me of something," Roger blurted. "Wait up, Bob!" he called after the latter, who had started on; he halted as a glistening blue-black creature the size of an M-20 tank hove into view. The rods were its antennae, the pointed thing a leg, of which, Bob quickly saw, it had six—their scrabbling on the concrete was the source of the sound they had heard.

"Ye gods!" Bob yelped. "It's some kind of giant bee-tle!" At his shout, the creature, for there appeared no doubt it was alive, shifted its bulk so as to bring an immense compound eye to bear on Bob. Then it lurched toward him. Greenish matter was trailing from a gaping wound on its abdomen.

"It's hurt!" Bob yelled, and fled up the steps. Roger followed, barely avoiding the advancing behemoth. Inside the lobby, he overtook Bob.

"It's one of those bugs invading Oob's level," he told the uncomprehending draftsman. "Only bigger."

"You mean there's more than one?" Bob demanded. "I'd call that overkill." He went back to the entrance to peer out at the plaza.

"It's gone," he reported. "It couldn't have gotten clear that fast on its own, so it must have had help."

"Sure," Roger agreed. "There's millions of 'em, all sizes from step-on to anti-tank gun."

"Where'd they come from?"

"I'm a little hazy on that," Roger admitted. "From another energy level, is all I can say for sure."

"What's that mean?" Bob insisted.

"It's all these divisions in the Meniscus. They got in, and now they're invading in force. They tried to eat Oob."

"Roger," Bob said sternly. "Just level with me: why

didn't I ever see one of those giant beetles before, if they've invaded in force?"

"They're not all giant," Roger explained. "You've probably seen and squashed lots of small ones. And the invasion just recently happened. I guess. Hard to say, with the temporal flux all mixed up like it is."

"Oh," Bob said. "Meanwhile, let's try to do something intelligent."

CHAPTER TWO

When Rusty Naill ran out of gas, he was about a quarter mile from the beach. He said "Damn!" without conviction and unshipped his oars. After casting a glance at the palm forest backing up the white sand beyond the surf, he settled down to pull strongly for shore. The wind wasn't helping any; looked like rain, too.

After half an hour of exertion in the noonday sun, he was tired, blistered, totally fed up, and in trouble in the surf. A six-foot comber had half-swamped his flat-bottomed skiff, and when he had lunged to save his tackle box, which went anyway, he managed to fall overboard. Dog-paddling frantically across the face of a comber, he caught a glimpse of the small boat upside-down before it was smashed down on the hard sand. Doggedly, he swam for shore. When his feet touched bottom, he stood and waded the rest of the way, or at least until a breaker slammed his back and knocked him down. His groping hand made contact with his tackle box, which he clung to as he got to his feet. The lid had been knocked open and the box was empty. He tossed it aside.

Cursing silently, Naill plodded up onto dry sand and sat down. He glanced idly out to sea and was startled to see what at a distance looked like 'one of those old galleons or whatever; closer, pulling hard for shore, a big rowboat manned by swarthy fellows in head-bandannas like movie pirates. One of them even had an earring.

Rusty eased over behind a clump of palmetto and lay flat, wondering why he was hiding. Probably the idea of pirates, he scoffed at himself.

The rowers drove the heavy whaleboat through the surf to ground its prow on the beach. The men, harangued by a big fellow with bristly black whiskers, lifted a large and apparently heavy steamer trunk over the side of the boat and staggered with it high up the slope of the beach, almost to the palms, until Blackbeard—" 'Blackbeard,' ha!" Rusty said sarcastically to himself—yelled; then they dropped the chest and the other men came forward with shovels. Sand flew as they plied their digging utensils enthusiastically.

One man stepped back, wiped his brow and spoke to the whiskery fellow, who drew from his waistband a long-barreled pistol of antique design and fired it, point-blank, into the other man's midsection, throwing the victim three feet onto his back.

The other men paid no attention at all. Rusty scrooched down even closer to the itchy white sand. "They must be making a movie!" Rusty told himself, not believing it. He looked around as much as he dared, without lifting his head. The view was of totally deserted beach in both directions. "No cameras in sight," he reported. "Must be some kind of telephoto equipment." He felt uneasy for a moment, wondering if the electronic eye was on him, then reminded himself that if there were cameras, there was nothing to worry about.

Just then one of the men came striding in his direction. Rusty scrooched even closer to the sand. The fellow came directly up to the palmetto, and urinated two feet from Rusty's head. Funny, he thought, how a fellow always liked to pee *against* something; probably went back to the instinct to mark the territory.

The little group on the beach had finished digging,

and were lowering the box into the excavation. Then they tumbled the dead man in, and refilled the hole. When the spot was neatly smoothed over, the whiskery fellow yelled something, and the party fell in ranks and shuffled back to their boat and rowed out toward their galleon.

Rusty relaxed and even scratched a few of his insect bites. When the ship, all sails set, was a mere speck, he stood and strolled over to the scene of the minidrama. The gravesite was easy to see, being well marked with footprints. Rusty stood looking down at it, trying to assimilate the fact that a man was buried there—a fellow who, only ten minutes ago, had been alive and scratching, just like him. . . . This line of thought led nowhere Rusty wanted to go. He looked around again for the concealed cameras, and saw nothing. He decided to go up over the sea-oats and out to the highway, flag down a car, and get to the sheriff's office to report the murder. He plodded upslope, the dry sand squeaking under his boots, and from the top of the slight rise, looked at the dense growth of sabal palms ahead.

"No road," he remarked to himself. "That's funny." For a moment he felt disoriented, as his memory automatically pulled back to his reason for being down at the beach in midmorning, when he ought to be out setting his nets before the damned tourists in the cattle-boats stirred everything up.

Nothing; except he'd gotten his boat swamped as if he was some tourist instead of a licensed captain. He looked, saw the skiff upside down above the tide-line; the oars were nearby.

"Dammit!" Naill swore. He must have been hung over to let a thing like that happen. He took inventory of his aches and pains: Nope, not hung over; feel good. Better get back. He set off toward his boat, idly wondering why he couldn't make out the Don-Ce-Sar up the beach. The old dump was hard to miss since they gave it that new pink paint-job last year. He glanced up at a sound; a lumbering Coast Guard Consolidated PBY flying boat was cruising past, just like during the war. Rusty watched a ghost crab duck into its hole. A fifty-pound jewfish was attracting flies just above the surf-line.

"Damn red tide again," he thought, resentfully. "They oughta spend some money curing the tide, instead of shipping cargos of cash to places most folks never heard of to buy gold beds for local gang-leaders."

That reminded him of the crew in the rowboat. He glanced out to sea, and it looked like—by God, the boat was coming back! Must have seen him! He went past the sea-grape bushes and over the rise and, having no choice, into the palm jungle.

CHAPTER THREE

It was two A.M., and Julian was sitting at a table on the sidewalk across from the farmer's market, eating his onion soup and reflecting on the curious events of the day: first, that crazy old woman at the pension, yelling broken French at him and flapping her apron as if she were shooing away geese, when he came down for break-fast. Then the crowd in the street, clustered around some shop; looked like it just had paintings in the window, but people were yelling and even throwing things. He had skirted the crowd, netting a few dirty looks from the fringe participants, and had strolled on over to the river, and pretty soon a clatter broke out up the side street, and a horse with big blinkers on his head, and broken harness-straps flying, came galloping down and across the grass strip and pulled up hard at the water's edge. Julian decided he needed a more peaceful spot in which to sit down and think, so he went along past the usual rank of sad-looking fellows displaying awful bad paintings on easels, and into a bookshop. A big, burly fellow with a mustache was examining his own right fist, while a slender, artistic-looking young fellow harangued him.

"I'm telling you, Wemedge," the latter was declaring
vehemently. "He's *great*! Some day—"

"Skip it, Scott," the burly man snapped, and walked
away. Julian looked at the books on the nearest shelf.
Brand-new dust jackets gleamed in garish colors. Above,
dull cloth bindings bore almost illegible titles in faded
gold-leaf.

"*A History of the Pre-Raphaelite Movement* by Felix
Severance," he managed to decipher. He was about to
take the old volume down when a sprightly dark-haired
young woman came up and inquired, in English, if she
could be of help.

"Oh, I see you know Felix's work," she changed the
subject. "*So* sensitive! Too bad he doesn't know what to
be sensitive about."

"Sylvia, that sounded like a dirty crack," the artistic
fellow in the gray flannel spoke up. "Felix is just a little
ahead of his time."

The big man playfully punched his shoulder and said,
"Come on, Scotty; time for an aperitif."

Julian took the chair offered by Sylvia and took a deep
breath of calm, peaceful bookstore air.

"This is what I like about Paris," he told himself. "This
could be almost any day in the last two hundred years,
except for the clothing styles, of course, and the cars."
Just then a car backfired in the street outside. Julian
looked around to see a beautifully-restored Citroën, from
about the twenties, he guessed, cruising past, chauffeur-
driven. The driver was hunched over the big sticking-
straight-up steering wheel, his mustache bobbing as he
spoke to the machine.

Julian rose, thanked Sylvia and went back out into the
fresh-ground-coffee and fresh-baked-bread aroma of the
street and crossed over, ducking another restored
antique—must be some kind of old-car do going on, he
realized—and into a café.

His coffee was superb, and the croissant as light as a
feather boa. Julian sighed with contentment, then shivered as he saw *something*—he couldn't put a name to

it—came hesitantly through the door. At first he thought it was alive, then quickly realized that a thing like a bushel-sized rutabaga, with waving tentacles and spiky, lobster-like limbs, couldn't possibly be a living creature; then changed his mind when it turned its single large, blue eye on him. He rose and backed away as it veered to come directly toward him.

"Hi, Roger," said a glutinous voice, which Julian was forced to acknowledge came from a foot-wide mouth like a sabre wound.

"I'm n-not Roger," Julian told the entity. "I was just browsing, you know. . . ."

"No, of course you're not Roger," the thing acknowledged readily. "Wrong locus entirely. But still, perhaps you'd be able to assist me in any case."

Julian rose hastily and fled back to the bookstore. "S-Sylvia," Julian called. The dark-haired young woman was at his side at once, making soothing sounds.

"Sorry about yelling like that," Julian said, "But what is *that*?" He pointed to the rutabaga now jittering in the doorway. Her eyes followed.

"Oh, that's just a little rough spot I'm having planed and refinished," she said as if in explanation. "People used to trip over it."

"I don't mean the *floor!*" Julian cut her off sharply. "For heaven's sake, Sylvia, I mean *that!*" His finger was almost touching Oob's nearest tentacle.

"It's so rude to point," Oob snapped. "She can't perceive me, Roger. I'm in tight focus. Come along, my boy, we'd best talk in private." He went past the chair toward a curious line of flickering light that seemed to have sprung up in mid-air. The line swelled, like an edge-on disk rotating to face him, Julian thought. Oob approached it—and abruptly the outré creature was gone. Julian sat down on a low table of paperbacks, rubbed a hand across his face, and looked appealingly at Sylvia.

"Didn't you *see* it?" he pled. "It was like a rutabaga, only bigger, with tentacles or something, and an eye at the top, and externally-jointed legs below. It *spoke* to me, called me 'Roger.'"

"No, Julian," the woman said quietly. "I didn't see it, but it's gone now, isn't it? Let's just pretend it was never here, shall we?" She was backing away as she spoke.

Julian sighed and looked at the spot where the apparition had vanished. "Hallucinations," he muttered. Then. "Sorry, Sylvia, just a little game I was playing." As he spoke, he watched the tip of an externally-jointed leg poke out from nothingness, grasping as if for purchase, and a moment later the apparition was back, staring at him with its lone eye, now looking baleful, rather than benign.

"Come along, fellow!" it barked. For a moment, Julian didn't understand. He hesitated, one of Oob's tentacles made a grab, then wrapped around his arm and tugged, thrusting him toward the glowing disk. Julian tried unsuccessfully to avoid the shimmering surface, but was quickly pushed to it—and *through* it. He stumbled, but maintained his equilibrium. He stared around wildly: a complex structure of polished rods and crystal planes rose from a stretch of smooth-mowed lawn. He spied a bricked path and went to it. The rutabaga was nowhere to be seen.

He had to go back! Julian turned, saw the oil-on-water-colored patch hanging there, impossibly, two feet above the grass. He leapt for it, tripped over his feet, and fell heavily. At once hands grasped his arms, helping him up.

"Sorry about that, old man," an unctuous voice said almost in his ear. "We were trying to bag that Rhox, you understand, and somehow snagged you up, quite by accident."

"Sure!" Julian burst out, jerking free of the grip on his arm. "You're out collecting geological specimens, so my quiet afternoon turns into a waking nightmare!" He paused to take a breath and to look around for the rutabaga, but saw only a waiting stretcher and a small group of white-clad men and a few women—not bad, he noted, eyeing a truly lovely blonde girl. At once, he

smoothed his lapels, gave his slicked-back hair a swipe
of the hand, and arranged a more dignified expression
on his face.

Amazing! his every-action-observer-mind commented.
*At a moment like this, I'm automatically moving to give
her the impression I'm a dominant, self-assured male,
quite capable of providing food for a mate and her young!*

Even as he derided himself, he was elbowing past the
handsome if slightly jowly fellow who had helped him up,
to zero in on the blonde beauty. She smiled tentatively at
his intent gaze and shifted her pose slightly to emphasize
the curve of her hips (able to bear his son), her breast
(able to feed his son), and her thigh (able to outrun
predators, human and animal).

"Hi," Julian said, quite overwhelmed by the glossy,
pale hair and rose-petal cheeks (healthy female). "I'm
Julian." He extended a hand tentatively. *"Bon jour,"* he
offered. *"Je m'appelle Julian."*

"Why?" the beauty inquired.

Julian paused in his assault. " 'Why,' what?"

"Why do you call yourself 'J'lan?" she asked
interestedly.

"Well, I don't actually call myself," he improvised.
"But that's what Mater named me," he amplified, a bit
of annoyance in his tone.

"Oh, you needn't be angry, J'lan," the girl chided and
took his hand in her amazingly soft and warm one, tugging him imperceptibly (almost) closer to all those beguil-
ing charms.

"I'm M'liz," she told him, parting her poignantly
curved lips to show perfect teeth (able to eat and stay
healthy).

"Well, Liz," Julian stammered as he felt the pressure
of those well-formed mammaries against his chest. "Oh,
sorry!" he blurted, recoiling slightly. Her face was an
inch from his now. Her breath was as delicate as the
fragrance of a spring bouquet. Her lips were so soft, he
thought in delight. *And the way her pelvis fits against*

my belly and legs in amazing! Say! I like this place! What a red-hot mama this one is!

A firm hand on his shoulder tugged him back.

"Look here, fellow!" the male voice barked, not so oily now. "You're a stranger here, of course, but it so happens M'liz and I are about to sign a cohabitation contract!"

The girl snuggled closer; she nibbled Julian's ear. "Pay no heed, J'lan," she whispered. "R'heet is *such* a stick-in-the-mud."

The pressure on Julian's shoulder increased. Suddenly he resented it. He released M'liz and spun to glare face-to-face at the bigger man, whom he shoved violently, going into a boxer's stance. "Want some more, buddy?" he demanded in a taunting tone. Buddy took a step toward him and Julian left-hooked him. Buddy fell heavily.

M'liz caught Julian's arm. "Oh, you needn't, J'lan!" she cried. "R'heet doesn't mean any harm. He just didn't understand!" By now she was looking down stonily at Buddy as he lay on his back, blinking.

"He won't bother us again," she stated in a tone of command. She turned back to Julian, who hesitated only momentarily before embracing her warmly.

It's not fair! the jeering critic-mind cried. *I'm a damn fool to dally with this dame, but . . . that slim waist (emphasizes ample, child-bearing width of pelvis), those nice boobs! That golden hair! Precisely two eyes, one nose, a mouth that's the right size: a normal female of exactly the right species!*

"Don't I have enough problems?" he inquired of himself, savoring her sweet mouth, "without horsing around with some sugar-daddy's *petite amie*?" Her arms were holding him closer to all those goodies. Only a complete boor would use force to get away from her; beside which, she sure was nice!

The blow to the side of his head sent him reeling, his grip lost. His feet tangled in some damned vine; he hit face-first. At once, M'liz was kneeling beside him, cradling his head in her hands, and making cooing sounds. He tried to roll away, just as the pretty girl shrieked and reeled back. She was staring up past Julian, her hand to her cheek. R'heet stood staring stonily down at her, ignoring Julian.

"You—you *hit* me, you beast!" M'liz moaned, then scrambled up and rushed past Julian as he came to all fours. He twisted to watch her rush into Buddy's arms.

"You *do* love me!" she yelped, grinding her pelvis against his.

"Disgraceful!" Julian reacted. He looked again at the complex structure rising from the lawn like a power-company installation, but this one was no transformer station, and it supported no high-tension lines; it was a squat, nearly cubical structure, all alone in a clearing in a park. There were a dozen or so of the white-clad people; they had withdrawn a few feet and were watching M'liz smooching Buddy.

Julian went over to the nearest man and demanded: "Did you see the rutabaga?"

The man recoiled, adjusted his hearing aid and said, "Repeat, please." He seemed to have a trace of foreign accent—not French, Julian noted absently.

"What for?" he snapped. "It'll still be the same question: 'Did you see the rutabaga?'"

"Dear me." The man, a distinguished-looking fellow with a touch of gray at the temples, like the Dad in a high school play, fiddled with his hearing aid again.

"Damn translator's malfunctioning again: sounded like you asked me if I'd seen a rutabaga."

"I *did*!" Julian barked. "Well, what is it? Did you or didn't you?"

"Just wait here, and I'll see if B'lon can't stir you up some vegetables—though it's an hour, relative, yet till voom-time."

"I don't give a damn about voom-time!" Julian snarled. "And never mind any more blondes!" He grabbed the man's arm, which felt like an oak root, and was just beginning to realize that was an erroneous move when the arm moved suddenly, dumping Julian on his back.

"*Do* unhand me, fellow!" the middle-aged man ordered. "I'm Technor S'lunt, and getting your vegetables for you as rapidly as is practical, here in the Complex. Oob may pop up at any moment, and—"

What are you doing here? a silent voice between Julian's ears spoke up abruptly. *You're not even Roger! But then I don't suppose you're here by choice. . . .*

"I don't even know where 'here' is!" Julian yelled, clapping his hands over his ears.

He looked at Technor S'lunt accusingly. "That trick of throwing your voice or whatever is damned uncivil!" he stated hotly. "Of course my name's not 'Roger'! Who said it was?"

"My apologies, sir," S'lunt said urbanely. "As it happens, the last pest who intruded here in Culture One was a feckless chap much like yourself, and—"

"I guess I'm as feckful as anybody," Julian defended himself stoutly.

"What was that you were saying about Roger?" S'lunt prompted. "We have cause to be grateful to him, of course, so if he sent you . . ."

"I'm trying to find out where the rutabaga went," Julian insisted, "after he pulled me through the, ah, hole or something. Looked like a puddle of oily water, only it was standing on edge, floating in the air a foot from the two-for-a-franc table. Dreadful tripe! Gaudy paper covers with monsters, or scared-looking girls in front of old houses, or degenerates with bandannas tied over their mouths—that sort of thing. Fifty centimes, indeed! I'm surprised at Sylvia!"

"Oily water on the books, you say?" S'lunt queried. "Floods, eh? Pity. I *do* hope your loved ones are safe."

"To perdition with my loved ones!" Julian yelled. People were gathering around now. M'liz came over and put a hand on his arm. He threw it off.

"Can't any of you people understand?" Julian shouted, accusing them all. "It's just a simple question: 'Where's the rutabaga?" That's all. Simple and clear. Just someone answer me!"

"I've told you—" S'lunt began placatingly, but Julian cut him off.

"Then don't waste time telling me the same thing again! Did you, or did you not see the rutabaga?" Julian paused as if hearing his own words for the first time. "It's not really a rutabaga," he explained lamely. "It just sort of looks like a big rutabaga, or maybe a turnip; it depends on the color. He changes color, you know. Anyway, he's sort of a big tuber, except for the eye and the tentacles, of course, and the legs. Like crab's legs. Have you seen him?"

M'liz spoke quietly to S'lunt. "That sounds a little like that terrible Oob fellow, don't you think, Technor?"

S'lunt slapped his forehead with a sharp *smack!* "Are you telling me, fellow," he demanded, "that you've led the Rhox *here?*"

"I'm telling you nothing, dammit!" Julian snapped. "I'm asking—or trying to ask—a simple, reasonable question: Have you seen anything of the chap I described?"

"Certainly," S'lunt came back emphatically. "He's confined in a holding locus at Use One-Twenty."

"Oh, no, he's not!" Julian contradicted scornfully. "He's running around loose, pushing people through holes into weird places like this! That's what happened to me: I was right there in Sylvia's place, looking at some Aubrey Beardsleys, when he came in, and at once assaulted me!"

S'lunt turned to beckon to another man, no less important-looking. "What about it, G'mor? Is it possible the infernal nuisance is at the bottom of the present emergency? With his multiple extrusions into this plane—and other planes as well, don't forget—he could be anywhere—even here, as this poor fellow keeps insisting."

"I insist on nothing, except an answer!" Julian corrected. "And I'm not a 'poor fellow'! You seem to know all about the rutabaga, now that you've decided not to be so cagey about it! Is he here? He *has* to be here: he went through the hole—"

" 'Aperture,' " G'more corrected. "But that doesn't necessarily mean he arrived in the same locus as yourself. You see, the alignment is critical: a divergence of as little as a second of arc could land you ten parameters distant from him."

"Oh," Julian said, miming enlightenment. "I guess that clears that up. Now, how do I get back? I've got a tea date with Fifi in fifteen minutes, and she's a hellcat when forced to wait. So—"

" 'Get back,' you say," S'lunt intervened. "I'm afraid, my dear sir—my poor, dear sir—that is quite out of the question, at least for the present."

"I'll be damned if it is!" Julian countered hotly. "I'm right on the verge of writing the Great American Novel, you see, and I have to work in the congenial atmosphere of the Rue des Capucines! I can't stay here! Where'd he go?"

S'lunt turned away, motioning to a well-muscled young fellow in a tight white T-shirt. "Better take him over to the core, H'bul," he suggested.

H'bul moved in briskly; Julian put up his dukes. "Stay back!" he ordered. "You're not taking me anywhere. I go where I damn please. Now, where did the infernal rutabaga go? You admitted you've seen it!"

"Of course," H'bul soothed. "It's only one of the Rhox's silly third-order extrusions—"

"I don't care what you call it!" Julian cut in. "I just want to make it take me back where I belong!" His gaze was on the curious structure of chrome-plated pipes and crystalline planes set so incongruously on its patch of lawn in the primeval forest. "What *is* that?" he demanded. "Never mind!" he corrected himself. "Just show me the monster, and—"

A vast voice boomed from close above, or underfoot, or somewhere—Julian couldn't quite decide which:

TECHNOR S'LUNT! the immense words reverberated

in the still air, I HOLD YOU PERSONALLY RESPONSIBLE FOR THIS STATE OF AFFAIRS! YOU, WHOM I HAD APPOINTED AS GUARDIAN OF THE BORE, HAVE PERMITTED THE INSIDIOUS RHOX TO PERFORATE IT LIKE A ROADSIDE SPEED LIMIT SIGN! THIS IS INTOLERABLE! PRODUCE THE OOB EXTRUSION AT ONCE!

"UKR!" S'lunt blurted. "It's not my fault! I was doing my best, when the monitor station here began to signal multiple perforations of the flux wall! I couldn't be everywhere at once! I arranged to shunt the nearest extraneous entity here, where he can be dealt with. How was I to know he'd drag a civilian along with him?"

HAD YOU CONSULTED YOUR VRAM-DENSITY METER, AS IS S.O.P., EX-TECHNOR, UKR's immense, angry voice boomed, YOU'D HAVE REALIZED THE VRAM-FIELD WAS OVERLOADED; YOU COULD HAVE SHUNTED THE APERTURE ASIDE BY A SIMPLE ROTATION ON THE Q AXIS!

"What do you mean, 'ex-Technor'?" S'lunt called to the sky. "I received my appointment from the Committee in solemn council assembled! It can't be revoked!"

AN ASSEMBLAGE OF ORDINARY MORONS EXPERIENCES NO MIRACULOUS BOOST IN IQ, MERELY BY CONGREGATING! UKR stated loudly. I SAY YOU ARE CASHIERED, AND BANISHED AS WELL!

"Banished? Where to?" S'lunt moaned.

I SHALL LEAVE THAT TO THE INGENUITY OF OOB, UKR intoned. THAT'S JUST, DON'T YOU AGREE? YOU ALLOWED THE NUISANCE TO INFEST THE BORE, SO BE IT!

S'lunt yelled in fury. "That's yivshish!" he declared, and looked to his colleagues for agreement.

"Right!" Julian declared. "I don't know *exactly* what 'yivshish' means, or 'the Bore,' either, for that matter, but just letting things ride is clearly irresponsible in the highest degree!"

"Oh, boy, a space/time/vug lawyer," someone groaned.

"But he has a point, UKR; you can't just let disaster run its course on the pretext that somebody made an error. Do not we all?"

"Just tell me what this is all about," Julian begged.

"Well, you see, J'lan," H'bul supplied, "we thought we'd trick Oob into our hands, by setting a trap for him: we selected at random a point of permeability in the entropic Meniscus, and—"

"Hold it right there," Julian interrupted the recital. "Start on familiar ground, OK? Like with what that rutabaga was and where it's gone."

Julian peered upward among the complex of intersecting tubes and planes, glimpsed a flicker of motion, then realized he was looking at the lumpy form of the rutabaga, crowded behind a six-way intersection of pipes.

"There he is!" Julian blurted, pointing.

S'lunt and a few others turned to look upward.

"We've got him!" H'bul exulted. "He blundered when he entered the field of the vram-projectors! He can't whaffle now! Just keep an eye open for trickery—and M'lon: you and P'ty fetch a vug-net; hurry!" But even as P'ty and her lover trotted away obediently, Oob made a complicated gesture of his tentacles, flushed Day-Glo pink, and was gone.

"Oh, that's just Oob, or one of his silly third-order extrusions," S'lunt supplied. "You see, we discovered the existence of the Trans-Temporal Bore, and—"

Julian held up a hand. "You're doing it again," he pointed out wearily. "I don't know what a 'Transit-imperial Bore' is, but if it's anything like an art critic, the biggest bores I know of, I don't want anything to do with it!"

"That is hardly the point, sir," H'bul chided. "The Bore is the work of one UKR, a machine devised by the Builder, to enable him conveniently to assemble representative displays from a wide range of space/time/vug loci."

"I know about time/space," Julian put in. "I read about Professor Einstein's work, but 'vug' is a new one on me."

H'bul didn't steeple his fingers, but he did assume the expression that one normally associates with didacticism. "Let us begin at a more elementary level," he proposed. "Space is a medium which, while it remains stationary, permits free movement within its parameters. Time, on the other hand, is in continual flux, but we are unable, normally, to alter either the rate or the direction of our apparent temporal movement, which is matched to that of the temporal fabric. Vug, on the other hand, is the malleable aspect of what we usually refer to as 'reality.' It is as rigid as space, yet flows like time, and we are at liberty to modify it, and our relation to it at will, employing the appropriate equilibrium of vram-forces, of course."

"Oh," Julian said numbly.

"When the Builder cut the Bore across the continua," H'bul went on imperturbably, "he, or she—never mind that, I'm not referring to gonads in any case—in order to avoid compromising the local integrity of the temporal Meniscus—the force that tends to keep one era apart from another, so that persons, objects, and phenomena do not wander from their native orientations—in order to avoid compromise of local Meniscal integrity, I say, he erected a series of monitor stations along the Bore, which keep tabs on the entropic membrane lining the Bore, and when detecting any irregularity in the problyon flux, at once supply temporal energy sufficient to reestablish the entropic equilibrium. Unfortunately, some time ago, relatively speaking, an entity known as the Rhox penetrated the Bore, quite by accident, and at once perceived the possibility of exploiting the channel for—unthinkably—its own entertainment! It found that by tampering with the monitor circuits, it could cause the repair function to alter its orientation so that, far from resealing weak points in the Bore, it merely pinpointed them, so that at these points of weakness, he could perforate the membrane readily! Dastardly, don't you agree?"

"I'll agree to anything, except looking at Matisse or that Picasso phony," Julian agreed eagerly. "If you'll just stick to plain English and leave out all those Menisci and Bores and things! Where am I? Who *are* you? How do I get home?"

"One can hardly omit the subject of one's discourse," H'bul carped. "As for my identity: I am Sub-inspector H'bul, working out of the third Aspect, on detached duty, with full pay and allowances, at Monitor Station One, which is suspected of malfunction. I'm here to set it right. When I've done so, with the help of ex-Technor S'lunt and these other folks, we can set about returning you to your native locus."

"Whew!" Julian sighed. "That time you almost *said* something. I like the part about returning me to my native locus. I didn't know I even *had* a native locus. Is that anything like Sylvia Beach's shop in Paris?"

"Whatever aspect of your tiny slice of time/space/vug you choose," H'bul said reassuringly.

"You said you tricked that rutabaga—Oob, you called him," Julian reminded his mentor.

"To be sure," the sub-inspector agreed. "We set up a number of permeable zones, to attract him. Unfortunately, that was unwise, as it developed. It resulted in a certain amount of local confusion of loci: tumbrels rumbling past commune roadblocks; Prussian troops crowding the sidewalk cafés where the AEF was accustomed to gather, singing 'Parley-voo'; enraged crowds stoning exhibitions of early Impressionist work, well after it was discovered that the rags Van Gogh wiped his brushes on were masterpieces—all that sort of thing."

"A 'masterpiece,'" Julian pointed out, taking his turn at didacticism, "is not the crowning achievement of a lifetime—it's student work: the piece a journeyman makes to demonstrate his readiness for promotion to the rank of master."

"You know what I mean," H'bul dismissed the pedantry. "Anyway, this Oob was attracted, just as we'd planned, but, alas, he fooled us, by utilizing one of the illicit perforations made in the Bore by the malfunction of this ungrateful device"—he waved a hand at the rod-and-plane construct behind him—"and ducked through just as we were about to lay him by the heels."

"He doesn't have any heels," Julian pointed out. "And why did he drag *me* along, and why is he perched up there now, and what's he doing? Why don't you grab him?"

"You'll soon see!" Oob's glutinous voice spoke up from a new niche, still higher on the monitor station. All eyes turned his way.

"You blundered, you fools!" the Rhox gloated. "You imagined you could herd me here, and by use of brute force, inhibit me in the orderly enfoldment of my destiny. Well, you can't do it!" He wrapped a couple of tentacles around a projecting stub just below a net-like arrangement of chrome-plated wires.

"You know what will happen when I destroy this node-guide," he taunted. "Hold on to your hats, kids, it's going to be a bumpy epoch!" With that, he wrenched hard at the node-guide. Darkness closed in.

"Hold dead still, everybody," S'lunt's cool voice spoke in the dimensionless ambience. "We mustn't lose our orientation," he continued. "It appears the locus has been shifted to null status. We must act with care. First, establish a firm grounding: quasi-down is *that* way. Right; now we'll all turn to face the technical installation, the position of which we still recall. Now, we'll walk slowly toward it until we can all link hands. Arms outstretched, everybody. Proceed!"

Even as Julian wondered who the take-charge voice belonged to, he was extending his arms and turning to face the unseen structure, keeping his feet firmly against the springy turf. After three steps, he bumped his knee on something hard. He groped, felt a smooth metal rod. Seemed farther away, he reflected, but re-extended his arms, groping for contact. He found a limber finger, which at once curled around his own in a caressing way.

"M'liz?" he inquired quietly. The finger held fast as

he made a tentative effort to free his thumb. The finger
pulled with surprising strength for a girl; he yielded. No
one touched his other, left hand.

"Very well," S'lunt's bossy voice spoke up again from
a few feet to his left. "Now, we mustn't allow the Rhox
to dart between us. That's his scheme, clearly, plunging
us into darkness so we can't optically observe his movements on the station. Just keep close together, and grab
anything that tries to pass."

A yelp from Julian's right was the only audible
response.

"You *fresh* thing!" an indignant female voice twittered.
"Can't you just wait a few minutes until we can be
alone?"

"No nonsense now!" S'lunt snapped. "H'bul, is that
you, trying to feel up T'wit? Stop it. We're in a grave
situation here, and we *must* keep our attention on a uni-
fied effort. Envision, now, everyone! Envision!"

" 'Envision,' he says," Julian muttered, as the tugging
became more imperative. "What *I* envision is a table
in the shade on the sidewalk in front of Vladim's, and
a nice little chateaubriand with a slice of tomato and a
glass of claret!" The tugging grew even more insistent, and
Julian had to take a step sideways to retain his equilibrium.
His knee bumped something less unyielding than the steel
pipes. At the same moment he became aware that the
clutching finger had now incircled his wrist. He yanked
hard, to no avail. He groped with his free left hand and
encountered a writhing mass of slender tentacles, one of
which was holding him fast.

"Oob!" he yelled. "I've got him! Help!"

"Hold fast, outlander," S'lunt's voice urged. There
were sounds of reaction: gasps, muttered curses, a
scream, quickly stifled, and a rush of feet toward him.
Abruptly, the tentacle was wrenched away; the sounds
were cut off as by a breaking tape. He stood alone in
pitch darkness.

"Hey!" he yelled. "I was envisioning like you said, and—"

Something nudged the backs of his knees and he sank

down into a hard but not uncomfortable chair. There were sounds of feet hurrying past, of motor vehicles close at hand, a babble of voices, speaking French, Julian realized, his eyes screwed shut. He opened them. On the plate before him was his nicely scorched steak. He grabbed the red wine and swallowed it at a gulp. The chair on the opposite side of the table was occupied by the rutabaga, a dismal dark blue now. It blinked its oversized eye at him solemnly, and the great gash of a mouth opened.

"Foolish of you, sir," it said. "Don't you realize that the Cosmic All is in a highly malleable state when the vram-coil has been switched off without the usual check-list items being performed? First, the tilk-suppressor should have been activated, then it's essential to power up the framistractors, and—"

"Skip all that," Julian dismissed the recital. He had just noticed that the patch of sidewalk under the striped canopy ended just beyond Oob's chair and on his side, extended barely past the legs of the table. He clutched the seat of his chair, looking straight down into a bottomless abyss.

"More!" he specified. "I wasn't envisioning just the patch under the table! I meant the whole thing! The street, the buildings, the people. I can hear—" The street sounds cut off suddenly, and again silence reigned. Julian tried to relax. The tiny island on which he was perched was not alone, he realized. Nearby at other precariously supported tables, he saw S'lunt, and H'bul and M'lix as well, all looking across at him.

"Foolish of you," remarked the bossy voice, which Julian saw belonged to a plump, officious-looking fellow at the nearest table. "Why in the world didn't you erect more conspicuous parameters?"

"I guess I just didn't feel like it," Julian replied cockily. "What are you going to do about your pal Oob here?" He looked back across the table. Oob was gone.

"He did it again!" Julian complained. "If you people decoyed him here, didn't you have in mind some way of restraining him after he arrived?"

"Certainly," S'lunt confirmed imperturbably. "M'lon will be along with a most efficient entropic stator any moment now. You see, we hadn't included *you* in our calculations: your presence upsets the problyon balance severely."

"Pity," Julian spat. "Suppose I just go along home now and let your problyons get back to normal." He looked expectantly at the former Technor, who shook his head sadly.

"We'd love to assist you in that," he assured Julian. "But, alas, so long as Oob remains free, we can't balance our circuits, eh?"

"Then catch him!" Julian directed sternly. "Time is passing, and I've told you I have a previous engagement!"

"To be sure," S'lunt agreed, nodding pleasantly. He turned and called, "Uh, P'ty! Where the devil's she got to?"

"You sent her off to get a vug-net, don't you remember?" Julian taunted.

"Yes, of course, but—no! Dammit, I *told* everyone to look sharp for a locus of permeability here in the vicinity of the station! The malfunction can easily have opened one nearby! B'lob, do you see anything?"

"Afraid so," B'lob answered. "M'lon darted past me just now, and when I turned to speak to him, he was nowhere to be seen." He stooped and picked up what appeared to be a fragment of palm-frond.

"Poor chap," he murmured, "and poor P'ty, too: lost. Randomly pitched down the Bore, to emerge, Flonk knows where/when!"

"Very well," S'lunt barked. "I've been stripped of my rank, but not of my awareness of my duty! You, B'lob, shape up these people, and prepare to link with me in erecting a Probe-field. We'll find them! And Oob, too," he added.

Oob, the Rhox, was perched in his saddle at the center of his Control Apex, his tentacles busily poking buttons on the console before him, as he repeatedly consulted a chart tacked to the board conveniently mounted at eye level.

"Drat!" he muttered to himself, and peered more closely at his chart. "I'm going to have to risk activating the random-grab circuit," he informed himself reluctantly. "R'heet won't like it, but it's the only way, since that tricky fellow Roger Tyson has played me false." Apparently satisfied with this rationalization, he hauled down on a large, red-painted lever, eliciting a groan from the panel; pink sparks jumped all across the banks of persistors behind the console, and wisps of smoke arose.

"Double drat!" Oob snarled. "I fear the overload kicked in the automatic scan and reverse accessory!" he explained to himself. "The fat's in the fire for fair this time . . . ! 'The fat's in the fire for fair,' " he repeated, savoring the alliteration. "It scans," he decided. "So be it!" Before he could throw in the oops-circuit, the dim light about him faded, leaving the idiot-lights on the panel glowing vividly in the darkness.

"Quadruple drat with pepper on!" Oob moaned. "This will have those confounded Culture One upstarts down on me in a couple of trices. UKR, too, I fear." He jittered for a moment, then he leapt clear as the Apex folded inward about him, reverting to an unrealized state, having been, Oob realized, eliminated from the Fabric by his impetuous action. Oob reached frantically, barely caught the escape lever with an outstretched manipulatory member, and hauled himself to temporary safety, at the cost of using the one-way panic door, which quite excluded him from regaining the Apex. He peered into the surrounding darkness, barely made out the outlines of a curious rectilinear structure, and scuttled toward it on his short ambulatory members. He reached the rude hut, and crouched beneath the lone window. He sniffed an odor of woodsmoke and well-rotted garbage, snorted and glanced at the illuminated dial of the Vugmeter strapped to his median carapace.

"Infinite drat!" he groaned. "Missed! By seven hundred temporal units! This is disaster!"

Squatting disconsolately in the darkest corner of the hovel, Oob waited impatiently for the hag's return. It was quite unfair, the way she'd attained mastery over him, just because he'd accidently forgotten to balance the chronic fields to maintain her in status quo. Doubtless, she'd castigate him severely for some imagined shortcoming before petting him and fixing him his bowl of sour milk mixed with chicken blood, which he'd have to pretend to be grateful for as he took it outside, not to consume—ugh—but to dispose of in the swine-pen. The temptation to do an unauthorized TSV shift was strong—too strong to resist. Oob cinched up his sphincters, closed his median eye, and uttered the mantra. On the instant, darkness was dissolved in brilliant light. He opened his eye to assess the situation. It was worse than he'd feared: R'heet and that pest S'lunt were standing nearby looking directly at him without approval.

"Go ahead and slap the inhibitor on the rascal," S'lunt urged. R'heet complied, and Oob felt his perception in the beta range fade and die. He made an abortive lunge for freedom, was caught up in a vortex of unleashed vram energies and whirled away to—where?

CHAPTER FOUR

When Rusty Naill reached the barrier of the densely packed sabal palms, he took out his fish-knife and slashed at the barricading undergrowth of palmetto, clearing a point of entry. He took a step, paused to slash again, took a final look back at the quiet beach behind him, noted that the sun was getting low. The site of the murder had already reverted to anonymity; Rusty realized; he couldn't be sure just where those fellows had buried the treasure— *Treasure!* he snorted. "Probably their accumulated garbage." After all, the days of Long John Silver and Captain Kidd were long past.

His eye wandered to the vessel out on the gulf. It had swung around to lee'ard, and he was pretty sure she was moving out to sea. *Well, never mind that. The thing to do right now is to get to the highway and flag a car, and report the killing.*

He had gained another ten feet when he heard the voices: a woman's shrill one, complaining, and a man's reply: "Just be calm, my dear, and I'm sure—"

"You're not sure of anything, you big dope!" she cut him off.

Rusty made a megaphone with his hands and called. "Hello! I guess I'm lost, and could you direct me—?"

His call trailed off as the palmettos to his right shook and burst outward to reveal a pert little burnette in an amazingly spotless white tennis outfit, it looked like. Behind her, a distinguished-looking but similarly clad six-footer looked curiously at Rusty.

"I say," he said. "Have you seen anything of the Rhox hereabouts?"

"No rocks around here," Rusty grated. (Must be a tourist.) "All sand; ground-up seashells, you know. Maybe a little lime-rock outcropping here and there; that's just more seashells, turning into limestone. I guess in a few million years . . ."

"No, no, you don't understand," the stranger interrupted.

"You can say that again," Rusty stated fervently. "How far is the highway?"

"I'm sorry," the newcomer said. "We're strangers here ourselves; I was hoping you could direct us to the nearest entropic fix."

"Need a fix, eh?" Rusty queried contemptuously. "Beats me; I never got into the dope end." _Say!_ his thought continued silently. _Those fellows on the beach! That's probably what's in that box! Holy Moses! I'd better get to the sheriff fast!_

The girl had come closer to him, her well-formed bosom prodding his arm gently. He looked down at a cute face, a little like Debbie Reynolds, he decided, with big blue eyes, and disconcertingly black hair. Her kissable lips were parted, showing china-white teeth. Her hand was on his arm, warm and soft. She wasn't even sweating in this heat, he noticed.

"What are you folks doing out here in the palmetto scrub?" he mumbled then thrust out his hand. "Rusty's the handle," he stated.

The man looked curiously at the proffered palm, and finally grasped it. "I'm M'lon," he said. "And this is P'ty, R'sty."

"That's 'Rusty,' " Naill corrected, "not 'Ars-tie.' Gladda meecha, Patty and you, too, Milon. Look, this is no place for two nice folks just down from . . . Michigan?" he hazarded. "Mighty lonely stretch, here. I guess you parked up above and figured to take a short-cut to the beach, eh?" Even as he spoke, he was wondering why they'd be coming to the beach in tennis outfits—ladies' outfits at that, both of em, little skirt and all. Kind of weird, but if their car was just up on the road . . .

"Wonder if you folks could give me a lift," he wheedled. "Got to get to town right away." He had been about to mention the dope smugglers, but decided against it. After all, if they were here to make the pickup, he might not be out of the woods quite yet.

"Sorry, R'sty," Patty said in a melodious voice, the harsh edge he'd heard earlier quite absent now. Trickier than she looked, Rusty reflected. Turns it on and off like a light.

"I know it's a lot to ask, you folks being all set for a nice swim and all," Rusty gobbled. "But it's a matter of"—he decided not to say "life and death"—"importance. My boat—"

"Oh, splendid, you have a boat," Milon cut in. "Suppose you just run us to the nearest settlement."

"What 'settlement'?" Rusty queried. "There's Holiday, about fifteen miles south, not much of a town, but I wouldn't call it a settlement. Istachatta Springs, that's twenty miles north—"

"That will be just fine," Patty said, taking his hand confidently.

"Except my boat's swamped, motor'll never start," Rusty managed over Mel's effusions. "She's washing around in the surf over there, actually. Lost my gear, too. Let's get going. Like I said, I need a lift, and—"

"Look here, R'sty—"

"It's not 'Erstee,'" Rusty corrected again, this time a bit impatiently. "Must be foreigners. "'Rusty'! See? Simple. Like a rusty nail. Fact, that's my name. Rusty's just a handle, o' course, real name's 'Clarence.' But nobody calls me that except my folks, and they're both dead now. Rusty, OK?"

"As you wish, Arstee," the man said. Rusty decided not to contest the point further.

"Let's get back to your car," he urged. "Skeeters will be getting fierce pretty soon." He slapped the side of his neck as if in illustration. P'ty looked at him concernedly. Her expression reflected sudden resolution.

"Listen carefully, Rusty," she said, getting it right at last. "The Rhox is at large near here. He must be apprehended. He's running wild, punching holes in the Bore with perfect abandon: the most irresponsible creature imaginable. Are you *sure* you haven't seen him?"

"No rocks here, Honey," Rusty told her for the second time. "The geology of Florida—"

" 'Florida'!" M'lon exclaimed. "I've heard of it: a swampy island in Channel Eight!"

"Nothing like that," Rusty contradicted. "I'm not talking about some TV show! U.S. Nineteen, actually, is just a short distance." He pointed. "In that direction, as you know."

P'ty shook her head, looking troubled. "We know nothing of a Use Nineteen, do we, M'lon?"

"Nothing at all, sir," the man confirmed.

"Even the advanced Survey has investigated only as far as the Ninth Phase; nothing at all is known of 'Use Nineteen'; and actually, the place is not yet classified as Useful."

"You are in error, sir!" Rusty waved his hands against the verbal barrage. "OK, OK, doesn't matter what you call it: Gulfshore Drive, or whatever. The highway is all I mean."

The two in white exchanged glances, had a brief, whispered conversation; then the man turned grimly to Naill.

"Sir, are you, by any chance, a native of this locus?" he inquired.

"Well, I grew up down here since age ten," Rusty told him. "I guess that makes me *practically* a native. Born in New Jersey, but never been back. Folks came down, here after the Boom, you know."

The girl gasped audibly. "You know about the Boom?" she squeaked.

"Everybody knows about the Florida Boom in the Twenties," Rusty replied.

" 'The Twenties'! A moment ago it was only the Nineteenth!" M'lon protested. "Are you having us on, sir?"

"It's 'U.S. Nineteen,' " Rusty said patiently, hearing the futility of his explanation even as he spoke. "And 'Nineteen-Twenties.' No connection. Let's get up to the road, OK?" He started to whack at the obstructing fronds, but M'lon put out a restraining hand.

"The less disturbance we create here the easier it will be for Technor S'lunt to get a vram-fix on us, and carry out a Retrieval," he said as if imparting information.

"I don't know anything about some guy named Lunt." Rusty was growing more and more impatient. "I just want to get in out of these damned bugs, so what say we shove off? And I don't need anybody getting a framfix, or whatever, on me. I told you I don't use the stuff. Come on, I won't rat on you." He pushed past the girl, accidentally brushing his forearm across those nice breastworks, *blump, blump.* After a few steps he realized the strangers weren't following him. He turned to look back at them, a snappy wisecrack all ready. Damned tourists!

His mouth remained open, but silent, for a full thirty seconds. There was nobody there. Suppressing an impulse to get cold shivers, Rusty lunged back down the rude path he had cut and shied violently at a sort of spiderweb thing hanging over the trail. *That* hadn't been here a minute ago!

He paused to examine the irregular, slightly iridescent patch closer. There seemed to be nothing holding it up. It looked like it ought to be transparent, but the play of rainbow color flowing over it obscured the view behind it.

He brushed at it, as if to wipe it aside, as if it *was* a spiderweb. His hand went all blurry for a moment, but he felt nothing. *Just an optical illusion,* he assured himself. *My eyes . . .*

He put a hand over them and took a deep breath. Nothing to get excited about. First, the movie pirates— no, just drug smugglers, he corrected. *Then the tennis players—funny, no rackets—and now this!* It was turning into a crazy day. There had been that squall, too, that blew up out of nowhere, swamped his boat, and disappeared.

Better take it easy, Clarence, he cautioned himself sternly. *No use standing here feeding the skeegies and looking at a patch of dirty window with no glass.*

He forged ahead, right through the funny patch, tripped and almost fell. The dense stand of palm trees was gone, and Milon and Patty were nowhere to be seen. Instead, he was looking across a broad, paved plaza with a fountain in the middle, to the facades of a row of immense buildings.

They sure run them new hotels up in a hurry. Rusty formed the thought, then dismissed it. *Nobody can clear jungle, fill in the bay, and put a coat of pink paint on a ten-story condo, all in total silence, while I'm trying to get a sensible answer out of a couple of lost tourists. Said they was from Michigan, I think—*

Even as his reason rejected the plaza and the tall structures lining it, he was walking briskly toward the latter. From the corner of his eye, he noticed movement. A squat, lumpy-trunked palm beside a flowering shrub seemed to move minutely. *Just the breeze stirring the fronds,* Rusty told himself, just as the tree sidled over, crossed the curb and darted in among the ground junipers. *Oh, boy! Walking trees, already.*

He did a hard left and approached the ambulatory plant. Up close, he realized its "fronds" were actually palmetto fronds, freshly cut and held in ropy gray tentacles, as camouflage. Behind their partial screen, he saw an immense eye gazing at him. He shied, and took off at a full run toward a man who had emerged from the central building.

As the man hesitated as if about to turn back, Rusty yelled, "Hey! Just a minute!" The stranger glanced back toward him and stopped.

Rusty came up, winded, and gasped out: "—the tree! It moved! I know it sounds crazy, but—" He turned to point out the peripatetic palm and gulped hard. It was ten feet behind him, coming directly toward him, its pointy, jointed legs twinkling as it came.

"Look!" Rusty urged. "It's chasing me! Help! Look, pal, I'm R—Clarence Naill, I'm a licensed skipper, and my boat— Never mind. It's *coming!*"

"Do calm yourself," the local's urbane voice urged. "This is a matter for the Cell." He patted Rusty's arm comfortingly. "It likely won't actually attack," he told him. "Just try to ignore it," and he was off, hurrying back up the broad, shallow steps. Rusty uttered a yell and jumped aside as the monstrosity almost touched him.

"No need for panic, Roger—" Oob said in his clogged voice. "No, sorry, but all you fellows *do* look alike, you know. I only want to make an arrangement with you. Shall we talk like reasonable beings, before old F'shu comes back with a pack of beadles?"

"No!" Rusty barked. "I don't talk to hallucinations! Get away!" He kicked at the thing; his toe impacted on a texture like a giant potato. He kicked again, and the creature shied, grabbed for his ankle with its wormlike tentacles, but stopped as Rusty backed off.

"Talk about what?" he demanded. "I don't know what you are, but you're on a bum lay! I'm a stranger here myself!"

"Aren't we all?" They gluey voice of the dull-brown potato rejoined. "So many continua, so many beings, so much time: how can one find one's true niche?"

"My niche is on the last stool to the left at Sparky's!" Rusty yelled. "A big schooner of that English ale he has on tap, and maybe a corned beef sandwich would be real fine, right now, on rye. And prolly in a few minutes that Suzy will come in—to make a phone call like she always says—and she'll have one with me, and life can be beautiful!"

"Quite so," the vegetable agreed. "Nothing's so comforting as the prospect of perpetuating one's genes. All in good time, Mister—?"

"Naill," Rusty supplied. "And who—or what—are you?"

"Why, I'm merely a third order extrusion of Oob, Chief Counselor of the Rhox. Pleased to meet you." It extended a tentacle, which Rusty declined to shake.

"Why are you chasing me?" he demanded. "I saw you back there in the palm grove when I was talking to Patty and Mel—then they disappeared!"

"Things are getting a trifle out of hand," the monster told Rusty. "I admit I was partially at fault. I panicked—opened an Aperture without proper preliminary research, and neglected to nullify the vram energies, too. Pity. It was the threat to the integrity of the entire Bore that rattled me. Surely my attempt to oppose the disaster is commendable, even if I did lose my head a bit." It paused as if awaiting congratulation, then resumed. "Already, there've been at least three hundred unclassified entries, and a major displacement, to say nothing of the disturbance back at Culture One!"

"'Culture One'!" Rusty repeated the lone familiar phrase. "I've heard of that! Mel and Patty were talking about—"

"And just who are Mel and Patty?" the voice like a mouthful of sorghum interrupted.

"I asked you who *you* are, first!" Rusty accused.

"Oob's the handle," Oob said patiently. "As I told you only a moment ago! Short attention-span. Problem with all you fellows."

"Oh, I didn't realize 'Oob' was a name," Rusty explained. "I thought it was an adjective, meaning 'objectionable' or something."

"Every lexeme means *something*," Oob declared. "Except of course, for . . . No, I'd better not get into all that. Let us endeavor to communicate at a basic level of primary intent."

"What's this place?" Rusty demanded, waving his arm to indicate everything in sight. "It wasn't here five minutes ago!"

"Certainly not," Oob agreed comfortably. "Not when viewed from a certain perspective. Change, my boy, constant change, fluctuation across the entire spectrum of the unrealized potential! Such is the nature of being, vug energies being what they are."

"That's OK." Rusty waved away the philosophy. "But this is solid concrete I'm standing on, and it takes a few hours to set, for openers!" He stamped his foot to dramatize the solidity of the pavement on which they stood.

"Careful, lad," Oob cautioned. "This is a very fragile construct—they call it the Final Configuration. It's quite theoretical, of course—held in pseudo-stasis only by the emanations of the problyon generator yonder." He pointed a pale green tentacle toward the building where F'shu had disappeared. "Actually," he went on, "our being here is a serious breach of local security; we've intruded an uncontrolled element into a most precisely balanced equation. Doubtless we'll be spontaneously ejected at any moment."

"Swell," Rusty replied, sounding less sarcastic than he had intended. "I better go in there and explain matters to this Shoe fellow!" He started up the steps, noticing idly that they were cut from slabs of marble in which fossil scallop shells could be seen.

" 'Explain,' eh?" Oob's unctuous voice pursued him. "Just how do you propose to explain a compound violation of every section of the Code without condemning yourself to the Fate?" he jeered.

Rusty ignored the bothersome fellow. As he reached the top step, he stumbled on an unseen discontinuity, retaining his balance with quick footwork. He reached for the big brass-framed door and it revolved easily, palming him out into the lobby of an ornate, old-fashioned hotel, complete with cigar counter, barber shop, and breakfast room. A bellhop in a natty uniform with a pillbox cap looked him over carefully.

"You Mr. Philip Morris?" he demanded impatiently. Rusty denied the charge and headed for the neon sign reading BREAKFAST ROOM. Inside the cozy restaurant, he saw an unoccupied table just where he'd hoped, with a view of the door, in case that damn potato followed him.

After a ten-minute wait, which he spent watching a group of six waitresses gossiping in a corner, a female ex-Belsen-guard type came over and demanded to know who had told him to sit there.

"Nobody, sister," he came back, without hesitation. "I'm so damned smart I figured out where I wanted to sit with no instructions."

The lady wrestler grunted, muttered something about a waitress, and went away.

"Another nutty place," Rusty groaned silently. "They expect the customer to come in and stand around waiting for orders." Before he could further explore the absurdity of the concept, a slattern in a dirty yellow pinafore came over, unlimbered a pencil from behind an ear like a bagel, and demanded his order.

"Cuppa java," he told her. She snarled and walked away, to return a moment later with a globular container of murky fluid with which she overfilled a cup already in place on the bare, damp table. She deposited a paper napkin and a spoon beside it and turned away.

"Any cream and sugar?" Rusty inquired.

"Oh!" the lady exclaimed. "You want sugar and milk?"

"Why are you asking me that?" Rusty wanted to know.

"Well, you said—" she started, but Rusty cut her off.

"If you know what I said," he told her, "there's no need for me to repeat it. Cream, not milk."

Thereafter, Rusty was afforded fifteen uninterrupted minutes in which to ponder the nature of things. Then the tough old broad came back and put a paper cup of bluish fluid before him, plus a chipped bowl half full of clumped white grains. She added a simper like a goosed orangutan and gave him a ponderous flirt of an oversized butt as she withdrew. Somehow, Rusty felt he had gotten off easy. He diluted the brown guck with the blue-white guck, and added some lumpy white stuff. After stirring the mess, he sipped cautiously, put the cup down hastily, dropped a quarter on the table, rose and reentered the world of great affairs. Out in the lobby proper, he noted a fellow almost lost in the depths of a grossly overstuffed chair, pretending to read a dog-eared newspaper—the *Tranton Bugle*, he noted—but actually watching him, or someone behind him, with a beady eye. Rusty went over to him, paused and said:

"OK so far?"

The paper went down like a collapsing tent, and the beady eye and its mate looked up indignantly.

"You can't get away with this," a thin voice snarled. The face that went with the beady eye and the voice was small, mean, knuckle-scarred, with a mouth that twisted like a cartoon character's close-up. Rusty sat on the arm of the chair and looked down at the top of the lumpy, going-bald head.

"You in on this deal, Pig-eye?" Rusty muttered, as if to avoid hearing himself.

"Well!" Pig-eye snapped. "Would Lefty of sent me if I wasn't? By the way, I'm not Pig-eye. He's over Syca-more, on the Jones lay. Barfy's the moniker." He offered a callused hand, which Rusty ignored.

"You can tell Lefty I said his muddah wears GI shorts," Rusty said. "I got to blow now, Piggy. What's new in Trenton?"

"How the heck would I know?" Piggy snapped. "You better get over Smitty's before ten A.M. this morning," he added.

"How about ten A.M. tonight?" Rusty suggested.

"Whattaya, wiseguy?" Piggy demanded, coming out of his chair to stare fiercely at where Rusty's third shirt button would be, if he'd had buttons on his shirt. Actu-ally, he noticed in surprise, he was wearing a striped black-and-white shirt with a detachable white collar and gold studs, plus a yellow silk tie.

"If you know what's good for you, Mr. Lepke," the little fellow grated, "you'll cut the comedy and hand over the stuff. Now! Lefty don't like waiting around!"

"I'm getting tired of this," Rusty told his new friend. "Good-bye!"

He walked across the faded pseudo-oriental rug to the far side of the lobby, where a sign on a counter read TRAVEL AGENCY. A clerk with a face like a surprised fox terrier eyed him brightly and said, "Yessir, return for Schenectady today?"

"I'm flying to Tibet," Rusty corrected. "What's this Schenectady stuff?"

"Well, sir, after all these weeks, I've come to know my regular customers' habits rather well. You usually—"

"You mean you've seen me before?" Rusty demanded.

The narrow, whiskery head nodded emphatically. "Every Tuesday, sir, as regular as clockwork! Five ninety-nine, as usual, sir!"

"Is this Trenton, New Jersey?" Rusty asked, warily. "What's the date?"

"Why, no sir; I suppose you're joking, Mr. Lepke. We're right here in Brooklyn! It's the seventeenth . . ." His voice trailed off.

"Of what?" Rusty pressed him.

"Eh? 'of what,' what?" The flustered clerk gobbled. "Oh, of August, sir. Most amusing sense of humor, Mr. Lepke."

"Who's this Lepke?" Rusty asked. "What year?"

"Why, sir, you're a prominent local entrepreneur, of course, known to one and all. Nineteen twenty-three. Superb weather we've been having, wouldn't you agree?"

"Beats me," Rusty answered. "I haven't been outside for ten minutes."

"Oh, dear me, yes," the clerk agreed dazedly, fanning himself briskly with his slender, manicured hand.

"Seen anything of a forty-pound potato with legs?" Rusty inquired casually.

"Why, ah, as to that, Mr. Lepke . . ."

Rusty saw the clerk's weight shift as he stepped on a

signal button. Rusty turned; two uniformed house dicks were bustling importantly toward him. The first to arrive, an unshaven Neanderthal with a gold-colored junior high class ring with a big blue glass knob on his middle finger, hitched up his gun belt and said heavily to the clerk:

"OK, Mort, what's the beef?"

"Why, no actual beef," Mort hastened to assure his interlocutor. "Just thought perhaps you boys could assist Mr. Lepke."

"Yeah?" The cop looked at Rusty with an expression which neatly concealed any approval he may have felt.

"Got any eye-dee on you?" he demanded.

Rusty had his mouth open to explain that he'd lost his wallet when his boat swamped, but at that moment he saw from the corner of his eye a furtive movement behind a potted plant.

"See you later," he blurted, and fled.

CHAPTER FIVE

Russ Ganth was dozing behind the wheel of his cab when the crazy man yanked the door open and jumped in beside him.

"Go!" the fare barked. "Hurry up! It's right behind me!"

Russ craned his neck to look past the nut, saw nothing but the usual crowd on the sidewalk.

"Where to, mister?" He grated, and gave a huge, square Lincoln a scare pulling out into traffic.

"The airport!" the fare barked. "In a hurry!" He showed a faded document like a railroad schedule. "The ten-fifteen for Spokane takes off in fifteen minutes!" he stated.

Russ thought that over. "You mean a aeroplane?" he asked, politely enough.

"I don't mean a balloon!" Rusty/Lepke snapped. "Can't you get any more speed out of this thing?"

"Yeah, sure, but they got cops, you know." Russ seized an opportunity to cut around a bus on the right side. Rusty felt like a passenger on a runaway freight train. He struggled to speak over this Lepke guy, to no avail.

" 'The ten-fifteen fer Spokane,' you said," Russ accussed. "That's in the state o' Warshenon, right? Pretty good, pal. How's about the next flight to Paris, hey? Heard some guys are planning to try that, too."

"Lindy, in twenty-seven," Rusty muttered. "Is this really nineteen twenty-three? Warren Gamaliel Harding is president?"

"Sure, I kinda like the guy," Russ affirmed. "Called his own speeches 'bloviating'; neat, huh? Guy's got a sense o' humor. He'd like about the ten-fifteen to Spokane!"

"Tell him I said to stay away from Japanese crabs," Rusty grunted.

"Huh?" Russ countered, peering into his rearview. "I don't get it. What's that 'pose' to mean?" He braked sharply. "If you think you're gonna crack wise about our presydent, you can run the rest o' the way! Out!"

"It's just that I heard they're bad for you," Rusty explained, "and he likes 'em."

"Yeah, well . . ." Russ offered. He glanced at his dash clock. "If we're gonna make that ten-fifteen, we better haul ass," he commented, and burned rubber.

"Lost off Tortuga in the seventy-eight," the deep voice intoned. "On the bottom in sixteen fathom o' green water." Andy Scute winced at the words. He wondered for a moment who had said them, then realized that *he* had, when the old woman had told him to "reexperience some of your deaths." That was spooky, Andy reflected, and somewhere far below the Andy-consciousness, Rusty Naill struggled to surface; then he relaxed and observed. " 'Reexperience my deaths,' hah!" Andy barked.

He stood up and the old woman nodded and said, "Yes, go on."

"It was that little red bastard with three wings," he responded quickly. Then, "Fire in the aircraft!" He fought the controls for a moment, then set up a sideslip to blow the billowing flames away from his face. The little isinglass windscreen was already cracked and twisted by the heat. He craned his neck to find the triplane, but it was gone.

In the distance, just under the cloud cover, he saw

two Nieuports. Good timing! The Spad was responding sluggishly to the controls, the engine wasn't the only thing that Jerry had hit: but he spotted a pasture below, and wrenched the little craft around for an approach into the wind—from the north as indicated by the cattle down there, who always faced the wind. *Crackk!* A bullet ripped through the fuselage behind him somewhere. A Nieuport flashed past him. The damned Frogs were shooting at him! He took evasive action, and it looked like he might make it OK, but—

Rusty let out a breath and got his mind back on matters at hand. *The old devil must be ninety!* he thought, feeling desperate, because for all his spindle shanks, and the silly little peruke sitting awry on his wizened head, he was a master of the épée. *There! Nicked me again! He's as fast as a snake. But I've got him doped, I think; just wait until that next riposte, and go in under his blade, and—*

God! Who would have thought it would be so cold!

The assassin stepped out from behind the column and struck—but he missed! *The fool must think he's dealing with some fat old senator.* There were two more, one of them, Mars be praised, good old Junius—and he was armed. A duck aside, tap the smelly lout, move in, and— Junius! No! It couldn't be!

Rusty woke from a troubled sleep to find the old crone still sitting across from him, fumbling with the cards in her claw-like hands. She gave him a penetrating look.

"You'll feel better now, Andrew my lad," she said in a voice that was cracked like a dropped egg.

"Better than what?" Rusty croaked. "Who are you?" He looked around at the low, smoke-blackened ceiling beams, the walls of mud-mortared, whitewashed rubble, at the greasy candle guttering in its earthenware saucer.

"What *is* this place?" he appealed. "Where am I?"

"You're safe here with Mother Goodwish," the

crotchety voice assured him. God, she was ugly—that nose—like a warty brown pickle hanging out over a mouth like a torn pocket—and that one isolated black stump of a tooth. He got to his feet; the three-legged stool fell over. His eyes went to the shadows in the corner beside the rough fireplace. *Something* bulked there— the lumpy body, the drooping tentacles, the single huge eye, closed now, with surprisingly long lashes.

"Oob!" Rusty blurted. The beldame put out her withered hand.

"Don't exercise yerself, me pretty," she cackled. "That's only my familiar, Catkin, sleeping, he is. Don't wake him—he mislikes to have his repose disturbed!"

"I'll repose his disturb!" Rusty grated; he grabbed up an iron poker and brought it down hard on the monster. It made a *splat!*ing sound, and carroty substance splattered. The old witch screeched, and Oob's gluey voice said blandly,

"Naughty boy, Clarence! I should think you'd have realized by now—" Rusty stopped dead, staring down at the overturned creature, its tentacles hanging limply except for an occasional twitch, while its multi-jointed legs kicked a few times and were still.

"It's still *alive!*" Rusty/Andy choked. "Let me out of here!" He turned and, brushing the old woman aside, charged out into the sunshine. He stared wildly around at an irregular, muddy trail that meandered past squat half-timbered huts with smoke trailing from mud-plastered chimneys. Hogs rooted in the street and around the houses. A fat girl dressed up in some kind of peasant costume that squeezed her breasts up into view was emptying a wooden bucket from a doorway.

"Hey!" Rusty yelled. "Miss—can you tell me—?" The young woman looked up, dropped her bucket, and fled back inside. The shaggy head of a discouragingly large man poked out, staring across at Rusty with no apparent approval. Rusty put his head down and strode doggedly across toward him. The big fellow stepped out to meet him.

"Pirthee, Master Andrew," the big fellow said in a surprisingly high, squeaky voice, "canst forgive the wench? She's but new come to our town, and knows naught of the ways of the great world."

"No sweat," Rusty grunted.

"My master is clement," the pro-wrestler-type squeaked. "How can Hugi the Camp-follower serve thee, m'sire?"

"Just tell me what place this is," Rusty requested wearily. "Tell me anything you know. I don't know anything, except my name's Rusty, or Clarence, really, Naill, or maybe 'Lepke,' and my boat was swamped and since then—"

"The witch has addled thy wits, then?" Hugi answered. " 'Thy boat,' thou sayest. Where, pray, didst thou ply thy vessel here in the New Forest, leagues from any water?"

"On the gulf," Rusty supplied. "Out of Bayport. Not much of a place—used to run booze in there, back in Prohibition times. Just thought I'd catch a few mackerel for a nice breakfast. Usually I'm on my thirty-footer, but I had a fuel leak, and—"

His voice trailed off as he realized he was talking to himself. Hugi had ducked back inside. Rusty turned to look behind himself to see what had spooked the big fellow. It was his erstwhile hostess, scrawny in billowing black skirts with sort of saddlebag things at the side, hurrying toward him with a look of fury on her wizened face.

"Stay, varlet!" she snarled. "Or I'll put a geas on ye'll close yer throat that tight a sup of small beer won't pass it for a fortnight!"

Rusty held up a hand. "Don't do that," he pled, not knowing what she was talking about. "I'm sorry about Oob. . . ." Once again he left his sentence unfinished as he saw Oob himself scuttling along in the old bag's wake, with no sign of a wound on his potato-like body.

"Roger!" the Rhox called. "Do stop complicating matters! You've forced me to perforate the Bore repeatedly, at points not indicated on the Grand Chart!"

"Gosh," Rusty said in mock repentance. "Why don't

you go mash yourself and leave me alone? And I'm not Roger!"

"Of course not, dear boy," Oob agreed. "As for leaving you alone, I can hardly do that! You took it upon yourself to cross over the Meniscus, and—"

"Like hell I did!" Rusty challenged. "It was those tennis players, Patty and Mel! They . . ." He fell silent as he recalled the spiderweb in the path, and that the tennis buffs were already gone when he encountered it.

"OK," he conceded. "I blundered in here on my own, but how about directing me back home?"

"Pity," Oob said, fading to a bilious yellow. "Once in, you've become a part of the equation, and cannot be neglected. There's no telling what anomalies you might introduce into the order of the cosmos!"

" 'Order'?" Rusty queried. "First I'm in some kind of fantastic shopping center, and the next thing I know, I'm a hoodlum in Brooklyn, then I'm being psyched by a witch!"

During this exchange, Hugi had come back out, and now sidled up beside Naill.

"Prithee, Milford, canst force yon demon to lead thee to gold?"

"That's a swell idea," Rusty snorted. "Don't I have enough trouble without planning a bank heist?"

" 'Twas but a thought," Hugi pointed out. "To take a demon's hoard is no sin. Indeed it could well be counted a blessing!"

Oob was crouching a few feet away, waving his tentacles over his tuberous body in a complex pattern. The old crone had come up behind him, her eyes fixed on the almost hypnotic weaving of Oob's flexible manipulatory members. She collapsed beside him.

"Oh, Catkin! How I've missed thee. Art well, my pretty? Didst yon felon injure thee?" She was on her knees, studying the unbroken greenish hide from which the tentacles sprang.

"Get back, Nell!" Oob ordered brusquely. "I'm perfectly fine, and I mislike to have my zoog complex fussed over! Back to thy hut, miserable one! I'll attend thee ere cockcrow!"

The old woman slunk away, after giving Rusty a dagger-like look. Hugi gobbled and followed her, apparently begging for a handout.

"Now, let's get a couple of things straight here," Naill said to Oob in a no-nonsense tone. "All I want out of this deal is me! OK, I stumbled into something that was none of my business; just let me out!"

"I see no advantage in keeping you here in Faggotsby," Oob conceded. "I myself must thread the maze back to my Control Center, of course, but as for you, poor lad, you may go where you will." He waved a few tentacles, sketching a ragged circle in thin air, which at once gelled over, and Rusty saw the familiar rainbow hues playing across its surface. Without awaiting an engraved invitation, he stepped through it.

It was bitterly cold, and an icy wind probed the edges of his coat, biting at his neck like flaying knives. Rusty readjusted the double-breasted pin-striped garment, put his head down, and slogged toward ... *Toward what?* the question seemed to mock at his efforts. *Wait a minute*:

Lepke wondered confusedly how he'd gotten out in a blizzard. He'd been in the cab ... That was it—it was a set-up. Boss must've planted the hack to kidnap him and drop him here. He halted and looked around. Where in Hell was *here*? *No point in plowing through snow-drifts when I don't know what direction to go.*

Skip that! he retorted. *Keep going!*

He squinted through the darkness, saw a point of yellow light over *that* way. He started toward it, noticing that he could no longer feel any pain in his toes—or anything else, either. *Got to get to shelter,* the city boy told himself sternly.

The light didn't seem to get any closer. He ignored that, and went on doggedly. After a long time, he realized he could see that the glow was rectangular. It was a lighted window! Swell, only a little farther now. . . .

Rusty picked himself up again. Not for the first time, he realized, or the tenth.

His breath burned in his throat. His bones had frost on them. The yellow window—he could see the mullions now—was definitely closer; but if he just took a little nap here first . . . Lepke's thought went back to his last meeting with Lefty. It was a bum rap: practically accused him of skimming the take—him, the most loyal guy in the rackets! Well, maybe he *had* sidetracked that ten gees he'd beat out of old Carboni, but that was his own idea, in a way—but skip it. Lefty was sharper than he'd figured. He'd picked a hell of a way to knock a guy off—froze to death in a blizzard. But—

With a yell of anger, Rusty lunged to his feet—or *somebody's* feet. They were ice-cakes. He managed a step, then another. Closer to the window, he saw that it was set in a wall of weathered clapboards. The room inside seemed to be a store, with shelves neatly stacked with canned goods, tobacco products, and items of clothing, like caps and gloves. He fumbled along the wall to a door, thumped on it, pushed, met resistance. There seemed to be no doorknob. He pounded again, managed a hoarse croak. The door swung inward suddenly, and warm air gushed out. For an instant he hardly noticed the woman standing there. She was tall, slender, not quite young, but quite beautiful, with reddish hair put up on top of her head. She had high cheekbones, slightly hollow cheeks, and she said, putting a hand to him,

"For heaven's sake, do come in!" He took a step toward her. The closer he got to her the more she looked like Katharine Hepburn. Those big, expressive eyes, that no-quite-disapproving mouth, the scarf wrapped around her neck . . .

"Katharine!" he mumbled, "I mean, Miss Hepburn! How? What?"

She had to tug him inside, then steady him as he made his way to the big chair beside the potbellied stove. She was speaking quietly to him, in that familiar, perfectly modulated New England voice. He sank down in the chair and let it all go. There was an instant of wrenching pain. Rusty/Lepke opened his eyes.

He was back in a chair in the hotel lobby, with a cold draft blowing on his neck. Must have dozed off, dreamed about the blizzard. He got up and went out through the revolving door into the street and was in a vast, unfamiliar plaza.

CHAPTER SIX

Roger Tyson looked around at the amazing plaza he and Bob had so abruptly discovered in the middle of Brantville.

"Thought it was the bank," Bob muttered. "Used to *be*! I've been in the First National before. This is all something . . . !"

"I know," Roger soothed the dismayed young fellow. "Look, I'm Roger Tyson. I've been through this kind of thing before. Don't get upset: it's just the holes in the Trans-Temporal Bore."

"You keep talking about this bore," Bob complained, but he put out his hand to Roger. "Bob Armstrong, glad to meet you, Mr. Tyson. What *is* this place? Look, there's somebody now. Where'd he come from?"

"We'd better be casual," Roger counseled. "We don't want to upset him, talking wildly, you know." They strolled across to meet the man, a husky fellow of early middle age, with sun-bleached hair and a weatherbeaten complexion. He was standing, staring back up the steps. Before they reached him, he abruptly went up, and pushed through the doors. For a moment they stood, feeling disproportionately let down; then the door opened and he re-emerged, looking around as if amazed.

69

"He looks as lost as we are," Bob remarked, then, raising his voice slightly, "Say, fella, you live around here?"

The redhead glanced at him in a relieved way, and hurried over. "Thank God for a normal American," he said fervently. "Rusty Naill's the handle! . . . I think," he added doubtfully. "For a while there I was a hoodlum named Lepke, and then I met Katie Hepburn and she—" He offered a callused palm. "Say," he went on, "you'll never believe what—"

"Sure we will," Bob assured him. "We went in the bank, and here we were! Where *are* we, anyways? There's nothing like this in Brantville!"

"What part of Florida's *that* in?" Rusty asked. "I was in a blizzard," he hurried on, "and Katharine Hepburn—"

"Yeah," Roger chimed in. "We saw the glacier, but it's gone now."

"Glad of that," Rusty said. "Before I met Kate, there was this sort of medieval village, and old Mother Good-wish, or 'Nell,' somebody called her; she called *me* 'Andy'; she had this pet demon—really! I *saw* it! Thing about knee-high, dirty green, with legs like a spider and wavy tentacles at the top—"

"Oob!" Roger blurted.

"How's that?" Rusty said. "Thing was alien, had this big eye, and it and the old dame were pals. She called it 'my pretty.'"

"That's just Oob, the Rhox," Roger explained. "And I don't mean 'rocks,' like stones. It's kind of an outlaw life-form that's found its way into the Trans-Temporal Bore somehow, and is raising Cain! Old UKR and the people in Culture One are trying to capture him, but that's tricky, because all we ever meet is just a third-order extrusion. Does no good to smash it flat, or whatever, either; it just extrudes another one."

"Oh, I see," Rusty said doubtfully.

"No, you don't," Roger contradicted him, "but that's OK; it's important to forget about trying to understand,

and just go with the flow. If we can just make contact with the Builder, he'll straighten this out in a hurry."

"You didn't say about this builder," Rusty pointed out.

"I was just getting to that," Roger assured him. "You see, we're all part of the Builder, so we have authority. UKR will follow our orders."

"Not so fast, Mr. Tyson," UKR's disembodied voice spoke up, less loudly than usual. "Only such orders, or I prefer to say, 'suggestions,' as are in consonance with the Final Concept will be acted upon. Kindly keep that in mind at all times."

"Swell!" Roger enthused feebly. "Now, if we just knew what this Final Concept was. . . ."

"All in good time," UKR reassured him. "Remembering, of course, that time is an insubstantial construct of the human intellect—the *limited* human intellect—in the pre-Builder stage of evolution."

"Perfect!" Roger commented. "We don't know what we're supposed to be doing, and if we did, it would turn out to be imaginary, or worse!"

"Good boy!" UKR congratulated him. "Now you're getting the idea!"

"He *is*?" Bob and Rusty said almost in unison with Roger's, "I *am*?"

"Just for the 'present'—another meaningless concept—" UKR proceeded, "what are your wishes?"

"I'd like to be back home, with Q'nell and that damned couch!" Roger declared fervently.

"I want to just go on with a usual day, like I was, up until I saw that fake iceberg!" Bob offered.

"You can put me back in my skiff with plenty of gas and no cross-chop," Rusty suggested.

"Pity," UKR replied. "That's quite impractical, inasmuch as the ever-widening repercussions of your blundering about in the Matrix will have to be nullified first, of course."

"Oh, of course!" Rusty said sarcastically. "They can't let me get back to work until the Matrix is nullified!"

"Not the Matrix, Clarence!" UKR reprimanded sharply. "The *disturbance* to the Matrix!"

"That's what I meant," Rusty insisted.

"How about canning all this hot jazz and doing something useful?" Bob suggested in a reasonable tone. Just then Roger clutched at his arm and Rusty's, pulling both of them closer.

"Look over there," he commanded. They followed his glance and saw Oob creeping quietly closer, in the partial concealment of a planting box.

"What do you want now, Oob?" Roger called challengingly.

"It's old Nell's familiar," Rusty gasped. "She can't be far away. She's a witch, you know; a *real* one: had me reexperiencing some of my deaths. Spooky!"

"What *is* that thing?" Bob wanted urgently to know.

Roger's tone became didactic.

"That's only a third-order extrusion of a critter known as Oob, the Rhox. He had a lot of big ideas about using all of human history as some kind of sideshow. It doesn't do any good to squash him, either. He just comes back. Even the boys at Culture One couldn't deal with him. But I've got an idea that producing all those extrusions is wearing him down. His color's not good. He's faded out to a sort of dirty magenta, you can see, and I don't think he has as many feet as he used to."

"Do I not?" Oob retorted, and in a sudden rush on twinkling legs, was at Roger's side. Then, his tentacles drooping, he sighed. "I'm a tired being," he confessed. "And a disappointed one. Alas," he went on, "I was forced to abandon my conception of the Ultimate Sideshow, when that spoilsport UKR came along with his ridiculous notions about you people being ancestral to the Builder. Ergo, I have no further interest in sampling your short and dreary history."

"Say," Rusty spoke up, addressing Roger, "do you understand what this spud is talking about, fella?"

"Tyson," Roger supplied. "Roger Tyson. Not really,

but I've discovered you don't have to understand to get caught in the trap here, and—"

"What trap?" Bob demanded.

"The Time Trap; that's what we're in," Roger explained. "Only it's not really a trap; I mean we're in a laboratory slide, being examined under a chronoscope by the scientists in Culture One. Only it's not really a lab, more of a filing system. See?"

"Nope," Bob and Rusty replied promptly.

"Neither do I," Roger confided. "I once had a hypno-briefing, and for a while I knew a lot of stuff about things like the reinforcer, and the null engine, and something called Turnabout. That last was pretty weird: all of a sudden everything's twenty-four hours earlier; then you repeat the day, otherwise there'd be no limit to the size of the displays."

"Twenty-four hours ago," Bob remarked, "I was on the job at the plant, goofing off, you know: just finished my coffee break—fifteen minutes, from ten-thirty to eleven forty-five. I remember old Jed was looking at me when I got back behind the board—I'm a draftsman, you see, and I was just—"

"Bob," Jed said in an overloud voice; people were looking. "You been away from that board over half a hour. Got a good mind to dock you."

"No, Mr. Pawkins," Bob protested. "I just stepped out for a cuppa. Have this detailing finished up in a minute! You know Mr. Kumchett counts on me to furnish the answers when the Service Board calls—"

"OK, I hand it to you, Bob," Jed conceded. "You *do* come up with the idears. I guess we got to allow you a little leeway on the coffee break." He lowered his voice: "But try to be a little sneaky about it, OK? Don't want these other folks to start getting ideas. . . ."

"Sorry about that, Mr. Pawkins," Bob reassured his supervisor.

"Call me 'Jed,' like you always do," Mr. Pawkins urged, coming up alongside Bob. "How do you do it, anyways, Bob?" he wheedled. "Seems like every time the engineers design theirselfs into a corner, you take a look at the sketches and come up with a gadget—like that overunder clip last week—that makes it work. Then the big-domes ack like that's what they had in mind all along. Too bad you can't patent some of the stuff you come up with on comp'ny time. You'd be a rich man today."

"If I wasn't so dumb," Bob mourned, "I'd be a genius, eh?"

"Not what I said, Bobby," Jed protested.

"Say, isn't it about time for lunch?" Bob changed the subject abruptly.

"Just came back from coffee break," Jed pointed out.

"Right," Bob conceded. "Being in the drafting room more'n about five minutes inhibits my creativity." He headed for the snack bar, with Jed's complaining voice trailing off behind him.

"—what you're trying to do, fella!" Rusty's voice was still nagging.

"Let him be," Roger Tyson suggested. "He'll be all right."

Bob, with a sudden rush of panic, sat up and yelled, "*You* guys again? I thought *that* nightmare was over!" He looked around at the broad plaza, the rectilinear planting beds—the bulbous form creeping into the concealment of a bush with green flowers ... "Say, fella," he addressed the nearer of his two fellow suffers.

"Tyson, Roger Tyson," the latter told him. "Take it easy," he added, a trifle smugly, Bob thought.

"It's *him*, or it!" Bob shouted. "Look here, I was back at the plant, right there in the drafting room, and Jed was chewing my ass, just like every day—and now I'm back here, in this crazy dream, with Oob the Rhox sneaking up on me! Roger, you seem to know something about all this! How about explaining what's going on?"

"Easy, Bob," Roger soothed. "I've been in some weirder ones than this. Once somebody stepped on my tail, and a little later they amputated my antlers; talk about a headache!"

"You look better without them," Bob reassured him. "How do we get out of here?"

"We have to be careful," Roger said. "Once I managed to shift out of a pre-material state and into a death-cell, run by blue men who glowed in the dark—reverse polarity, or something."

"Yeah?" Rusty put in. "How'd you do that?"

"It was mostly Q'nell," Roger admitted, "but I helped. I remember: she told me to get my parameters aligned, and to try to coalesce the gray stuff you see when you close your eyes. . . ."

"Doesn't sound too easy," Bob remarked, and closed his eyes. The gray stuff was there, all right; so far so good.

" 'Coalesce,' Roger said," he reminded himself. He tried. The gray was shot through with little whirling red specks, he noticed, and some bluish globs down there. . . . He reached, and was falling out of the gray mist into total blackness.

"Hey!" Rusty yelled. "What happened to Bob? In fact, what happened to everything? I was in this cab, an old Reo, it was, only like new, and the driver was taking me to the airport, in Toledo, or maybe Brooklyn, and—"

"I know," Roger said wearily, holding up a hand. "I think we've gotten into one of these pre-material loci, very malleable, you know, and everything we think about becomes real—sometimes even things we *don't* think about, like the time Q'nell and I were horses—" Roger broke off, blushing at the recollection. "She was so, *horsey*," he explained. "Very distracting. So we have to be careful. As for Bob, no doubt he was dwelling on some idea or other, and accidentally triggered it into pseudo-realization."

"Look," Rusty cut in, "I went inside the big doors up there, and it's a hotel lobby, kind of run-down, like the old Statler in D.C. The cops were after me—and Oob was there, still sneaking around—and my name was

Lepke. Funny, I was Lepke, but he wasn't me, if you know what I mean."

Roger nodded. "I do, sort of," he comforted the confused seaman. "Don't worry about it. It was something to do with falling into atunement with the wrong ego-gestalt. Could happen to anybody."

"Later," Rusty mourned. "I was in this blizzard, and met Katie Hepburn—!"

"Sure," Roger soothed. "Don't try to rationalize it. It's not rational. But something you did while you were Lepke *had* to happen, to align the parameters, or something," he finished uncertainly.

"And there was Andy Scute," Rusty added. "*He* was a nasty piece of business! But all of a sudden—I was me again! I'm afraid I left old Nell in the lurch; ran off her familiar, Oob. He was quite content there, it looked like. Should have let him be."

"That's bad," Roger told him. "You see, Oob has this idea it's up to him to police the Bore, the Trans-Temporal Channel, you understand—"

"Nope," Rusty cut him off. " 'Understand' is just what I don't!"

"Neither do I," Roger confessed. "But it isn't something we have to understand, we just have to ride along with it."

"Oh, sure," Rusty replied. "Just like life."

"That's the idea," Roger seconded. "It's kind of like when you're first born: everything was perfect, then all of a sudden you're dumped in this strange place where all kinds of new and unpleasant things start to happen, things you never heard of before. But you have to adapt, and settle to down to yelling, and dirtying diapers, and saying 'goo-goo' and 'Daddy,' and stuff, and later, falling off bikes and getting the cold shoulder from the cutest girl in third grade, and all that."

"I can do it," Rusty declared. "Only what's next?" He looked up the flight of stone steps. "It was just as real as this," he muttered. "Realer. I kind of liked it: they had everything right there in the lobby: rapid dry-cleaning, cigars, a lunch counter, bakery shop, stores, really convenient. It was 1927," he concluded. "How come life was better in those days? What's different now?"

"It's called 'The Golden Age Effect,'" Roger informed him. "As the memory gets a little hazy, we start remembering the good things being better than they were and we forget the bad parts; but the fact is, we were younger: we *felt* better, and there were lots of things we didn't notice, and it all seems more solid and meaningful. Take the thirties: Clark Gable wearing black-and-white shoes, all ready to make a new picture; brand new Deusenbergs and Model B Fords, and the airplanes: the Aeronca K, and the Eaglerock and the StaggerWing Beech, and the Gee-Bees and all the Wacos—all classics, brand new and available, cheap, at the nearest dealer. But—at the same time, the Depression was going full blast. Nobody's nostalgic for that. Which brings me to my point: when you start visualizing something, then bringing it into experimental focus, you know, you have to be careful to get the good part and leave out the bad stuff. Put yourself in the first row of the balcony eating popcorn and seeing *Mutiny on the Bounty* for the first time, not standing in a bread line in the rain."

CHAPTER SEVEN

The motion of the vessel was sickening, Roger realized for the thousandth time, and the rough-hewn oak deck planking was already slippery from all the barf that had been deposited there by landlubbers who hadn't quite made it to the taffrail. He lost his lunch suddenly. "Small loss," he reflected. "Hardtack with weevils and bilge water with green scum."

A hoarse voice yelled, "Avast there, Mr. Christian!" With a start, Roger realized the captain was addressing *him*! He turned, and Charles Laughton, his face red with thespian effort, bawled: "I've warned you for the last time, mister! No more daydreaming when there's a keel-haul to see to."

"You'll have to excuse me, sir," Roger heard himself saying. "Able Seaman Trotwood fell asleep at his post because he'd been on duty continuously for thirty-nine hours; it was more than human flesh and blood could endure. Anyway, when you keelhaul a fellow, he's not much good after that, with all his hide scraped off by the barnacles, if by some miracle he hasn't drowned."

"I'm master abroad this vessel!" Laughton bellowed. "Now, get over there, and carry out your orders!" He glanced down at the mess on the deck, his jowls vibrating with actorly rage, or with something that made them quiver. Chuck really ought to lose weight, Roger reflected. Just then, with a yell and a heave on the line, the crew brought poor skinny little Trotwood over the side, stripped of his rags, and as bloody as a skinned beef. He made a feeble movement and said, "Goddammit, get them damn ropes off me. I'm reporting this to AGVA! You damn near drowned me!"

"Easy, Fred," Laughton said gently. "Save the histrionics for when the camera's not on you."

"Oh, sorry," Fred said and slumped to the deck and lay, unmoving.

"Trotwood was a good man, Captain!" Franchot Tone spoke up at Bligh's elbow. As always, Roger wondered how such a funny-looking fellow had ever made it in Hollywood. Well, maybe he could act, Roger reflected. *That's the part I hate,* he thought distastefully: *when they start* acting.

"All right, people!" Somebody yelled through a megaphone. "That was OK, all except Fred writhing around and cracking wise when he was supposed to be dead. We'll have to dunk him again, and *this* time, Fred, for chrissakes go limp. You're dead, see! Captain Bligh has murdered you! That's what sets off the mutiny! OK?"

"I won't go back in that tank," Fred muttered, getting to his feet and dabbing at the water on his face.

"What's this, mutiny?" the megaphone yelled.

"Well," Fred offered, looking suddenly abashed, "maybe for time-and-a-half."

"You're fired, Fred!" was the response to this effort. "And you can tell AGVA—" The megaphone dropped as a pert girl in a tailored gray suit tugged at the arm holding it.

"What I'm tryna say," the same voice went on, unmegaphoned, "is whatever good old AGVA says, goes!"

"Damn right!" Fred said inaudibly, as he wandered off, dripping. A man in shirtsleeves hurried past, waving a sheet of typescript.

"Poor Fred," Laughton commiserated. "If he'd only

known when to keep his mouth shut—and when not to wiggle around—he could have had a great career. He dances a little, they say, and he has that sad, 'I need mothering' look that drives the ladies wild. As for myself, I never needed mothering. I made it on sheer talent— and guts! Once at a party I had to kiss that Davis witch; ugh! I think I'll like being Quasimodo better; nearer the real me, you know." The actor seemed suddenly to notice Roger, to whom he had been talking for a full minute.

"Here, who're *you*, lad?" he demanded. "Where's Clark? Tourist, are you, sneaked into the set to see the magic up close, eh? We'll be lucky if you're not in that last medium-shot, standing around in your gray flannel— abominably cut, too, I must say—amongst my cutthroat crew. I recall once we had a row of telephone poles in a dolly shot of the Via Flamina—ancient Rome, you know. It's the details that make the verisimilitude, you know."

"Gee, sir," Roger offered. "I thought you were great as Henry the Eighth. The way you said 'Granted!' every time Elsa made another demand . . . And as Rembrandt, too."

The portly actor grinned. "I've been wondering whether to essay that one," he told Roger. "I suppose this is Manny's way of nudging me, eh? Very well, you may tell him I've decided to do it!"

"Gosh," Roger heard himself mumbling. "Does this mean if it hadn't been for my interference, he never would have made that one . . . ? And just when I was telling myself to be careful . . ."

Everyone was breaking for lunch, Roger realized. He went along, automatically falling in beside an incredibly cute girl with a clipboard, who reminded him a little of Q'nell. Poor kid! At home, alone, except for that Oob character, and poor old Charlie, wondering what in the world had happened to him. His thoughts wandered on, to the great empty plaza, and Bob and Rusty, poor chaps; he hadn't meant to abandon them like that; just when he was cautioning them not to do anything hasty, too . . .

But here was here and now was now, he reminded himself sternly. The present space/time/vug matrix was as valid as any, it was only that he had arrived in it, well, sort of sideways instead of the usual crawl-straight-ahead progression. He had thoughtlessly dumped himself back in about 1935, on a movie set in Hollywood, in the middle of the Golden Age. Well, how about seeing some of it, instead of just standing here looking down the script girl's cleavage! Roger strode determinedly to the head of the line and was promptly knocked down by Whit Bissel, looking mousy, but with a mean left hook, Roger had to acknowledge. He muttered his excuses and got up.

"Sorry, Mr. Bissel," he managed. "Gee, I've enjoyed you in all your pictures. You know, it's the fellows like you who're the *real* stars!" But if he's here, it must be later than 1935, Roger thought.

"Cut the crap," Bissel snapped just as Emmet Vogan passed, giving the two a cool glance.

"Hey!" Roger gulped. "Vogan just bucked the line, and you didn't—"

"Emmet's been around a while," Bissel pointed out. "I don't think I've seen *you* before—a great mistake, young fellow—you've got to acquire the knack of being noticed. Now, in my first picture . . ."

"I'm not an actor," Roger put in.

"*That's* obvious," Whit told him. "But I always hate it when they start *act*ing."

"Me, too," Roger agreed. "Do you remember in that Kate Hepburn pic, *Keeper of the Flame*, I think it was, when the horse reared and she started *act*ing? I hated that."

"Say, you must know *some*body," Bissel offered. "There's not half a dozen people that know about that property. I thought it was still at the treatment stage, and you've already seen the rushes, eh? Sorry if I was a bit rough with you there, but I'm tired of people pushing me around because I always play quiet little fellows."

"This is all an illusion," Roger stated. "It's all unreal, I know that, and yet—"

"Don't knock it," Whit suggested. "It's a living."

Roger made a gargling sound. "I didn't mean—" he managed.

Bissel said, "Excuse me," and hurried away. Roger gazed in awe as Marlene Dietrich strolled past, garbed in a gauzy pink thing, with a makeup man trotting beside her, trying to dab at her cheek on the run.

"Lay off, buster!" she snapped with a heavy Teutonic accent.

"As long as I'm here," Roger told himself, "I might as well see all I can." He headed for a cluster of brilliant lights far across the cavernous sound stage, and came up on a street in London, circa 1875. Robert Donat or somebody like that was strolling past a shop with black urns in the window, and a sign that said REMOVALS FROM ASYLUMS AND HOSPITALS.

Not too cheery, Roger reflected. He saw a sign ahead with a large head of yellow cheese painted on it; he turned in. There was a smell of toasting cheese and good English ale, and a muffled surf-roar of conversation. The place was hardly lit at all, except for the small-paned windows and a few candles guttering on tables. He pushed through the crowd of periwigged extras, and took a table in the corner.

A heavy-set man with a big untidy brown bag-wig reluctantly scroonched over to make room.

"Wow," Roger commented, studying the brown-with-age notice tacked on the oak-paneled wall announcing a race meeting at Ascot. "Some of these directors really waste money, eh? Like paying all you fellows to sit back in here in the dark where the camera will never see you."

"Are you, sir, by chance, addressing me?" the coarse-featured old fellow inquired, not as if it mattered. "Your speech, sir, has something of a colonial ring to it."

"Sure," Roger confirmed. "I was saying about the way they waste money putting monogrammed underwear on the Hussars, and all."

"As for the excesses of foreigners," Roger's new acquaintance said with distaste, "a reasonable man can hardly hope to fathom such follies. The same, I fear, applies to you colonists. I have heard that even now the confounded upstarts propose to metallize a road the entire length of their town, New York, I believe they call it. Damned insult to His Grace the Duke—the name, I mean."

"That's not true," Roger countered. "There are no metal roads in New York, unless you mean the railroads, of course."

"Hah!" the old fellow snorted. "I've heard of some madman up-country who proposes to lay iron rails and operate some sort of horseless carriage thereon. Folly, sir!"

"It worked," Roger told him. "Steam power, you know."

This netted another snort. "I find no reference, sir, in Scripture to 'steam power.' One sees a trickle of steam from the spout when brewing one's tea," he went on. "I fail to see the connection between that frail emanation and the drayage of cargo on or off iron rails! Ridiculous!"

"Well . . ." Roger started to explain, then fell silent as he realized he didn't know doodly squat about steam engines.

"What about internal combustion?" he offered. "That's a lot more successful."

"The term, sir, is meaningless," the old fellow dismissed the idea. "And superfluous. The whole idea of the horseless carriage: why, for Heaven's sake, do these madmen propose to eliminate the horse, which Divine Providence has suited so perfectly to its God-given role, and is everywhere readily available?"

"Neater," Roger supplied. "No harness to mess with, and no getting spooked, running away."

"I see you know little of our modern London post-chaise system," the domineering local snapped. "No more perfect form of transport will ever be developed, as none is needed."

"Good morning, Doctor," a tenor voice broke in, and a dandified young fellow in a long coat of claret velvet bustled up, and bobed his head at the older man, giving Roger a resentful glance.

"May I have a seat, sir?" he inquired diffidently.

"By all means, Jamie," was the reply.

"Sir!" the newcomer blurted, smiling broadly as he seated himself. "I'm overwhelmed! You never before so far unbent as to call me 'Jamie!' Thank you, sir! This is a red-letter day for me." He paused. "Yesterday I was bad," he confessed. "I owned to the spleen, I fear, in conversation with Miss Henderson—Captain Henderson's pretty sister, you'll recall. By the way, sir, how did your dinner go with the rabble-rousing Mrs. Robinson?" He took out a notebook and jotted, then looked expectantly at the doctor.

"I told her," the doctor replied, seeming to suppress a smile, "that I was quite a convert to her republican principles, and prayed that she might allow her footman to dine with us. She will never like me now, I fear. And yourself, dear Boswell, how is your Plan succeeding?"

"Capitally, sir!" Boswell replied. "One of my strictures, you'll recall, is to curb my tendency to chatter on at length—"

The old doctor nodded. "I recall," he growled. " 'Don't rattle,' you command yourself. Excellent advice."

"—at tea last fortnight," Boswell was still gushing. "I was a few moments late, you see, and Miss Williams said, 'Why, it is a part of his Plan!' They twit me, you see, Doctor. I told them I had resolved to forsake idleness and folly. They laughed." Boswell smiled ruefully, and resumed the small talk.

"What other sacrifices does your Plan require of you, Jamie?" the doctor asked gently.

Boswell paused uncertainly in his discourse, and replied, "I mustn't own to the spleen. And I'm determined to respect Father."

"Laudable aims, Jamie. How goes your journal?"

"I bring it up every other day," Boswell responded, and again fetched out the hardbound notebook from an inner pocket. "I shall note, Doctor, the particulars of this happy meeting, sir, as soon as I return to my rooms."

"Excellent," the doctor said, and gave Roger a quizzical look. "You were speaking, sir, of curious artifices. Internal steam, or the like," he explained to the young fellow.

"I've heard of it!" Boswell exclaimed, looking directly at Roger for the first time. "Some sort of scheme for propelling one's coach without horses, eh?" He cocked his head expectantly.

"It's not 'internal steam,'" Roger corrected. "You see, steam is raised by *external* heat, and internal combustion is just the opposite: the fuel is burned *inside* the engine."

The doctor wagged his heavy head as if in understanding, but his meaty features reflected only incomprehension. "You call this apparatus an 'engine,' eh? Most appropriate. The etymology—"

"Sure," Roger agreed. "You see, the gasoline is squirted into the chamber, and detonated by a spark plug; that drives the piston down, which gives the crankshaft a push via the con-rod. Very efficient, with proper valving and timing, you know."

"Incredible!" Boswell cried. "And who, sir, do you imagine would consent to remain in the vicinity of an exploding 'engine'?"

Roger tried to explain; meanwhile, he was looking for the camera. A door opened nearby, and he caught a glimpse of a steamy kitchen, where costumed extras bustled as if preparing food.

"This is ridiculous," Roger reflected. "Not even von Stroheim would go *this* far supplying background detail nobody can see." He paused, struck by a thought. "Can it be," he inquired of himself, "that I've done it again, without the Aperture? Stumbled into the *real* eighteenth-century London, and it's *not* a movie set?" He caught the old gentleman's rheumy eye. "Beg pardon, sir, but would you be the famous Doctor Samuel Johnson? In the flesh?"

"Too much of it, I fear," Johnson replied jovially. "You

call me 'famous,' sir. Am I then known on the other side of the Atlantic?"

He turned to Boswell. "This gentleman, Jamie, is a colonist. Seems quite civil, though a trifle eccentric," he added quite audibly behind his hand.

"I've a great interest in the plantations," Boswell said eagerly. "One could make one's fortune there, I think. Do you agree, Mr.—?"

" 'Tyson,' " Roger supplied. "Roger Tyson. Yes," he continued, "the opportunities are unlimited. The timber, and the completely virgin oil fields, and the gold in California and Alaska, and—" He fell silent as he realized the Londoners were staring raptly at him.

" 'Calaforny,' " Johnson repeated. "I've heard of it. An island far to the west, is it not? How would one journey there, sir? Round the Cape, I suppose; a perilous voyage. Still, if there's gold to be had . . ."

"Only ten hours by air," Roger blurted without reflecting. The madhouses of this day were no place to be locked up, he told himself, resolving to watch his conversation from now on.

Boswell tittered, and Johnson uttered a rumble that could have been a chuckle.

"You have a keen sense of humor, sir," the latter remarked. "You colonists are flying now, are you? Just how is it done, sir?" He stood and flapped his arms awkwardly. "That about it, eh?"

"No, you don't understand," Roger contradicted the dignified old fellow. "One doesn't actually *fly*, like a bird; one rides in an airplane, *it* does the flying. You just sit there and a pretty stewardess brings you your dinner."

"Capital, sir!" Johnson boomed. He clapped Roger on the shoulder. "I fear, sir, I failed to catch the name."

"Tyson," Roger said, "Roger Tyson."

"Oh, of course, I confess my memory is not all it once was." He turned to Boswell. "Jamie, this is Mr. Rogers, or Tidings. Be sure to note this meeting in your journal. Mister Tidings, my young friend is James Boswell. He is a Scotsman, but he cannot help it."

Then he added: "Good sirs, we must away i' the instant! I saw Beelzebub but now, lurking in the shadows yonder."

Roger's gaze followed the doctor's gesture and caught a glimpse of Oob, just easing in behind a screen placed before the scullery door.

Boswell offered his hand. Roger shook it with a sense of unreality. Still, he reassured himself, the aroma of freshly toasted cheese was as palpable as the rattle of pewter tankards and the hubbub of bibulous voices. How the devil had he done it? He was just talking to Rusty and Bob about being careful . . . *Quiver*.

"Roger!" Rusty's voice intruded on his ruminations. "How did you do that?"

"Do what?" Roger inquired, and opened his eyes. The featureless plaza extended to the distant facades; nothing had changed. How long had he been gone?

"One second you're over here," Rusty complained, indicating a position on his right, and *zap!* you're behind me. How'd you do it?"

"Beats me," Roger confessed. "I've been all kinds of places since I saw you last. I was aboard the *Bounty*, the movie one, you understand, and I saw Marlene Dietrich up as close as I'm seeing you right now! Then I chatted with Boswell and Johnson for a few minutes, and—" He gripped his head with both hands. "This is terrible!" he groaned. "Now I'm flitting around from one exhibit to another, without—"

LOOK HERE, LITTLE CREATURES! a vast voice boomed down out of the cloudless sky, which, Roger noticed absently, had a distinctly green cast. THIS MEDDLING MUST CEASE AT ONCE, RELATIVELY SPEAKING!

"It's UKR!" Roger gulped.

"Who's a sucker?" Rusty demanded. "Nobody's fooled *me* for a minute! *I* know it's just a nightmare because of eating too many soft-shelled crabs last night at Sparky's!"

"In that case," Bob spoke up feelingly, "what am I doing in *your* nightmare?"

"It's not quite a nightmare, fellows," Roger attempted to elucidate. "UKR is no dream, he's this machine, you see—"

"Nope, I don't!" Rusty snapped. "What machine? I don't see any machines!"

"The voice," Roger explained. "The big voice in the sky. He was built by the Builder, and—"

"It figures," Rusty said coldly. "The Builder built it. OK, but where *is* it? Talks out of the sky, you say?"

"Didn't you hear it?" Roger yelped. "It was loud as thunder; it said, 'Quit meddling!' "

"Suits me," Bob contributed. "Suppose I go inside and look for that F'shu. Maybe he knows what's going on."

"No use," Rusty told him. "It's just a hotel lobby, like I said. Some guy thought I was a big shot, probably crooked, named 'Lepke.' And he said it was 1927. But when I went back outside—"

"You didn't come out," Bob said flatly, and looked to Roger for confirmation.

"That would be about the time Bissel socked me," Tyson explained. "I didn't see . . ."

As the three disputed the matter, F'shu re-emerged from the door alone, and came briskly down the steps. He appeared not to notice the bedraggled trio awaiting him at the bottom.

"Say, F'shu," Roger halted him as he started past. "Could you—?"

F'shu whirled and gave him a stern look. "How is it you know my name?" he snarled.

"You told us," Roger blurted.

F'shu frowned. "I seem to have a vague recollection of . . . but that was so long ago—absolute," he finished vaguely.

" 'Absolutely' *what*?" Bob demanded. "Lay off the run-around, OK?"

"Snag number!" F'shu snapped.

"You're from Culture One," Roger stated, ignoring the cryptic remark. "You can tell us how to get out of the

Bore and back to the boring. Especially since UKR is getting impatient with us."

"Culture One was—or will be—abolished in the third phase of the Reorganization," F'shu said shortly. "How is it you know of its existence?"

"It's a long story, F'shu," Roger said wearily. "Couldn't we just get on to the substantive part, the rescue? We're all innocent victims of circumstances beyond our control."

"Ah, yes, M'ron's famous axiom, in which he claimed to have summed up the human dilemma. Sheer yivshish, actually! How is it you know I originated in Culture One? It appears, sir, you've been prying."

"Oob told us," Roger replied. "It's Oob that's causing all the trouble," he added. "Just stick Oob back in his Control Apex, with a suppressor focused on him, and the meddling will cease."

F'shu folded his arms across his Charles Atlas–type chest, and looked searchingly at Roger; then his gaze wandered to Bob and Rusty, who were standing behind Roger, looking belligerently back at the white-clad official.

"You got something to do with ruining my day?" Bob wanted to know.

"And swamping my boat?" Rusty contributed.

"Now, calmly, gentlemen," F'shu soothed. "Suppose we just drop back to a pre-activated state and take stock of affairs?"

"I don't like the sound of that!" Roger objected. "Just show me the nearest Aperture, and we'll take our chances."

"Not practical," F'shu dismissed the suggestion. "The Alignment, you know, is badly out of sync."

"Swell!" Roger snorted. "The big Alignment's out of sync, so we're supposed to spend the rest of our lives dodging Oob from one nutty stage-set to the next!"

"Still," F'shu pointed out, "there *are* compensations: there is no finite termination point to these aberrant lines. You shall live, subjectively, forever."

"You mean we'll spend Eternity like this?" Rusty

groaned. "Look, since you seem to know all about this stuff, why not just put me on that stool at Sparky's, and let me go on slowly dying? OK?"

"I'll take a transfer to Design Section," Bob offered. "That's not much to ask, after six years with Jed in the drafting room."

"Quiet down, fellows," Roger suggested. "This may be the break we need. I never heard of a 'pre-activated' state before, but it sounds promising. Go ahead, F'shu." He directed his remark to the white-clad Inspector, who nodded absently.

"Already done, of course," he reproved quietly. "As Grand Monitor of the Ultimate Apex, I don't propose lightly, while in a pre-material state—and I urge *you* to take no precipitous action."

"Gulp," Roger replied; he turned to Rusty.

"You want to be on a bar stool, you said," he stated. "We're now in a malleable context, so, judging from my past experiences with the Bore, I'd say just scroonch your eyes shut, and visualize what you want: the human imagination is a powerful vector in an indeterminate Cosmos. You see, it all goes back to the instant of the Big Bang, when everything was pre-material and the vector provided by the human conceptualizing ability gives things a shove in . . . well, in the direction they went."

"But there *weren't* any humanity at the 'time of the Big Bang'!" Bob objected. "I know that much!"

"Your conception of relative time is an illusion," F'shu put in. "That which is, *is!*"

"Alas," Roger said, "most of what we 'know' is illusory. Anyway, that's part of the big puzzle. If there was no time or space, or even vug, who's to say if man was present?"

Rusty duly closed his eyes, as did Bob, who had listened closely though uncomprehendingly to the dialog.

"Yeah, that's it," Rusty murmured.

He opened his eyes and squinted against the glare from the glassy blue-green water extending to the horizon, just past the chrome-plated rail of the thirty-one-foot

Mako he'd always meant to have someday. He heard a gentle *tinkle!* and turned his head to see Candy at his elbow in her scantiest bikini, offering him a tall glass with ice cubes. "I'm going below for a nap, dolling," she cooed.

He watched the nice hip-action as she strolled away. "Say!" he said aloud, "this is the real stuff! To heck with Sparky's. I've got my own sources of supply!" He smiled contentedly and closed his eyes, enjoying the lift and slide of the gentle seas. "Probably from a typhoon six thousand miles away," he thought. *Quiver!* He grabbed for dear life as a limb of the tree he was perched in sagged, hesitated, and leaned farther. He opened his eyes and saw a debris-littered beach below him. *Damn! I really hafta be careful what I think about,* he realized.

The shrieking wind had already torn his clothes from him, and he was getting chilled fast—even here in the tropic latitudes. The house had gone at the first gust; then the tsunami hit, and he'd been darn lucky to be tossed into the tree, about the only one still standing, he realized, squinting his eyes to get a glimpse of the storm-ravaged beach. *There's Jim's Chris-Craft, stove in bad,* he noticed, *fifty feet above tideline, too.* Not much hope for his own brand-new Mako, even back in Cap Bob's boat-shed at the Pass. *Or was I—* He felt a surge of panic. Where was poor little Candy? *Quiver!*

At Rusty's yell, Candy came running across the deck. She was still wearing half of the bikini. "Dolling!" she squeaked, "I was just dozing off, and I heard you yell. What's wrong? Where's your clothes? How'd you get soaked? You fall overboard, or what?"

"Forget it," Rusty urged. "Just a little slip."

"Oh, you *did* go over the side. Thought you's a better seaman than that, dolling. Better put on some clothes—guess you shedded 'em in the water, eh, so's you wouldn't get drowned."

"I must have," Rusty temporized. "I'm a little hazy. Speaking of clothes, where's yours?"

"Oh, dolling, did I forget—?" She fled. Rusty got to

his feet, established the deck firmly underfoot, and said aloud, "OK, wise guy, cut the comedy!"

"You have only yourself to blame," F'shu replied testily. "I warned you!" Rusty opened his eyes. Roger and Bob were standing ten feet away, at the foot of the broad steps, looking at him with unreadable expressions. F'shu was frowning. "I warned you," he said sadly. "Luckily, I noticed your plight and retrieved you. I don't like to use the field retriever unnecessarily you know; upsets the stat computer."

"Thanks," Rusty said. "You can tell the computer to stick it."

"Are you—? Did you—?" Roger stammered. "Glad you're all right, Rusty. I should have warned you to be _very_ careful. I remember one time I ran into a subhuman oaf named Bimbo, who was intent on tearing me limb from limb. He thought I was his new play-pretty. He was only about six-four-six, but he had arms like a gorilla, a skull like a cannonball, and a temper like a wolverine! I remember when I killed him one time, knocked his eye right out of the socket; that _really_ got his goat!"

Quiver. Roger paused as he realized Rusty and Bob both were making urgent _shush!_ing motions and backing away. He sniffed, got a whiff of well-rotted goat-hide, and turned just as Bimbo lunged.

"Belay that!" Roger commanded. "Armored plate-glass!" The giant rebounded from the invisible barrier, rubbing his flat nose, from which blood was flowing. He crossed his close-set brown eyes in an effort to look at his hurtie. He shook his bullet head and wandered away.

"Whew!" Roger sighed. "That was close! I better take my own advice! Now, Bob . . ." He turned his attention to the earnest young fellow who was staring at him with a dazed expression.

"Did you see him?" Bob gasped. "That was a real, live _Homo erectus_, or I'll cancel my subscription to _Scientific American_! He was just jumping at you and he changed his mind—where'd he go?" Bob interrupted himself. "He was right here, and—"

"It's the pre-activated state," Roger told him, wondering what he was talking about. "I didn't need him anymore, so . . ."

"Well, the next time you need an ape-man, check with us first, OK?" Bob looked to Rusty for agreement, but Rusty was nowhere to be seen.

"He's done it, too!" Bob yelled. "Now don't *you* go disappearing on me again, Roger!" he appealed.

"Don't worry, I won't," Tyson assured him. "I just wish Q'nell was with me instead of you. No offense." Had he felt the *Quiver!*?

"Gosh!" Bob said, "Morning, ma'am." He looked wildly around. "Now they're doing it the other way!" he carped. "First it was people disappearing: now it's half-naked ladies popping out of nowhere!"

"Half-naked?" Roger blurted and turned to see Q'nell's slim figure half in a slinky negligee. She had a startled expression on her perfect face. "Roger!" she wailed. "Did you—?"

"Not me," Roger cut in. "At least not intentionally. Awfully glad to see you, girl, even though I hate to see you mixed up in this. I didn't mean—"

"Roger! Don't!" Q'nell cried, throwing herself into his arms. "You have to be *very* careful in these silly pre-activated states, you know that! Why, you almost—"

"Thanks for stopping me," Roger gulped. "I guess I don't know how to be careful. What happened to F'shu?"

Q'nell shook her head. "He reverted to an unrealized state, one Basic Minute after he set up the pre-activated field," she told Roger. "That was careless of *him*. You see, he comes from the Ultimate Culture, some millennia in the relative future."

"Too bad," Roger said. "We were hoping he could help us."

"'We,' Roger?" she said with in interrogative inflection. "You're quite alone—except for Oob, of course."

CHAPTER EIGHT

When Bob eased back into the drafting room, Mr.
Kumchett, the big boss, from Concept Approval, or
somewhere, was just entering by another door.

"Oh—Armstrong, isn't it?—there you are," he called.
"Just looking around for Jed. Have you seen him? Damn
fella's never on the job when I want him."

"He said something about lunch," Bob improvised.

Kumchett looked at his Zolex strap-watch. "Not lunch-
time for another twenty minutes. Can't stand a fellow
who shaves his break-time! Now *you*—Bob, isn't it?—
here you are, right on the job! When you see Jed, tell
him he's fired. You're the new supervisor, Bob, isn't it?"

"Sir," Bob faltered. "C-could *you* tell him? If I'm to
be promoted, sir, how about a shot at Design, upstairs?
I have a few ideas."

"Capital notion, Armstrong, isn't it?" Kumchett waved.
He made a note on his cuff and strolled away.

For a moment Bob stood bemused, sniffing the familiar odors of vellum, shaved cedar, and Pink Pearl. Design
Section, hooray! His thoughts turned briefly to Roger,
whom he had last seen ogling the lovely brunette who
had popped out of nowhere, half-dressed, and grabbed

94

Roger. Well, if that was trouble, may we never have tranquillity! Roger'll be OK.

With that cleared up, Bob put his instruments back in his tackle-box, pulled the cover off his board and the almost finished longitudinal section of the proposed Culture Center. Those suspended acoustical panels were a bitch, but he could leave that to the new man. Whistling, he strode out of the drafting room—for the last time? he wondered if he dared to hope—glancing pityingly at Dick and Dave, crouched over their boards like elves toiling in a cave under the mountain . . . *Quiver.* "Stop it!" he reprimanded himself sharply, dodging a stalactite. *Or is it* mite? *Oh, yes: "Ants in your pants: the mites go up and the tights go down." Quiver!* Dammit! He'd done it again!

The doorman at the entrance to the once-fashionable Dorian ducked his head and held the portal wide to admit Sweet Manny O'Rourke and two of his close associates. Manny tightened the belt securing his camel's-hair overcoat and strode through, his eyes taking in the details of the wide lobby in a quick left-right flick.

Upstairs, he barged through the door to Suite 7-C.

"Jeeze, Boss," Lefty, his right-hand man grumbled. "I woulda—"

Manny took a step into the garishly papered room and peered through the layer of cigar smoke at the four men seated at a card table under a glass chandelier.

"Where's Lepke?" he barked.

"Cripes, Sweets," a bald, weasel-faced runt whined. "Give the guy time; it's only two minutes after."

Lefty shouldered forward. "Don't try to tell Mr. O'Rourke no advice, Popsy," he grunted.

"Yeah, but where *is* the mug?" a beefy fellow who had forgotten to shave demanded, rising from the table, his eyes fixed on Lefty.

Manny put out a hand. "Take it easy, Hymie," he urged. "Lefty don't mean no—"

"Lay off, Doc," Lefty urged.

"I don't care what Lefty don't mean," Doc Condon snapped. "And don't call me 'Doc'; that's 'Mr. Condon' to you, Lefty," he ordered the latter.

"I guess if you can call me 'Lefty,' Lefty offered, "I got a right to call you 'Doc,' like ever'body elst."

"OK, OK," Doc reversed field, taking a step backwards, "Call me 'Hymie,' OK? I just don't want nobody to get the idea I'm mixed up in the Lindy snatch."

"Sure, Hymie," Manny purred. "But where's Lepke at?"

"Oughta be here any second," a small, bookkeeperish fellow suggested.

They waited, adding steadily to the smoke layer.

Roger Tyson kept his eyes tight shut for a long time. "Don't go messing it up this time," he commanded himself impatiently. "This may be your last chance. The prematerial state won't hold up long, with F'shu gone." He waited grimly for a certifiably good idea to occur to him. "Just as long as that Oob nuisance isn't crouched back of a rubber tree, watching every move," he specified. "How about just being back home, in that hideous living room, but oh, so cram-full of cozy joy and crowned with a woman's love . . . ?

"Don't go thinking about the shooting of Dan McGrew," he cautioned himself. "A fellow has to *learn* from his mistakes. Lucky Dan was too drunk to shoot straight that last time . . ." *Stop! You're doing it again. Don't woolgather! Concentrate! I need to get back to Culture One, and get them to focus a suppressor on Oob, and—Quiver.*

—bumped into someone, a cute little number whose name, he remembered, was P'ty. "Sorry, dear," he mumbled, putting out a steadying hand. Big M'lon suddenly loomed up behind her.

"Take your hands off my intended," he commanded.

"But I was just—" Roger explained.

"I saw you doing an illegal displacement, right in front of me," the big fellow cut him off. "What do you think this is, just a jungle, where unmonitored personnel can blunder around and damage the whole entropic fabric at will?"

"That's what it seems like," Roger pointed out hotly. "I was sitting peacefully at home, and—" He looked around, observed that he and the two Culture One citizens were alone on a small terrace apparently topping a very tall tower. At a similar long-stemmed table a few feet away, a young fellow in a beret was sitting alone. Funny how you could always tell an American, he mused. There wasn't even a handrail, Roger noted as M'lon towered over him in a menacing way, thrusting the giggling P'ty behind him, both being crowded onto the very edge of the tiny island.

"Just take it easy," Roger suggested, easing his chair back, but not too far, he cautioned himself. "Don't you Culture One people do anything to stop this Oob except accuse his victims of being responsible?" he inquired in a voice with a tendency to slip into a falsetto. "And why do you spend so much time flagpole-sitting?"

"Oh, yes," M'lon replied, slowing his advance, "I'd forgotten all you primitives are claustrophiles. Perhaps a change of apparent context . . ."

Roger got to his feet. He was back in the Plaza with Bob and Rusty—and another fellow. . . .

Mr. and Mrs. Horace Potts stepped down from the raffish taxi which had squealed to a stop at the curb.

"Oh, Horace," Delia Potts squeaked, gazing at the crowded sidewalk. "It all looks so . . . so . . . Parisian!"

"Quite naturally, my dear," Potts replied, overtipping the surly, unshaven cabbie, who snarled and departed. "It is after all, Paris," Horace stated firmly.

"Oh, look!" Delia yelped. "They're evicting the restaurant! See? They've put all their tables out on the sidewalk! It seems so cruel!"

"It's all right, Dellie," Horace soothed her. "It's what you call a sidewalk cafe. See? The people are sitting at the tables eating and all."

"Let's speak to that nice-looking young man," Mrs. Potts suggested. "I'm sure he's an American. Isn't it odd how you can always tell an American in these foreign places?"

"It's those pinkish-tan sort of raincoats," Horace said grumpily. "Catch *me* wearing one!"

Julian looked up as the plump, still-pretty woman came up and said, "Pardon me, young man, I'm Mrs. Horace Potts, and this is my husband!"

"*Mister* Horace Potts, I don't doubt," Julian replied, lifting his rear an inch from the chair. "Do join me."

"Oh, I knew you were an American!" the lady squeaked. "And you've heard of Horace! Isn't that nice, Horace, the young man has heard of you! Yes," she went on, "I'm quite proud of Horace's success. Thank you. Sit down, Horace, don't dither."

"You in the Market, sir?" Horace inquired ponderously, as he sat and tucked a napkin into his shirt-front.

Julian shook his head, "Actually—" he began, as Mr. Potts continued.

"—pity one can't be everywhere at once," the broker was ruminating. "Had a ticker office aboard ship, you know, but it's not quite the same as actually being on the Floor! I've taken a strong position in International Wicker; expect great things from that stock. What was the name, sir? I'm afraid I didn't catch it."

Julian shook his head. "I didn't mention it: 'Julian'—"

"A bit of advice, Julius," Horace was saying. "Sell all those newfangled 'electrics,' or whatever, and get into sorghum futures!" Horace looked satisfied until a short, fat waiter appeared and jabbered at him in some damned foreign tongue.

"Just coffee," Horace barked, and looked expectantly at Dellie.

"I'll have what Julian is having," she cooed.

Horace looked around sharply. "Julian? Who's Julian?"

"Why, Horace," Delia said gently.

"That's *my* name, Mr. Potts," Julian told him.

"Call me Horace, Julius," Potts commanded heartily,

offering a well-manicured but powerful hand, which Julian gripped and released.

"Did you know," Julian began, "that that gesture goes back to a time when two strangers meeting showed an empty hand, to demonstrate they weren't holding a weapon—?"

"Told them fellows," Potts growled, "when Potts says 'buy,' you *buy*, dammit! Got to be a bit brusque at times," he nodded with an apologetic look at his wife, "to keep the damned ducks in line! Act like *they* were giving the orders! Sorry, Dellie, you know how I hate shop-talk. Tell us about yourself, sir," he switched his remarks to Julian. "Live here in town, do you?"

Half an hour later, while Julian was still trying to explain to Horace Potts that "Julian" was his *last* name, and there wasn't any other last name, the waiter approached nervously, and addressed Julian:

"M'sue, I fear w 'ave ze, how you say, 'gas leak'; one must vacate ze premises." He fled.

Julian rose and assisted Dellie from her chair.

"Here!" Horace grated. "What'd that fellow say?"

"There's a poison gas leak, dear," Mrs. Potts told her spouse. "We're to, oh, vacate the premises."

"Damned nonsense!" Horace barked. "The war's over, been over for years! I'm sitting right here to have my coffee in peace! Sit down, Dellie! You too, sir, if you don't mind; mustn't let these foreigners try to bully honest Americans! Damn waiter probably just wanted to clear us out of the table so he can gouge a big tip from somebody by producing a table on command!"

Julian was looking at what appeared to be a probing finger of a translucent bluish substance. He fanned at it with his hand; it continued to probe; indeed, he realized, it was forming up into a more solid texture. It touched the table and stopped dead. Odd sort of gas.

"It seems he was right," Julian told the Pottses. "We'd better get out of here." He looked around at the other tables. No one else seemed disturbed, and it appeared there was only the one probing tentacle of gas. The thought of a tentacle reminded him of something. He ducked to look under the table. Potts was muttering, but getting to his feet. Just as Julian was about to suggest they cover their faces with napkins, the blue phenomenon disappeared.

"Well, folks," Julian began, "I guess the scare is over." Just then he saw a flicker of motion and turning his head quickly, caught a glimpse of Oob's pointed feet just disappearing from view under Dellie's chair. He also saw a final flash of the blue mist.

"Wait!" he blurted. "It's—!" His voice faltered as he realized he didn't really know *what* it was, either the leg or the mist. But he was sure this would be a good place to vacate, at once.

"Come on," he muttered and took Dellie's arm, tugging her away. Potts fell in alongside, and abruptly the bluish mist was rising in a thin column before them, then widening into a shimmering bluish disk, like a pane of flawed glass, Julian thought, just as his momentum carried him against—no, he corrected himself—*through* into another place. Gone were the cracked sidewalk, the bright-colored awnings, the worn-out taxis. There was no city here; they were standing in a broad grassland, spotted with gnarled, flat-topped trees—and a large, black-maned lion with fleas moving on its muzzle, just coming to its feet under a tree a few feet away. The big cat looked lazily across at them—

"Here! How the devil did you do that, Julius?" Potts demanded angrily. "My wife—!"

"Get back!" Julian barked. He took a step back himself, and shied as the multi-legged tuber jostled him, emerging, it appeared, from thin air.

"Stop where you are, Roger!" the wide mouth ordered. All three had already frozen.

"Are you addressing me?" was the best Julian could muster, after suppressing a tendency to gibber.

"No more disturbance of the temporal fabric, mind you, now," Oob ordered. "You've already upset my parameters quite sufficiently, thank you; so if you'll just hold on briefly, and give me an opportunity to orient you—"

"Love to!" Julian agreed. "I've had one bad shock after another ever since I first saw you! Now, what's going on?"

"There are forces," Oob recited patiently, "which, when maintained in a state of equilibrium, give rise to an illusion of stability in the infinitly complex and ever-shifting continuum you fellows call space/time/vug. When random vectors are introduced, the pseudo-orderly matrix collapses, and there appear incongruous justaposi-tions of grossly inappropriate nature, which, of course, precipitate still further impediments to orderly entropic decay."

Oob paused, and Potts said loudly, "I get it! It's some kind of promotional scheme for a circus or whatnot! Well, we've had enough of it! My wife—"

Before Julian could deny it, Oob cut in, unctuously. "Sir, Kindly spare me your remonstrances! I am not the source of your misfortunes; I am merely a well-inten-tioned bystander, attempting to assist you! Unfortunately, your kind's innate ferocity and xenophobia render that difficult in the extreme! If we could just chat quietly for a few moments—"

"'Just chat,' eh?" Potts yelled. "Look here, you damned turnip! We were sitting quietly at our table, bothering nobody, just trying to soak up a little of the so-called Parisian ambience we paid plenty for, and all of a sudden we're lost on a prairie full of man-eating tigers! I'd like to know what 'chatting' is going to do to fix *that!*"

"Sir, quietly, I beg of you," Oob appealed. "You see, an irresponsible person named Roger Tyson has once again penetrated the Temporal Meniscus at a point of weakness engendered in the Temporal Bore by the unbridled activities of a number of meddlers such as yourself, and—"

"I'll meddle *you!*" Potts yelled, and kicked Oob hard in the bulge of his torso, netting himself a painful toe-sprain, while the Rhox simply faded a few shades to a chilly blue tone. Meanwhile, one of the lions stretched out under the acacia tree had raised its head and was staring across at the little band of unfortunates. Julian was the first to react.

"Stay put, folks," he urged. "Motion will attract them, especially any hurried retreat. So we'll just . . ." he trailed off, wondering what he had been about to say.

"Have no fear," Oob put in quickly. "The demise of any of you in this locus so far-removed from your native coordinates would introduce serious distortion into the vug-fabric." He made a quick motion, as if sketching a six-foot circle in thin air, and miraculously a film like a soap-bubble hung there, shimmering. "Kindly follow in an orderly fashion," he remarked, and turned toward the Aperture, hopped upward toward it, and was gone.

"Look out," Julian warned. "We have to be careful—"

"Well, that's a start," Potts interrupted. "With that damn hallucination out of the way, maybe we can find the way out of this stunt."

"It's not quite so simple, sir," Julian cautioned. "We're apparently in Africa, at about any time in the last hundred million years. Not much going on; probably that's why whoever is manipulating us chose this spot to dump us. We have to do as Oob said."

"You mean jump through that hoop, or whatever?" Potts demanded. "Some trick: I wonder how he did it." He leaned close to the rainbow-shimmering surface, ran his hand across the edge and behind it, pausing to give Julian a puzzled look.

"No wires, no nothing," Potts announced. "My hand disappeared when I put it behind it. It's opaque." He walked around to the other side of the curious phenomenon. "Looks the same from this side," he reported. "Only I can *see* something in there . . ." Then he was gone.

"Mr. Potts!" Julian spoke up sharply. "Don't—!" Mrs. Potts wailed and fainted. Julian caught her; not until she was steady on her feet did he go around the Aperture. There was no indication that Potts had ever been there,

other than some trampled grass. Julian wheeled at a sudden sound of frantic hooves; a lone eland galloped past, directly toward the pride, which it had quite apparently failed to detect, the wind being at its back. Dellie wailed again. The foremost lioness darted forward to intercept the big buck, which shied violently and spun to charge straight toward the two who stood watching in horrified fascination.

"It's awful!" Dellie moaned, clutching Julian's arm. "I've heard about zoos where the animals run around loose, but at least they had a moat or something. These beasts are right here in the same place *we* are! There's no fences or anything! And where's Horace gotten to? He's always going off to investigate some shop or something without a word. Horace! Where *are* you?" Her voice broke down and she wept quietly. Julian patted her shoulder.

"Now, now, Dellie, if I may so address you, it's going to be all right. Oob won't leave us here; he told us that would confuse his parameters, so I'm sure Horace is all right."

"But that tiger!" Dellie protested. "It's going to eat that inoffensive deer. I can't watch! It's too dreadful!"

"No," Julian corrected, as he stepped out and flung his arms wide almost in the face of the terrified eland, which swerved and bolted directly through the Aperture. The lioness executed a skidding turn and followed. Dellie looked up just in time to see it sail through the iridescent film into—nowhere.

"It disappeared!" she cried. "Oh, Mr. Julian, what in the world? Is it in there with poor Horace?"

"I doubt it," Julian consoled. "They approached from different sides; probably ended up in locales many frames of reference apart."

"Sh-should I, I mean we, jump through there, too?" she quavered, looking up appealingly at Julian. He looked around at the empty horizon and the other lions under the tree and nodded.

"I guess we'd better," he told her. "Shall I go first, or would you prefer to precede me?"

"Be left here all alone?" she yelped. "Not on your life, Mr. Julian. Give me a hand up." He linked his fingers to provide a stirrup, and Dellie stepped up, poked, looked, leaned, and tumbled through.

Julian was alone under the vast, yellowish sky. He studied the aperture from a distance of six feet: it seemed he could make out vague, flickering images moving beyond the slightly reflective surface. He moved around to view it edge-on; it almost disappeared, becoming only an insubstantial line. On the other side, he moved in closer, watching as a sixty-foot allosaurus leaped at an iguanodon twice its size, snapped its jaws to tear a fifty-pound chunk of red meat from the huge, fleshy tail, and jumped away before the ponderous herbivore could twitch the injured appendage, flattening trees up to eight inches in diameter.

Julian backed off; then, on impulse, went back around to the other side of the diaphanous disk. This time, the scene vaguely visible beyond the membrane was a peaceful city plaza. Three men stood chatting at the foot of a wide flight of marble steps.

"That looks civilized," Julian commented to himself, and hunching his shoulders as one expecting a blow, he dived headfirst through . . . something. There was a sensation like a tough soap bubble resisting minutely, then bursting. He struck, rolled, and came to rest sitting on a smooth, seamless pavement. The men he had seen through the aperture were standing ten feet away, staring at him.

"Hi, fellows," Julian greeted them. "Where have I got to now?" He scrambled up as they came slowly toward him. One extended a hand.

CHAPTER NINE

"Tyson," he said, "Roger Tyson. This is Rusty, and that's Bob. We're in the Grand Plaza of Culture One."

"Boy," Bob spoke up, "old Kumchett was just about to mellow and move me up to Design, and I blew it! All of a sudden here I am, and Jed must be wondering where I skedaddled to all of a sudden. There goes the old promo."

Julian introduced himself, inquired after the Pottses (no one had seen them), and tried to listen as all three men began simultaneously to explain matters to him.

"I'm having this series of hallucinations, see?" Rusty told him. "And you're just part of them, so don't worry: it doesn't matter."

"I've been overworking," Bob contributed. "I guess this is what it's like when you black out and can't remember it afterward."

"Actually, Julian," Roger Tyson prevailed, "we're all victims of some irresponsible meddling by Oob, the Rhox, with the Trans-Temporal Bore, itself an experiment being conducted by the people here in Culture One." He looked up the steps where F'shu had last disappeared through the high bronze doors. "At least I think that's what F'shu said," he added. "But there's more to it than that. It's the Builder who controls the whole Axial Channel; uses it to check on his work, you see. We have to talk to him."

" 'Fraid not," Julian replied. "Don't see, I mean. What about that ambulatory turnip fellow who's always dodging around when things go wrong?"

"Oh, that's just Oob," Roger reassured him. "Means well, but not too bright—except for an IQ around the million mark, of course. He's the one who came along and started puncturing the Temporal Meniscus while trying to fix it, and started people wandering back and forth out of entropic context. But UKR is on to him, and he'll straighten things out. Now, right now, we're at the Terminal Coordinate, the end of the line, so to speak: the final state of Culture One, just before it disappeared. There's a fellow named F'shu who was going to help us, but he disrealized himself accidentally."

"Oh," Julian said. "Will things start getting comprehensible pretty soon?"

"Not to our impoverished third-order intellects," Roger supplied. "But to the Builder, everything is perfectly clear. Unfortunately, the attainment of the Greater Order requires that we suffer these minor inconveniences, but—"

" 'Minor,' hell!" Rusty growled. "I had a date with the hottest little number in Bayport. She's never going to believe all this! Fact is, I'm not even going to *try* to tell her."

"As," Roger cut him off grandly, "*I* was *try*ing to tell *you*—well, I don't exactly understand, you understand, but I have great confidence in UKR. He's a machine, you see, and thus can function externally to the grand pattern of organic unfolding. Say," he raised his voice, "UKR! Take over, will you? I'm about out of glib explanations."

I WAS ABOUT TO DO SO, UKR's vast voice boomed out, then modulated to a more normal level: "Everything that's happened to each of you, and many others as well, is a part of a larger pattern that is under the continuous scrutiny of the Builder: in due course, all will be resolved to that state of perfection toward which the Universe has been evolving for twenty billion years, local. The construction of the Bore seems, perhaps, an error. But the Builder is incapable of error. We must all, and that includes myself, go forward in good spirits toward our eventual apotheosis. Calm yourselves, gentlemen, all will yet be well."

"Say," Bob commented when the oracular pronouncement had concluded, "how did you do that, Roger?"

"Say, UKR," Roger yelled. "Where's the big emergency you were talking about on the phone?" Roger inquired.

ALL IN GOOD TIME, ROGER, UKR came back. PRAY FORGIVE ME IF FROM TIME TO TIME, SO TO SPEAK, I BECOME A TRIFLE CONFUSED WITH REGARD TO YOUR ARBITRARY NOTIONS OF CAUSE-AND-EFFECT, PROGRESSION, AND THE LIKE. ACTUALLY, I WAS JUST ABOUT TO PHONE YOU REGARDING THE EMERGENCY. IT'S THE INVASION, YOU KNOW—

"Damn if I know!" Roger interrupted. Oob showed me some dark blue beetles is all—"

THE VRINT ARE QUITE ENOUGH, I ASSURE YOU, ROGER, UKR stated impatiently. THEY ARE, LIKE YOURSELVES, ORGANIC BEINGS, BUT UNLIKE YOURSELVES, HAVE NOT YET ACHIEVED THEIR APOTHEOSIS, BUT CONTINUE TO ACT AT RANDOM AS INDIVIDUALLY MOTI-VATED UNITS, EACH BENT ON ITS OWN PETTY DESTINY. I MYSELF, ALSO BEING A MECHANI-CAL ENTITY, THE PRODUCT OF YOUR OWN FULLY EVOLVED SPECIES, AM NOT EQUIPPED TO DEAL WITH THEIR IRRATIONALITY. I MUST THEREFORE HAND OVER THE PROBLEM TO YOU, WHO WILL BE ABLE TO FATHOM THEIR ORGANIC MOTIVATIONS AND RESOLVE THE DIFFICULTY.

"Oh," Roger replied dazedly. "It's a problem your

superhuman intellect can't handle, so you expect *me* to fix everything up? Have I got that part right?"

EXCELLENT, UKR intoned. WHAT ARE YOUR SUGGESTIONS FOR IMMEDIATE ACTION TO AVERT FINAL DISASTER?

"Is that the straight dope?" Rusty inquired belatedly. "It's all part of a pattern we can't see? Like the time that damn tourist in the Cigarette boat cut my line when I had the Tarpon Roundup cinched with an easy three-hundred-pounder, and it turned out he was a zillionaire and he came back and made it up to me? Boy, did he make it up to me! Bought me a Mako, and . . . after that, I don't remember the details," he concluded.

"That's right," Roger sighed. "It seems inconvenient to us, but then it's not for our convenience."

All four men shied abruptly as a galloping eland leaped past them, then a young lioness in hot pursuit.

"Ye gods," Julian said reverently. "I wondered where they'd gone. But Mr. and Mrs. Potts ought to be along in a second; they were the next through. I was worried they'd run into the lion."

F'shu came hurrying down the steps and up to the four wayfarers. Roger started to address him, but F'shu ignored him.

"Gentleman," he gasped, out of breath. "Forgive the delay. About forty years local, I believe. I'm afraid there's been a little difficulty. You see, I accidentally relegated the Center here to an unrealized state, and it's taken some time to re-evoke it, perceptually speaking."

"Say," Bob put in. "Is that Oob vegetable still hanging around? Shouldn't we—I mean, shouldn't you . . . ?"

"Later," F'shu brushed that aside. "What I'm about to report rather changes the complexion of matters."

"The suspense," Roger intoned, "is killing me. I want to ask you: what about that lion?"

"It appears," F'shu bored on, ignoring all interruptions, "that the situation has deteriorated to the extent that our usual techniques for realigning the entropic vectors have been rendered nugatory. Events have taken on an entropic momentum all their own. I have no protocols for dealing with the chaotic interpenetration of temporal filaments. The Bore is hopelessly compromised, affecting the Matrix itself."

"Oh, that happened some millennia ago," UKR said casually.

"It's funny," Bob commented to Roger. "Every time one of these weirdos 'explains' matters, I get more confused."

"Me, too," Rusty agreed.

"What was all that the big voice was saying about an invasion?" Rusty put in.

"And what about us, or rather you, Mr. Tyson, being expendable?" Julian contributed.

"That's odd the way old F'shu reappeared," Roger mused, "after he'd supposedly eliminated himself, along with Culture One. But maybe that comes later," he suggested. "I have to remember chronology is flexible in a pre-activated state."

While the chap in the scandalous white dress was talking to the other Americans, Horace Potts busied himself patting his wife's shoulder.

"Dell," he said quietly, "we made a mistake, taking this trip. I've always heard things were pretty strange in Europe, but I never figgered they'd be *this* damn strange. Sorry I got you into this, girl."

She sniffled and turned to look up at him. "It's not your fault, Horsey," she squealed. "It's all the fault of that awful creature—I *feel* it. We were just fine until *it* appeared, except for the waiter. Horsey, do you suppose it's the Devil?"

"You haven't called me 'Horsey' for years, Dell," Horace said in a tone of reminiscence. "Remember the day we met, girl?"

Young Horace Potts felt pretty swell, cruising past the high school from which *he* had graduated last June, leaving childish things behind. The brand-new '69 Cougar ragtop Pop had given him purred as sweetly as a kitten—a

Cougar kitten, like they showed in the "Cat with silken sinews" ads. The metallic green hood gleamed in front of him, the smell of XR-7 leather was all around him, and that little gal sitting on the steps beside the concrete lion was—wow! She must be a new sophomore: he sure hadn't seen *her* before. She glanced past him, unseeing, and stood up. My god, what a body! And that face—as cute as Debbie Reynolds in that old flick *Singin' in the Rain*.

He braked a little. There ought to be a law, he assured himself, against girls being so totally mind-blowing. Look at that sweater, not huge, but shaped just right! And the gray flannel skirt, the way it curved out and then along that thigh . . . Man, how could a man keep his mind on what he was doing? She glanced his way—and her glance held, for a miraculous full second, before she looked down at her feet. He pulled to the curb, not even meaning to.

"Hi," he said. "Want a lift? I'm Horace Potts; I graduated three months ago." He hoped it didn't sound too much like bragging. She was holding a stack of books; the same old books he'd finished with forever. . . .

"Come on," he urged. "I'm not a dirty old man." He reached across and opened the passenger-side door.

"Oh, no," she said in a voice as sweet as a waft of perfume. "I *know* that; it's just that Dad . . . Oh, OK!" She jumped in and settled down on the solid leather.

"I love your car," she said in her voice of an angel. "I'm Delia Robinson."

He took her soft, tender little hand. He'd much rather be kissing that heartbreaking little mouth, he realized, but he restrained his arm as it responded to an unbidden impulse to slide across the sweet gray-angora shoulders. *Don't rush it!* he commanded himself. Wow! His eyes drifted down over her shoulder and down her front. Wow! How about a fellow running his hand over *that* stretch of angora! He gulped silently. She smelled nice: perfume, and just a touch of girl-sweat.

"Where to, my lady?" He'd almost said "madam," but

"madam" means "my lady," so he said "my lady" instead. She glanced up at his face with a hint of a smile on those cute features. He wondered briefly if she had a brother. How could he stand living in the same house with this rare creature, and not being able to— He pictured her getting into the shower. Wow! The (male) human mind can't even grasp a concept like that, he realized. "I asked you, 'where to'?" he reminded her gently.

"Anywhere, Horsey," she said, and leaned her angelic head on the solid leather seat-back. He switched on the radio. He had it set on FM 103, the cool music station. Noise banged out, too loud. She reached and dialed to FM 90; the sweet sound of violins came in, perfect for the mood, Horace realized, although usually he resented that classical stuff and all.

"You like that?" he asked her.

She nodded. "Fritz Kreisler," she murmured. "*La Gitana;* that's '*The Gypsy Girl.*' "

"Nice," Horace commented, not feeling hypocritical, he realized. It *was* nice.

"Could you take me to the YW?" she asked softly. "No hurry; I'm meeting some girls. . . ."

In an instant, a vision of naked females of nubile years wreathed in the mist of the shower-room flashed before his imagination's eyes; then he took command, sternly. *She's probably very intelligent,* he told himself. *She likes classical; even knew about Chryslers.*

"Do you really like Kreisler?" she asked shyly.

"I'll settle for my Cougar any day," he responded forthrightly. "Got it for graduation. You a sophomore?"

She nodded again. "We just came to Brantville," she told him with an easy intimacy that thrilled him. "My dad's in the Army, you know. He's a chicken colonel. Stationed at Camp Crook, of course. He's hoping to make general on this assignment. He's DCS Engineering; the last three DCS/E's have all gotten their star when they transferred out."

"Sounds like an important man," Horace responded. Wow! A general's daughter! Fred would be impressed when he got back from the Army next month. Fred was a "buck sergeant" now, whatever that was. A *lot* lower than a general.

"A general's a pretty big man," Horace hazarded.

Dellie nodded once again. "He's only forty-five," she said. "He's not a West Pointer, but nowadays that doesn't matter so much."

Staring, paralyzed, at that heavenly profile, Horace realized he couldn't stand it any longer. He used his knees to steer while he put his right hand on her cheek and turned her face toward him. She leaned closer. Her lips were sightly parted, showing china-white teeth. Her mouth was as soft as a marshmallow, Horace realized abruptly. He almost pulled back, but her hand on the back of his neck restrained him. And her hand was on *his* knee! His thoughts went whirling.

Quiver. He opened his eyes and looked, seeing nothing; for a moment he felt confused, as if he were falling through space. He struggled to get his bearings: then he took charge, dammit, and remembered where he was. There was nothing in sight but another of those damned plazas or places the foreigners always had in the middle of their towns where a commerce center ought to be; and this one was plainer than most. Some of that modern architecture, it looked like, with no regular doors or windows or roofs or chimneys and stuff to make it look like somebody lived there. But Dellie was right here beside him: her face looked a little puffy or something, and she was wearing a gray wig, but she was still the prettiest thing a fellow ever saw. He embraced her tenderly, and she said, "Oh, Horsey, in spite of everything, I'm glad we came."

Suddenly remembering something about a big turnip with legs, Horace slammed on the brakes, netting a hoarse yell from a guy in a dented pickup. He wondered briefly why pickups were always dented, and usually had brown mud caked on them. Dellie clung to his arm, and murmured, "Now, Horsey, be careful."

"What say we just go for a drive, honey?' he blurted on impulse.

To his astonishment she wriggled closer and breathed, "I'd love that, Horsey."

They drove the Cougar on into the perfumed night, wishing the moment would never end.

CHAPTER TEN

"Say, Roger," Rusty spoke up. "Do you understand what all that stuff the voice said is s'pose to mean?"

"'Fraid not," Tyson admitted. "But—where've the Pottses got to?" He looked around; the couple was nowhere to be seen.

"I was on'y about six or seven, I guess,' Butch Bachelor said, "when I seen the fline soster."

"Oh," the interviewer commented, folding his notebook. "I'd understood it was more recently."

Butch wagged his hand. "Just a kid," he repeated. "Prolly don't remember too good. You know that crazy ideas kids can get: invisible companions, and like that."

"But that ... *thing* you showed me," the reporter objected. "That's an actual artifact! It must—"

"Just foolishness," Bachelor countered. He aimed the play ray-gun he'd found on the bench at a scraggly azalea bush by the waste receptacle; the plant flickered and was gone. Some dead leaves remained on the ground.

The reporter—from the *Sun*, Butch thought, or had he said the *Independent-Courier*? Didn't matter—he hadn't noticed anything. These clowns always got everything wrong; never listened. He dropped the gadget back in his pocket. The *Sun* man was standing over the hole in the dust where the dead-looking bush had been. He turned to look squarely at Bachelor.

"H-how did you *do* that?" he said in a self-consciously shocked voice.

"Do what?" Butch riposted.

"Make the plant disappear," the stringer gulped.

"What plant?" Butch demanded.

"Why, the, ah, azalea, I believe they're called," the interrogator supplied.

"Where?" Butch challenged.

"Well, it *was* right there!" The fellow pointed to a hole in the ground.

"What's that got to do with me?" Butch said belligerently.

"Y-you *made* it disappear!" the little man stated defiantly.

"You accusing me of stealing city property?" Butch challenged. "If I got it, where'd I hide it?" He lifted his arms as if inviting a search.

"No, no, you didn't *take* it!" the excited scribe corrected. "You just . . . disappeared it! It vanished, just like that!"

"What's that s'pose to have to do with me?" Bachelor dismissed the silly accusation.

"That . . . gadget!" the confused reporter blurted. "You put it in your pocket! What *is* it?"

Butch patted his pocket, felt something, and fetched out a thing like a plastic kazoo, or whatever you call it— a musical sweet potato, it looked like. He remembered he'd picked it up off a bench where some kid had left it; thought he'd turn it in at the Lost and Found. He handed it to the nosy guy, who recoiled as if he'd been offered a live rattlesnake.

"What *is* that thing?" he hissed.

"Take it easy," Butch suggested. "It's some kinda toy, I guess. I was *gonna* turn it in."

"You'd better take that *directly* to the police station,

Mr. Bachelor," the newshawk commanded in a stern voice.

"That'll be the day," Butch dismissed the order. "Look, pal, I'm a law-abiding, tax-paying citizen, and I *never* had a good experience with a cop."

"D-does it work on *anything*?" was the next question.

"Work how?"

"Like before. You just pointed it, and *zap!* the bush vanished."

"That's dopey," Butch informed his accuser. "Stuff doesn't just vanish."

"Not usually," the scribe admitted.

At that moment, two surly-looking young fellows wearing scruffy fur jackets and torn jeans carefully modeled after the wardrobe of the motorcycle gangs you see on the telly came up and paused by the bench. "You tired, Lump?" one asked the other.

"Yeah. Let's sit down a while, Moose," the smaller one said. "Got this empty bench right here. I'm tired." He made a move as if to sit in Butch's lap; Butch thrust him aside.

"Hey," the lout yelled. "Being fat and dumb is one thing, getting belligerent's another!"

"Tell him, Moose," Lump urged, as he kicked the reporter's foot in the process of shoving him aside.

"Look here, you scum!" the writer spat. "You can't—" The rest was cut off by Moose's smelly hand, placed firmly over his mouth.

"Sumbitch is spitting on me," Moose mourned.

"What's yer name, trash?" Moose changed direction abruptly. "Calling me and my pal 'scum' ain't a good idear. I ast you a question." He poked the cowering newsman's chest with a finger like a callused banana.

"Hawkins," the poor little man gasped. "Cass Hawkins. I'm a reporter. You can't—"

As Lump turned away, he noticed Butch. "Got you a play-toy, hey?" he jeered, as he reached for the kazoo. "Gimmee!"

Butch avoided the grab, aimed the thing like he had

at the bush, and punched the white button. Some soiled clothing fell to the concrete walk, along with a shower of pale dust, some greasy black hair, and a full set of finger and toenails.

"Good work," Cass blurted, rising, only to be pushed back by Moose.

"Whatsa idear?" the youth snarled. "Where'd Lumpy go? Where's he at?"

"Observing the activities of moronic clods has never been a hobby of mine," Cass told the agitated lad. "Now get to hell away from me before I tell my friend to do it again." Moose took to his heels, as the saying goes, though he was in fact running on his toes.

" 'That's a real handy gadget,' as the actress said to the bishop," Cass said to Butch. "Now you *really* better go to the cops."

"I didn't. . . ." Butch stammered, staring at the recently vacated boots and garish bikini underwear heaped incongruously on the brick path.

"Sure you did, sir, and a good thing," Cass encouraged him. "We were being mugged, and you— Well, I don't know what you did, but that thing belongs in the hands of the Army. Let's go." He rose and strode off along the walk. Butch followed, muttering.

Oob stopped dead some yards short of Bob and Rusty, as an uprooted bush came blowing across the tiled pavement. An instant later, Dirty Bimbo fell at his feet, followed after a moment by a second primitive hominid; both were stark naked. They eyed each other and thrust out their right hands.

"Lump's the handle," the more hairy of the two blurted. "Don't think I seen you around, bud. Where's your bike?" Bimbo scratched his lumpy scalp with a fingernail like a black-rimmed banjo-pick. He took a swing at Lump, who leaned aside and took an elbow-breaking grip on the proffered member. Bimbo howled and went to his knees.

"I like yer style," Lump told the kneeling anthropoid.

"But you got to learn a few tricks. You must be new inna neighborhood." Lump paused to look around as if suddenly noticing his surroundings, and his nudity. "Where's Moose?" he yelped, going into a crouch. "And the two cubes? Wheresa park? This ain't—"

NO, IT CERTAINLY IS NOT, a giant voice spoke as if in answer to Lump's incomplete remark. LOOK HERE, SMALL ORGANISM, THIS MEDDLING MUST CEASE! YOU'VE CREATED YET ANOTHER POINT OF ATTENUATION IN THE MATRIX. NOW, GIVE ME THE RELEGATOR AT ONCE!

Oob, sidling to stay behind Lump, cast a despairing glance at Bob and Rusty.

"Oh, dear, this is catastrophe!" he wailed. "It's the Relegator; I lost it somehow. When the crowd gathered and began throwing things at me I became rattled and fled on foot; it must have come unclipped from my harness! In the hands of fools like yourselves, or worse, it can inflict damage that will be quite beyond my skill or even that of the Final Authority to repair. Imagine the chaos if the entire entropic membrane were to collapse: stampeding bison in Central Park, early Celtic tribesmen swarming in the dirt streets of Lugdunum, mammoth herds cropping suburban lawns in the Midwest—"

"That's it!" Bob yelled. "I *saw* one on Marv Blum's lawn, and—"

"Oh, dear," Roger sighed. "Right in Brantville?"

Bob nodded.

"Yes, yes, easy now, gentlemen," Oob urged. "I should not have spoken so precipitately. I'd momentarily forgotten your species's unfortunate tendency to leap on a horse and ride off in all directions. It can be fixed, I'm sure, or at least I hope so. Can you imagine the static I'll have to take if the ice cap wipes out the Final Authority's Terminal State? Unthinkable! I've got to get that Relegator! Excuse me, gents, I'll be back five minutes ago!" He sketched with writhing tentacles a rough circle about himself. The circle shrank and Oob was gone.

"That's a relief," Bob said. "That critter gives me the willies!"

"He was our only link with wherever he was a link with," Rusty mourned. "I wonder . . . ?" He went over to examine the spot whence the Rhox had so abruptly departed the scene; saw only a vague shimmer in the air. "Here goes, pals," he said over his shoulder, and leaned.

Bob and Roger were suddenly alone.

Hiram Pawkins lowered his rifle. The wagon came out of the dust cloud and his coughing fit ceased at the same moment. The horizon was clear.

"Damn hostiles are gone, Martha," he called up to the seat of the Conestoga, spitting mud. "Something must have spooked 'em," he rambled on. "Tell you the truth, girl, I was just about to save you from a fate worser'n death here." He patted his ex–Union Army Springfield and sighed. "Glad I never fired," he finished. "What say we pull up and you rustle some eats. I'm plumb tuckered."

You think yer the only one tuckered? his mate thought, but said, "Jest as you wish, Mr. Pawkins." She reined in the team, and the swaying, creaking wagon came to a halt.

"Hey, Ma!" a juvenile voice yelled from behind her. "Is the Injuns still here? Are they gonna scalp us, Ma, huh?"

"Hush up, you Jedediah," Martha snapped. "Course they ain't here. Yer pa'd never of tole me to stop if they was."

"Heck," was the reply. "I never got a good look, 'cept fer the one Pa shot off the tailgate—" The sound of a palm striking flesh cut short Jedediah's complaint.

"Got to wash yer mouth out with boiled soap again," his outraged mother carped. "Don't know whereat you younguns get that kinda language. Lucky yer Pa never heard you!"

"Heard what?" Hiram inquired as he swung up on the

wooden seat beside her. "That Jedediah been taking the Lord's name in vain again?"

"Not *that* bad, Harm," his spouse reassured him. "Jest said— Sorry, I can't repeat it."

"I heard the little devil," Hiram admitted. "Said 'heck!.' Got a mind to give him a good hiding, soon's he's watered the stock." A mournful *mm-nyuh!* from the cow tethered behind the wagon seemed to acknowledge the reference.

"Gee whiz, Pa," Jedediah started, and his Pa's slap sent him reeling back inside the canvas-covered shade.

"Told you, boy, a thousand times if I told you once, all them citified badwords, 'shucks' and 'goshdarn' and all that, excuse me, Martha, are jest as bad in the ears of Our Lord as if you come right out and said real bad-words. You watch yer mouth, boy!"

"Pa," Jedediah persisted, "when you was into the Army, at Vicksburg and all, during the late rebellion, didn't the brave soldiers talk thataway?"

"Sure-bob did," Hiram confirmed. "Air was blue with foul language. Hurt me to have to listen; old general tried to put a end to it fer the sake o' their immortal souls, but soon's he went back in his tent, they'd start up again. It was 'gosh' this, and 'heck' that, all day and half the night!"

"Mighty disturbing, Harm, I know, being in the war and all," Martha commiserated. "But you lived through it, praise His Precious Name, and now we're going to Oregon and find us a fine farm, and you can put all them horrors outa yer mind. Now, Jedediah Pawkins, you jest fergit about the war and all that; yer a lucky boy yer was safe in Minnesota where the Johnny Rebs never set foot, thanks to yer paw and the other brave soldier-boys."

"I wisht *I* could been bigger so's *I* could be in the war," the lad persisted.

"Lucky you weren't," Hiram told him unfeelingly. "I mind the time we had to cross over the river, the Tom-bigbee, it was, in the night, with Rebel calvary all around us in the dark. Lost over fifty mules and a number of boys, too, that time. Once I slipped and nigh went under. Them packs was heavy. I prayed so hard the Lord thought I was Jesus!"

"Harm!" Martha rebuked sharply. "Fine example *you* set fer the boy!"

"Can't a man have a little peace in his own home?" Hiram demanded of the universe.

"Some home!" Martha retorted. "Nothing but this here prairie full o' wild injuns. A body can't even sleep good nights!"

"One thing I swore I'd never stand," Hiram stated loudly, "is a nagging woman. I'm done! I hope you and the boy can find Oregon all right!" With that, he jumped down, turned an abrupt left-face, and stalked away across the flat grassland. He didn't glance back until he had passed the lone cottonwood tree growing beside a pitiable trickle in the bottom of a mostly dried-up creek-bed. When he did take a look he stopped dead and scrambled back up the bank; the wagon and team were nowhere in sight.

He uttered a hoarse yell and ran along his back-trail, clear in the tall buffler grass. He found a small heap of bovine dung, but no other trace of his family and his worldly goods. Totally bewildered, he sank down on the ground and went to sleep.

He slept uneasily, dreaming of crowds of strange-looking people, all staring at him as they crowded past, most of them yelling. One fat lady in a scandalous short dress that showed her bulging knees planted herself before him and yelled, "You with the Shriner bunch, or what?"

He tried to tell her he didn't hold with none of them un-Christian clubs nor nothing, but the fat exhibitionst had hurried away.

"Humph!" Hiram snorted, watching the lady's retreat. "Could of at least been a purty young gal. Hard to see how she got all that ham into that there scandalous garment." Other bypassers were casting curious glances at him, so he got to his feet and saw his Conestoga—no—another one, too new to be his, sitting fifty feet away,

with something painted onto the canvas: OMAHA PIONEER
DAYS.

He went over to the comforting familiarity of the covered wagon, and found two fellows with brand-new store
clothes and funny hats up front, messing with the harness
on a fine pair of grays. Acted like they didn't know a
Marlowe hitch from a square knot. He took the straps
from one fellow's hand and quickly ran them through the
rings and buckles and cinched them up snug.

"You with the Junior Chamber?" the younger of the
two city fellers asked him.

"I ain't with nobody, looks like a body could see,"
Hiram snorted. He looked around, saw a few other prairie schooners, all too new-looking to be *his* rig.

"Where's Martha and the boy at?" he demanded.

"Better check with the Grand Marshal," the older,
taller of the strangers told him, and they hurried away.

"Hey, don't go yet!" Hiram called. "Leave a feller out
here alone amongst the hostiles! Last I seen of 'em—"
He broke off as he realized the two slickers weren't listening: they had stopped a big-bellied man wearing some
kind o' Stetson, and all three were laughing. One pointed
at him, and they laughed some more.

Riled, Hiram stalked over toward the two. None of
'em was packing a pistol, he noted, while he had Becky.
He'd show 'em they couldn't laugh at *him*, just because
he was kind of lost . . . He squeezed the well-worn wal-
nut stock of the rifle and felt confident he'd soon
straighten this out.

"Where'd all these fancy people come from?" he was
demanding of himself for the umpteenth time, making
his way through them. One minute he was lying down,
all alone; a minute later he was waking up in the middle
of some kind of jamboree, it looked like.

Two middle-aged ladies in decent clothes and sun bon-
nets came over toward him and the younger one said,
"Excuse us, sir, can you direct us to the ladies' facility?"

Hiram stopped dead. Up close he could see they had
paint on their faces. Scandalous! He backed away. Should

of knowed it! Scarlet wimmen! How'd they get out here, a hundred miles west of Kansas City? All these folks seemed like crazy people.

A tall, bronzed fellow with a seamed face and a bald head accosted Hiram.

"You with Howie's bunch?" He grunted. "Marshaling point's yonder. Got five minutes." He pointed vaguely.

The two "ladies" were still standing looking uncertainly at him. He wondered what a "facility" was. *Prolly one o' them houses of ill repute you hear about.*

"Never been in one o' them places!" he blurted. The ladies looked shocked.

"Well, I should think not!" one said.

"Can't hardly stand to think about what you wimmen do in a place like that!" he added for good measure. If he could shame 'em, maybe they'd change their ways. They fled.

"Ast you if you's with Howie's bunch," the bald stranger repeated. "Better get going, pal. Getting late."

Hiram gulped and nodded and set off the way the fellow had pointed just as if he knew where he was going. Must be he'd stumbled onta some kinda outdoors asylum. All these people were crazy. Look at that fellow, tacking up a sign that said: ALL VOLUNTEERS TO PINK AREA NINE SHARP.

What'd that mean? Volunteers? He'd done his time as a volunteer. Maybe a reunion going on.

He followed the little pink-arrow signs to a big pink "9" nailed to a post. A few people were hanging around, mostly females, he noted. Couldn't be no militia volunteers!

A man wearing a sort of a white shirttail thing with short britches stitched to it that showed his bare legs, was standing to one side, staring at the other people. He looked as mixed up as Hiram felt. Hiram went directly to him, and asked in a tone intended to communicate overtaxed tolerance:

"Whereat's Martha and the boy?"

The man jumped and looked curiously at Hiram. "I

beg your pardon, sir," he said smoothly. "I know nothing of them. Are you—?"

"No, I ain't with Howie's bunch, nor no Shriners, neither!" Hiram barked. "What's going on here, anyways? The wagon was right there, and I looked back, and it was gone!"

"Oh, dear," the white-clad fellow murmured. "Another of Oob's unregistered Apertures—or possibly a new rent in the Meniscus itself. Just where did you last see them, sir?"

Hiram pointed. "'Bout half a mile yonder," he grunted. "You can see, ain't nothing there now."

"One of the wagons, you say," the stranger said, nodding thoughtfully. "Why was it out there? The parade—"

"Not 'one of the wagons,'" Hiram corrected. "Just had the one, brand-new Conestogie that cost me most of what I got for the farm. Can't afford to lose that! And Martha and the boy, too, not to say nothing about the stock. . . ."

"Sir, as you can readily see," the man in white protested, "there are over a dozen of the wagons. Look about you. Are you sure . . . ?"

"Reckon I know my own Conestogie," Hiram muttered, glancing at the rank of covered wagons lined up nearby.

"Wait here, sir," the stranger said. "I shall see what can be done." He hurried away. Hiram removed his hat to scratch his head and sauntered over toward the nearest wagon. A short, fat man, also in brand-new store-clothes, was peering under the wooden bed and looking baffled. He brightened as he saw Hiram.

"Oh, you'd be one of the experts from the Old Square," he said happily. "I can't seem to find the thill-bolts I'm supposed to tighten up. Could you . . . ?"

Hiram gave the man a contemptuous glance. Durn city feller, out here trying to mess with stuff he don't know nothing about. He ducked under, stared in amazement at a steel frame covered by weathered wooden veneer visible from the side. And leaf-springs, just like a fancy gentleman's carriage! He stepped back, and shook his head.

"Somebody's messed this here vehicle up bad," he said. "Got a lot of arn under there. You just watch: won't hold up under the long haul, and rusts bad, too. And heavy; you'll wear out yer team."

"Gee, thanks," the little feller said.

"Watch yer language!" Hiram snapped.

The man in the white get-up came back, looking kind of upset, Hiram thought.

"Well, where're they at?" he demanded as soon as he figgered the feller could hear him over the crowd.

"Have no fear, sir," the slicker said. "I've located your loved ones, and—"

"Who said anything about love?" Pawkins demanded. "That wagons' worth good money!"

"Oh, if it's money you're concerned about," R'heet replied, I can—"

"Never said I was worrit," Hiram corrected promptly. "*Ever'body* needs cash!"

"Permit me" R'heet said perfunctorily. He reached into a pouch slung over his shoulder and brought out a stack of that "stage money" you hear about. Pitcher o' George Warshenon on it and all, but it was too little; not much of a fake, even. Hiram pushed it away when R'heet proffered it.

"I'll take gold," he snorted. "Two-and-a-half-dollar pieces. New ones. Always thought they was purty," he explained. "Don't get me wrong, brother," he added, as he thrust his hand into the cloth bag marked DENVER that R'heet had pressed on him. "Don't mind them cartwheels, just that—" He let a stream of the bright-yellow, quarter-sized coins trickle through his fingers back into the bag, which he then peered into suspiciously. "OK," he stated. "Any more?'

"How much more can you conveniently carry, sir?" R'heet inquired, offering a second, larger canvas bag, brand-new, like the first. Hiram almost staggered as he took it. That rascal's heavy! He put the first, smaller bag on an adjacent open tailgate and opened and looked into the new one. Gold gleamed in the dark depths. He reached in, scrabbled, and brought out a fat coin. He tried it between his canines and snorted with satisfaction. "Real stuff," he commented. "What'm I s'pose' to do fer this?"

"Just go on being your own sweet self," R'heet dismissed the query. "It's Service policy to alleviate suffering where possible without disturbing the entropic Matrix."

"Don't know nothing about no mattresses," Pawkins grated, " 'less you talkin' about the scarlet wimmen's."

"By no means, sir," R'heet reassured him. "It's just that, considering that you'll soon be gone from this entropic locus, you can hardly disturb the Meniscus in any significant fashion, no matter to what use you put the funds I've provided. Are you sure you can carry all that?"

"Sure-Bob can," Hiram reassured the donor of his new wealth.

At that moment, Martha appeared, dragging young Jedediah along behind her.

"Never thought Oregon'd be like this here, Harm," she stated disapprovingly. "Whyn't you tell me where you was headed, 'steada walking off like you done?"

"Enough, woman!" Hiram cut off her recriminations. He handed her the smaller of the two bags. she hefted it, held it up to stare at it, then looked inside. She brought out a brand-new coin and bit it, nodding in satisfaction.

"You *said* where we'd get rich in Oregon Territory," she said hesitantly. "But I figgered it'd take some time. Harm, you ain't robbed the Mint, have ye?"

He gave her the contemptuous look the remark deserved, and turned to the strange feller in the tricky white duds, but he was gone. "Well, now, Martha," he said instead of the introduction he'd been about to offer, "I met this here feller, and he seen I was the kind o' man they need here, and he give me a little something to get started on. Come on, let's find the Land Office."

CHAPTER ELEVEN

When Roger Tyson and his snazzy little wife both disappeared like they done, Charlie Schlumph backed toward the front door. Better get clear o' this place, 'fore the cops come in and start in accusing a feller of murder. Too bad; he'd meant to show his gratitude and all with something more bankable than conversation. His eye was caught by the strange window set in a box that Roger had been messing with when he done whatever he done to disappear; the window seemed to glow faintly in the glare of late afternoon. Charlie went to it and peered into it. He saw vague shapes moving beyond the shiny glass surface. It looked like a bunch of people—a mob, you might say—all yelling, though silently, and surging around, like them Frenchmen yelling "*Feeny la Gare*" in Pairsst, when the forty and eight taken us there. As he stared, if seemed he could *hear* faint sounds, like somebody yelling, "No, dammit! I meant the Rhox *Control* Apex! Not this infernal traffic jam!" *Quiver*.

Charlie's eye was caught by the fellow who seemed to be doing the yelling; at first he thought it was Roger, but, no, this was a little younger fella, even, and not *quite* as shell-shocked. He seemed to be staring straight at

Charlie, Charlie realized, and *coming* toward him, pushing people aside.

He reached out. Charlie recoiled as a hand emerged from the shiny glass window and groped toward him. Then the whole arm came through, and the clutching hand closed on Charlie's sleeve. He yanked at the same moment he yelled, but the arm pulled him, resisting furiously, toward the winder, and—

Charlie tripped, went to all fours, breathing hard. He was looking across a broad plaza at a group of civilians: one of them, he saw, was the one who'd dragged him out the winder. He'd see about that! He came to his feet in a rush, pushed at a youth in his way and met a blow which knocked him on his back. Roger was standing over him wearing a ferocious look, which faded as he stared at Charlie's bloody nose.

"Par' me, pal," Roger said. "I thought it was that damn ape-man again." He offered a hand which Charlie spurned, getting awkwardly to his feet unassisted. He thought about taking a swing at the whippersnapper, but decided against it when he put a handkerchief to his nose and remembered how bad it hurt.

Another man came over, hand outthrust. "It's all Oob's doing," he told him. "I'm Rusty Naill." Charlie shook his hand.

"He's been popping up and causing trouble," Roger explained, "and then he's gone again! It's made me a little jumpy, I guess. Here, let me look at that nose."

"You'll get a look at that nose about the time I kiss the Kaiser," Charlie growled. "Lemme be, boy, I got no beef with you. Gladda see you, in fact; where'd you go? It's OK, just a mistake like you said."

"Where's Martha?" a stranger demanded.

Charlie said, "Who's that?"

"Ma waff, that's who!" the old boy snapped. "She disappeared on me here, her and the boy, too."

"That's disturbing, I know, sir," Roger put in, "but you'll just have to get used to things like that, I'm afraid, until we get all these holes in the Bore fixed up. She's probably quite all right, just confused. To her, doubtless, it will appear that it was *you* who disappeared; you've slipped into diverging planes, or loci, you see."

Uncomforted by this news, Hiram stalked over to where a group of men were engaged in conversation with a great big turnipy sort of thing, looked like it was alive; kept wiggling a bunch of wormy things on top, and jittering on a set of legs like one o' them lobsters. Wasn't jest no foreigner; nope, this was some kinda demon come from the Bad Place. Hiram squared his shoulders and kept going toward the group.

When Lepke hadn't appeared after ten—no, make that fifteen minutes, Manny O'Rourke stubbed out his cigar in the chipped saucer serving as ashtray, with an air of finality.

"I guess he don't want to deal after all," he commented heavily. "Looks like the poor boob wants to go head-to-head. Well, I guess I can fix that."

"Hold it, Sweets," Doc Condon urged. "Let's not go getting a lot of good boys kilt just because Lepke's hack got jammed in traffic or like that."

Manny nodded heavily, and brushed at the spiderweb that he had just noticed. There seemed to be nothing there, just a kind of shimmer, sort of interfered with a fellow's vision. He batted at it ineffectually until Lefty eased up and muttered, "Better take it easy, Boss; you're upsetting the boys, right?"

"Upsetting my left hind gaboochie!" Sweets burst out. "Help me! The damned thing's getting bigger!"

Lefty seized his boss's arm and pulled him back. "Boys get the idea you went bonkers, there'll be war for sure, Boss! Remember it's the whole South Side at stake here! Right, Boss?"

"Somebody pulling something, Seymour," Manny told Lefty. "They're tryna cover up—"

"Ain't nothing there, Boss," Lefty insisted. "Just set and let's talk it over till Lepke shows up, OK? How come you called me 'Seymour,' anyways? I'm yer old pal, Lefty, right?"

Manny lunged past Lefty's attempted block and fell. . . . He hit hard, and came up tugging his Mauser from its holster in his armpit, looking around wildly to see what Doc and his boys had in mind next. He gaped. He was alone on the beach: Looked like Coney Island, only not as dirty and no people. Musta fell out the winder! Funny he wasn't kilt, five stories up. He stood, brushing sand from his knees. He looked out to sea, then around at the dirty-brown beach and the jungle behind it. No buildings in sight. Then he saw a couple of people in some kind of white outfits, a guy and a doll—not bad. He fixed an ingratiating smirk on his face and sauntered over.

Gotta play it cozy till you know who you're talking to. Might be the local cops. Like that time he pushed the little guy with the scar outa the way and grabbed his cab. Come to find out later it was Al Capone! Lucky Al was in a good mood that day. . . .

The pair in white were just coming out of the bushes— prolly having a quick roll in there. The thought upset Manny. He was an extremely prudish fellow, the Sisters having pounded a set of conventional sexual mores into his skull, though omitting to provide him with any knowledge of geography.

"Prolly California," he told himself as the couple paused and looked curiously at him.

"Hope I ain't breaking up nothing important," Manny greeted the two, aware of his own graciousness. "Go right ahead, don't mind me—'cept, where am I? Sounds pretty dumb, but I got lost, see, and wound up here." He couldn't quite tell them he fell out of a window and landed here.

"Another one, P'ty," the man said with a funny accent, neither Irish nor Yiddish, nor even Spanish, Manny knew; he'd grown up with those.

The girl nodded. "Yes, M'lon, I can see him quite well. Did you notice that he materialized right there, in contravention of Policy 978-J?"

"Sure did," M'lon replied, and advanced toward O'Rourke, his hand outstretched. Manny took it and heaved hard. You wouldn't catch Sweet Manny O'Rourke in a sucker play like that!

He hit face-first and sat up spitting dirty brown sand. He looked up at Mel. This sucker was full of surprises.

Manny came to his feet with a lunge, and a hand grenade exploded in his face. He lay for a while wondering if his brains were blown out, then drew a deep breath and opened his eyes to find the girl—stacked nice, she was, for sure—looking down at him. "Sorry about that," she said curtly. "But old M'lon might have hurt you. He hates it when feeble little third-order beings try to get tough."

"Tripped," Manny explained. "Call me 'Sweets,' like my pals." He got up and took another look along the beach. It still looked like a beach. But in the water, a couple hundred feet offshore, a snake as big as a keg of Al Bonanno's home brew was sticking its head out of the water. But it wasn't exactly a snake. Manny amended his first impression as the elephant-sized body rose clear of the water and came, on four tree-trunk-like legs, toward shore. Manny yelled and the girl shushed him.

"Don't attract its attention," she ordered. "It's more frightened than you are."

"Who, me, scared?" Manny gobbled.

M'lon came to Manny's side and said in a no-nonsense tone:

"You absolutely must avoid further distrupting the orderly realignment of the entropic laminae by getting yourself devoured at this point in the Unfolding. Our very presence here places intolerable stresses on the Meniscus. We took the risk in order to alleviate a point of trauma as indicated on the Master Plot. Now why did you intrude here, fellow, just under two hundred million years, relative, prior to the legitimate commencement of your personal vital fiber? It's irresponsible in the extreme, and I must insist—"

Manny was not to know what M'lon insisted, since the

snake-elephant in the surf had angled its twenty-foot neck with the undersized head with the oversized jaws to look squarely at him, first with one yellow eye, then the other, like a bird inspecting a worm. When it started toward him, he yelled and ran, pelting across the loose sand toward the shelter of the trees. He thought he heard a yell behind him. *Prolly the snake's got old Mel. Hope Patty got clear.* His lungs felt as hot and dry as that dead sponge over there, washed up above high-tide line. He stumbled, and it seemed like it took an hour to fall and roll and come to rest waiting for the elephant-snake's fangs to chomp into him. After a while, he raised his head and took a look. The elephant-thing was stretched out on its side, breathing hard, the long, snaky neck and an equally long tail stretched out full-length. The eyes were open, at least the one that was looking at him. Mel was standing astraddle the neck and little Patty was a few feet away.

"Pity," Mel called, "The entropic stress of displacement was too much for this harmless fellow. He's dying, I'm afraid."

Manny got to his feet and went toward Mel, almost forgetting to saunter. He could smell the thing now: the stink of dung plus the cucumber-smell of the snake house at the zoo.

"Whattaya mean 'pity'?" he demanded. "That thing shunt of been let outa the zoo in the first place."

"You don't understand, sir," Mel said, sounding tired.

"That's what they'd call the understatement of the year," Manny agreed. "What *is* this place? How'd I get here? And who're you?"

"A previously uncharted stretch of the Jurassic, via an illegal Aperture. Inspectors of the Final Authority," Mel replied promptly if incomprehensibly.

"Well, skip that part," Manny dismissed the matter. "How do I get outa here? I got important business. If Lepke shows up and I'm not on hand, it'll be war in the ward!"

Gotta avoid that; louse it up for everybody. It was

all those gang wars that had made the bigdomes repeal
Prohibition. Sure, there was still a market for hooch in
"dry" counties; and there was plenty of money to be
made from protection, loansharking, and the numbers—
but it wasn't easy street, like the good old days. . . .

Feeling rather proud of both his social consciousness
and his group loyalty, plus, he had to admit, his elo-
quence, Manny gave Mel a no-more-crap look. "You and
yer moll down here on vacation or what?" he demanded.
"I got no time for vacations! How do I get back to Chi?"

"Shigh is temporarily off-limits, of course," Mel replied
snappily. "It's part of the Prohibited zone, due to the
invasion, of course. Even such as *you* should know that!
Perhaps you're responsible in part, eh, for the disaster
which has befallen Shigh!" He turned to the girl, "P'ty,
place this offender under arrest!"

Manny sneered. "That'll be the day." He dismissed the
matter. "Now, I ast youse a question: how do I get
home? And what disaster?" he demanded out of context.

P'ty reached over and secured a grip like a pipe
wrench on Manny's arm. He attempted to shake her off
and yowled in pain. "Hey, leggo, sister!" he yelled, looking around to see if anyone was looking, but saw only
the dying mesosaur.

"Hey!" he yelped. "What's it all about, anyways?" He
ducked as the girl yanked him closer, giving him a stern
look. "Attempted resistance will only make it worse for
you, sir," she grated, as she slapped the handcuffs on
him. He uttered a hoarse yell and turned to run. The
mist that had suddenly come up obscured his view along
the beach, but he could see well enough to skirt the
immense corpse of the saurian and run like hell along
the water's edge.

"Look, fellows," Oob said in a wheedling tone. "This
misunderstanding has gone far enough. The time has
come for reasoned discourse." He was squatting out in
the open, not bothering to hide behind the flowering
arbutus in the shrub pit near the center of the plaza. His

lone eye had a wild look, Roger thought, and his color was a medium gray-green, indicating ... what? Roger didn't know, but there seemed no harm in yielding to the Rhox's appeal.

"Go ahead," he urged. "Say something that will make it reasonable that I fell into my TV and came out in a city-sized nuthouse."

"You were the only one at your level I could talk to," Oob moaned. "Of the few who had, at that time, experienced vug-displacement, you were the only one who had some slight grasp of the enormity of the misfortune which has befallen the Cosmic All. Both the insidious UKR and I have clarified the situation for you, and on that basis I now appeal for your active cooperation in restoring, to the extent possible, the integrity of the entropic Meniscus. Is it to be yes, or no?"

"If I can do anything that will get me back home with Q'nell, I'll be more than glad to do it!" Roger hastened to assure the Rhox. "And what was that crack about UKR? He's OK; helped me last time, and he'll do the same now, I bet. Oh, UKR!" he raised his voice to call to the pale sky above the plaza. "Help, it's me, Tyson, Roger Tyson. Get me out of here!" *Flicker.*

There was a world-encompassing *blap!* and Roger was standing alone on a sheet of glass that stretched in every direction, shimmering confusingly along a band where the horizon ought to be. Uh-oh, Roger thought; I'm back at the Ultimate Locus. Not far away, a single object rested on the glass. Roger recognized it: it was the brand-new Schwinn he'd wished up that time, smashed by the impact as it had fallen from the sky at his command. No matter—what use would he have for a forty-foot bicycle, anyway?

"I have to be more careful this time," he cautioned himself. He raised his voice to call, "Car!" then added, "Parked by the bike, in perfect running order, with gas in the tank."

Without so much as a *whoosh!* of displaced air, the normal-sized '31 Model A-400 appeared, its convertible sedan styling as snappy as the day Edsel okayed it. Roger went over, looked inside at the shiny new fake leather upholstery in a fine shade of blue to match the shiny Washington Blue paint job. The sight gauge on the dash (fine idea, that!) showed F, with actual gasoline sloshing around the numbers to prove it. He got in, set the spark and gas, pulled out the choke, pushed the starter button with his toe; paused, switched on the ignition, and tried again. The little four-banger came to life with a contented "I think I can, I think I can."

Roger scanned the stretch of glass ahead for a hint as to which way he should go, saw something over *that* way and drove toward it. When he got close, he saw that it was *another* sixty-foot bicycle, smashed just like the other one. He turned to look back. There was no wrecked bicycle behind him.

CHAPTER TWELVE

"Oh, no," he groaned. "Back in the trap!" He goosed the Ford, which chattered steadily along, but he noticed no change in the scene, no wind in his face. With nothing by which to gauge speed and direction, he might as well be sitting still. In fact, he decided impatiently, I probably *am* sitting still!

He opened the door and stepped out onto the running board (fine things, running boards; why had they done away with them?). He glanced down at the familiar glass surface and stepped down and fell hard on his face while the Model A went ticking on its way, far too fast for him to catch it; then it wasn't there. Just like that. "Damn!" Roger snarled. "I did it again!"

He turned at a sound behind him: the A was coming directly toward him, nobody at the wheel, the door hanging open. Roger stepped back, gauged the trajectory; as it passed, he swung aboard. Back in the seat, he slammed the door and gripped the wheel. He still didn't seem to be getting anywhere, he noticed, but what the hell! It was better than walking, in spite of no air and music.

Up ahead, he saw a hint of movement from the corner of his eye. A man in a suit and felt hat was running on an interception course, waving both hands. Roger swerved away from him, then relented and curved back to meet him. He was a big, beefy guy with coal-black eyebrows and an unshaven jaw, Roger noted as the fellow covered the last few yards and almost fell into the seat beside him, uninvited.

"Get me to the Dorian, fast!" the newcomer ordered. "Get going! Time's a-wasting!"

"No sweat," Roger replied affably. "I'm Tyson, Roger Tyson; who're you?"

"I'm Sweet Manny O'Rourke," the domineering stranger stated importantly. "Move this heap, pal, and I'll make it worth yer while." He showed Roger a rubber-banded roll of oversized greenbacks that would—Roger gulped—choke the proverbial horse.

"Which direction?" he inquired politely.

"The Dorian, I said!" Manny snapped. "All you guys are s'pose to know the town before you get yer license, right?"

"I seem to have misplaced the town," Roger pointed out, ostentatiously looking left and right across the polished plain of glass.

Manny started to nod, then went stiff. "I thought I was outta that fit I was having," he mourned. "*Now* where'm I at, hah?" He turned fiercely on Roger. "What'sa idea, pal? I—"

Before he could complete his period, both men shied as a fat lady on a moped steered wobblingly across their path. A pet chicken with green-dyed feathers and a red ribbon on its neck was perched on the cargo-rack behind its owner's ample rump. She glanced idly at Roger and yelled, "Look out where ya going, ya bastid!"

"We must be in New York," Roger commented. "Or maybe Paris, except she spoke English, sort of."

"Whattya talking?" Manny growled. "I'm right here in Chi!" He looked around as if noticing his surroundings for the first time. "I see what Mel meant about the disaster and all," he remarked. "You know what happened, pal?" he inquired of Roger.

" 'Fraid not," Roger answered. "Look around. Does this look like Chicago?"

Manny made a throwing-away motion. "Beats me, pal," he admitted. "Just lemme off at the corner, OK?"

Roger started to say, "What corner?" but suddenly realized that the drugstore ahead was indeed on a corner. CUT RATE DRUGS, the sign said. On impulse Roger pulled to the curb and switched off.

Manny was already out of the car. "Vo-dody-oh, bub," he called cheerfully, and strode away.

Roger got out and went toward the green-framed screen door. Inside, it was cooler; the floor was made of little hexagonal bathroom tiles, and there were gray-streaked marble-topped tables with wire legs. Large bottles of colored water ornamented the dark-varnished counter, and in back there were elaborate glass-paned, wood-framed cabinet doors with patent medicines behind them. A youngish fellow with thinning hair and an inadequate jaw said, "Yessir?" in a challenging tone.

Roger took a seat at the first table, noted that the salt-and-pepper shakers were empty, and replied. "You serve lunch?" Manny sat down opposite him.

"At six P.M.?" the chinless fellow inquired without interest, according Manny a cool glance. "Got some sandwiches, apple pie, stuff like that," he added, waving a listless hand at the display on the counter.

"I'll have a *Chateaubriand avec pommes frites*," Roger ordered grandly. "Rare. And a half-bottle of a nice little Beaujolais."

"Sure, soon as I get my Rolls-Royce back from the shop in London," the wise guy replied, "I'll run over to Delmonico's and pick it up. Meanwhile, how about a nice pastrami on rye, just made yesterday? Coke with that?"

"Interesting," Roger told the servitor after he sampled his lunch. "First time I ever had hot Coke. This sandwich: where do you get the mummified mammoth meat?"

The waiter ignored the provocation and swept from

the room, head held high. He din't have to stand around and take no crap offa wise guys, come in here and mess up the tables.

Manny was sitting astride the adjacent chair, staring at a ketchup stain on the table. It looked a little like a naked dame kneeling over. His gaze drifted upward and was caught by a sort of dirty string hanging in the air. Reminded him of the thing at the meet before he fell out the window. He shoved his chair back. "Wait a minute, pal," he growled. "What's this s'pose to be?" He gestured at the aperture.

"Oh, that's just one of Oob's Apertures," Roger replied brightly. Manny almost asked what was holding it up, but philosophical speculation had never been O'Rourke's strong suit. His attention wandered until, rising, he found the thing—kinda spiderwebby—right in his face. He brushed at it and felt a sensation of extreme cold in his hand. He put his fingertips in his mouth and nearly crossed his eyes trying to get a good look. Sort of like dirty glass, it was now; something reflected on it.

But it was not his own countenance that Manny saw; it was more like a window into some kinda store. A old dame—no, maybe not so old, was putting stuff on a shelf. Must be a flick; looked like Katie Hepburn. Manny had always appreciated from afar Miss Hepburn's delicate beauty and flawless diction. He leaned down for a better look and stumbled, din't see the steps, blundered against a flour barrel, and fetched up against the counter behind which Kate was now turning with a surprised expression on her face.

"I beg your pahdon," she said quickly. "I don't think I saw you come in."

"Never *come* in," Manny blurted, and turned to look behind him for the door he must have come through someway. No door; just a blank wall made of two-by-fours with planking on the outside. "Where'd the lunch room go?" he blurted.

"I'm sorry, sir," the Hepburn said. "I've no dining facilities here. Insufficient trade, you know."

"But what're *you* doing here, Miss Hepburn?" Manny demanded. "A big movie star like you! I seen *Morning Glory*; you was swell! I'm Manny O'Rourke," he added, offering a paw. "The boys call me 'Sweets,' " he went on. "You can, too, if you want."

"That's very friendly of you, I'm sure, Mr. O'Rourke," Kate replied. "But candidly, I rather disapprove of this 'instant first name' business. Now, with what can I help you?" She looked at him inquiringly.

Jeez, what a face, like one o' them old statues of a goddess, Manny thought, but he said, " 'With what can I help you?' Oh, boy, what a elegant way to talk, right?"

"I'm sure the locution is quite regular," Kate replied coolly. "Is there something you wanted? Perhaps a fine pair of warm gloves," she suggested. "It's down to thirteen below out there, and not a great deal better in here, I fear."

Manny was nodding, "You bet, Kate. How'd ya guess?" He was rubbing his bare hands together, miming the discomfort of a fellow who needed gloves. Kate fetched a flat box down from a shelf above the canned soup and took out a pair of fur-lined leather gloves. Manny grabbed them and put them on, then took one off and reached for his wallet.

"What do I owe you, Miss Hepburn?" he muttered. "Still can't dope why a movie star is selling dry goods at the North Pole."

Kate smiled. "I don't remember you, Mr. O'Rourke," she told him. "But you seem to know me very well, even my secret daydreams."

"Now that *Sylvia Scarlett*," Manny muttered. "Tell ya the truth, I din't like that one so hot. Yer the best-looking dame inna world, s'pose to be some punk kid. When Cary Grant called ya 'he,' you hadda wonder if the guy was nuts."

Kate nodded. "I saw the play in Boston; like you, I thought it silly. But how do you know about my foolish fantasy of the stage?"

"Ain't no fantasies, Miss Hepburn," Manny told her,

looking soulfully into her lovely, expressive eyes. "I seen you on a silver screen plenty times. You're the top. Whereat's the nearest town, eh?"

"That would be Gamecock, some fifteen miles east," she told him. "Alas, the road is snowed in; no mail for two days now. Thank heaven for the PC."

" 'The PC'?" Manny repeated uncomprehendingly.

Kate unclipped a cigarette-pack-sized black box from her waist, held it to her lips, and spoke softly into it:

"Henry? Kate here. . . . Yes, of course. I have a gentleman here who'd like to get into Gamecock. Don't you think if you came round by the old farm road you could get through? . . . No, he hasn't a machine; get Archie to come along to drive him in. . . . Thank you, Henry. You're a dear." She returned the thing she'd been talking into to its place at her hip and gave Manny that flashing smile. "He'll be alone in about a quarter-hour, Mr. O'Rourke. Would you care to sit by the stove there? Why, you haven't even an overcoat!" She came around the counter and fussed over him, getting him seated just right, so he got the heat from the pot-bellied coal-burner, then offered him a cup of tea.

"Moving pictures, you say?" she said absently.

Manny started to ask if she didn't have anything stronger, but instead, accepted the cup and saucer and sipped the hot water. "It's peaceful," Manny reflected. "I'll say that fer it. But how'd I get here?" The problem held his attention for a fraction of a second, before a sound behind him brought him to his feet in a crouch, one hand inside his wide-lapelled jacket. But it was only a kid with a red nose and a knit cap pulled down over his ears.

"Hi, Miss Katie!" he was greeting the proprietor enthusiastically. "I figgered I could make it OK!"

"Bobby! Did your father *let* you come out in this weather?" Kate gasped.

"Naw, not exactly," Bobby admitted. "He thinks I'm in the attic. He give me a old trunk to look through, said it was his grandma's 'mystery trunk' and all. Had some old clothes in it, and some snapshots showed a guy in a brass Model T beside some kinda covered wagon or like that and I climb out the winder."

"'Climbed out the window,'" Kate corrected, not sharply. The boy nodded.

"What I said," he stated with a trace of impatience. "Got any of the new Moon Pies?"

"Certainly, Bobby," Kate told him. "After all, one doesn't go back on one's promises." She went behind the counter and handed over the saucer-sized brown cakes.

The boy was close to the stove now, and Manny could smell the wet wool. "You live aroun' here, kid?" he asked. The boy gave him a contemptuous look. "Naw, I just walked over from Boston," he stated sarcastically.

"Don't wise off, Junior," Manny advised him. "Ever see a gun?" he went on, in a clumsy effort to be ingratiating. The boy's lip curled even more. "Got my own twenty-two fer Christmas," he told the strange man scornfully. "Pa said he'll show me how to shoot it soon's the thaw."

"I mean a real gat," Manny insisted, "like you shoot guys with that wanna muscle in," he explained, and took out his thirty-eight-caliber Beretta. Kate yelped and grabbed for it. Manny was so astonished that he merely gaped as she threw the weapon into a galvanized garbage can by the door.

"There, now, Bobby, it's all right," she told the lad, hugging him. "Mr. O'Rourke didn't mean to frighten you."

"I ain't scared," Bobby assured her. "Prolly jest a cap-gun, anyways. I wanna look at it." He pulled free of her embrace and went to the receptacle and reached inside.

Manny jostled Kate getting to the boy first. "You lay off, kid!" he yelled, as Kate caught the boy's arm and pulled him away.

"Bobby!" she rebuked him. "Do you want another pie, or do you want me to PC your father and tell him you've been naughty?"

"Aw, you don't hafta *call* nobody," Bobby suggested. "I just wanneda *look* at it."

"Of course," Kate said, giving Manny a disapproving glance as he pocketed his heat. "Now let's just forget all about it," Kate said; she went behind the counter and busied herself shifting the positions of cans of beans and soup.

"Hey," Manny spoke up. "I fergot to pay fer the mitts and all." The boy went past him and put a quarter on the counter.

"Thanks, Kate," he said. "Sorry I got you riled up."

"I'm not riled at *you*, Bobby," she assured him, and handed over two dimes in change, giving Manny a look that was clearly disapproving.

"Say, Miss Hepburn," Manny said. "How can I square things? I never meant—"

"I'm sure there is nothing to 'square,' Mr. O'Rourke," she told him. "Except for the gloves, of course," she added.

"Sure," Manny said eagerly. "I just ast ya bout that, Miss H, I said you fergot to collect for the mitts and all."

"That will be sixty-eight cents," Kate told him, and he handed over the coins. She glanced at them, then looked more closely. She picked a quarter from among them, studied it, and looked coolly at Manny.

"I'm sorry, Mr. O'Rourke," she said. "I'm nawt amused."

"Sure not, nothing funny," Manny agreed. "What's the beef?"

"A rather foolish counterfeit," the slim beauty told him, giving him a keen look. "You say your name is 'O'Rourke,' but you're no Irishman. And this quarter: how do you expect to fool when it's dated '1989'?"

"Real name's Goldenberg," Manny explained. "Ed Goldenberg. Hadda change it when I got inna rackets. My folks din't approve. 'Draggin' the name inna mud,' Pop said. So I changed it."

"Really?" her eyebrows went up. "And what, pray, is disgraceful about working in pictures?"

"Nothing at all," Manny hastened to assure her. "I think yer great—and so does everybody else! Is that why yer hiding out like up here in the North Pole? Ye'r ashamed o' yer work?"

"Vermont," Kate corrected. "*My* work? I was referring to your own excellent characterization in *Little Caesar*."

"You got me wrong, Kate," Manny blurted. "That was a big flick last year, I seen it. Eddie Robinson; that guy, 'Little Rico,' " he went on scornfully. "He was a mug to get hisself shot up that way. Them Hollywood guys don't know nothing about the real rackets."

"Pity," Kate reproved briefly. "I wondered why you kept referring to the moving pictures, pretending you thought I was an actress. I see now. You were hinting in hope I'd recognize you."

"I don't get it, Miss H," Manny protested. "I seen you in *A Bill of Divorcement*, with that 'profile' guy. I got to admit I envied him when he got to smooch ya."

"Oh, now I'm playing opposite John Barrymore," she said in a tone of mockery. "Are you shooting here in Gamecock—or at least near it?"

"Me? Shooting?" Manny objected. "Look, Miss Hepburn, you mean about the gat—naw, you don't want to believe all that stuff you see inna flicks!"

Bobby, who had been standing by, staring, with his mouth open, bolted for the door and barged through it, into a flurry of snow. Kate's call after him was lost.

"Poor child," she commiserated. "His mother's dead. And his father drinks. Would you mind, Mr. O'Rourke, just going along and seeing he's all right?"

"Me?" Manny started to expostulate, but, melted by her cheekbones, he nodded and blundered out into the bitter wind just as a spidery black Model T came chugging up, snow-caked chains on the skinny tires. A spry little man who resembled his car stepped down, lifted the ear-flap of his plaid wool cap, and called to Manny: "You the fare Kate called about?"

"You seen a kid?" Manny called back.

Henry pointed. "That one?" he inquired. "Looks like old Bob Whadkey's boy. What's he doing out in this weather? Come on." He climbed back into his high seat and employed the new self-starter to set the four-banger in clattering motion.

"Be right back," he yelled down to Manny, and pulled away toward the lad struggling through the banked snow.

Manny yelled "Hey!" and gave chase. The tall, narrow vehicle seemed to be gaining on him. He ran harder, passing the spot where he had seen Bobby, and still the Ford receded. He could see its tracks in the snow. It was hard to see through the whirling curtain of snow-flakes ahead.

Manny slowed; no use getting a heart attack. He yelled, weakly. No response. The car was gone. He was alone in the snow.

Up ahead, he saw a glow of light, looked like a window. He struggled toward it. It was *cold* out here! He pulled his collar close around his neck and by now he could make out the shape of the small, white-painted clapboard building. How'd he get *behind* it? The T was parked in front of it. He'd fix that Henry wiseguy when he got ahold of him! It was only another few feet, but he was soooo tired; he could hardly breathe! His feet were fifty-pound blocks of ice.

As he reached the door, it opened. Kate, charming in a fur coat and hat, was just coming out. She gave him that dazzling smile:

"Oh, Mr. O'Rourke," she said, sounding surprised to see him.

"Henry got the kid," Manny mumbled. "Gotta get back inside, Miss Hepburn. 'Fraid the cold's gettin to me."

"I should think so!" she said emphatically, hugging herself, a chore Manny would have been glad to perform for her. "You should never have come out in this, in only a lounging suit," she admonished him, as she held the door open.

"Well, you know," Manny muttered. "Kind of a sudden trip, you might say."

She nodded. "I see," she assured him. "Do come in." He stumbled into the cozy warmth and the smell of coffee.

"I was thinking," Kate told him, "after you left, I mean. It's so curious seeing *you* here in this remote place, and knowing my most cherished fantasy, too. Remarkable! Could you— I mean is there possibly a minor role for me in the picture? The opportunity may never come so close again."

"Another cuppa that hot tea, Kate, and whatever you say goes," Manny gasped out. She hurried away.

CHAPTER THIRTEEN

Jed Pawkins looked up disapprovingly when Bob came in, fifteen, almost twenty minutes late. The boy looked like he'd been drinking—at this hour! Too bad, just when he'd been thinking about recommending him to Mr. K for promotion to Design.

"Oh, Bob," he called in what he thought was an ingratiating tone. "Would you come over a moment?"

Bob gritted his teeth; any time Pawkins used that smarmy voice it meant somebody was in for a lecture about his great-grandpa and the pioneer days and how he founded the bank, and if it hadn't been for the Depression, Jed would have been rich, all the rest of it. Bob glanced at the wall clock. Damn! It was a good five minutes fast, and he was already running a little late.

Bill Hutchens was having another. His new friend Tom Something was getting tiresome. The convention was a bore. Tom was still yakking; Bill wasn't really listening.

"—seen it, I tell ya!" he insisted. "It wasn't them wise guys from Acme Metals, neither. Like a big tuber, sorta pink, with these legs and all like a spider—and tentacles on its head—if it hadda head! Hey!" he interrupted himself. "There it goes—out the door!"

"Thought you said a tuber," Bill objected indifferently. "Make up yer mind: a tuber or a spider?"

"Both!" Tom insisted. "Listen, Bill, the damn thing jumped *out* at me! Scared me, in that dark hall—kinda spooky. Now it's out inna parking lot." He started after it.

"In the dark, you couldn't see a tuber jumping out at you," Bill said to Tom's back.

Just then Walter Shield came along and Tom collared him. "Listen, Fritz," he demanded. "I seen this here monster-thing inna corridor! Can't get nobody to listen. It's right outside!"

"Prolly just those wiseguys from Acme," Walter suggested, disengaging his arm from Tom's clutch. The convention was getting worse by the moment. First, the big boys from Consolidated failed to show—he only *came* to see them; then the lousy banquet—instant indigestion. And a lotta nobodies coming around taking up your time—and now this Tom Something, talking crazy.

"Gotta go, Tom," Walter explained and fled. After ricocheting off three broads that weren't as unattached as they looked, Walter had had enough; this finished it. He went on out. His car was right by the door. Enough was enough. He was wishing he hadn't told Myrtle all about the big deal he was sure to cinch with Mr. Collier at Consolidated. Now he'd be coming home with his tail between his legs—two days early.

He snarled at a couple of Jaycee types who were clogging the doorway. Somehow that reminded him to check out. His bags were already in the Chrysler. He went over to the desk and paid up. Wasted money.

In his car, he gunned angrily out of the lot, saw the Route 40 sign, and did a hard left to get into it ahead of the pickup. He drove angrily, got clear of town and onto the open road. The night was clear, the highway empty. He was making good time. Too bad about not getting a chance to bend Collier's ear, but what the hell. Even old Bill had acted like a stranger, all cozy with that

Tom Something. Even the booze at the bar was bad, at two bucks a shot, too! Crap!

Walter settled down to driving. Lonely out here, a long way between towns. He jumped, startled at a sound—a sort of *creak!* from the back seat; it sounded like. He turned his head for a quick look. Nothing there but his hanging suits and the sample case. Nothing to be jittery about, he told himself. He heard another creak, and said aloud, "OK, so the old crate creaks. So what? Got a couple good years out of it." He had only bought it because Chrysler was in trouble and he hated to see another old-time car company go under; so much for charitable impulses.

When Mrs. Gelbfleisch got to the Acme Market that morning, there was already a crowd there. Mrs. Murphy was over there, always pushing to be first in line. Yep, the word was out: rutabagas were going to be in short supply because of some kind of crop failure—and they were Mr. Gelbfleisch's favorite, too. Mrs. Murphy knew that—she'd laughed when she'd heard—so she ought to be nice enough to let a person go first!

Mrs. Murphy was looking back over the crowd. She spotted Dottie Gelbfleisch and called, "Oh, Mrs. Gelbfleisch! I've got something for you! I know your Morris loves rutabagas, and I heard there was a shortage, so I picked up some nice ones for you. Seventy-nine cents."

Dottie Gelbfleisch was speechless—almost: "Why, Gertie, you should be so nice!" she simpered at last, handing over three quarters and four pennies, wondering as she did how much commission the fat mick had added to the price.

"It's terrible, isn't it, Dottie," Gert gushed. "The poor farmers—their whole crop ruined by a plague or something!"

"No, Gert," Dottie corrected. "Plagues are for people. It was more of a blight. 'The rutabaga blight,' the paper said. Another example of government mismanagement. Prolly radioactive fertilizer or like that."

"Me and my Pat won't use 'em," Gert said complacently. "Anybody wants to eat—" "—tough roots," she almost said, but caught herself before precipitating a tirade about prejudice.

"Spikking rutabagas," Dottie said. "Look at *that* one." She was staring along the aisle, and Gert's gaze followed. Oob, the Rhox, was squatting on his externally-jointed limbs like a forty-pound potato in a collapsed deck chair, Gert thought wildly. But it was alive! The snaky things on top were twisting around.

"Dottie!" she gasped, wondering about Freudian symbols, "you see that thing?"

"You think I'm maybe blind, or what?" Mrs. Gelbfleisch riposted. "Come on, Gert, let's look into this." She tugged her old pal's arm and together they marched up to the thing. It had an eye, Mrs. Murphy realized, and the eye was gazing directly at *her*. She stopped dead. "Let's call the manager," she gasped. "An *eye!* It winked at me! The nerve!"

Dottie, however, was intent on confrontation.

"Here, you, nice doggie," she offered, wondering if that big, wide mouth had teeth. "Nice doggie," she repeated. "Just step aside once, OK, and let a lady pass." She thrust Gert ahead to dramatize the need to make room for a lady to pass. Oob sidled a few inches to the left. Gert balked.

"If I might have a word with you ladies," Oob suggested tentatively, "perhaps I could clear up a part of this situation right now. You see, my Relegator has fallen into unauthorized hands, and I fear further mischief will be done unless someone quite uninvolved and thus bearing a minimal entropic charge, such as yourselves, will volunteer—"

"That's it!" Gert yelped, retreating. "My boy Mike, the one that's in the service told me, 'Never volunteer, Ma.' That's what he said. And he *knows*. He's what you call a top sergeant, entirely!"

"I'm sure the boy was right, Gert," Dottie agreed

dully. "But what if a giant rutabaga's blocking your way? Then what?"

"Hardly 'blocking your way,' madam," Oob objected. "I stood aside, just as you requested. But I warn you: don't get too close to the, ah, the wavering line you may have noticed just in front of you. It's what we Rhox call an Aperture. You really mustn't pass through it."

"This blathering rutabaga's tryna tell us what to do, Dot!" Gert barked. "Why, the back o' me hand to the spalpeen!" She stepped determinedly forward—and wasn't there anymore.

Dottie uttered a sound and collapsed. Oob fled, just as:

Rusty Naill staggered: the floor of the store was six inches lower than that of the plaza which would occupy the space in another two million years. Rusty hastened to assist Dottie in getting to her feet.

"Sorry if I startled you, ma'am," he offered. "I was just . . ." He ran out of explanation.

"Where's Gert?" Mrs. Gelbfleisch demanded. "One minute she was standing right here with me, looking at the rutabaga! The next—she's gone!" Dottie looked accusingly at Rusty. "And *you* pop out of thin air, like a—!"

"Did you say 'rutabaga'?" Rusty interrupted. "A *big* one, with legs like a lobster?"

"That's the one!" Dottie seconded, nodding accusingly. "I'm calling the manager! You stay right here, you . . . rapist!"

"Hold it!" Rusty urged. "I'm not, I mean I didn't— that is, I just *got* here—wherever 'here' is!"

Slightly mollified, Dottie hestitated. "This is the Acme, on Third," she stated. "There was this— Where's it gone? The rutabaga, I mean? I mean, it wasn't really a rutabaga. Who ever saw a rutabaga as big as a bushel potatoes, with legs already, like you said, and these—" She put her hands to her head, fingers extended and waggling.

"That's Oob, all right," Rusty assured her. "You say

he's around here? He likes to hide and then jump out
at people."

"I'll jump out at *it*, the low-life!" Dottie asserted, staring around belligerently. Then she looked keenly at
Rusty. "Just where did *you* come from, Mister, spikking
jumping out at people! And where'd Gert go?"

"Why, I was there at the Final Concept, F'shu called
it," Rusty stammered, "and—well, I don't know. Bob
Armstrong was there, fine fellow; he had *no* idea what
was going on; and a rather bossy fellow called Roger
Tyson. We were just talking, but after that it gets a little
vague. . . ."

Abruptly Oob was there before them, jittering on his
pointy feet. "I warned you, Clarence!" he said in his
gluey voice. "You've confounded the confusion still further! Now you've involved these charming ladies—"

" 'Ladies,' plural?" Rusty challenged. "I only see *one*
lady."

"Disaster," Oob stated as crisply as one can speak with
a mouth full of syrup—or so it sounded to Rusty. "More
interference," Oob added coldly.

"You keep blaming us, your victims," Rusty said. "It's
you that's causing all the trouble!"

"Where's Gert?" Dottie insisted.

"That, madam," Oob began, "is a function of ten to
the twelfth variables, none of which is consistent in any
practical sense. It is extremely doubtful that she will ever
reappear at this precise energy level."

He leapt as Gert yelled: "Hey!" directly behind him.

"This vegetable still here?" she demanded. "Listen,
Dot, begorra, you won't be after believing what I been
seeing at all these last few days, entirely!"

"What few days?" Dot challenged. "You ducked outa
sight maybe ten seconds ago, and this gentleman popped
up instead, then the rutabaga's back again, talking mean."

"Forget all that, Dot," Gert urged. "Now, if you'll be
listening to me, I'll be after telling you all about it: first,
there was this nice young man, 'Julian,' he told me his
name was. He invited me inside this palace-like, for a

snort. It was *some* place, Dot! Big as the train depot, with white marble columns and statues of naked women, and a black-and-red marble floor big as a football field (that's a hundred yards) slick as glass. Over on the side, we went out on a balcony with a view like the Grand Canyon. Disperate nice out there: springtime, it was, and nice music, and we got service like we were the visiting royalty, entirely! The eats were a little on the light side; some kinda salad greens with crabmeat or like that. The booze was good stuff. I only knocked back a couple, and I was flying!"

" 'Drunk,' you mean, Gert," Dot put in. "Disgraceful!"

"No, bejabbers, it takes more'n a couple pink ladies to inebriate a Doyle (I'm born Gertrude Doyle, you know). I mean I was *really* flying. Like through the air, bedad! Julian was right there, for a while, then he went off someplace and I was just after drifting and sailing amongst the clouds, and God spoke to me! He says:

" 'GERTRUDE! THIS IS A GRAVE MISCALCULA-TION! YOUR ARE IN DIRE PERIL. KINDLY CON-CENTRATE YOUR MIND ON THE LAST MUNDANE SCENE YOU CAN RECALL.' "

"Yeah?" Dottie encouraged. "So what'd you do?"

"I told him I couldn't remember what I was doing last Mundane," Gert supplied. "So he says:

" 'NEVER MIND; I SHALL INSPECT YOUR COR-TEX FOR THE NECESSARY DATA.'

"Well," I said, "nobody's messing with *me* corset, even if I'd be after the wearing of one!"

"Plenty chutzpah, considering it's the Lord you're talk-ing to," Dottie observed.

"I dunno about that, matter of fact," Gert explained. "Just this big voice it was, coming out of the sky. Figured it was God, only He wouldn't be inspecting a lady's corset!"

"What'd he do next?" Dot prompted.

"Said 'JUST RELAX, AND RECALL WHAT YOU WERE DOING JUST BEFORE YOU RUPTURED THE MENISCUS.'

" 'Me? "Ruptured"? The idea!' I tells him," Gert went on, caught up in her recital. "Next thing, here I was."

"That's s'pose to be a coupla days, you said," Dottie challenged. "Sounds to me like maybe half a minute."

"Ladies!" Oob interjected. "We must recall that third-level temporal coordinates become irrelevant in the context of the Final Concept (a misnomer by the way), so doubtless you both are correct in terms of your own personal entropic orientation."

" 'Recall,' it says," Dottie huffed. "How can I remember a bunch nonsense I never heard of? Hah?"

"Never mind, Dot," Gert interceded. "I think all he means is like time passes fast when you're having fun, or whatever."

"Precisely," Oob seconded. "Have fun, ladies."

"Fun, is it?" Mrs. Gelbfleisch snorted. "I'll fun *you*, you galloping turnip!" She aimed a blow with her rolled umbrella, impacting Oob right between his eye. Carroty material spattered, Oob's legs went limp, as did his tentacles, which hung limply down across the pale-gray bulge of his bulbous form.

"You killed it!" Dot screeched.

"All I done was give it a light tap to teach it some manners!" Gert objected.

Rusty stepped between the ladies, risking wounds from their dagger-like stares.

"It doesn't matter in the least," he told them soothingly. "It's only a third-order extrusion. See, it's already fading."

Indeed, Oob's bulk had diminished to the size of an ordinary vegetable, and was a pale, almost translucent gray, which faded and was gone.

"Whew!" Gert sighed dramatically. "Just as I thought: it was only me imagination after all. Bejabbers, that's after being a disperate relief! Saints be praised!"

"Then how come I imagined the same thing?" Dottie demanded. "Anyways, I got shopping I should do; thanks for the rutabagas, Gert. I'll be seeing you."

"Just like that, you'll be going off, like nothing

happened?" Gert complained. "Nobody's ever going to be after believing me when I tell 'em—"

"Don't," Rusty urged. "Don't even try. We're mixed up in some kind of future research project, Roger told me," he explained earnestly. "But the Builder has it all in hand, and if we just go along quietly and act reasonably, it will all work out."

"Bedad!" Gert exclaimed. "That's after bein' just what Father Flaherty was after saying last week! You mean we're all just being tested by Divine Providence?"

"Sort of," Rusty conceded. "You see, the Builder made up this sort of mock-up universe to try out some ideas. It didn't work out too well, and when it finally evolved into Culture One, they decided to try to do something about it; they built the Temporal Bore, I understand from what Roger said—he was prolly confused himself—so they could examine the whole extent of time and see where things had gone wrong. Then the Rhox showed up—an intelligent life-form who stumbled into the Bore from some unrealized (on this plane) potential level—and they, or he, mixed things up even worse when it tried to sort out the incongruities and all, and now—Well, if Oob is around here—" He paused to look around searchingly. "Anyway," he went on, "his damned Aperture is focused on this level and it's working—that's where your friend went; she's lucky she got back here and isn't stuck in Sherwood Forest or something, so we'd better try to do something about that."

He paused and raised his voice slightly to speak again. "Oh, UKR, are you there?"

WHERE ELSE, CLARENCE? the great voice, somewhat restrained, replied promptly.

"How do we get out of *this* one?" Rusty called to the ceiling. There was no response. Dottie tugged at his arm; Gert crossed herself, made a few extra passes in the air just for good measure, and said, "Now, don't be after doing no voice-throwing, entirely, fella-me-lad. I had a cousin, Feenie, he called himself in vaudeville, used to make a mule's rear talk like that! Stop yer fooling and *do* something!"

"I'm trying," Rusty protested. "I'm playing by ear; but we've got UKR to help, if he'll answer."

"Oh, Mister Ucker," he said, or so it seemed to Gert, as he addressed the air conditioning duct overhead. "Sir," he went on, "we've been the victim of some sort of mistake. I was right there on the beach—"

" 'Beach,' ha!" Gert cut in. "I'm right here in the Acme Superette with me friend, Dot, and all of a sudden this oversize carrot or whatever ye'd be after callin it—"

"That's Oob," Rusty supplied. "A lady has stumbled through his Aperture, quite by accident. Couldn't you put her back here?"

NOTHING EASIER, UKR said loudly. I'LL DO IT FIVE MINUTES AGO. KINDLY STAND BACK FROM THE UNAUTHORIZED APERTURE.

"That's that thing like a sort of glowing string hanging there in midair," Rusty explained.

"That's ridiculous, Mister Ah," Dot snorted. "How could . . . ?" She advanced to confront the shimmering disc. "Now suppose I—" As Dottie stepped forward, she vanished before Rusty's astonished gaze.

He stood staring at the string as it rotated slowly, widening into a patch of blurry iridescence. Then it exploded.

CHAPTER FOURTEEN

When Walter (Fritz) Shield passed the CHURCH OF
THE NAZARENE sign for the third time, he gnashed both
his teeth and his gears and braked hard, shoving the
shifter into low. This time he'd really *creep*, and if there
was a turn he hadn't noticed (which was impossible) this
time he'd damn well notice it. The light rain pattered on
the windshield, just enough to keep him switching on the
wipers and then switching them off again when their
clop-clop started to annoy him. The new road went along
perfectly straight, directly toward the lights from over on
U.S. 18, up ahead. Beside him, the black barrier of pine
and oak trees was unbroken. There was no place he *could*
have turned. Maybe this time he'd come out on 18, like
he ought to. Grimly, Walter drove on. He came to the
low spot and crossed it without difficulty, although the
exhaust sounded like a motorboat, bubbling underwater.
There was the little house again, only this time there
were lights on inside. Walter started to turn in at the
unpaved drive, but sternly decided against it. No point
in confusing the issue, he told himself. Straight ahead,
and if that damned church popped up again . . . Well,
he didn't know *what* then . . .

* * *

Professor Mary Tomkins was upset. The paper *still* wasn't here: that Whatkey boy was so unreliable it was an outrage! His mother had been such a pretty lady, too, though there were rumors she was a little *too* friendly with a number of men. . . . Bother those malicious rumors, she admonished herself, though she *had* seen her going into apartment F-69-B1 that time, when she *knew* Sarah was out. Anyway, Fred always liked to find his paper laid out right there on the hassock by his chair, and if that impossible little urchin didn't get here in the next sixty seconds, she'd have to call the paper and complain. Wasn't as if the Whatkeys needed the money; Old Bob Whatkey had all that money from the Veterans and all—so . . .

The paper wasn't all, Mary told herself. She was starting to feel a little indignant now: the TV was out, and Fred's lamp wouldn't go on. She *click!*ed the switch four times, and went for a new bulb. The fridge was *whirr!*ing away, so it wasn't the power again. The clock stood at 3:05, which was at *least* ten minutes slow, but the second hand was moving.

She marched into the pantry, where the circuit breakers were, and flipped the switch. Nothing. Well, she had a flashlight back here, just in case: she groped for it, switched it on, feeling competent and foresightful, and was shocked at how shabby her neat and orderly shelves of canned goods looked in the wan beam. She quickly checked the breakers. All in the ON position, so she'd have to call Sunshine Electric and have that awful man come out. She still felt uncomfortable every time she remembered the time the porch light was out, and she'd changed bulbs, put in a brand new one, right out of the carton, and it still didn't work, and she'd called and he came and took out her new bulb and threw it away over her protests and put in one of his own, and dammit, it worked. He gave her that insolent grin and charged her twenty dollars! Now it would probably be the same, just some silly little thing . . . She brushed at a cobweb, feeling enraged at her own inadequate housekeeping.

With a shock like an ice-cold wave breaking over her, Mary stared into the stalactite- and stalagmite-studded depths of a dark cave that seemed to go on and on into pitch darkness. She took a few steps, peering in vain for a bit of light. She stopped dead and turned all the way around, thereby getting herself completely disoriented, and *thought* she saw a faint glow in *that* direction. She started toward it, and almost tripped over a ridge in the floor. If she only had a light!

She felt a moment of comfort when she remembered that a flashlight was precisely what she had in her hand. She switched it on and played the brilliant white light over a red-and-yellow curtain of stone filaments that almost blocked her way. Good thing, too, she realized, stepping back hastily from the edge of a sheer drop. One more step and she'd have fallen into that pit, thirty feet across, at least, and she couldn't find a bottom with her light.

She shrank back against a giant column of wet stone and sank down so as to sob more comfortably. She was having some kind of spell—like old Aunt Henrietta in her last years—only *she* wasn't in her nineties, or even old! She was right here in the storeroom—no, Fred wanted her to call it the pantry—looking at the cans of tomato aspic that had started to leak and make black rings on the fresh shelf-paper, and then, suddenly, she was in the cave of the Great Evil, all alone.

Abruptly, she was shivering, not only from the chill of the stone against her body, but from the thought of the monster. He was taller than a man, and hairy, with that giant, snarling dog's face and the obscenely long, black claws. *Ursus speleus*, she thought; still, her ancestors had stood up against the beast, with only a sharp stick, and made decorative arrangements of their stacked skulls afterward.

Why, only the other day Moog had killed one of the monsters with a rock he pushed over a cliff on it, and dragged home the body—and with a little black cub that snuffled and sniffled into everything—including the pot

of foul, bubbling, scum-covered water left over when
Heg hadn't washed the pot after she made the bread.
Um the Afflicted drove the cub off and *drank* the horrible mess, and went into a spell of his own, yelling and
chanting and wanting to grab every woman he saw.

So that was how beer was invented, Mary reflected:
the by-product of bread-making; the same ingredients,
exactly. The revelation had almost taken her thoughts off
her ridiculous situation for a moment.

She got to her feet; she was *still*, impossibly, in a damp
cave. The foundations of the house must have been dug
right next to it, and the wall had finally caved in without
anyone noticing, and she'd stumbled in; but her store—
pantry—was only a few feet away, so she'd better get
busy and find it, staying well clear of the sinkhole, of
course.

But perhaps Fred would be along soon, looking for
her. *He* wouldn't let fear of the Monster keep him away!

Her head ached, she noticed. Suddenly she was thinking of the willows that grew in profusion by the river
bank; acetylsalicylic acid: they were full of it—aspirin!
She could gather leaves, extract the juice and help those
poor souls of the tribe, with their rotting teeth and
arthritic joints and untreated cuts and bruises. How
happy they'd be to have a pain-killer! But right now, the
thing was to get out of here. She sidled around the edge
of the pit and made her way toward the glow dimly
visible through the screen of stalactites.

Something—no, someone—rose up in her path, the
form of a man—a shaggy, brutish man. He stared at her
and growled. Mary stamped her foot. "No!" she stated
firmly. The Tribe . . . but, no again! It couldn't be! But
the "memories," if that's what they were, were so clear!
"Shoo!" she commanded. "I don't believe in *Homo
erectus* wandering around in the woods, or the Sasquatch,
either, or Yeti or whatever."

She continued steadily toward him, holding his small
yellowish eyes with hers, and flashed her light full in the
gorilla-like face. The brute whimpered and fled. Mary

stopped dead, sat on a rock, and pondered. Magic! She was a witch-woman, she knew that, but she was also Professor Mary Tomkins, and she remembered her life with the tribe—undoubtedly *Homo erectus*, she had to admit to herself—but she also remembered her cozy home in suburban Brantville, with Fred. There was no simple explanation, she realized, unless her mind was gone. If so, so be it. She'd be damned if she'd sit here and cry. She got up and went toward the light.

Walter Shield set the climate-control lever a bit higher. Getting *cold*! His gas gauge was on the edge of the red part now, and no lights in sight. He felt in his pocket again, fingering the thin stack of currency; no point in counting it again—he knew he had twenty-one bucks, no more, no less. Enough to top off—but he needed to stop at a motel; he was tired, and he needed a good meal. He envisioned pulling into a Holiday Inn, registering with a clear conscience, and strolling into the dining room to order up a pretty good steak, if he could convince the waitress he wanted it rare, not brown all the way through. And a tall draft.

Damn, why had he been fool enough to get himself stranded out here on the interstate far from any town, hungry and broke and out of gas? He couldn't remember.

The convention hadn't been a lot of fun, and he'd been among the first to leave—in the early evening, which seemed days ago, but was actually only about three hours, he reflected. After that, things were a little vague. He remembered that damned Route 40 sign that took him the wrong way; eighty miles in the wrong direction before he took a good look at the map and discovered that the next town (Brantville, five miles) on 40 was *east* instead of west. Dammit! That had shaken him, and that was probably when he'd failed to look at the gas gauge.

He could have cashed a check at the Con, but hadn't thought of it. Now he had twenty-two bucks with which to eat and sleep *and* gas up—if he could find a gas station before he ran dry. He peered through the darkness—

and saw the baleful blue point of a distant mercury-vapor lamp, off to the right.

He slowed, looking sharp for the exit, found it, and fetched up at a sign reading "MILTON 5" to the right, and "BINEBERG 3" to the left. There were no lights to beckon him down the road, so he decided on left and swung into the narrow road and drove off into pitch blackness.

Swell: now he was broke, tired, hungry, and out of gas—*and* on some back road. At least on the interstate there'd been a little traffic in case he ran dry. He looked at the gauge: the needle was well into the center of the red. (Hey, dum-dum, you're outa gas!) Great! Walter was sweating, in spite of the fact that his toes hurt from the cold.

Hey! There was a light—an Amoco sign—almost hidden behind trees. He pulled over in front of the pumps. There was a light inside the office! He got out and went in. There were some tired-looking sandwiches in plastic wrap. He picked one up, took a Coke from the cooler, and paid up.

"I need gas, too," he told the slack-jawed youth behind the counter. "Will you give me twenty dollars' worth of the regular, please?"

The boy looked pained, stretched in a leisurely way, and went outside. Walter decided to wait until he was in his motel to eat. He could pay that by check, he hoped.

"Wouldn't take twenny," the lad reported. Walter was happy to accept two dollars in change. He took the next entry to the interstate.

After another hour of drumming along southward, Walter noted a large, illuminated sign reading, "HOWARD JOHNSON—THIS EXIT."

"Damn nonsense!" he muttered. "There *isn't* any exit here! They mean 'next exit'!"

"Except," he reminded himself, "that for some reason 'next' is coming to mean 'the one *after* next.'" In Old English, it was "nigh, nigher, nighest"; that gave us "near, nearer, and next." If one of those "next-means-the-one-*after*-next"-people were standing at the head of the line at the bank, and the teller said "next," would he step aside for the fellow behind him? Nope, it was selective. Like "next Friday" means "a week *after* next Friday" to a lot of people. So much for logic. So the people that put up signs have caved in to the minority, and say "next exit" when they mean the second exit. Dopey.

Walter was enjoying resenting the mangling of the language, reminding himself of how the past participal suffix -*ed* was fast disappearing, thanks to the laziness of sign painters, presumably: "air condition homes" (*houses*, dammit!), "devil crabs" "old fashion fruitcake," even "use cars." Even the plural -*s* was on the way out—and why did the analphabets have to put an apostrophe in a simple plural: "USE CAR'S 4 SALE"? You'd never convince those fellows that 4 didn't spell *for*. And the useful expression, "I couldn't care less"; made meaningless, or counterindicative, by modifying it to "I *could* care less." People didn't seem to realize that words were supposed to *mean* something.

In Hollywood armies, the top sergeant is forever reporting, "all present *and* accounted for." Wrong!!! Its *or*, not *and*! The idea is, if Kablitski's in the brig and Jones is in sick bay, the rest are present. So Kablitski and Jones, though not present, *are* accounted for. If they're present they don't *need* to be "accounted for."

And Walter wished that someone would explain to Hollywood that the Southern "y'all" was strictly a plural—"all of you"—and was never, never, not *ever* used in addressing an individual, except when meaning "you and your bunch"; it seemed easy enough.

Walter was feeling warmer, having worked himself up to a fine state of indignation, which worked to his disadvantage, alas, when a yell from behind him caused him to jump wildly and wrench the wheel hard left. Just then a hot-shot in one of those squatty little cars shaped like something you'd scraped off your shoe shot out of an access road right in front of him and slowed down. Walter said a badword and gunned past the damn fool.

As he did so, he saw the trestles with BEN'S BARRIERS stenciled on them; he braked hard, went into a slide, and banged over the edge of an eight-inch drop-off where the pavement had been dug up. He hurtled down a slope, fighting the wheel, but flipped and came to rest upside down.

"Damn good thing I had the old harness fastened," he told himself as he figured out how to release himself without falling on his head. He managed it, but found the door wedged tight. The electric window didn't work.

Suddenly he was thinking of upside-down gas tanks, and sparks from the electrical system. Sitting on the headliner—and especially hard perch, he realized, due to the transverse metal ribs under the vinyl—he tried the other door. It opened easily; indeed, it felt as if it were being pulled outward. Walter scrambled out, and in the glow of his one still-functioning headlight, he saw the squatty red car parked beside him.

"I apologize, sir," a foreign-sounding voice was saying. "I'm not yet fully familiar with all the complexities of your curious unspoken code of vehicular precedence."

"Aw, that's OK,' Walter started to say, in a momentary feeling of magnanimity occasioned by the fact that the guy *had* stopped to help. But instead, he said, "Least I survived." He turned toward the voice that had come from behind the open door, and literally staggered as Oob stepped forward.

"Cripes!" Walter muttered. "Am I dead and seeing demons in Hell?"

"By no means, sir, another department entirely," the Rhox hastened to assure him. "Pray be calm," the monster went on easily. "I shall be glad to transport you to a pest-house if you're in need of the ministration of a chirurgeon."

"Thanks a lot," Walter replied, having turned to look at the surprisingly shabby-looking underside of his '84 Chrysler. The rear end had gone out the first week, and then, when his oil idiot-light failed, the new engine. He'd spent plenty on that bus, and now just when he'd gotten it in pretty good shape, it was a total loss. Unless the demon was prepared to pay up.

"A good twenty-four thou," he said reproachfully, "to replace her. You feel like reimbursing me?"

"Check, gold, or folding money?" Oob inquired insouciantly.

CHAPTER FIFTEEN

"Say, how do you do that, anyway?" Walter inquired, as he realized suddenly that he was being made sport of. Some kids, no doubt, damned juvenile delinquents, or those clowns from Acme, had fixed up this thing with the snakes on top, and the legs like a spider, and— That eye! It was staring at him steadily. And the voice—it had come from a mouth like the flap on a mail sack. Why'd they go to all the trouble? Walter had from time to time suspected that he had secret enemies; now he had proof of it.

The idea, he figured, was to con him into giving the cops a story about being forced off the road by a turnip in a Maserati; some joke! Well, he'd fool 'em: he'd never say a word about this.

Just then a brilliant beam of light probed down from the embanked road above. Walter peered, trying to see where it was coming from. He made out a white-clad figure—in shorts, it looked like, in *this* cold—coming down toward him.

"Good evening to you, sir," the newcomer said as he came up. Walter was staring. The guy looked like a movie star, practically, a little gray at the temples, but a build like Lex Barker. And that outfit; not shorts, but a sort of a kilt. This guy was as nutty as the rest of the day.

"Hi,' Walter said glumly. "Did you see that?"

"I witnessed your veering off the road in a panic just as I passed you," the stranger stated.

"Panic, hell!" Walter blurted. "The SOB pulls out in front of me," he informed the universe, "and did twenty, and I hadda go around or hit him!"

"What SOB is it to which you refer?" R'heet inquired, looking around, and holding his light on the red sports car.

"Well, how do I know who you are?" Walter demanded. "I'm driving along, minding my own business, and—"

"Pity," R'heet said, casting his light on Walter's inverted Mopar product. "I suppose your machine is beyond salvage?"

"So that's it," Walter blurted. "It's a put-up deal. You pick out a nice car, your pals run it off the road, and you buy up the wreck at a bargain price, and fix it up, or sell parts! It doesn't fly this time, pal! I wasn't born yesterday!"

"No, I suppose not," R'heet agreed solemnly. "I suppose forty or so of your local temporal units are required for the maturation of the newborn primitive organism. But aside from these arbitrary distinctions, just how the occasion of your entry to this plane of existence is germaine to the problem at hand, I fail to see. We must act effectively. Specifically, returning you to your planned sequence of actions with the minimal disturbance to the Matrix. By the way, have you seen anything of a little chap with—"

"Don't know what that's s'pose to mean," Walter replied cagily. Thought they'd trick him into talking like a nut-case, did they?

"Too bad," R'heet commented. "I'd an idea he was involved here, judging from an anomalous reading on my vug-meter. Been tracking the rascal, you know, and I have a pocket variance-suppressor with me with which to lay him by the heels."

"He didn't *have* any heels," Walter volunteered, to his own surprise. "I mean—"

"I understand," R'heet comforted him. "You feel the need to dissemble, in order to avoid the appearance of eccentricity. Fear not, I'm not here to pass judgment on your sanity. But where the devil did he go?"

"You some kind of cop?" Walter demanded.

"Not as you people ordinarily employ the term," R'heet corrected. "I am, however, an inspector of continua, duly appointed by the Council of the Final Authority."

"I never heard of any of that stuff," Walter dismissed the claim. "Not here in the good old USA! Anyways, the point is, right now I need to get to my motel; I've got a reservation, got to be there by midnight; so let's get going."

"I'm sorry, sir," R'heet replied. "These arbitrary temporal distinctions confuse me. " 'Midnight': that implies a centroid of a variable expanse of entropic decay. My instruments—"

"Oh, a musician, eh?" Walter put in. "Rock and roll, or country?"

"I fear, sir," R'heet said stiffly, "the references escape me."

"Sure, you foreigners wouldn't understand." Walter settled the matter to his own satisfaction. "What you doing here in the U.S. of A?" he inquired next.

"As I explained, sir—" R'heet began, but Walter interrupted.

"Call me Fritz; and I told you I don't understand the explanation. You some kind of a spy, or something?"

"I am, undoubtedly, 'something,' " the visitor from Culture One affirmed. "But not, by any means, a spy. I'm simply here in line of duty: the obnoxious Rhox led me here, and—"

Oob chose that moment to reappear, clambering up over the inverted chassis of Walter's car. "Kindly moderate your use of pejorative epithets," he demanded in a tone like hardening plastic. "I attempted to assist this primitive—of your *own* species, at an earlier stage, may I point out, Inspector; he was headed for certain disaster, due to the absence of a bridge formerly spanning the river ahead. He was in a savage mood, I noted, and unlikely to obey the rather minimal warning signs erected by the union workers as they went off-shift. He'd have been killed—

"Bah!" Oob interrupted his own glib explanation. "Why do I trouble myself to dissemble? The fact is, Inspector, a serious temporal discontinuity has developed here—"

"Due to your own multiple perforations of the Meniscus," R'heet put in.

"Be that as it may," Oob continued coldly. "Clearly, it was undesirable for this poor chap to plunge through the fault into an achronistic locus."

"But," R'heet said severely, consulting some kind of fancy pocket-watch, "it appears that is precisely what happened."

"Not my fault," Oob persisted. "I tried to help him, but he veered too sharply."

"So you ran me off the road and over a cliff!" Walter charged, looking up at the ten-foot embankment over which he had plunged. "Some 'assistance'! My car—"

"The machine will be returned to pristine condition, Walt," R'heet reassured him.

"Sure, that's OK," Walter countered, "but that'll take a week, *after* we get towed in and wait till Monday A.M. to start!"

"By no means, sir," R'heet contradicted. "When would you like it to be ready? Last Tuesday about right?"

"A weisenheimer, eh?" Walt retorted. "Look, just give me a lift to HJ's, and I'll call it square. No insurance company inna world is going to pay off for damage caused by a bushel-sized turnip!"

"No need," R'heet remarked absently, as he went over

to look at the dirt-encrusted underside of the elderly Chrysler.

"Amazingly primitive," he commented. "Still, it functioned, after its fashion." He did something with his fingers; Walter staggered back as the car rolled over to sit, crookedly, on its bent wheels. Then it moved forward, wobbling and made a sharp right turn. Walter's eyes were fixed on the steering wheel, spinning lock to lock, with nobody turning it.

"Hey!" he yelled. "There's nobody—" He shut up as the battered vehicle effortlessly mounted the near-vertical slope, smashed across the substantial metal guardrail, rolled up onto the road, and parallel-parked on the shoulder. The engine, Walter noted dazedly, wasn't even running.

"How," he asked numbly, "did you *do* that?"

"Merely a matter of exploiting the slight energy disparity in the Woof, set up by the disturbance thereto by Oob's interference," R'heet replied blandly.

Walter, clambering his way up to the shiny vehicle parked on the shoulder, was staring unbelievingly.

"The fender!" he shouted. "Got that smacked the same day I took delivery! It's straight! And the paint job looks brand-new! There's no wear on the tires!" After a look inside, he commented, more calmly. "The cigarette burn that damn fool Joe made when it was new—it's gone!"

"I took the liberty," R'heet confessed, "of returning the artifact to its original state inherent in its aura. I hope you find that satisfactory."

"Do I?" Walter exclaimed. "Man, that's marvelous! Does she run as well as she looks?" He got in and cranked up. The V-8 purred sweetly. He tried the electric window beside him; it worked.

"Better!" he informed himself. "Had trouble with that window while she was still in the showroom." He put the car in gear and drove off, whistling, enjoying the new-car smell.

It was half an hour before he remembered the helpful

stranger back there. Walter wondered only briefly how he'd happened to be out here in the country. He braked. Better go back and pretend he'd just been giving her a little test flight.

After a slow return trip, his headlights revealed the break in the guardrail. He stopped; the little red car was visible down below. That fellow had taken a chance driving down that embankment—but where had the monster gotten to?

The thought brought Walter out of his blissful state. The fellow in white was gone. Too bad. Time to get to the motel and catch up on his sack-time.

He gunned around in a U-turn, just in time to watch a light-flashing, siren-howling cop-car pull up. It ignored him; he drove quietly away, his lights off. Watching the mirror, he eased on down the road. Some passerby must have seen the cars off the road and called in.

He was watching the shoulder ahead for the man in white; the Inspector, some kind of cop after all. But it was the monster that kept prompting his subconscious to break into a cold sweat. Was he, Walter Shield, cracking up? The Inspector had seen it, too—unless he had also imagined the man in white. It was too much for Walter.

He had almost succeeded in putting the matter out of his mind when a voice that sounded as if it were speaking through a mouth full of molasses said from behind him, "Never mind, Walter, R'heet has resources. He's back home by now, doubtless inciting further persecution of myself, a harmless, gentle, benign being—"

Walter missed the rest, because at the first syllable, he had swerved violently, almost losing it, and braked to a halt beside a sign reading "BRANTVILLE 3" He turned to look in the backseat. Oob was perched there, his tentacles waving aimlessly; his integument was a pale dusty-rose now, Walter noted *en passant*.

"Pray carry on, Walter," the Rhox directed.

"I'm not your damn chauffeur," Walter returned hotly. "And my name's 'Mr. Shield'! How do you know that feller's OK? Where'd he get to?"

"He returned to Culture One, as I have already informed you," Oob stated impatiently. "Although no longer an accredited inspector, he retains many of the OUO devices issued to him in his official capacity, all inconspicuous, of course, in order to aid in concealment of his identity while in the field."

"What was he doing out there in the sticks, at this hour?" Walter demanded.

"Again, you require me to repeat myself," Oob pointed out mildly. "He was attempting to follow me, and—the rest you know. It was my sudden detection of his spy-ray which occasioned my abrupt maneuver which resulted in your coming to grief."

"So it's all *his* fault, now," Walter said sarcastically, noting the sign reading "BRANTVILLE 3."

"Hey!" he blurted, braking, "I already passed that—or was that before I turned around?"

"Pay no attention, Mr. Shield," Oob urged. "It's merely a faulty suture, a minor manifestation of the cyclic pattern induced in this filament of the Woof, due to certain unfortunate acts of meddling by certain irresponsibles I shall not demean myself to name."

"Oh, Walter said numbly. He drove on three more miles, and sure enough, there was a sign that said "BRANTVILLE CITY LIMIT"—or had it? He stopped, backed up, got the sign in his headlights. It read "BRANTVILLE 3."

"This is nuts." Walter drove on. "I'm driving around in a circle in a brand new ten-year-old car, talking to a pink turnip!"

He looked back at Oob. "OK, pal, you've had your fun. Now how about you lay off the tricks and get me into my motel, which if I don't get there pretty soon, they'll cancel my reservation."

"Turn in here," Oob directed airily.

"How can I? There's no—" Walter started, but stifled the objection as he saw the motel sign, perched high on the bluff beside the highway. He looked in vain for the driveway; finally, at Oob's direction, he spotted a dim sign reading ENTRANCE, well hidden behind a hedge.

"He was lying," he muttered. "There's no bridge out."

"Perhaps in another plane," Oob suggested.

"Guy laid this out was nuts," Walter muttered. He drove up to the well-lit entry invisible from the highway and stopped under the overhang. Inside, an old woman with a face like last week's laundry looked him over without approval and demanded, "Got a reservation?"

"Sure have," Walter replied cheerfully, producing documentary evidence thereof. The hag glanced at it, rifled a spiral-bound book and commented, "You cut it close, Mr. Shield. Mostly they get here before six."

Walter briefly considered telling her he'd been delayed by a fatal car-crash, and that this was only his astral projection she saw, but decided against it. He felt a touch at his knee and looked down. Oob was beside him with his two-suiter, concealed from the sight of the old hag by the counter. Walter made a face, miming, "Keep out of sight—she'll never give me a room!"

She clattered a key with a large plastic tag down in front of Walter and muttered, "One-oh-six. You want a wake-up call?" and turned away without awaiting a reply.

"No thank you, Madam," Walter said to her back. Oob was almost halfway to the door. Walter followed and they found 106 around to the right, all the way at the back.

"Seems like the old bat could have given me something a little handier," Walter commented silently, as he went back out to the new '84 Chrysler and drove it along to the door.

Inside, he found the usual HJ decor, no newer and no shabbier than all the others. The TV was attached to the wall by an armored cable. In effect, the management was saying, "We know you're a damned thief, but we intend to thwart you, wiseguy." In the bathroom the usual undrinkoutofable plastic cup was in place, cocooned in sticky Saran Wrap. He took the tissues from the chrome-plated box and put them by the bed, which had enough heavy covers for Antarctica.

Once settled on the hard mattress, Walter took stock: OK, he'd finally made a few points with Mel at the con, and got bored and left, and covered the first hundred miles of the drive home with no difficulty. Then the damn fool in the red Maserati had run him off into a construction site and flipped him. Lucky he wasn't hurt. Then the rutabaga reappeared, and the fellow in white, and all of a sudden he had a valuable restored car. There'd been a little funny business with the city limits sign, but all seemed normal now. Walter relaxed and went to sleep.

He got an early start, in spite of no wake-up call, and soon cleared the city limits. The Chrysler hummed sweetly. Even the damned windows still worked, and the radio sounded better than ever. A fruity voice said, "And about that alien spaceship that landed on the White House lawn: no response has yet been made public to the ultimatum handed to the president by the aliens. In other news—" Walter switched off. Why did the damn fool assume everybody'd had his gear glued to the radio all night? *What* spaceship? *What* ultimatum? " 'In other news,' " he said aloud to savor the idiocy of it. "Just give with the news, bub," he retorted. "If it's the same news, I'll be able to tell!"

He settled down to watch the scenery. Nice fall trees; odd, in the middle of April. He had just achieved a halcyon state of communion with Nature when Oob spoke from the back seat, almost precipitating another one-car accident, just missing the SCENIC VIEW sign. "They figure I won't notice the view, but I'll see the sign," Walt muttered angrily. The next one said "HILL." "Yes," Walt muttered, "I noticed. And there's a tree. Funny, no sign on it reading 'TREE.' "

His peace thus shattered by the double assault of Oob's continued presence and the stupidity of the bureaucrats who spend the taxpayers' money on dopey signs, Walter reverted to a state of barely repressed hostility toward whatever might dare to transpire next. *Quiver.*

The mood was nugatory. What happened next would have been sufficient to enrage a monk at his matins. A flash of light like a bomb-burst in front of him caused him to wrench the wheel hard to the right, then brake hard as the car slammed across a six-foot-wide ditch and smashed through ten feet of dense underbrush before climbing to rest aimed directly at an immense tree, one of a host of native chestnuts, Walter noted in amazement. As a woodworking hobbyist, he fully appreciated the superior working qualities of mellow, golden chestnut wood, as well as its unusual beauty of color and grain. Also, he knew, the tree was virtually extinct in North America, due to the nineteenth-century chestnut blight. And here was a virgin stand. How the devil had it been overlooked?

Walter was out of his car and picking his way across the layered leaf-humus to put a hand on the fissured gray bark of the forest giant. He looked around furtively. In the gleam of the headlights, he could see dozens, hundreds of the great trees, and not even a sign to say hands off. His greed was fully aroused. If he could buy up this patch of land—cheap—he'd have timber to last him the rest of his life, and planks left over to sell at a fancy price. "Oh, boy," he gloated, moving in among the giant boles. There was no light in sight, not a sign that a human being had ever ventured here before. He paused and looked back to see if the turnip-monster was behind him.

There was no rutabaga, Walter saw, but there *was* something: a lithe, straw-colored form that glided silently behind a thick bush. In the momentary glimpse he'd gotten, it appeared to be a big cat of some kind—one of those mountain lions, or panthers, or maybe cougars you called them. Only bigger. He had caught a glint of reflected moonlight on formidable bared fangs, he was pretty sure. He wasn't *too* scared, he noted with satisfaction. Probably a tame one from some nearby zoo or whatever.

Standing quite still, he watched the bush. There was no further movement from the cougar—if it *was* a cougar. He eased around behind the big chestnut, savoring the comforting texture of the bark, envisioning the magnificent things he'd make of the wood: a rocker, a bookcase, a bedside table. Lovely.

The animal moved out of cover, took a look at Walter, just as he was sliding from behind the tree, and yawned.

Saber-toothed tiger! Walter's memory-of-pictures-in-books screamed. *I thought they were bigger*, his conscious mind commented, *and extinct*, it added, *just like the chestnuts*.

Holy Moses! If he could capture this critter he could sell it to a zoo for a fortune! Funny it'd be wandering around here, so close to the highway. Walter noticed just then that his headlights had gone off. He had to get inside the car; maybe he could even back it out of here . . .

"Quite impossible, I'm afraid, Roger," an unctuous voice said at his elbow. "Your—or rather your machine's—fuel line is ruptured, and all your hydrocarbons have drained out. Pity, that: quite poisonous to the soil, you know."

Walter had spun at the first syllable and was standing with his back against the chestnut, staring into the darkness of the forest. There was no one there. He suddenly smelled gasoline. Whoever the invisible man was, he was right about the broken gas-line, Walter realized. He started toward the car again. It was barely visible by the glints of moonlight reflecting from the newly polished brightwork. He had actually forgotten the stabbing cat when it bounded across his path and disappeared among the trees.

"Keep going," the voice urged. "You're quite right to seek shelter in your conveyance."

Again, Walter turned and stared in vain into darkness. "Who's there?" he croaked. "Where are you? Stop playing hide-and-seek! You're making me nervous!"

"No need to be nervous, Walter," the suave voice reassured him. "I've sent the feline on its way; it wouldn't do at all for an out-of-context vital filament to be violently terminated just now."

"Oh," Walter replied feebly. " 'Inconvenient,' eh? Well, Mister, if that's *your* pussycat, they've got a few laws about leashes and that, so you better quit playing games with me!" He halted and put his fists on his hips.

"Now just come out where I can see you, Buster," he commanded. "I get tired talking to nobody." Oh, it was the guy in white back again.

"Hardly 'nobody,' Walter," the no-longer-disembodied voice corrected. "I am Senior Inspector of Continua R'heet, on detached duty to Locus Ten billion, Four Hundred and Four Million, Nine Hundred and Seventy-one Thousand, Six Hundred and Two, Third Level, of course."

"Oh, o' course!" Walter mocked. "I don't know about all the arithmetic, pal, but you got no right walking your wildcat in this country, let alone this state, nor even anywhere in the U.S. of A!"

"I assure you, Walter—"

"Where'd you get this palsy 'Walter' stuff, bub?" Walter cut in. "That's 'Mr. Shield' to you!"

"Very well, Mr. Shield," R'heet repeated patiently. "I regret the slip; I sometimes forget the petty ego-motivated imperatives of third-level life-forms."

"If that's an apology, it flops!" Walter barked. He was examining his valuable restored Chrysler. The short trip through the underbrush had apparently not damaged it visibly. He got in and cranked up: the engine ran for ten seconds and stopped dead.

"Damn!" he muttered. "I forgot: no gas."

R'heet slid in beside him. "Look here, Mr. Shield," he said heavily, "Oob is abroad somewhere close by, well away from his Control Apex, fortunately, and thus powerless to manipulate the entropic membrane. His Aperture won't function in this temporal enclave. He can't escape. We should therefore cooperate to capture him. We mustn't allow this opportunity to pass!"

"All of a sudden, it's 'we' this and 'we' that," Walter carped. "I don't remember us being partners."

"That honor is conferred upon you, willy-nilly, sir," R'heet informed him, "by the happenstance that it was you who wandered into the enclave first."

"I didn't 'wander' anywhere," Walter objected. "The explosion forced me off the road, that's all."

"Ummm," R'heet mused. "Yes, I *did* note a discharge

of entropic energy; a natural spontaneous equalization of
the accumulated stresses occasioned by multiple violations of matrical integrity."

"Swell," Walter conceded sarcastically. "You admit
there was an explosion. That makes me feel heaps better."

Before R'heet could respond to this sally, there was a
sound of a body crashing through underbrush just outside. As Walter hastily pushed the button to run the open
window up, a disheveled figure stumbled into view from
the bushes. It was a woman of early middle age, he
noted, wondering what a fairly cute little housewife was
doing out here in the wilderness in the middle of the
night, alone. No, not alone, he corrected, as a second
shapely matron appeared in the wake of the first. Before
Walter could open the door to inquire if the ladies
needed assistance—running the risk, he knew, of an
insulting rejection—the monster appeared, jittering in
the path of the ladies.

"There he is!" Walter blurted, as R'heet said.

"Stand fast, Mr. Shield. We'll take him this time."

"It's the rutabaga again!" Dottie yelped, unlimbering
her rolled brolly, which she carried in all weather, under
the impression that it was elegant.

Gert caught her arm. "Better wait, Dot. Somebody's
watching."

"Say, Gert," Dottie interrupted. "Do you feel kind of
funny? As if you were lighter, maybe; kind of young and
full of the divil?"

"I feel all right, Dot," Gert replied. "Say, all this exercise is good for you! You look . . . slimmer."

"I just noticed *you* don't seem to be carrying as much
flesh," Dot said, sounding shocked. "Do I—?"

"Never saw you look better, Dot!" Gert cried. "And I
feel good! I don't know what happened, but I kinda like
it, rutabaga and all!"

"What's a car—nice one, too, only a little back-dated—
doing out here in the woods?" Dottie demanded, returning
her attention to the situation at hand. "Some o' them
degenerates in there, I bet, jump out at young girls and

all that! Come on, Gert, we don't fall for that!" She turned sharply toward the left and Gert followed.

Walter was out of the car by then, calling after them, "Ladies! If I can offer any assistance . . ."

"Don't bother," R'heet advised. "They have their biological integrity to think of."

"Yeah, but maybe they could tell me—" Walter started, but broke off to make a grab at Oob, who was sidling off into the underbrush. Walter secured a grip on one steel-hard leg and hauled hard. Oob made a lightning-fast movement. Walter felt a cold stab in his chest, and darkness closed in.

"Now you've done it, Oob," R'heet said sternly. "You terminated a legitimate thread of the Warp and thus invalidated a patch of the Fabric extending thousands of parameters in all pseudo-directions. You've also carelessly laid yourself open to restraint by conventional means. I abjure you: go into stasis at once, and remain in that condition until we can reknit the fabric!"

Oob, having flung off Walter's feeble grip, darted aside, seemed to strike an invisible barrier, and rebounded to roll a few feet and lie supine, his legs twitching. His tentacles scrabbled at the leaves in vain; then R'heet stepped on the creature's prime manipulator, pinning him in place. Not until then did the Rhox go catatonic and limp at R'heet's feet, his single eye open and staring.

He started as Walter stepped up and said, "We better tie it up."

"You're alive!" R'heet gasped.

"No thanks to you, pal," Walter remarked. "Watch it: it's tricky."

"No need," R'heet assured him. "He's quite helpless."

CHAPTER SIXTEEN

When Henry dropped young Bobby Whatkey at his doorstep, the snow and all had stopped. From inside, old Bob yelled, "Hey, Henry, that you?"

The boy muttered a grudging "thanks," and went to the side of the house to make a stealthy entry via the outside stair to the attic. He reached the warmth of the cavernous old garret and draped his wet cap and muffler over an old chair with broken rungs. He began to rummage listlessly in the old trunk Pa had told him to stay away from.

He heard feet on the ladder and the old man yelled: "Boy! You up there?"

"Sure, Pa," Bobby replied. He looked at and threw back a lone high-topped shoe, well-worn; carefully examined a rusted metal object—looked like some kinda can-opener, he thought. He wondered why his grandpa or anybody else would ever keep all this junk. He thrust aside a small, leather-bound book, full of crabbed hand-writing, he saw when it fell open. Then he saw one of those musical sweet potatoes or whatever, and grabbed it. He tried it and was unable to elicit any sound, but it looked kind of like a gun. He wondered briefly if that gun the stranger had in Kate's store was real—maybe the guy was one of them gangsters. Bobby was glad he'd left—but poor Kate was still there, all alone. He aimed the potato-gun at a visualized hoodlum and said, "Bam!"

Manny fell heavily, then picked himself up awkwardly. "Damn! Sorry, Katie; I guess I slipped," he muttered.

"How is it you know my name?" the New Englandish voice demanded.

"Well, you know . . ." Manny began and abruptly realized he was alone. He looked around. He was back outside, on a warm day, in some kind of big open space. A few guys standing around was all: no store, no Kate, no blizzard.

"That will be quite enough!" a stern voice barked behind him. He spun, his hand going to his gat. The man facing him was taller than himself and well-muscled, but dressed in some kind of little trick outfit, white, with a short skirt. An identical short skirt looked swell on the gal behind him; or the legs exposed by the skirt, Manny corrected.

"Aw right, what's going on?" O'Rourke demanded. "Where's Kate at? You must be with the pitcher company, hah?" He wasn't aiming the gun.

The man in white made a swift motion and plucked the Beretta from Manny's grip and threw it aside.

"You may consider yourself under arrest, sir," R'heet said mildly. P'ty stepped forward and cuffed the astonished Manny.

"Now," R'heet went on, "how you expected to escape undetected while making use of a Q-zone field in contravention of article four of Policy 978-J, I cannot imagine; and my instruments indicate that you have, by repeated violation of the Meniscus, created a persistent matrical flaw: most dangerous. What have you to say for yourself?"

Manny was pointing with his chin at a spot behind the Inspectors.

"It *moved!*" he blurted. "It's doing it again! I seen it! Keep that thing away from me!"

Oob, creeping into the garret on Bobby's heels, dived

for the open trunk. The jar caused the lid to slam. Oob
pushed, but found himself neatly trapped. He struggled
to get into position for a vooj-transformation, but was
unable to get his prime manipulator in contact with his
yatz-patch. He relaxed. Might as well activate another
extrusion and catch up on his sleep. He dozed . . .

The two Culture One agents exchanged glances, then
turned as one and pounced. Oob attempted to flee, but
made the error of darting directly toward Manny, who
yelped and kicked out, impacting the Rhox's sensitive
yatz-patch, causing the creature to lapse into a deep
paralysis. P'ty scooped him up in a stasis-sack, which was
a part of her standard field equipment. R'heet joined her
in sealing the container, within which the captive thrashed
his limbs frantically.

"Nice work, sir!" R'heet congratulated Manny. "Fortunate that you knew the precise position of the yatz-patch.
Otherwise he'd have led us a merry chase. We are in
your debt, sir." He offered a hand.

Manny ignored this as he held out his hands to be
freed. "What *is* this place?" he grated. "Whereat's Kate?"

R'heet looked thoughtfully. "After your abrupt depar-
ture, she feared her sanity was being affected by her
isolation; she will leave, or has left, the Gamecock area
to go to the mythic Isle of California," he told Manny.
"There she had, or will have, a brilliant career as something called a 'movie star.'"

"Jeez!" Manny said reverently. "You mean if I
wouldn'ta come along and kinda jarred the kid outa her
rut, she never woulda went inta the flicks?"

"Your interference, plus the activation nearby of an
unauthorized Relegator, precipitated the reweaving of
that particular fiber of the Woof," R'heet acknowledged.
"Still, no harm was done; the realignment, by good luck,
is more in consonance with the Master Plot than the
previous pattern. It appears the orderly unfoldment of
the lady's destiny, or Woof-line, had been aborted by the
scandal, during her childhood, of the disappearance of

two women from a New York grocery store. Her parents read of the incident, and refused her permission to go to New York to go on the stage. In defiance, she fled to the wilds of Vermont and opened a store of her own; that filament was reabsorbed by the incidents I mentioned. So, insofar as that particular expanse of the Fabric is concerned, you, quite fortuitously, are absolved. I congratulate you, sir."

"Yeah," Manny muttered vaguely. "If that Lepke would of showed up on time, I never woulda got into this."

"And that would not have come to pass had not the personality field of Clarence Naill merged with your own because of abnormal stresses in the Meniscus."

" 'Clarence Naill,' " Manny replied. "Say—that almost reminds me of somebody!"

"Not now, sir," R'heet appealed. "An out-of-context reversion at this point would tie a square-knot in the warp!"

"Take it easy," Manny urged. "I guess Clarence was just a guy I useta know."

Roger Tyson and Bob Armstrong came over, across the Plaza, Julian trailing them.

"Say, R'heet," Roger called. "What are *you* doing here? What's in the box? Why aren't you back at Culture One, tricking some poor gal into a cohabitation contract?"

"Running down a hot lead," R'heet replied icily. "Oob and I resent the implication."

"Go ahead and resent it!" Roger defied the Inspector. "It's a fact!"

"Nix," Bob advised Roger. "Maybe this guy can help us, so lay off bugging him, OK? What's a 'cohabitation contract'?"

"It's a lousy deal where some poor guy that isn't getting any tries to tie up all the nice young stuff around, just so nobody else can get any," Roger explained cynically, as Bob shushed him in vain.

"That, sir, is a gross exaggeration!" R'heet barked. "Now, unlike this gentleman"—he indicated Manny—

"you, both of you, have repeatedly violated the code, and I now call upon you, sir, for an accounting!" His eye was on Bob.

"Don't get tough," Bob retorted stoutly, and moved in, his fist cocked.

Roger grabbed him. "That would be a mistake, Bob," he advised the young fellow. "All these Culture One guys are experts at tai kwan do or something!" But Bob, incensed both by R'heet's cop-like remarks and Roger's interference, lunged at the inspector, jostling the latter and causing him to lose his grip on the stasis-sack. At once Oob was out—and gone.

"Damn!" Roger said feelingly. "You had him and you let him get away!"

"*I* 'let him get away'?" R'heet countered. "Had this young idiot not attempted to assault me—in itself a Class One offense—" He broke off, looking around keenly.

"The wretch can't have gone far," he told Roger. "Here in the Final Concept, he is of course unable to introduce any significant modification into the Fabric, it having been sealed. So I need merely conduct a scan . . ." He stopped talking to unclip a device from his brief garment and start tinkering with it and frowning.

"He must have slipped away along a plane of matrical weakness created by this fellow's latest illegal transfer!" he said glumly. "I need merely—" R'heet's voice cut off like a broken tape as he made a half-turn and disappeared.

Bob, Roger, and Julian stared at the vacant spot where, a moment before, the Inspector had stood.

"That's a new trick," Roger stated glumly. "I've never known him to just go out like a light before."

"It was the entropic detonation," Oob explained, having popped up at Roger's elbow. "Pity; the potential had built up to a high level, you see, due to the irregularities, and it took only a slight prod to set off an explosive release, propelling us and other vulnerable entities across the parameters to who-knows where/when. Now I have the dull task of determining just where I've been deposited. Botheration!"

"What about me?" Roger pled. "You ought to at least help me get back into known space/time/vug."

"I have no responsibilities whatever regarding you, Roger," Oob told him coldly, "since you refused to come to an accommodation with me when I offered you the opportunity." He turned away.

Roger heard a deep *Boom!* He looked around at a dense forest that now surrounded him—right where the plaza had been. This time he was *really* lost.

He heard crashing sounds nearby, and an eland came bounding between the trees, a saber-toothed tiger in hot pursuit. Roger took refuge behind a giant tree, and saw the rusted-out chasis of an automobile, overgrown with brush. Pretty odd. But wasn't everything?

Letting that one go, Roger went over to investigate the hulk. An old Chrysler, he saw.

He froze at a sound. Something was approaching from over *that* way—probably another saber-tooth. But it was a slim, rather attractive woman of early middle age who came into view, incongruously clad in a tattered but once stylish frock and scuffed high-heeled pumps. She stumbled, looked up, and saw Roger.

"Oh, you're not—" she blurted.

"Absolutely not, madam," Roger confided, with a bow. She tittered.

"I seem to have gotten lost," the lady told him. Her eyes went to Oob. "Ohh, Catkin, there you are!" she gushed.

"Haven't we all?" Roger responded rhetorically. "I'm Tyson, Roger Tyson." He offered a hand, which she first looked at suspiciously, then took. "Sorry," she said. "It's been so long. I'm Mary Tomkins," she added softly. "Professor Tomkins, actually, but I've never before been absent-minded. There's a cave back there," she went on. " 'The Cave of the Great Evil,' it's called. 'The Cave of the Lesser Evil' is over that way."

She gave Roger a confused look. "I seem to be suffering some sort of identity crisis. I'm a perfectly normal inhabitant of Brantville, Ohio—and at the same time I'm

Witch-Woman, some sort of shaman to a tribe of early
transitional *Homo sapiens*. I met them in my first day
here. When I was lost in the cave. Luckily, a young fellow
named Boog the Bold was snooping around in the taboo
cave and led me out.

"The poor things were living in terrible conditions.
Awful mud-and-stick huts they were always accidentally
burning down, and getting terrible untreated burns in
the process. The able-bodied ones, that is; they always
ran and left the old, the sick and the babies to burn alive.
They ate carrion and tubers and berries that gave them
diarrhea. They were drinking polluted water, and freezing in winter and sweltering in summer, and they were
forever scratching themselves. I did a few simple things
to help, and they thought it was magic.

"But that's not all: I found I somehow knew their
language, and all about them! It was as if I'd always lived
among them—and at the same time I was Mary Gay
Tomkins, an archaeologist. Just having the scientific
approach enabled me to do remarkable things for them.
They were *so* dumb: if their hut burned down it wasn't
because they'd dumped the old bedding—leaves mostly—
beside the fire: it was because the fire-demon was in a
bad mood. I started watching for fire hazards and the
huts started lasting longer.

"I showed them how to make a fire-hardened spear-
point by laying a pole across the fire so it would burn in
two. Scrape off the char, and you have two hard-pointed
spears. I didn't know much about archery, but I got them
started. I made them build a kiln and harden their pots
so they could boil their water; some simple folk-
remedies, like aspirin and fuggie-bush leaves—perfectly
good vermifuge, you know.

"I even air-conditioned Chief Lug's hut; that was fun.
I showed them how to make goat-skin bellows, and baked
clay canisters for pressure vessels. We pumped them full
of compressed air and cooled them with snow from
the mountains, and when I opened the plugs—ice-cold
air rushed out and expanded: bitter cold. Mixed with

the ambient air, it was nice and cool. I was just being selfish, I suppose: I couldn't stand being so uncomfortable.

"We found some ores and started smelting metals. Iron is easy: just pile up a mud-brick furnace, fill it with chunks of dry wood and ore, and let it burn. Liquid iron runs out the bottom into channels in the clay ground.

"Today I came out to get some mold I found in the cave—I think it's a *Penicillium notatum* or close to it. And now I've somehow got myself lost. . . . It's all so strange."

Roger nodded. "What's happened," he began to explain, "is that the Temporal Bore set up by the Builder, or maybe UKR, or the Culture One folks, I never got straight on that point, has been entered by some trouble-maker, or -makers, called the Rhox, who've compromised the integrity of the Entropic Fabric, or the whole Matrix, and it's getting everything scrambled up. This superimposition of the Pleistocene on th twentieth century seems to be the most extreme dislocation I've encountered. Bob—that's Bob Armstrong—you *did* say Brantville? Bob's from Brantville, too, and that's where I was living when—Never mind. It seems to have hit the Brantville area hardest. But we're working on it—UKR and I, and maybe Oob, too, for all I know. He says he's trying to help, but now there's been *another* invasion, by some big—or little at times—blue beetles he calls the Vrint. Seems they have a high IQ, and they kind of like the facilities humanity has constructed, which they see as being provided solely for *their* benefit." Roger froze suddenly, staring at the ground, where a large, shiny, dark-blue beetle was crawling over a bare patch. He stepped hard on it.

That was a mistake, vermin! somebody who seemed to be perched in a tree boomed out through a megaphone. *We cannot permit any plea of ignorance to prevail, since we have repeatedly explained our preeminence to any number of your units. Yet you persist in your nihilism!* Mary recoiled with a cry of fear.

"I don't know anything about that!" Roger yelled back. Mary put a hand on his arm.

"Thank heaven you hear it, too," she said in a voice taut with anxiety. "For a moment I feared—"

Roger patted her hand. "No, it's all right, Mary," he soothed. "It's just another player stepping out onto the board. I think UKR will deal with it." He raised his voice, "UKR!" he called. "You'd better step in here, before my warp gets so snarled up in my Woof we'll never get the old Fabric back into shape!"

Mary caught Roger's arm and ducked, just as a crude spear, twigs and leaves still attached, came whanging past him to glance off a tree. He ducked and looked toward the source to see a squat, heavy fellow with a bullet head half-concealed in the underbrush.

"Its Moog," Mary whispered urgently. "He's intent on killing me, since I interfered with his beating his children to death. Get down, Mr. Tyson!"

"I know him as Bimbo," Roger told her. "He's single-minded, but easy to bluff." He rose and made shooing motions, reinforced with the spoken command, "Go on, shoo, you big dummy."

Just then Lump Oblumski loomed up behind the *erectus* and clobbered him with a knotty length of heart-of-pine. Bimbo fell heavily. Lump came forward, his club poised.

"Hi," Roger greeted him. "Nice timing. He was trying to kill this lady, Professor Tomkins." He turned to her, ready to proffer a formal introduction.

"Jeez, it's Witch-Woman," Lump muttered.

"Good heavens, it's a new face," Mary mourned. "I suppose he'll take over the clan now," she predicted. "There's no other healthy young male to dispute him, except Goob the Toothless, but he's no threat. Ever since the python crushed his jaw, he's been rather timid. Can't eat well, you know, so he's grown weak."

"You can tell this Goob I got no beef with him," Lump volunteered. "Long as nobody bugs me, I'm cool. Now, you, bub," he addressed Roger, "you can split now. I wanta talk to yer lady friend here."

"Hold it right there!" Roger ordered, picking up Bimbo's spear, from which he quickly stripped the foliage. "The lady's not interested in talking to you. Get lost!"

"Oh, yeah?" Lump jeered. "Hey, where's Moose gone?" he interrupted himself. "And the sucker on the bench?"

"UKR," Roger barked between gritted teeth as the grinning lout advanced. He aimed the spear-point at Lump's chest. "Scat!" he ordered.

CHAPTER SEVENTEEN

"Is that nice, after I went ahead and taken out this feller for ya?" Lump demanded, prodding Bimbo's fallen form with his foot.

"I appreciate that," Roger conceded, "but Professor Tomkins is under my protection. Just go along now, and there'll be no trouble."

"Yer aiming that spear at me," Lump grieved. " 'Under yer perteckshin,' hah? Boy, I guess *that* makes her safe!"

"Damn right," Roger agreed, and prodded Lump's chest with the crudely hardened point. Lump looked shocked, grabbed the spear, and pulled it toward him, turning sideways to avoid the point. A movement off-side caught his peripheral vision, and he was turning toward it when a baseball-sized rock impacted against the side of his bullet head. He fell across Bimbo, snoring.

"They make a lovely pair," Mary remarked as she kicked the stone aside. "I wonder where he came from. Come on, Roger," she urged, starting along the faint path. "I'll introduce you to the clan. They're an uncouth lot, but we'll perish on our own here."

"How do you know about—? I mean, you said—" Roger blurted. "You don't seem to be a stranger here at all," he mumbled. "How . . .? I'm sorry, I think maybe

190

I understand. Once I was even a horse, to say nothing of Q'nell. I mean I was *her*, too, for a while. It seems you've meshed with another personality—that can happen when you slip out of your natural locus, you know. Even old Rusty was telling me—"

"I don't understand at all," Mary told him. "But what the hell! Who said I have to understand anything?"

"That's the spirit," Roger congratulated her. "Let's see, where were we when Bimbo came along?"

"You were just clearing your throat, as if about to embark on a speech," Mary told him.

"Oh," Roger said blankly. "You mean like this: 'UKR'?"

"Yes, yes." Mary nodded impatiently.

"I *wasn't* clearing my throat!" Roger snapped. "I'm sure I told you UKR is a vastly potent machine-entity, devoted to assisting people like us."

BE CALM, the vast, reassuring voice of UKR boomed out.

"That's a different one," Mary commented. "How many disembodied voices do you know, Mr. Tyson?"

"Just the one," he replied. "I don't know who that first one was. This is UKR, a highly capable machine designed by the Builder to monitor the welfare of humanity."

"Oh, dear," Mary said as if to herself. "Are you feeling quite well, Mr. Tyson? After all, one's heard of a *deus ex machina*, but a *machina ex deo* is quite another matter. We *must* be rational about all this."

"Wrong!" Roger declared firmly. "Rationality has nothing to do with it. Now," he raised his voice, "I'm being as calm as circumstances permit."

MATTERS ARE BECOMING COMPLEX TO THE FOURTH ORDER, UKR told him. THE ENTITY WHO SPOKE TO YOU A MOMENT AGO IS, LIKE MYSELF, A FOURTH-LEVEL INTELLECT, PARTLY ORGANIC IN NATURE, A MECHANICAL-ORGANIC CONSTRUCT, ACTING ON BEHALF OF A POTENT GROUP-MIND KNOWN AS THE VRINT. WE MUST CONDUCT OURSELVES WITH CIR-CUMSPECTION. THE VRINT SUBSCRIBES TO

NO HUMANLY IDENTIFIABLE CODE OF LOGIC,
ETHICS, OR RATIONALITY. IT CAN BE DEALT
WITH ONLY ON THE BASIS OF RAW PRAGMA-
TISM. IN ANY SITUATION, ITS CONCEPT OF
ADMIRABLE BEHAVIOR IS TO DO WHATEVER IS
EASIEST, AND CALL IT A VIRTUE.

"Oh, I see," Mary responded. "They're liberals."

"That's a bit harsh, isn't it, Professor?" Roger objected.

"Well, after all, *they*'re invading *our* time/space," Mary
reminded him. She saw another of the scuttling blue-
black roaches and pointed it out to Roger, who, rather
than stamping on it, shoved it away. Then he saw another,
many more.

"This place is swarming with the horrid creatures,"
Mary wailed. "I saw one in my kitchen yesterday. 'My
kitchen,'" she repeated in a tone of wonderment. "It's
so strange, Roger," she confided. "I'm Witch-Woman,
and I know the forest trails as well as I know the temper-
ature fluctuations of the last cycle of glaciation, and yet
I'd be perfectly at home with my refrigerator, my micro-
wave, my air conditioning, the auto-timer on the stove,
the vinyl floor, hot running water, and glass window!"

"Sure, it's weird," Roger agreed. "And it's made even
weirder when all of a sudden the Pleistocene shifts over
a little and encompasses the Holocene."

"Is that what—?" Mary started and clutched Roger's
arm. "Those awful blue beetles." She changed tack. "Just
look at them! They're attracted by Bimbo and the other
one! Dreadful! Shoo!" She advanced toward the heaving
dark-blue blanket of beetles, which was now half-
covering the unconscious pair.

"We can't let even Bimbo be eaten alive," Roger
blurted. He caught up a fallen leafy branch and began
to beat at the crypto-insects. They swarmed up the bough
and attacked his hand savagely. He uttered a howl and
pulled Mary back, away from the fierce carnivores.

"They're worse than army ants!" he yelled. "Let's get
out of here!"

One moment, the booming voice of the Vrint rang out.

I have explained to you that we are not about to stand by whilst you savage my forager-units! Take care, lest we retaliate in kind. Suppose I should eliminate the Greenland ice cap, raising sea level two feet, and inundating every major site on this aspect of space/time/vug? What about that, eh?

"You wouldn't!" Roger yelled to the sky. "UKR, you wouldn't *let* it, would you? All I did was swat a few filthy bugs, anyway," he finished lamely.

Enough of your perjoration! the Vrint yelled, a truly awesome sound.

LET BE, ROGER, UKR commanded. Then, continuing in a quieter voice, "The Vrint is a most puissant entity, not lightly to be challenged. Suppose you just let it have this aspect of STV, and I shall do what I can to divert its attention to a vast swath of unrealized continua in a wild area we call Use Nineteen."

"I never heard of any place you called 'Use Nineteen,' or even Use One," Roger countered. "How do I know it won't turn out to be my hometown?"

"I've been wondering," Mary put in, *"apropos de bot,"* just what part of the world I'm in. It's clearly not Ohio, or even North America; *Homo erectus* never penetrated there."

"Don't count on it," Roger cautioned her. "In another aspect of STV, the New World might not have split away from the old until just recently, say a few hundred thousand years, and Peking Man could have come across Berengia. Nothing's fixed and absolute, and that reminds me: everything we intruders do here, out of context, has repercussions that go echoing down to later ages. Just stepping on that bug could have results we could never foresee."

Poor example, petty creature, the Vrint spoke up. *"That bug," as you put it was His Superb Uttermost, Commanding General His Imperial Highness the Lord of the Puce. His unhappy demise will not be allowed to pass unrequited! Now, what would be a fair exchange, by your distorted value-scales, for Puce?*

"How about all the guitar-pickers in Nashville?" Roger proposed.

Inadequate, the Vrint dismissed the idea. *While that is, indeed, a group which has imposed truly cosmic-scale cacophony on the tiny patch of STV accessible to it, this achievement pales in comparison with that of Moonshine Bob and his Rocky Mountain Rockers.*

"I'll throw them in," Roger volunteered.

Perhaps, petty creature, you fail to grasp the stupendous majesty of the entity, myself, which you have savaged but now, the Vrint riposted.

"Well, what more do you want?" Roger demanded in exasperation.

I once had the misfortune, the Vrint intoned, *to tune in on a debate in Congress: each windy politician in turn stated, with reference to the previous gasbag, that "My distinguished colleague, Mr. President, [as if he were speaking privately], is a damned liar and a fool to boot!" The utter emptiness of all that campaign rhetoric repelled me to a degree that Moonshine Bob had only approximated. To expunge such an excrescence from the Cosmic All would give us great satisfaction.*

"It wants to eliminate debate in Congress?" Mary gasped.

"Nope," Roger corrected. "He wants to eliminate Congress." He raised his voice slightly. "Done! Just take a moment to convert their former buildings into cozy apartments for hardworking taxpayers made paupers by the confiscatory levies enacted there."

Easy enough, the Vrint agreed. *And I, and indeed all conscious beings everywhere, are grateful to you, minibeing though you are.*

"It was a pleasure," Roger assured the Vrint. "By the way, why do you refer to me, and presumably the entire human race, as 'mini-beings'? We're a lot bigger than your cockroaches."

Oh, yes, as to that, the Vrint replied insouciantly, *the matter of scale is, after all, quite amenable to variation. We chose the size you've observed for convenience in*

infiltrating your simple domestic structures. The matter
can easily be rectified.

"Oh, yeah," Roger countered scornfully. "What does
it matter? A bug an inch and a half long isn't much
different from one half an inch long."

"Roger," Mary intervened anxiously. "Don't you think
a modicum of discretion at this point . . . ?"

Tyson waved that away. "Big voices out of the sky
don't bother *me!*" he declared, and turned toward a
*crash!*ing sound from the jungle to his right. Something
huge was moving there, he realized.

Lump had awakened and kicked away a beetle which
had nibbled his callused foot. He shook Bimbo. "Hey,
wake up, buddy," he exhorted. "Damn bugs are getting
us!" He brushed away another insect which was crawling
across Bimbo's apelike face.

Lump looked up, scrambled to his feet, and dived for
the underbrush, while, twenty feet away, a truck-sized
creature with a glossy blue-black carapace and six-foot
horns on its fore end came 'dozing through the thicket,
uprooting six-inch trees as it came directly toward Roger.

"Holy Moses, it's like the one we saw in Brantville,
only alive!" He leapt in front of Mary.

"Run, Professor!" he yelled. "I'll distract its attention!"

"Nonsense," she replied coolly. "I'll attend to this."
She went past Roger, stopped squarely in the path of the
immense beetle, and raised a hand.

"Aroint thee, wretch!" she said clearly. "Get hence,
I abjure thee, by the authority of Catkin, my beloved
familiar!"

The giant beetle paused, while uprooted timber fell
around it. It waved its antennae vaguely.

"Begone to Use Thirteen!" Mary cried. The Vrint's
fading voice wailed, *Dirty pool, mini-being!* just as the
behemoth scrambled, executed a one-eighty, and fled.

"That's not all," Mary called to the sky. "You shot your
last wad with that one, Vrint!"

"Mary!" Roger faltered. "What—? How—?"

"Never mind," she said competently. "Just a little trick I picked up from Nell. She got it from Catkin."

"Didst speak my name, Mistress Goodwish?" Oob's gluey voice spoke up, as Oob himself emerged from a flowering arbutus. "Hi, Roger. Oh, sorry, I realize you're not Roger, but you see, all you fellows look—"

"I *am* Roger!" Tyson yelled. "What do you mean, 'You're not Roger'?"

"Never mind," Oob said curtly. "Matters are getting out of hand here," he explained. "The Vrint tricked you, it appears: they tapped your impressive charge of entropic energy, my boy, and employed it to create a major discrepancy, conservation of vug–wise, in the Fabric. I could hardly allow that to pass unrebuked. They had already introduced a myriad or so of their units into Third Level contexts, all of which units naturally expanded geometrically in consonance with the archetype evoked here—a grave error, since it blew their cover completely. One or two 'bugs' which had hidden away in base cabinets swelled in a trice to the size of hippos, wrecking the kitchens which had up till then afforded them safe haven. Those Vrint in the street, in public view, were at once set upon and destroyed. There's little left of the Vrint, on Level Three, I think."

He leapt aside as a phalanx of giant Vrint slammed through a screen of shrubbery with astonishing abruptness, followed immediately by a horde of yelling relatives of Bimbo. By now, Bimbo himself had been assisted to his feet by Lump. They scrambled aside, then fell in at the rear of the folk, joining enthusiastically in the uproar. Mary drew Roger aside, into the shelter of a giant chestnut tree.

"I want to see this," Tyson objected. "Oob said—"

"Poor, dear Catkin is often wrong in his attempts at clairvoyance," Mary told him, over the uproar. "He complains of tuning in on the wrong band, due to some sort of sabotage. The Folk don't have much judgment, as you see," she confided. "They're quite accustomed to set upon great beasts with only sharp sticks as weapons.

They're unable to perceive that these immense insects could turn and rend them."

"Don't!" Roger shushed her. "We're probably in one of those malleable, pre-material states, and if you visualize something—" He cut short his plea as the nearest Vrint-unit spun and charged directly into the howling mob, sending astonished hominids flying, both literally, with tosses of their antlered heads, and figuratively, as the panic-stricken sub-men took to their heels.

"Pity," Mary said unhappily. "We were just getting a rather nice little town going. I was going to introduce barter in place of mugging, and rest rooms away from the communal dining area, and burying the dead instead of throwing them in a shallow cravasse at the back of the cave and snacking on them from time to time. Now we're set back to square one!"

"A good thing," Roger asserted. "Can you imagine the chaos it would have created in the ranks of your profession if a party of amateurs on a dig in Ohio had turned up not only *Homo erectus,* but Rotarians, fast food, and the telly?

"With the start you'd have given them, they'd have invented technology in a hurry, and upset the whole development of human culture. Imagine Ramses II going into battle with walkie-talkies, machine-pistols, and steel helmets, not to mention Gatling guns." He dodged aside as a steel bolt *whang!*ed into the tree beside his head. Beyond the rude path trampled by the stampeding Vrint, a swarthy fellow wearing a dirty cotton kilt and wrapped sandals spoke urgently into a hand-held field phone, in a language unknown to Roger.

"He's speaking ancient Egyptian!" Mary exclaimed.

"Damn! I did again!" Roger walked. "This overactive imagination of mine—"

Mary put a soothing hand on his arm. "Then why not imagine something pleasant, Roger," she urged. "Perhaps a cozy restaurant with a nice quiet corner table by a window with a view of the shore, and a superb menu and wine list."

"Sounds great," Roger agreed, selecting a hard roll from those in the wicker basket the waiter had deposited before him. He broke off a tough, chewy, hard-rinded chunk and applied butter liberally, then caught himself and offered it to Mary. The waiter was pouring red wine into their glasses from the carafe on the table.

"Not bad, Professor," he approved, looking around at the low-beamed dining room, with the big fireplace which looked as if it were actually used. No need today, he realized, though it was just a trifle coolish. The fire on the grate sprang up to a roaring blaze, the heat of which he felt immediately.

"It's mostly the sight of the fire that helps," Mary told him. "Very little actual radiation is palpable, and convection takes time. Most of the heat goes up the chimney. Just looking at it tells our primitive-level mind that we're safe in the cave with the fire-god."

"Don't!" Roger yelped, barely in time.

CHAPTER EIGHTEEN

"Roger!" Mary squeaked. "For a moment it looked—"

"I know! Forget it!" Roger snapped. "We're right here in Delmonico's, circa 1910, so don't even consider anything else. One has to be careful! *Very* careful!" He let it go as the short, plump, cheerful waiter came up with a loaded tray balanced on his fingertips.

"You folks see the big bug?" he inquired genially. "I never *seen* it, but the crowd inna street—! A cop come inside tole me it was big as a Pierce-Arrow. Right there on Madison Avenue. Some kinda stunt for advertising, hah?"

"Beats me," Roger mumbled. "Is it gone?"

"Guess so." Andy (his name was embroidered on his pocket) dismissed the topic. "Now about the *consummé au beurre blanc*?" he went on. "Charlie's making a new batch, so it'll be a minute, OK?"

"Swell, Andy!" Roger agreed enthusiastically. "Fine bread," he added and raised his glass to the servitor.

"Jeez," Andy stammered. "Don't mind if I do." He picked up the carafe and chugalugged it. "To yer health and the lady, too," he gasped when the vessel was drained. "Don't worry, I'll get another one." He swiped the carafe from the next table and put it before Roger with a flourish.

"Nice place," Mary murmured. "It reminds me of what I've read of life in the early twentieth century."

"Nineteen-ten," Roger agreed, chewing. The rare prime rib arrived and both diners pitched in while Andy beamed nearby.

"Why did they throw away such a delightful institution, and such excellent food and service?" Mary wondered aloud. She leaned closer to Roger. "Except for Andy guzzling our wine, I mean."

"I invited him," Roger reminded her. "Did you know that until quite recently, a lady couldn't touch her wine until a gentleman raised his glass to her? Or the gents, until the host did?"

"Barbaric!" Mary snarled in a ladylike way.

"Nineteen-ten," Roger mused. "The food was great, and the grand estates, too, but the seven-year-olds in the coal mines weren't having much fun."

There was a sound from the arched entryway, and Roger looked up to see a gang of dirty-faced urchins in long black stockings with holes in the knees crowding into the room shepherded by a lean, hatchet-faced fellow in a tight-fitting black suit.

"Now, Reginald," he chided one of the larger lads, who had lifted two rolls from a serving table, putting one in his pocket and gnawing at the other. "We want to be little gentlemen, remember! That was the agreement! Now, Clarence, you may sit here. . . ."

He pulled out a chair and two boys promptly sat on it, kicking at each other. The lean gentleman attempted to intercede, receiving a stray kick in the kneecap; while he was distracted, the rest of the dozen and a half lads collected by the Rescue League spread out over the room, trying out chairs, looking out the windows, yelling at each other, wiping their noses on the linen napkins, and sampling the bread on the serving tables. Two, whose noses needed blowing, fetched up beside Roger and stared meaningfully at the slab of tender, fragrant beef before him. He cut a piece and offered it. The recipient grabbed it and threw it on the floor.

"Raw meat!" the tot yelled, turning to relay the news to his colleagues. "This sucker's eating raw meat! And the dame, too!" Instantly, the diners were ringed in by the entire cadre of rescuees.

Their mentor tried in vain to regiment them. "I'm so *dread*fully sorry," he appealed to Roger. "You mustn't let this unfortunate incident—"

"It should be done a trifle more gradually," Mary stated severely. "I think a wash first might have been in order," she amplified, giving the shepherd a disdainful look.

"Well, madam, I'm Chester W. Chester the Third," he stated as if conveying impressive information. "I was just—right there in my study, you understand—discussing plans with Mrs. Meriwether Post, and we were musing over how pleasurable it would be to bring the boys up out of the mines and offer them the first good meal they'd ever had—and all of a sudden—"

"I know, Chester," Roger comforted the distracted fellow. "It's the malleable state, you see. Because of a number of factors, the integrity of the entropic Meniscus has been severely compromised. As a result, the vram barriers which normally restrict phenomena to their native loci are in shreds: whole eras have suffered displacement, shedding entities as they go. Thus it is, we're here in the Pleistocene, presumably on the Eurasian land-mass, while a defunct Chrysler, one of the last built before their inevitable demise—they couldn't overcome the compulsion to cheat the public—lies not a hundred feet away. You see, the limits which usually bind a topographical locus to its STV substrate have been broken over a wide expanse, so that when one is displaced entropically, one tends to fetch up at a different set of geographical coordinates. After all, the planet is traveling about a million and a half miles per day in its orbit, plus the fact that a point near the equator is doing one thousand mph around the axis as the Earth rotates, plus the motion of

the Solar System as a whole within the galaxy, while the
movement of the galaxy within the local group—"

"I understand about the motion," Chester put in agi-
tatedly, "but what's it got to do with me walking in my
sleep—" He interrupted himself to look down at himself.
"Thank heavens I'm not wearing those horrible pajamas
Aunt Lettie gave me for Christmas—"

"No, don't do anything hasty," Roger tried again, but
a buck-naked Chester was already in full flight, pausing
only to whip the tablecloth from under the elevated noses
of a pair of worn-out old bags nursing two centiliters of
gin.

"Heavens," Mary said mildly as Chester returned,
wearing the tablecloth like a toga. "The poor man," she
concluded, as he halted before her and inclined his head
in a Prussian bow.

"Pray forgive me, madam," he requested. "It is not my
custom to appear naked in public. I was only—"

"Don't, dammit, do it again, you idiot!" Roger yelled,
as the urchins, their curiosity as to what people were
eating having been satisfied by staring open-mouthed into
the faces of the diners as they chewed, now clustered
around Chester, poking each other and observing that,
"Ol' Chester ain't got no clothes on, only that bedsheet.
Let's take it." The lads seized upon both the suggestion
and the linen rectangle as one, and instantly Chester
stood revealed in all his beauty. He did a half-crouch,
like a marble nude in the museum and bleated, "Oh,
dear! I'll probably be thrown in jail!" As the last word
hung in the air, Chester wasn't there anymore.

"Now," Mary said calmy, "wouldn't it be nice if Mr.
Chester were safely at home and these little nuisances
were back in their coal mine with their pockets full of
money?" The hubbub of immature male voices was cut
off as if by a knife, and Roger returned his attention to
his prime rib.

"Nicely done," he congratulated her. "But we have to
hold that sort of thing to a minimum, since it further
degrades the integrity of the Matrix, you know."

"I think I'm getting the hang of it," Mary confided. "Actually, it explains a number of curious anomalies I've encountered in my work. When I was still a student, for example, I went on a dig in Florida, where a superb specimen of the mososaur had come to light. Unfortunately, it was clearly a hoax. Far from being a petrified skeleton, it was a rotting carcass, complete with internal organs, all intact and not more than a month old. I almost switched to engineering because none of the experts could offer any explanation, so I decided the whole science was a compendium of nonsense; if marine reptiles from the Cretaceous, thought to be extinct for over sixty million years could be alive and washed up on the beach in Pinellas County, what validity did any of the experts' ideas have?" Mary speared a chunk of asparagus and looked triumphantly at Roger, "But, of course," she went on, "if it's just a question of displacement through the Meniscus, why, it's perfectly clear!"

"Is it?" Roger queried hopefully. "But how did Bob and Rusty end up in the Plaza with me—of all the possible destinations in the STV—and that new fellow Julian, and the Pottses . . . ?"

"Clearly," Mary replied, "Someone, or something, is directing people there—to the Final Concept, didn't you call it?"

"I think you've got it!" Roger exclaimed. "It figures! But why?"

"Surely," Mary told him, "that is a question susceptible of logical analysis."

"But how did we get here?" Roger insisted, "and where is here? How is it you—? . . . and you mustn't get the idea that the Meniscus is fragile, it's tough as armor plate; it takes really tremendous force to penetrate it."

Mary waved that away. "Quite simple, really, Roger," she told him, "if one approaches the matter in a scientific way. One observes a phenomenon, one elaborates a theory to explain it, and one tests the theory's power of prediction. We're now at stage three, about to try the predictive power."

"Swell," Roger replied tonelessly. "How do we do that?"

"Simple enough," the professor assured him. "Doubtless, in view of Kepler's third law or something, any entity which undergoes a temporal displacement thereby acquires a charge of entropic energy proportional to the extent of the transference. Now," she went on, intent on her thesis, "assuming we're some fifty-odd million years out of our native locus, we must multiply that figure by our body weight, times a finagle factor yet to be determined, to discover just how much charge we're carrying. Clear?"

"Like ten feet of lead," Roger mumbled. "When did you pick up the jargon? I thought only UKR used all those expressions."

"From you, Roger," Mary said patiently. "You're forever trying to explain matters in terms of the incomprehensible."

"Oh," Roger said numbly, "I didn't realize. I was just trying to—"

"Don't feel bad," Mary urged. "The urge to explain to others what one does not oneself understand, in order to obtain some comprehension of the cryptic, is universal in human nature: ordinary life, especially since everything became so strange, is full of mysteries. For example, I told you about the curious matter of Faggotsby, where, in the thirteenth century, I was incarnated as old Mother Nell Goodwish, the local witch. It seems whenever I've been someone else, so to speak—"

Roger nodded encouragingly. "Go ahead, Mary. I know exactly what you mean: it's happened to me, and to a couple of other fellows I know, too."

"Well, people seem to sense something strange about me," Mary finished, "and decide I'm a witch."

"Sure," Roger agreed. "People are always jumping to conclusions."

"As I was saying," Mary resumed, "a fellow came to me as Mother Goodwish and demanded that I give him a share of my hoard of gold, or he'd go to the local squire and claim I'd put a spell on him. People were suspicious of *him*, too. I have a notion he was another displacee; he knew things he shouldn't, like the fact that the Earth revolves around the sun, and why the moon has phases, and that the planet is spherical. He even hinted at the existence of the New World. He scoffed at the villagers' superstitions, and at witchcraft—but he did seem to fear my familiar. That's one item I haven't been able to figure out. The strange creature came to me in my hut one night, speaking modern, twentieth century English and began telling me all sorts of incomprehensible things. You saw it: it followed me here. 'Catkin,' it told me to call it."

"That's just Oob the Rhox; that's R-H-O-X," Roger put in. "He's not such a bad fellow, really, just irresponsible and grasshopper-minded." Delmonico's was gone, Roger noticed; they were back in the jungle.

"Could he help us get away from here?" Mary inquired anxiously. She looked in the direction Lump and Bimbo had gone. "They'll arouse the villagers," she predicted. "I fear my peaceful life here is over. And Roger, those voices coming from above: what *are* they?"

I AM UKR, MADAM, he spoke up promptly. I HAVE DEPLOYED A FILAMENT OF AWARENESS TO MONITOR YOUR ACTIVITIES AND THOSE OF POOR ROGER. AT AN APPROPRIATE MOMENT, IF I MAY EMPLOY YOUR LIMITING HUMAN CONCEPT OF SERIAL TIME, I SHALL RESTORE YOU AND OTHER DISPLACEES TO YOUR PROPER COORDINATES.

"That business about the old witch," Roger addressed Mary. "Was that before you were an archeologist?"

"Actually," Mary responded, "I don't know. Things seem out of sequence. I was at home, in my store-room—pantry—and then I was in the cave. Just one step away from my sixteen-cubic-foot freezer, a shelf full of light bulbs, and a circuit-breaker panel, then—stalactites!"

"Yes, the transitions *are* rather abrupt," Roger commiserated. "Still, we're lucky to have each other for

company. Being here all alone would be even worse."
He thought that over. "Once I was missing my wife,
Q'nell—you'd like her—and I accidentally brought her
to me. The poor kid was very upset, wearing only a see-
through kimono or whatever women call those silly
overcoats. . . ."

" 'A negligee,' " Mary supplied. "I can see that would
be disconcerting. Lucky I was dressed for the walk into
town to the Post Office."

"UKR," Roger called, "can you get us back home right
now?"

I FEAR NOT, ROGER, UKR's disconcerting voice
rang down from above. THE DISTURBANCE TO THE
MATRIX OCCASIONED BY THE MASS INVASION
OF THE VRINT—

It's far from an invasion, Smarty! the Vrint's snappish
rejoinder drowned out the rest of UKR's pronouncement.
We think of it as merely a territorial adjustment, they
went on, *essentially to the orderly enfoldment of the Vrint
Destiny.*

AND WHAT DO YOU CONCEIVE THAT TO BE?
UKR persisted, with a hint of impatience.

I should think it would be obvious! the Vrint retorted.
*It is, clearly the burdensome fate of Vrint to undertake to
organize the chaotic fabric of space/time/vug in a fashion
conducive to a rational Final State.*

HOW DO YOU CONCEIVE THIS FINAL STATE?
UKR demanded.

*We perceive it as the symmetrical corollary to the Big
Bang.* The Vrint sounded a trifle smug, Roger thought.

"My God," he gasped. "The . . . what he said, to the
Big Bang would be the Big Crunch!"

Precisely, the Vrint confirmed. *The perfect solution to
all problems, none of which can exist in a post-Crunch
(or pre-Bang) context.*

"UKR!" Roger yelled. "It's time to *do* something!
Now!"

NOW, YOU SAY, UKR mused. YOU PEOPLE HAVE
ARBITRARILY DIVIDED THE TEMPORAL ASPECT

OF STV INTO TWO DOMAINS WHICH YOU DES-
IGNATE WHIMSICALLY AS "PAST" AND "FUTURE."
YOU CALL THE PLANE OF CONTIGUITY OF
THESE TWO FIGMENTS "NOW," AND DEMAND
THAT GREAT AFFAIRS BE BOUND BY THIS FIC-
TION. AS I HAVE TOLD YOU, I SHALL ACT AS
THOSE COORDINATES WHICH I COMPUTE TO
BE OPTIMAL ON THE HIGHER-LEVEL SCALE OF
OVERALL MATRICAL INTEGRITY. BE PATIENT;
THERE WILL SOON (ANOTHER OF YOUR OWN
CURIOUS CONCEPTS) OCCUR A RETURN OF
THE ICE, A CIRCUMSTANCE WHICH WILL
ENGAGE YOUR SIMPLE INTELLECTS IN PROB-
LEMS OF SURVIVAL, THEREBY DIVERTING YOU
FROM FECKLESS SPECULATIONS REGARDING
POTENTIAL IMPENDING DISCOMFORTS.

"Gee, swell!" Roger jeered. "I thought you were my
pal, and don't forget we're part of the Builder, and thus
your boss!"

"What does that mean, Roger?" Mary wanted to know.

"Eventually," Roger told her, "the entire human race,
at the culmination of evolution, will merge into a single
entity which will encompass every human intellect that
ever existed, thus embodying all the accumulated wisdom
of mankind. That entity is called the Builder. It built
UKR, you see; he's only a machine, and has to do what
we, as part of his owner, tell him to do."

"But what should we tell him to do?" Mary wailed.

"Easy," Roger returned crisply. "Get us out of here
and back to our own STV! Right now, not after the next
ice age!"

CHAPTER NINETEEN

"I wish I'd thought that over a little more carefully," Roger heard himself telling someone. Q'nell, or—no, it was that lady professor. But where *was* she? Had she already come and gone, or was that yet to happen? The whole cause-and-effect structure of his reality was shattered, he realized. But he could worry about that later, in the comfort of his cozy living room . . .

"Roger," Q'nell said, sounding anxious, "aren't you going to eat your cookies?"

Roger looked up, startled, "Of course, dear," he assured her, and ate one. Delicious! Poor Mary, he wished she were here now, safe and sound. He caught himself—a moment too late.

"Please excuse my appearance," Mother Goodwish said in her cracked voice. "You see, I was somehow trapped in a horrid Medieval village called Faggotsby, and the people—well, there aren't any smart little dress shops, you know. Excuse me. Oh, there you are, Mr. Tyson. I wondered." Then, to Q'nell, "I'm Mary Tomkins, my dear. I've had a terrible time of it. Could I freshen up?"

"Oh, you poor thing," Q'nell cooed. She gave Roger a sharp look. "You know my husband, I see. Just come along and have a nice hot bath, and I think my things will fit you." The two females went off, chattering. Roger sank into his chair and gave the TV an apprehensive look. "No *Daphne* tonight," he told himself. Q'nell returned.

"She's nice," she told Roger. "A professor, did you know? Where did you meet her?"

"In a patch of woods," Roger told her. "Where the Final Concept used to be—or will be, I'm not quite straight on that. I was in the Plaza, having a nice talk with Bob and another fellow, when R'heet—you remember R'heet—"

"Indeed I do!" Q'nell confirmed. "What's that lecher doing now?"

" 'Lecher'?" Roger echoed. "Did he—I mean did you—?"

"Never mind, silly boy." Q'nell massaged the back of Roger's neck. "That was all at a considerable temporal displacement, and on another filament entirely."

"He's lucky he disappeared!" Roger barked. "The skunk! Went off and left us there, too. Then ..." He paused. "Oob came along, as usual. It's confusing, there being so many of him. Anyway, all of a sudden I was in a forest—and Mary came along, and I remembered we were still in a malleable aspect, so I—"

"Certainly, dear," Q'nell soothed. "We're having chicken Cordon Bleu for dinner. Frozen, you know, and I think—"

"Let's eat out," Roger suggested. "I never learned to really *like* the taste of cardboard."

Mary came back just then looking radiant in little black nothing which Q'nell immediately regretted lending her. How was she to know it would make her look so stunning?

It was a restaurant Roger hadn't seen before, squeezed in between a shoe-repair place and an alley. The sign was one of those Olde English things, a board hanging from a wrought-iron spear, with a really crude picture of a yellow object painted on it. YE CHESHIRE CHEESE, the Gothic letters spelled out. "The aroma is fine," Roger noted, as they went in out of the chill wind, stumbling over the uneven threshold. Inside, it was warm, smoky, and noisy. Every table was occupied, it appeared, by overweight men in period costume: dirty ruffled shirts and jackets with stand-up collars; and they were all smoking long clay pipes.

"Look," Roger whispered to Mary. "That old fellow looks just like Sam Johnson."

"Indeed," she agreed. "And the young fellow with him: he's like Boswell."

Roger drew Mary aside. "We have to be very careful," he told her. "Not to disturb anything; the sequence of events, I mean. You see, probably that really *is* Johnson and Boswell: we've strayed into their space/time/vug locus, and if we interfere . . ."

"I understand," Mary assured him. "Boswell's taking notes right now. If we should disturb him, his *Life of Johnson* might never be written. But it's so fascinating. Couldn't we just get a little closer look at them?"

Roger shook his head. "Absolutely *not*," he told her. "Haven't you noticed, there are no women here? Just seeing you would upset Johnson: he's a notorious male chauvinist."

"Very well," Mary agreed. "Why in the world would a dignified old fellow like Dr. Samuel Johnson wear that horrid, frizzy wig on his head? It makes him look like a clown."

"That silly little peruke on Boswell isn't much better," Roger seconded her. "But that was the style then. I'd look like a fool here, with just my natural hair, if anybody noticed me."

A short, plump, heavily perspiring fellow in a red-and-white-striped vest jostled Roger.

"Sorry, sir," he mumbled, staring intently at the side of Roger's head. "I say, sir," he blurted. "Are you a returned colonist, perhaps, who's been scalped by the savages and survived?"

"Mind your tongue, my man," Roger responded absently, and lifted a mug of stout porter from the servitor's tray.

"Actually," he went on, after a revivifying pull at the pewter tankard, "I didn't survive. This is my ghost, revisiting the scene of former joys."

The waiter retreated half an inch. "Oh, I remember you now, sir; you're that sea captain fellow, Cook, I believe the name is. Back from the South Seas, eh? A table, gentlemen?" He fled.

"He called me a gentleman," Mary noted, accepting the chair Roger pulled out.

"And he thinks I'm a middle-aged sailor," Roger added. "But at least it got us a nice table, close enough for you to observe Doctor Johnson, but *do* be discreet! Lucky you're not wearing any makeup. That would really set him off."

The flustered waiter brought Mary a glass of port, and gave Roger another beer.

"Not bad," Roger commented. "They don't brew it like this anymore."

"This is just the time when tea and coffee were coming in vogue," Mary contributed. "In fact, they probably call this a coffee-house."

Roger tuned in on a snatch of the conversation at the adjacent table:

"—the famous surgeon, you'll recall, Doctor," Boswell was saying. "So I asked him, 'What ever became of that patient, sir? The lady who was grievously injured in the collapse of the stable?'

"'I mended her,' he told me.

"'But, doctor,' I replied. 'I thought her head was broken.'

"'And so it was,' he replied. 'Quite broken. But I mended it.' There, sir, is that not an evidence of the efficacy of our modern chirurgical science?" Boswell was nodding in agreement with himself.

"Bah!" Johnson dismissed the idea. "I read nothing in Aristotle of mending heads."

"Roger," Mary's soft voice distracted him from eavesdropping. "It seems so strange that we should be here—

two centuries and more before our time—and yet, it's so natural, so real, and matter-of-fact."

Roger and Mary observed closely as the two literary giants bustled away, and the scene faded around them.

"Don't even try to grasp it, Mary," Roger urged. "It's outside our paradigm. Things aren't as we always thought they were, that's all. We've become accustomed to compartmentalizing things as either past or future, or possibly now, and either here or there. As it happens, that has little to do with reality, whatever that is."

"You make it all sound so . . . insecure," Mary objected. "As if it didn't really matter much what we do; it's all a part of what *is*, whether we like it or not."

"Not quite," Roger disagreed. "In the early universe, *every*thing was latent, and began unfolding aimlessly, but humanity's appearance on the scene changed things in a major way. For some reason, we have the ability to manipulate the warp and woof of the Fabric, and weave it into patterns at variance with the Primordial Impulse."

"Such as?" Mary prompted.

"We developed hands and brains," Roger went on. "And that enabled us to make fire, and chip flint and make spears, and thus dominate animal life. We've gone on to dig canals and drain rivers, and add to the CO_2 in the atmosphere, and create mutations among living forms, and now we're about to ready to start terraforming the other bodies in the Solar System, and before long, we'll reach the stars, and our influence will increase geometrically then. Meanwhile, our remote descendant, the Builder, has created the Trans-Temporal Bore, and thus accidentally opened up all of STV to the Rhox and the Vrint as well. Now the whole fabric is in tatters, and our traditional segregation of past/future and here/there is breaking down. It was an artificial construct in the first place."

"Did you hear," Mary queried, "of Rhodesian Man? A skull of *Homo erectus* with an unmistakable bullet hole through it?"

"Never did," Roger grunted.

"And the Neolithic lithoglyphs that show astronomical bodies not visible without a telescope?" Mary persisted.

"What about the Peri Reis map?" Roger contributed. "A Medieval chart showing with good accuracy the east coast of South America, and Antarctica as it would be without ice."

Mary nodded. "I hadn't heard of that one," she said. "There are so many anomalies in the record, both temporal and spatial. Have you ever noticed the spectacles on people in many pre-Medieval paintings and sculptures? Now I begin to understand why."

"Those eight Wehrmacht men," Roger suggested, "who came out of a bunker in France in the seventies, for example. I'll bet they got into one of Oob's Apertures."

"And the Japanese soldier who surrendered on an island in the Pacific thirty years after the war," Mary added. "The poor man was probably lost in that same woods where I spent so many years. I wonder how he got back?"

"Perhaps they just envisioned their home-locus strongly enough to do the trick—even if they weren't in a malleable-state filament."

"Are *we* in a malleable-state filament?"

"I don't know," Roger admitted. "*I* was, for a while, but I accidentally shifted myself out of it into something worse. It seems I keep stumbling along farther and farther away from my destination, almost as if I were being herded."

HARDLY "HERDED," MY DEAR BOY, UKR's astonishing voice spoke up.

Mary jumped and clutched Roger's arm. "You *did* hear that, too, didn't you, Roger?" she quavered hopefully. "I wish it wouldn't *do* that!"

"Very well," UKR said in a normal conversational tone. "It's difficult attuning precisely to the arbitrary physical levels of your tiny lives, but since I upset you by communicating in my basal mode, I shall attempt to match entropies with you."

"What do you mean, 'hardly "herded" '?" Roger demanded impatiently. "Are you saying *you're* responsible for my jumping around like a grasshopper every time I happen to consider some alternative to whatever form of disaster I'm involved in at the moment?"

"You are less than charitable in your characterization of my influence, Roger," UKR commented sulkily.

"I thought you were my pal," Roger grieved. "The infallible mechanical servant of the Builder, namely, me." He brushed impatiently at the gentle buzzing under the overhanging foliage.

"While you do, indeed, embody one minute strand of the warp and woof which in time will become, or has become, depending on one's temporal orientation, the Master Builder, that fact does not confer on you any unique relationship to myself," UKR declared. "After all, Roger, every human psyche which ever existed participates in the entity known to the other First Level entities as the Builder."

"Including Mary," Roger pointed out. "So there's two of us telling—or asking you, if you insist—to get us out of this place and back where we belong. We must be creating intolerable stresses in the Fabric just by existing out of context."

"A telling point. How brave of you to volunteer to relieve the stress by ceasing to exist."

"I had no intention of doing anything brave," Roger objected. "And as for 'ceasing to exist,' that's the furthest thing from my mind. We just don't want to do our existing in this infernal wasteland!"

"Oh, I see. The distinction is a minor one, but I will observe it, since it seems of importance to you."

"Roger," Mary said hesitantly, "don't you think maybe you ought to give your conversational ability a rest now? Everything you say seems somehow to make things worse. Mr. Ucker," she raised her voice slightly, "couldn't you just whisk us out of this situation into a more civilized one?"

"VERY well, my dear, IF THAT'S WHAT YOU

desire," UKR responded in a voice which modulated from barely audible to deafening. Then, "Is this about right?"

"Fine," Mary confirmed. "But what about my request?"

"Such impatience," UKR grumped. "It's been less than twelve years, basic time, since you proffered the proposal."

"Don't worry, Mary," Roger reassured her, "UKR isn't on the same temporal wavelength as we are."

"Heavens!" Mary gasped. "Twelve years! Fred will have given me up for dead, and . . . I *do* hope he's found a nice wife. No, I don't, dammit! And, come to think of it, I spent, or will spend, at least ten years in Faggotsby. Why, I'd be sixty years old now! Roger, tell him to put it right!"

"All right, UKR," Roger addressed the unseen machine. "It's time for you to start showing a little consideration for the innocent victims of your strategy!"

"You have, perhaps, a point, Roger," UKR conceded. "Still, one must keep in mind the triviality of the objects of your commiserations."

"Do you suppose," Mary asked Roger anxiously, "he really *has*? Remarried, I mean."

"Probably not," Roger offered. "*He* hasn't experienced all those years objectively. Perhaps only a few hours."

Mary sighed. "If he has, by the Old Nick, Nell Goodwish will put a geas on her that'll lock her knees together so tight the fairest swain in Christendom'll not unlock 'em!"

"Now, Mary, don't be vengeful," Roger soothed her. "It's all academic, anyway, if we don't get out of here."

"Try," Mary suggested. "Maybe we're still in the malleable state you mentioned."

"OK," Roger acceded. "I'll try." He closed his eyes and attempted to firm up the amorphous gray of the vugfield. He evoked a straight line, rotated it to the horizontal. "OK so far," he reported. "Now I need to add some scenery." He thought of a Mercer Raceabout (circa 1912) perked under the elm trees in front of the First

National, and there it sat, gleaming yellow-and-brass. He took a step toward it and bumped his nose hard on an invisible barrier.

"Damn Meniscus has to be intact just when I don't want it to be," he muttered, and rolled aside as pounding hooves came rushing toward him. An immense bison charged past the Mercer, closely followed by a gigantic, shiny blue-black Vrint.

"Stop!" he yelled. A twelve-foot angel with a flaming sword interposed himself between the beetle and its prey. The bison halted and began to nibble the privet hedge in front of the bank. Roger got up and tried again for the car. He tripped over something he couldn't see, just as a battered covered wagon rumbled past, pursued by a crowd of Pawnees in war paint. Roger watched until they had all disappeared down the avenue; then he looked around for Mary. He saw her, sitting at a table set up on the sidewalk, deep in conversation with Julian. He started toward them and bumped his nose again.

"Hey, Julian!" Roger called. "Where'd *you* come from?"

The dapper young fellow looked up with a surprised expression. "Roger! Where's Gert?"

"I don't know any Gert," Roger told him grumpily. "I asked you an almost civil question," he reminded the tall artistic-looking Julian, then greeted Mary.

Mary got to her feet, but remained there, standing. "Oh, Roger, excuse me; this is Julian. Julian, Roger Tyson." Julian nodded.

"We've met," Roger said bluntly. He confronted Julian. "How did you get here?" he grated. "It's important, maybe. There must be a major rent in the Fabric nearby. That Conestoga—"

Julian waved a hand indifferently. "Somehow I seem to keep winding up back in Paris," he grunted. "I've given up trying to reason my way out of it," he told Roger. "Oh, here's Gert and Dottie now."

He stepped past Roger, who turned to see two smartly

dressed young ladies, looking somewhat the worse for a sojourn in the thicket from which they were emerging. "Oh, Julian," Gert caroled. "Saints be praised; it's you! It's a disperate time we've been after having, entirely, bedad!"

CHAPTER TWENTY

Julian went forward the greet the two, then led them
back to Roger and Mary, who had remained where they
were, perforce, since the unseen barrier still restricted
them to the spot at which they had arrived.

"Come and meet Gert and Dottie," Julian urged.

Roger shook his head. "Can't. Some kind of force-field
has me boxed in." He turned to Mary. "Well, it didn't
work," he said cheerfully. "I did manage to sort of stir
things up, but I can't break out of stasis. Perhaps *you*
could get to the car."

Julian and the ladies were asking questions, all of
which Roger waved away. "Be careful," he cautioned
Mary. "Don't bump your nose like I did."

She had taken a few steps and stopped, looking at the
Mercer, only six feet away. She turned back. "It's as if
there were a rope tied to me," she told Roger. "When I
try to go past that crack in the sidewalk, it stops me."

"Sidewalk?" Roger croaked, confusedly. "Here? Hooray! We've made it!" He scuffed his foot in the fallen
leaves littering the pavement.

Mary resumed her seat at the table. "Do take a cup of
tea, Roger," she urged. "It's very refreshing, you know."

"To me tea is like hot dishwater without the soap,"

Roger rejected the invitation ungraciously. The two new arrivals accepted, and sat down.

"Gert!" Dottie blurted. "That new diet you told me about—you look . . ."

"So do you, Dot," Gert replied, as she put a hand to her face. "It feels smooth," she said hesitantly. Now she was staring at the back of her hand. "My skin!" she gasped. "It's—!"

"Something's happened," Dot told her.

"I've been thinking, Roger," Mary spoke up, after a nod to her table companions. "Nell Goodwish has a few tricks: suppose I try the superb Black—the same one Merlin used to transport the sarsen stones to Stonehenge . . . ?"

"Don't!" Roger cut her off harshly. "There's enough confusion already, without getting into black magic!"

"I'll just summon Catkin," Mary offered. Before Roger could object, she did something intricate with her fingers and Roger felt something nudge his shin. He looked down to see Oob squatting there, his tentacles limp, his lone eye fixed on Mary.

"Well!" he croaked. "Have you no consideration? I'm in the middle of my regular every-other-millisecond invection, and all of sudden—! Dammit, I wish I'd never showed you those tricks! What is it you want?"

"Look here, Oob," Roger put in. "We need your help, I admit it. UKR doesn't seem to know what to do—"

"It's the rutabaga," Dottie yelped.

Julian was eyeing the Rhox dubiously. "I've seen that thing before," he said. "Just about the time everything went nutty."

"It's just Oob," Roger spoke up. "He's actually not a bad fellow at all; just misunderstood!"

"Why, Roger," the Rhox gurgled. "How nice of you to say it! Suppose we all move along to more comfortable circumstances and have a nice chat?"

"Wait!" Roger blurted. "First, let's discuss—"

But Oob had already deployed his vram-sensors, and was carefully feeling over the convoluted surface of the enclosing vram-field. He paused, said "Aha!" and twitched in a peculiar way. The light faded, as if reluctantly, leaving Roger sitting, alone, on a damp ledge of rock in the midst of a veritable maze of stalactites and stalagmites.

"A cave!" he blurted.

"The Cave of the Lesser Evil," Mary supplied. She was approaching from the left, charming in a garment of half-cured opossum hides. "I know the way out," she said complacently. "Shall we go?"

Roger looked down. He was stark naked. He shivered. "Must be Chester's lingering influence," he muttered.

"Don't give it a thought," Mary dismissed the matter. "At first, you'll recall, it was I who was undraped, and you gallantly volunteered your own rude garment." She paused to scratch. "Fleas and all," she added.

"I *don't!*" Roger protested. "Don't remember, I mean. And if I'd ever seen you in the altogether, I'm sure I wouldn't have forgotten it! How long have we been here, anyway?"

"I arrived first," she told him. "About an hour ago. Alone. I went on a little recon to be sure I knew where I was, and when I came back, here you were."

"Then," Roger mourned, "there's no way in the world to know how long it's been!"

Mary shook her head; she was intent on studying a small, growing column of translucent stone beside her. A drop of water fell, splattered on its blunt end.

"Less than ten years, I estimate," Mary said, "judging by the added deposit since I last inspected it. It's grown only about a tenth of a millimeter since I first saw it. That's very approximate, of course."

Roger groaned. "And while I'm gallivanting around from one crazy locus to another, poor Q'nell is back home all alone, wondering why I didn't come back! And meanwhile, the ice still advancing: it's probably dozed the house away by now, whenever 'now' is."

"Now, Roger," Mary said soothingly. "I'm sure it will come right in the end. I have a feeling, based on the little I know about all this, that some force or other is gradually realigning things to a minimum stress configuration."

"Meanwhile," Roger grunted. "you and I are stranded in a Neolithic cave we probably can't even find our way out of."

"I think I know the way," Mary corrected him cheerfully. "Come on, let's try." She tugged at his hand and he got wearily to his feet and stumbled along beside her.

"Damn floor's an ankle-breaker," Roger commented, then quickly put his hand over his mouth, "Sorry," he mumbled. "I'll try to keep my mouth under control."

"This way," the professor said, tugging him to the left of a major stone column.

"How do you know?" Roger asked.

"I can smell the fresh air," she replied. "I've had practice, during the past ten years or however long it's been. I remember Lig's baby was only a few days old the first time I saw him, and I cured his colic. Now he's a big, lanky teenager, always chasing the young girls. Anyway, I've had to rely on my sense of smell far more than I ever did before. As a result, it improved. Well, not really; I just started paying more attention. I can smell a stabbing cat at fifty yards, and spot spoiled meat in an instant. It's quite a different world, the world of smell. One tends to ignore vision and sniff continually like a dog. He looks at a bitch and doesn't notice she's a female, but when he smells her, he knows what to do."

Now Roger felt a minute draft of marginally warmer air. Slowly, in the darkness relieved only by a dim glow from a crevice in the ceiling of the cave, they made their way toward the source of the breeze, to emerge at last on a well-trodden stone ledge above a river, far below. Roger almost laughed aloud as he hugged Mary. "You did it!" he exulted.

Then he felt a hard hand on his arm and spun to see a hairy subhuman face snarling up at him: Bimbo's brother. The *erectus* was only five-three, Roger estimated, but mightily muscled. Roger tried to shake off the vise-like grip, but succeeded only in causing it to tighten.

"Let him go, Blug," Mary ordered calmly. Then, when Blug ignored her, she stepped in and struck him a hearty blow on the upper arm with the side of her hand. Blug's grip failed and Roger hid his bruised arm behind him.

There were other of the Folk crowding around now, exchanging grunting conversation.

"Mary, can you understand these people?" Roger demanded as a second native male came up and looked him over as if estimating his weight.

"Certainly," Mary replied. "It's very simple really. They haven't invented inflections yet. It's just a matter of memorizing the vocabulary—about about a thousand words. Some of them are remarkably like our familiar Indo-European roots. Very onomatopoeic. You'll soon know it as well as I."

Blug was keeping an eye on Roger, working his way around behind him, pretending to be intent on overturning rocks in search of succulent grubs.

"Uh-oh, Mary," Roger said. "Blug's going to try something—" He broke off as Blug lifted a flat stone overhead and turned to Roger, who had himself turned to face the ill-natured fellow. As Blug brought the big stone down, Roger leaned aside and punched the small Hercules hard in the solar plexus. Blug dropped the slab on his own foot and fell to the ground, yowling.

At once the tribe took up the howl, gathering closely around the injured man, not as if eager to help him, but rather intent on looking at his wounds.

Suddenly, the *Pithecanthropus* jumped up; he took a few halting steps, then paused. A thought wrinkled his narrow brow. He proceeded, limping theatrically around the edge of the crowd, muttering as he went. Just as he reached the cave mouth and ducked inside, a dull rumble started up from the depths of the cavern; it grew louder, interspersed with loud *thud!*s and *bang!*s from deep inside the grotto.

Dust boiled out of the depths of the cave. Mary went

to the entrance and called, "Blug!" followed by a string of grunting sounds. There was no reply from within.

"Roger," Mary spoke up softly, "do you remember that fissure in the roof of the cave the light was coming through?"

"Of course," Roger replied. "Lucky for us it was there."

"This one has one too," Mary said. "And," she added, "I have an idea the whole roof is about to collapse."

"Pretty tough on anybody who happened to be back in there when it does," Roger commented. By now, half a dozen of the Folk, mostly males, had gathered inside the cave mouth to stare, grunt, scratch, and stare some more.

"I'm surprised," Mary told Roger. "This is called the Cave of the Lesser Evil, and usually they won't go near it. But Blug ran right in."

Roger heard another clatter of falling rock from deeper inside. "It's going," he reported.

"Well, it seems Blug insisted on being first, as usual," Mary commented, "and has paid the price. Pity. I had almost managed to teach him to wait a full minute before pulling his fish-bait back out of the water."

"Maybe he's just stunned," Roger suggested, coming forward. "Let's go in and see. I think the collapsing is over for the moment. If the poor fellow is lying in there with a broken leg, pinned under a boulder, we have to—"

"Oh, very well," Mary agreed reluctantly. "I'd just about forgotten about things like compassion and help-fulness and so on. It's been every man for himself, for so long . . ."

"Must have been tough," Roger commiserated. "Come on. But watch your step." He led the way into the cave, its floor littered with rubble ranging in size from dust to a piano-shaped slab blocking the way to the deep cavern. Roger looked it over. "We're stymied," he announced. "if Blug's under that, he's finished; if he's on the other side, he stays there. There's not room enough for a ten-year-old to get past that, even if it wasn't all sharp edges."

Mary murmured her agreement, but she went to the biggest open space beside the fallen megalith and called. The echo was weak.

After a few more tries, she turned away sadly. "It's a terrible death even for a ruffian like Blug," she remarked as epitaph.

Just then Roger heard a muffled yell from beyond the barrier. He responded by calling Blug's name. The reply was a rock the size of a cabbage hurled through the opening.

"Smart fellow," Roger remarked as the missile missed his head and impacted on flesh behind him, eliciting a chorus of yells. He looked. One of the older women had a nasty gash on her knee.

"Ohh, Dunt," Mary said sighingly, and went to the old hag to tend her wound.

"Dunt's only about twenty-three," Mary told Roger. "It's terrible how they age so quickly. She was one of the first I was able to make friends with here. Poor thing."

Roger, meanwhile, had moved into position to throw a baseball-sized stone through the narrow opening, in hope of eliciting a response. He had climbed halfway up the barricading slab, and suddenly encountered a deep space between the barrier and the cave roof. He resisted the impulse to explore it and instead called to Mary: "I think maybe there's a route through here."

"Stay away from it," Mary counseled. "Blug may start bombarding you through it."

"Hey, Blug!" Roger called. Then, to Mary: "I don't need to go in: if he can reach it, he can come out. Maybe he hasn't noticed it yet. I'll try to get his attention." He called again and another stone ricocheted off the wall of the fissure, missing Roger by an inch. Peering into the dark cleft, Roger saw Blug's groping hand. He touched it to encourage the trapped fellow, and at once his wrist was seized in a grip like a bench-vise, and he was tugged headlong into the darkness, his face being raked painfully along the rockface. He yelled; it sounded muffled even to his own ears. Then Mary's voice spoke close by: "Roger, I'll get help. Hold on."

"Nothing to hold on to," Roger grunted. "Lucky I'm not claustrophobic. He's pulling me deeper. Hurry!"

A moment later he felt hard hands grip his ankles and pull. Inside the cave, Blug pulled back. Roger felt his joints creaking, or imagined he did. "None of that!" he commanded himself. "I'll think about something pleasant instead," he decided. "Like being back outside, in the sunlight, lying on the grass taking it easy." Nothing happened. Roger groaned, was entranced by the echo, and groaned again. The pain was mostly in his hips, he decided, where the femurs were being pulled from their sockets.

Suddenly Blug's grip relaxed momentarily, as he tried for a new purchase, halfway to Roger's elbow. Instantly the pull on his ankles hauled him backward, scraping him painfully in the process, but then he was free, gloriously free. He half fell to get his feet on the floor, and staggered back. At once, a jagged rock sailed through the opening and impacted in the face of a noisy fellow who had been jumping up and down and yelling. The others fled. Mary took Roger's arm. "You were so brave, Roger, so stoic! I'm proud of you."

" 'Stoic,' my left hind gaboochie!" Roger burst out. "I just couldn't decide whether to cuss or cry!"

One of the squat villagers emerged from the brush and advanced cautiously. He carried a dead rabbit, which he placed in the cave mouth. He darted a look at Mary and blurted something, then turned and ran.

"Poor Lug died," Mary told Roger. "And I'm afraid we've given rise to a new superstition: that rabbit is an offering to appease the demon in the cave. They've already forgotten about Blug." She paused in thought. "That's why they call it 'the Cave of the Lesser Evil,'" she realized. "No wonder! You see, it's the lesser evil because it happened to us and not them. The 'Great Evil' is an *Ursus spelaeus*. The cave bear, you know."

"But that must have been a long time ago," Roger reminded her. "They already called it that back when you first appeared. So— How weird," he amended. "I keep forgetting cause doesn't have to precede effect."

He felt Mary shiver, her slim body pressed against him. He patted her shoulder, then jerked his hand away as if it had touched a hot iron.

"All we have to do," Mary declared crisply, "is to consider the matter rationally."

"No!" Roger cut her off. "That's the last thing we should do! There's nothing rational about it!" On impulse, he called, "UKR!" There was only the cave's weak echo.

"That's funny," Roger commented mildly. "He's usually Johnny-on-the-spot. This is a fine time to let us down."

"Let's try to figure out exactly where we are geographically," Mary suggested. "As soon as it's dark, we can observe the positions of the constellations—"

"If they wiped the sky clean and put up a whole new set of constellations," Roger dismissed the idea, "I wouldn't even notice."

"That's all right," Mary said. "Before I decided on archaeology, I almost majored in astronomy. I love the stars. I have—had—a nice little six-inch refractor of my own, and—"

"Swell," Roger agreed. "So we find out we're in Antarctica before the ice—then what?"

"Greenland," Marty corrected. "That means at least a a couple of hundred thousand years B.P.—so to speak. I mean, if we're here in 300,000 B.C., 300,000 B.C. *is* the present."

"Why Greenland?" Roger inquired.

"I studied the stars when I first came here," Mary told him. "By extrapolating for the known movements of nearby stars, I was able to work it out—I think—at least approximately. It had to be Greenland. Just think, Roger: we're seeing lovely, habitable territory that was just recently buried under the ice and never thawed, back in our own space/time, uh, vug. I've a hunch early man crossed on the ice from Scandinavia via Greenland to the New World, a very long time ago. The red deer and the elk, too."

"You said three hundred thousand years," Roger objected. "There were no humans then."

"That's an approximation," Mary told him. "*Australopithacus boisei* was in existence by then, and just possibly they migrated north, as *erectus* did later. I'm only theorizing, of course. There are some anomalies, as well as gaps in the fossil record in North America, which my idea could explain."

"Stop," Roger objected. "You're starting to sound like UKR. Only," he mused on, "UKR probably doesn't—or didn't—exist in 300,000 B.C. There were no people to be the future components of the Builder."

WRONG, AS USUAL, ROGER, UKR corrected in its impersonal tone. THE BUILDER WAS IMMANENT IN THE ORIGINAL CONTEXT OF THE PRIMORDIAL EVENT.

"He means the Big Bang," Mary put in. Roger nodded impatiently.

YOU MUST, FOR YOUR OWN PEACE OF MIND, UKR went on, ATTEMPT TO RID YOURSELF OF YOUR PETTY AND IMPRUDENT TWO-VALUED TEMPORAL ORIENTATION. THE "PRESENT" MOMENT IN NO WAY DIFFERS FROM ANY OTHER RANDOMLY SELECTED ENTROPIC LOCUS.

"Whaddaya mean, 'my peace of mind'?" Roger yelled. "If you're concerned about my peace of mind—and Mary's, too—you can just shift us to some STV coordinates where things are a little more civilized!" *Quiver.*

CHAPTER TWENTY-ONE

Roger turned at a touch on his arm. Mary's gentle voice said, "Oh, Roger! It worked!"

He was feeling a little light-headed, he realized, and had his eyes squeezed shut. He opened them and saw about him a broad, cracked pavement, with weeds sprouting in the fissures, stretching across to a row of vacant-looking buildings—some of them crumbling about the edges, he noted.

"It's the Final Concept!" he yelled. "Only in ruins! Where's R'heet? Where the devil did he go?"

"Easy, Tyson," a calm voice said beside him. Bob Armstrong was facing him, a puzzled expression on his face.

"What happened, fella?" Bob asked in a soothing tone. Roger noted that the new fellow, Julian, was beside Bob; and a guy Roger had never seen before—looked like a retired hoodlum—was just coming up behind them.

"Aw right, whassamatta here?" the latter demanded. "We don't need no trouble." The burly newcomer's pig-like eyes were boring into Roger.

"What happened *here*?" Roger demanded. "It looks like—well, I don't know what it looks like, except everything's gone to pot! Where's R'heet gone?" Roger turned to look up the stairs where he had last seen the Culture

One inspector. The marble steps were chipped and the treads displaced, and tall stalks of dog-fennel grew between them. He went up; at the top he peered into the opening where the bronze doors had been, a gaping hole like the mouth of a cave.

"Funny," Roger found himself thinking, "out of one cave into another. But at least no stalactites this time." He went back down to Mary, and looked back up at the former doorway.

"Something's happened," he told Mary. "This place is in ruins—and it was supposed to be the culminating achievement of Culture One."

Something stirred in the darkness behind the corroded doorframe. A shiny, blue-black member groped outward; a vast shape loomed behind it.

"Ye gods!" Roger blurted, grabbing Mary's arm. "It's a really giant Vrint!"

"Never mind," she said casually. "I've a sovran spell for vermin."

"This is no time for spells!" Roger yelped. "Let's get going!" He hauled her back and along the cracked tile-work toward an adjacent vacant (he hoped) building.

"Look, Roger," Mary urged, resisting being dragged. He halted to expostulate, and saw what she was pointing at: a horde of six-inch Vrint, swarming from edge to edge of the wide avenue ahead, and on into the deserted plaza.

"There must be two kinds!" he declared. Just then someone—or something—emerged from the entry toward which he had been hustling Mary. It was a squat, bag-of-water-like torso, surmounted by a bump accommodating three heavy-lidded eyes, all of which were fixed on Roger. Its arms terminated in hands with too many fingers.

"It's got too many fingers," he told Mary.

"Nine on each hand," she noted.

A gelatinous voice, not unlike Oob's, came from the wide, lipless mouth. "Kindly stand fast, sir and madam," it said clearly enough.

Roger halted. "Why should we?" he demanded. "We're being pursued by a horde of meat-eating beetles!"

"By no means, sir," the newcomer contradicted. "I take it you refer to my quarry, the Vrint. They're trouble-makers, right enough, but they don't eat, you know, least of all alien protoplasm. Machines, you see." As he spoke, the strange being was hustling toward Roger on short but powerful-looking limbs.

"I'll soon have them under control," he added confidently. "Permit me to introduce myself," he said in a tone which assumed permission was forthcoming. "I'm Gom Blemp, roving Inspector for the Conglomerate. May I inquire . . . ?" He extended a nine-fingered hand.

"Tyson, Roger Tyson, and this is Professor Tomkins. Mary, may I present Mr. Gom Blemp?"

"Charmed," Mary murmured, placing two fingers across the squat inspector's proffered palm. "Are you by any chance related to my familiar, Catkin?"

Gom Blemp sighed. "As it happens, I *am* a congener of the scamp," he confessed. "It is precisely on his account that I am here. Our Monitor Service detected a veritable entropic froth in the incident problyon flux; I was dispatched to investigate it. My unit brought me here, too late, it appears, to confront the entities responsible for the meddling, unless perhaps you . . . ?"

"Innocent bystanders," Roger stated crisply. "What do you mean, 'too late'?"

"Why, as you can see," Blemp replied, "the inhabitants have fled, some time ago. Rather a pity, actually, since my instruments indicate that they had achieved an unusually harmonious accommodation of the manifold entrophic forces, resolving most of the stresses inherent in organic 'life,' as we call it. But I suppose you do, too."

"Do what too?" Roger demanded, evading the stranger's outstretched hand.

"Call it 'life,' " Mary supplied. "Yes, of course we do, Mr. Blemp. I assume you're an extra-terrestrial life-form?"

"Nay, more," Blemp corrected. "Extra-galactic. Little aggregation you folks call the Lesser Magellanic Cloud."

"And you came all this way, looking for Catkin?" Mary queried. Blemp twitched his cranial bump in what she assumed was a nod of assent.

"I'm sure I can fetch him for you," she volunteered, "if you'll promise you don't intend to harm him. He's a dear, actually. Reads to me in the evenings by the fire. Reads my mind, that is. All my eidetically-recorded memories, especially books I've read. I reviewed Ceramics 307 just last week."

"I assure you, madam," Blemp stated pompously, "injuring the scamp is far from my intention. I need merely to interview him, as a material witness. He seems to pop up whereever the anomalous flux is most apparent."

"Very well," Mary replied. "Excuse me, gentlebeings." She turned her back and Roger heard her muttering. There was a soft *plop!* and Oob was there, jittering on his pointy legs.

"Aroint thee, Nell!" he blurted. "I was in the midst of a most delicate finesse! I asked you not to use the recall mantra except in dire emergen— ... Oh, hello, there, Inspector."

He gave Blemp a sorrowful look, then looked sharply at Roger. "Had to yell 'copper,' eh?" he burbled. "I'd thought better of you, my boy. As a matter of fact—"

"That's enough, Oob!" Blemp cut in, as he caught the Rhox's prime manipulatory member and clamped a single cuff on it. "Now if you'll behave yourself, boy, I shan't be obliged to place you in a comatose state."

"Don't worry, Your Honor," Oob gobbled. "I'm a reformed fella, I was only—"

"Save it for the Tribunal," Blemp cut him off. "First item, turn over the stolen Relegator you whipped from Classified Storage."

"Don't have it," Oob muttered. "I'm sorry to say it's fallen into the hands of a particularly unsavory native of this locus, who has fled out of reach."

"Doubtless," Blemp commented briskly, "that dereliction on your part was instrumental in bringing about the disaster the evidences of which we see about us."

"Gosh, chief," Oob objected. "You gonna put the whole ball o' wax on _my_ plate?"

"You must excuse this benighted fellow's dreadful mixed metaphors," Blemp murmured. "He's unsophisticated."

"Forget his mixed whatchamacallits," Roger retorted hotly. "It's his mixed-up ideas about who's responsible for the trouble that gripes _me!_"

Mary put a calming hand on Roger's shoulder. "Please be reasonable, Roger," she suggested. "It's certainly not Gom Blemp's fault." She gave the latter a gentle smile. "What about the Vrint, Mr. Blemp?" she went on to inquire. "Why are they here in such numbers?"

" 'Gom' Blemp is the preferred style," the alien corrected gently. "When we Vosplishers detected their advent, from the Big Cloud, you know, there were a few hundred Batch Masters. We attempted to isolate them, but a few escaped here. Thereafter, to our surprise, they proceeded to reproduce in vast numbers. Therein lies the crux of the problem."

"Oh, swell," Roger commented. "You loosed a plague on the world—and now you're trying to make _me_ the scapegoat! That's ridiculous!" He turned his back to see a six-foot Vrint approaching across the weed-grown pavement. He grabbed up a three-foot stick from the rubble on the ground; waved it at the machine, and said "Shoo!" The mighty Vrint halted, twitched its feelers uncertainly, and clumsily heaved itself around to change course by about fifteen degrees, Roger estimated. It continued its advance, bypassing him, to trundle off down the avenue. Roger threw the rotted stick after it, which was ignored, and turned back to confront Blemp.

"How about it?" he demanded. "Because of _your_ blundering, the whole manifold is infested with these bugs, or machines, or whatever! What do you propose to do about it?"

"Pity, I haven't a relegator about my person," Gom Blemp replied, then, "Hark! I thought I heard—"

"As indeed you did, Gom," the gluey voice of Oob spoke up brightly. "My distress call, quite inaudible to these insensitive locals, I note. I've been crying for help continuously for some days, to stoop to local concepts of STV, with no result. I'm grateful you've come, sir. I surrender myself to your good offices."

"My 'good offices,' indeed!" Blemp scoffed. "I'm placing you under close arrest; don't imagine your attempt to sneak away whilst my attention was diverted passed unnoticed!"

"Who, I, sir?" Oob objected, displaying his prime member, bearing Blemp's restraining device. "I'd not have gotten far thus encumbered! A fine way to treat a fellow being, marooned so far from his native climes . . ."

"Don't lay that palsy routine on *me*, Oob!" Blemp admonished the saucy fellow. "You're going home, all right, to the Lye-vats at Pronk!"

"No, kind sir, not the lye-vats!" the humbled Rhox begged. Blemp spurned him with his pedal extremity. "Roger," he said, "I shall depute you to keep an ocular on this scamp. He'll try to delude you in any way he can, so be alert. Now I really must be off to attempt to repair some of the damage lately done to the Fabric by this criminal. *Hej sä länge!*" The nine-fingered hand gave a jaunty wave and the inspector strolled off toward the nearest dilapidated building, ignoring Roger's objections.

"What am I supposed to do with Oob?" he appealed to Mary. "I can't stay awake all the time."

"Let's truss him up," she suggested. "Apparently his unusual abilities are severely inhibited by the gadget Mr. Blemp attached to him. Now, Catkin," she addressed Oob directly, "you behave yourself— Oh, dear, here comes another giant beetle!"

"You may as well forget that 'Catkin' business," Oob grunted ungraciously. "I played along because it was convenient to have food and shelter provided in return for a few trifling manipulations of the local entropic membrane, to enable you to astound the locals, but that's over now. Though," he continued, "I confess it was a halcyon time, there in peaceful Faggotsby, so long ago, so far away . . ." As his voice faded, so did he, until only a ghostly grayish-white blob remained in view.

"So *that's* your scheme!" Mary cried. "You've forgotten the Elegant Copper!" She caught up a piece of rotted matter and tossed it at the vanishing Rhox and uttered something unintelligible which sounded to Roger like 'Wavery, quavery, solid as rock! Be still, thou mumble, as one in the stock!'"

A syrupy groan came from Oob, and again the Rhox jittered before Mary's complex gesticulations. "Treachery!" he moaned. "When I taught you the Elegant series, I trusted you! Will you betray me?"

"Damn right," Mary confirmed with satisfaction. "Don't think I don't know it was you who messed up my Magnificent Puce that time, and nearly got me strapped to the dunking stool!"

"A mere momentary inattention on my part," Oob pled. "Stay your hand, Nell, and I'll show you wonders yet undreamt of in your philsophy!"

"With Gom Blemp's inhibitor clamped to your prime member?" Mary jeered. "Save it, Catkin. I'm on to you now!"

Oob subsided, muttering like a pot of boiling mud.

"Matters are deteriorating, Mary," Roger told his companion in misfortune. "This Gom Blemp fellow—seems harmless enough—but he's an alien, not even from our galaxy! The flaws in the Matrix are bigger than I thought."

"But it's fascinating," Mary countered. "An alien culture! Think of how we both could benefit from an exchange of knowledge!"

"I've seen some strange things, lost in the Time Trap," Roger pursued his thesis. "But nothing as strange as Gom Blemp!"

"What about Catkin?" Mary persisted. "He's actually just as alien as Mr. Blemp."

"Yeah, I guess so," Roger conceded. "But he sort of blended: I mean, *he* never mentioned Vorplish."

"Why should he?" Mary asked, and seeing the alien in question exiting the building, approached him, asking briskly, "How old is your civilization? Ours is about six thousand years."

"Eh?" Gom Blemp seemed surprised at the question. "From the days of the early planetary explorations, I assume you mean? That would be almost forty thousand units, in your local reckoning. 'Six thousand years,' you say? Odd; we'd not noticed your activities until the present epoch."

"We didn't actually have space travel until quite recently," Mary elucidated. "I meant from the beginnings of civilization: writing, cities, money, lawyers, that sort of thing."

"As to that," Blemp responded uncertainly, "I fear we know little—all destroyed in the Wars, you know, when the planetary surfaces were mostly fused."

"How terrible," Mary remarked.

"Oh, you'll see for yourself," Blemp assured her. "You're just now approaching that exciting phase of your evolution. The pattern is unavoidable," he added, unemphatically. "Seen it a hundred times, starting with a minor world we called 'Splurch,' a name said to be derived from the sound evoked by a planet-wrecker striking atmosphere. Not much left. Pity. You simple folk seem to have made a promising start in a surprisingly brief period, but that's the way things are, eh? A culture begins to discover its powers of mutual destruction, and of course the urge to make use thereof is irresistible, so—*blooie!* or *splurch!*, and it's all back to square one!"

"You seem cheerful enough about it," Roger contributed.

"Of course," Blemp easily admitted. "*Our* time of strife is long past, it's merely *your* era of devastation we're talking about. Actually, I have an assignment from *Trivia Today* to describe your death agonies for the delectation of the masses. I 'timed' my arrival to enable me to observe the opening events of the inevitable holocaust; beyond precise calculation, you understand, so I'm quite pleased to have at least preceded the event. Damned uncomfortable if I'd come along just as the first hell-bombs were falling: nary a safe spot on the planet for organic life then, eh? But I made it with a comfortable margin—several centuries yet, or perhaps minutes; there are so many of your curiously arbitrary subdivisions of monolithic STV. A rational being finds it quite confusing: 'gigayears,' 'milliseconds,' and the like . . ."

"Skip that part," Roger dismissed the complaint. "You're saying that the entire Earth is on the verge of self-destruction, and all you're concerned about is your silly book report or whatever!"

"A report, sir," Blemp intoned, "which will be delivered along with the morning Gulpies to over ten trillion sentient beings. More, if you include such poor relations as the Rhox, the Vump, the Zilp, and perhaps the Bloont."

"Are you *all* ghouls, gloating over other people's agony?" Roger demanded. "Doesn't anyone care? Why not use your technology to help us avert this disaster?"

"There is indeed such a movement among the fuzzy-encephaloned," Blemp admitted. "But it has been successfully suppressed."

"Not quite!" a hard voice spoke up from an undefinable source. "Stand where you are, Gom Blemp! My jailers will take you in hand momentarily!"

A phalanx of blue-black beetles, poodle-sized this time, emerged from the nearest doorway and closed in around the little group. Oob yelped and attempted to flee; he was swarmed at once and wired to a tree.

"Does this mean," Roger called to the unseen speaker, "that you're here to help us?"

"That aspect of the operation is incidental," the Vrint boomed out. "Our purpose is to maintain the integrity of the Fabric, which requires that both Vorplish and its satellites remain aloof from this spatial aspect of STV for the present era. You are in luck, tiny being!"

"Vrint!" Gom Blemp blurted, "I abjure you to cease this meddling at once! You have no business here! Go home! Get on with it! Pay no attention to the locals; they're negligible!"

Roger ignored Blemp's insulting remark. To Mary he said in an aside. "This puts an entirely new face on matters. Up to now I've been concerned only with getting back home to Q'nell; now it seems that unless we can *do* something, we're all doomed to self-destruct. Any ideas?"

"Surely your friend UKR won't allow that," she suggested.

"How about it, UKR?" Roger called, with a glance upward toward the point whence the machine's voice always seemed to emanate. "Are you going to sit by and let it happen?" he challenged. "It's time to stop being coy, and *do* something that works!"

"Don't be pushy, Roger," Mary suggested, then, "Oh, Mr. Ucker, do be an old sweetie and prevent the collapse of everything."

CHAPTER TWENTY-TWO

EH, WHAT'S THAT? came the response. SORRY, I WASN'T PAYING ATTENTION. SPOT OF BOTHER WITH A SERIOUS EGO-DISPLACEMENT, ON YOUR VERY OWN FILAMENT, AS IT HAPPENS. SEEMS SOME OUTLAW FELLOW HAS DISAPPEARED AND HIS COHORTS ARE ABOUT TO PRECIPI-TATE A PRIVATE WAR. WHICH WILL LEAD, OR HAS LED, QUICKLY TO THE GENERAL COL-LAPSE OF SOCIETY. THEN, TO FURTHER COM-PLICATE MATTERS, ANOTHER CHAP HAS ACCIDENTALLY SLIPPED THROUGH THE ANEU-RISM LEFT BY THIS LEPKE'S TRANSFER, LEAV-ING BEHIND AN APPARENTLY LIFELESS BODY, INCREASING THE INTERPERSONAL STRESSES TO BURSTING POINT. MOST DISTRESSING. I'VE PUT A TRACER ON THE FELLOW LEPKE, AND IT APPEARS HE MERGED IDS WITH A FECK-LESS CHAP WHO HAPPENED TO BE ADRIFT IN THE ENTROPIC STREAM. IT WILL REQUIRE SE-RIOUS MEASURES TO SET THINGS BACK ON TRACK, DISMAL THOUGH THAT PROSPECT MAY BE: A SEMI-MAJOR TEMPORAL REVERSAL. I DON'T LIKE RESORTING TO SUCH DRACONIAN

MEASURES, BUT IT CAN'T BE HELPED. SO AS YOU WILL READILY UNDERSTAND, I SHALL BE QUITE FULLY OCCUPIED FOR SOME TIME— THOUGH NOT MORE THAN A CENTURY OR TWO (LOCAL SUBJECTIVE) I HOPE. *AUF WIEDER-SEHEN* FOR NOW, OLD CHAP, AND YOU, TOO, MRS. TOMKINS. UKR OVER AND OUT.

"Swell," Roger commented, bitterly. "No time to save the world, because some two-bit hood is in trouble."

"No, Roger," Mary chided. "I'm sure it's more than a gang rumble Mr. Ucker is talking about. Do try to be philosophical."

"I'm to be philosophical about having everything I've ever known and loved destroyed in a worldwide disaster of unspeakable nature?" Roger expostulated. "Think of it: no more big, juicy steaks, no more popcorn, no wines quietly maturing in their charred oaken kegs! No more starlit dawns, no voices mingled with laughter, singing the harvest home! No pretty girls, no gallant warriors, no sunshine filtering through leaves to cast their patterns on the velvet lawn! No more elegant chateaux surrounded by vast immaculate gardens. No cozy cottages in the sub-urbs with a shiny new car in the driveway, no new movies or old music. Imagine! Never again to hear *Nessun dorma*, or *Un bel di*! It's intolerable! And so much more—"

"That's sufficient, Roger," Mary told him. "I too shall mourn the passing of peer review, tenure, and faculty lunches, of course; but on the other hand, no more TV commercials about armpits, no shabby merchandise, no loudmouthed liars promising everything and delivering nothing—"

"Politicians *will* be small loss," Roger interjected.

"I was thinking of evangelists," Mary corrected. "No more cars breaking down on lonely roads in the rain—"

"That's how I met Q'nell!" Roger burst out. "And Oob too," he added. "It seems there's good and bad in every-thing, so it's not a simple matter to know what to ask for."

"No more quacks," Mary went on.

"No more falling in love," Roger contributed.

"No more headaches," Mary countered. "No fires on the hearth in winter."

"No spring," Roger complained.

"No head colds," Mary reminded him.

"Dammit!" Roger snapped. "No moonlit lagoons under a tropic moon!"

"No liberals, bitching about colonialism," Mary pointed out.

"No more libraries full of man's accumulated knowledge," Roger groaned.

"No more illiterates ignoring all that knowledge," Mary amended. "No more pronouncing caramel as 'carmel,' nobody talking about 'counterparts,' or 'viable alternatives,' or saying 'on balance,' or 'the congress' instead of 'Congress,' or saying 'eyether' instead of 'either'; we'll never again hear some ignoramus use 'fortuitous' as if it were a fancy new way to say 'fortunate,' nor 'plethora' as if it just meant 'plenty,' without the connotation of a disastrous overabundance, nor 'dollars' instead of 'money,' nor use 'media' as a singular noun, nor a thousand other irritating ignorantisms."

"There *is* that. But it's scant compensation for losing Van Gogh and Puccini and Clark Gable and restored Deusenbergs . . ." His voice trailed off.

"But, also no Picasso or Matisse, no acid rock, no *Bell Song* from *Lahkme*, no overrated Chaplin, no Edsel, and so much more."

"Sorry," Roger grumped. "I can't drum up any enthusiasm for all the misery I've done without: I could have been born with no limbs, but I don't rejoice that I wasn't. I could have been killed in the war, but the thought that I lived to get into this mess doesn't make me happy. I guess that's not very philosophical of me."

"But very human," Mary reassured him. "But just think: no more war, poverty, laziness, greed, or hypocrisy; no confiscatory taxes to punish the industrious; no starvation, no ignorance, no sickness, no moronic petty officials interfering with their betters—"

"Yes, that's a comforting thought. All those paper-pushers pushing their way into oblivion. Nice. Still, I'd like to kiss Q'nell in the moonlight, down by the shore when the orchestra's playing, and even the palms seem to be swaying. . . ."

"No more silly song-lyrics," Mary put in. "No more terrible restaurants where the service is even worse than the food."

"No model sailboats on the pond in the park," Roger mourned. "No pond; no park. You know, Mary, we had quite a lot of good things we didn't appreciate enough. For every bad restaurant in Hicktown, USA, there was a great one in France. Don't get me wrong: I'm no slavish admirer of all things French, but you couldn't find a bad restaurant there if you tried. I remember a little place we found one day on a bicycle tour of the countryside; sort of sunk into the ground, and rose-vines growing all around the door. I think it actually had a dirt floor. We took a table by the window. There was a planting-box on the sill, with geraniums. Van Gogh could have painted it. And the chow!" *Quiver.*

Mary buttered a piece she had torn from one of the hard rolls in the basket and took a sip of red wine between nibbles. "Ummm," she murmured. "I didn't realize I was so hungry, Roger."

"Uh-oh," Roger grunted. "I was talking about finding a bad restaurant: I hope . . ."

"You didn't find it," Mary reassured him, sipping a spoonful of her soup. "It's marvelous. Do eat, Roger, we don't know how long—"

Roger complied. "It's strange," he remarked contentedly, "how often when I accidentally actualize a locus, it's a restaurant."

"Good thing, too," Mary told him. "Actually, I hadn't had a good meal in years. The folk fed on well-rotted squirrels and bitter roots, and overripe or green berries, but I had to search a long time to find a stand of wild celery or a fig tree, or catch a live squirrel I could clean and cook. That was one of the things about me they couldn't understand: they were much impressed when I shared my food with the Fire God. After a while some of them started to do the same."

CHAPTER TWENTY-THREE

"Ye Gods!" Roger exclaimed. "*You* invented cooking!"

"Not really," Mary demurred modestly. "I learned it from my mother."

"Sure," Roger agreed. "After it was passed down by your friend Dunt or somebody to *her* kid, et cetera."

"Roger," Mary objected mildly. "You make it sound as if I influenced the whole course of human cultural development."

Roger was nodding vigorously. "Right," he said flatly. "That's why we have to be careful what we do when we're in a locus where we don't belong."

"You mean all this jumping around is just time-travel? Everybody we see either has happened or will happen?"

"Not quite that simple," Roger corrected. "We move in space, too. Now we're in France any time in the past couple of centuries, but it's our jumps in the vug dimension that are creating most of the upset to the Matrix."

"I remember a fellow named Andy Scute," Mary remarked thoughtfully. "That was when I was in Faggotsby. He was an odd one, seemed to sense that he and I had something in common; I gave him a job as a handyman. Most people were afraid of him. It's pretty clear in retrospect that he was another displaced person from the future. It's odd both of us should wind up in the precise same STV locus, don't you think?"

"Not really," Roger pontificated. "I think we're being manipulated by UKR, to rearrange the warp and woof to correct the flaws that have built up in the Fabric."

"Is that the same as the Matrix?" Mary asked.

"Not quite," Roger informed her. "The matrix is poly-dimensional; 'the Fabric' refers mainly to the common-place structure of STV we think of as here/now, and its extensions, future and past. 'The Matrix' is a concept that includes at least a dozen other dimensions, including the vug." Roger paused to deal with his Chateaubriand.

"Tell me about the vug dimension," Mary appealed.

"Well," Roger temporized, "it's not all that simple; but, by analogy: Space is expanding, but otherwise stationary, at least on the small scale; we can move about freely in all three dimensions of it. Time, on the other hand, is in constant undirectional movement, but we're stuck in its single dimension, and can't change the rate or direction of our movement (except, of course when we step outside the Fabric, like *we*'ve done). Vug is flowing, like time, but we can move around in it, like space. Things aren't fixed and immutable in vug. All sorts of influences can modify our relationship to vug. That's why things disap-pear and are never seen again, and why psychics can foretell coming events—sometimes—and lots of other lit-tle odd, inexplicable things that happen."

"Like our getting mixed up in all this in the first place," Mary contributed. Roger nodded, chewing. He raised an eyebrow and the waiter was at his side.

"Please refill madam's glass," Roger requested. "No telling when we'll have another chance at an exceptional little vintage like this," he pointed out.

"Oh, dear," Mary sighed. "You're *not* one of those dreadful snobs who talk about 'playful little vintages,' and 'noses' and being 'a good traveler,' I *do* hope."

"Nope," Roger reassured her. "If I like it, it's a great wine. If I don't, skip it."

Mary sipped. "It's not at all fruity," she commented, "and I find it quite endearing."

"Now *you*'re doing it," Roger charged.

"Just trying to describe it," she replied. "But hadn't we better get on with saving the world? Look!" she interrupted herself. "There's one of those horrid bugs!" She pointed. The waiter noticed and promptly stepped on the tiny creature.

"Oh, oh," Roger muttered. "That was a bad move, I fear."

A lean, middle-aged man wearing a frock coat of a familiar shiny blue-black had entered the restaurant; he came directly across to Roger's and Mary's table.

"See here," he said in impeccable English. "I can't have you people going about destroying my field units." He halted, staring down at Roger with an unmistakable hostile expression.

"Are you, by any chance, connected with the Vrint, sir?" Roger inquired prudently. The stranger nodded curtly. "I *am* the Vrint," he stated grandly. "I've chosen this embodiment as one less likely to precipitate disorder than my usual efficient form."

Roger refrained from inviting the fellow to join them. Instead, he barked, "Why do you blame us for your bug's demise? We've been sitting right here, bothering no one."

"You drew attention to the harmless unit," Vrint charged. "Most others of your race can't ordinarily perceive them, you know. They see simply ordinary insects. The vram charge you've built up with your irresponsible gallivanting has endowed you with heightened perceptions."

"I wouldn't know how to 'gallivant' if I wanted to," Roger dismissed the charge. "And I don't want to: all I want is to go home and live out a peaceful life with Q'nell."

"Then why, in Heaven's name, don't you?" the Vrint demanded.

"I don't know how," Roger told him. "And in addition,

there's a little job of world-saving I need to attend to first."

"You refer to this, your own miserable, underachieving locus?" the Vrint inquired as if amazed. "Why save *this*? It's profoundly flawed, you know."

"Roger," Mary spoke up, "I understood you to say it was this Vrint person who was the threat to all we hold dear."

"I was a bit confused at the time," Roger explained. "At first I assumed—"

"Purely on the basis of appearances!" the Vrint put in.

"—that the beetles were the threat," Roger finished.

"Where," the Vrint demanded, "did you obtain that false impression?"

"Gom Blemp told me!" Roger reminded the machine.

"Oh, *that* meddler!" The Vrint dismissed the matter, and fell silent for a moment. "I've just been chatting with my colleague, UKR," he resumed, "and he pointed out—"

"*Your* colleague!" Roger yelled. "he's *our* colleague, if he's anybody's!"

"No, little being," the alien corrected patiently, "UKR is, like myself, a second-order entity. You are at best his client."

"That's not what UKR said! UKR! Speak up and straighten this fellow out!"

HE IS ESSENTIALLY CORRECT, UKR boomed. I CAN ASSIST YOU IN YOUR ENDEAVORS ONLY INSOFAR AS THOSE EFFORTS DO NOT OPPOSE ORDERLY UNFOLDMENT OF THE MATRIX, WHICH THE VRINT IS WORKING TO RESTORE.

"Swell!" Roger snarled. "Some pal you are! How about at least explaining what's going on here—or wherever?"

VERY WELL, came the voice from above—or not actually "above," Roger corrected his thinking. It just *seemed* to be spatially displaced in an "up" direction; actually it was coming from the vug dimension . . .

Mary's hand gripped Roger's arm. "It still scares me to hear ghostly voices coming from nowhere," she confided.

"Not ghostly," Roger corrected. "UKR's just a being of another order; he's not a spook. And not 'voices'—there's just the one voice, unless you want to count the Vrint's."

"I *do* count it," Mary confirmed. "Roger, you seem to at least partially understand all this: can't you *do* something?"

"I did," Roger replied a trifle smugly. "I asked UKR to explain what's going on."

"He didn't reply," Mary pointed out.

"He will," Roger assured her. "Remember his time scale doesn't match ours. Sometimes one of his moments equals twelve years of *our* time."

"That's not very encouraging," Mary commented, and herself called, "UKR! *Please* speak up, tell us what to do! Please!" Then she began to cry.

"Ordinarily, that would be good tactics," Roger said, "but I don't think UKR is wired to respond to feminine hysteria."

"That's redundant," Mary told him, " 'Hysteria' means 'essentially female.' Think of 'hysterectomy.' "

"'Par' me, perfesser," Roger said sardonically.

I DO INDEED RESPOND TO THE DISTRESS OF THE INNOCENT, UKR supplied. OK, HERE GOES, TO RECAP: THE GIANT BRAINS OF CULTURE ONE DECIDED TO CREATE A CHANNEL OF ACCESS TO THE MANIFOLD, OR MATRIX IF YOU PREFER, THUS VIOLATING THE PRISTINE MENISCUS WHICH HAD HELD STV TO AN ORDERLY UNIDIRECTIONAL ENFOLDMENT SINCE THE ORIGINAL EVENT, OR BIG BANG IF YOU PREFER.

"Never mind the choice of terms," Roger yelled. "Just stick to what we can understand, and get on with it. I know all about the Trans-Temporal Bore. Well, not *all* about it—"

"Roger, please," Mary squeaked. "Do be quiet."

"Well," Roger muttered, "if that's all the thanks I get for trying—"

"Hush," Mary said sweetly.

TO CONTINUE, UKR resumed. THIS DISASTROUS UNDERTAKING SEVERELY COMPROMISED THE ENTROPIC/SPATIAL INTEGRITY, ALLOWING ALL SORTS OF OBJECTS, LANDSCAPES, PHENOMENA, AND PERSONNEL TO STRAY FROM THEIR NATURAL PARAMETERS—OR "WARP AND WOOF" IF YOU PREFER—INTO NON-NATIVE LOCI FAR REMOVED FROM THE ORIGINAL AXIS OF THE BORE. THIS CONSTITUTES A CLASS THREE ANOMALY, CALLING FOR INTERVENTION BY THE BUILDER ITSELF! INASMUCH AS YOUR OWN PARTICIPATION IN THIS PROGRESSIVE DEGRADATION OF THE MATRIX WAS INADVERTENT, I DOUBT IT WILL HOLD YOU CULPABLE. IT'S A JUST ENTITY, THE BUILDER.

"Which reminds me," Roger spoke up boldly, "that both Professor Tomkins and myself are participants in the compound being you call the Builder, which entitles us to double consideration! Plus some respect and assistance from a mere second-order machine constructed by the Builder specifically for the purpose of lending aid to victims of blundering in high places."

Mary's restraining touch on his arm dissuaded Roger from further expatiation on his theme.

YOU TRY ME SORELY, ROGER, UKR intoned. I REMIND YOU THAT I HAVE SUBSTANTIVE MATTERS TO WHICH TO ATTEND. KINDLY EXCUSE ME.

Roger called again, but he knew it was futile; UKR was gone. He could *feel* the absence of the potent mechanical personality.

"Well, I guess I loused it up again," he told Mary apologetically. "Just as he was explaining what's going on, too."

"Never mind," Mary comforted him gently. "He was talking nonsense. I *hate* jargon, *all* jargons!"

"Me, too," Roger seconded. "How about critics' lingo:

'actorly,' 'architectonic' (medicine for sick draftsmen?), 'a painterly style,' 'passages of brushwork,' 'rhythmic lines' 'nice use of values,' all that gobbledegook . . . ?"

"Dreadful," Mary agreed. "But archaeologists, bless their hearts, are worse: they should be prohibited by law from naming anything in English. 'The Cave of the Heifer's Outwash'; pardon me, but who cares how old the cow was? And excuse me, but it sounds as if she had a bad case of diarrhea. 'A plaque of schist' means a piece of flat stone. That tacky French spelling makes it worse."

Roger nodded. "Since you're an archaeologist," he responded, "perhaps you can tell me why so many of your colleagues have names that are English words: 'Marsh' and 'Cope' in the American west, 'Dart' and 'Broom' and 'Brain' in South Africa, 'Leaky' and 'White' at Olduvai, 'Black' in Asia, and so on."

"Just a minor coincidence," Mary told him. "There are lots more, lesser-known ones. Do you suppose it has some cosmic significance?"

"Could be," Roger offered. "Once you start examining the warp and woof, you find out that *every* trivial event affects *all* subsequent events, everywhere. That's why our wandering around in all these random loci can cause large-scale disaster. We *have* to get clear of this!"

"Gladly," Mary agreed. "Just how do we do that, Roger?"

"Why am *I* appointed world-saver?" Roger carped. "*You're* the professor!"

"Unfortunately, my area of expertise seems to be quite irrelevant to the situation," she replied.

"Maybe not," Roger said eagerly. "Let's analyze things, and maybe we'll come up with an idea!"

"Let's start with your superhuman friend UKR," Mary suggested. "You say he's helped you in difficult situations. Why not now?"

Roger rubbed his unshaven jaw thoughtfully. "I don't know," he admitted. "I suppose it has something to do with the problyon flux."

"Try again," Mary prompted.

"He said he was bored, and then he disappeared," Roger reminded her. "I'm afraid he's deserted us."

HARDLY, ROGER, the disembodied voice of UKR spoke up. I WAS CALLED AWAY TO MEND A DISASTER ON ANOTHER DIRAC LEVEL.

"Oh," Roger replied in a sarcastic tone. "And who was it who was so much more important than us?"

YOU, ROGER, UKR told him. ON ANOTHER ENTROPIC TENDRIL, OF COURSE.

"Me?" Roger yelled. "What are you talking about? I'm right here—I've been right here all along!"

JUST HOW WOULD YOU DEFINE "RIGHT HERE," ROGER? UKR inquired implacably.

"Well," Roger temporized, " 'Here,' is well, *here*! Where I *am*! What else?"

PLEASE, ROGER, UKR returned. CONSIDER: THE NUMBER OF FIBERS CONSTITUTING THE COSMIC ALL IS INFINITE. YOU EXIST—UP TO A POINT—IN ALL OF THEM.

"What's this 'up to a point'?" Roger demanded.

ON SOME ENERGY LEVELS, YOU HAVE NOT BEEN SO FORTUNATE AS ON THIS PARTICULAR PORTION OF THE SKEIN, UKR told him. STILL, YOU SURVIVE ON MOST LINES, AND THIS CANNOT BE CONSIDERED A TOTALLY NEGLIGIBLE FACTOR. THE SAME, I MIGHT ADD, APPLIES TO MARY TOMKINS.

"What's that s'posta mean?" Roger yelled, feeling sick.

"Your demise has been various and colorful, Roger," the great machine supplied, in a normal conversational tone.

"You mean, I'm really dead—somewhere?" Roger croaked.

TO BE SURE, UKR confirmed, returning to the oracular mode. BUT BE NOT DISTRESSED, DEAR BOY: YOUR PRIMARY THREAD OF IDENTITY REMAINS INTACT—FOR YET A LITTLE WHILE.

"Yeah?" Roger challenged. "How— I mean, what killed me?"

MANY AND VARIOUS ARE YOUR DEATHS, ROGER, AND YOURS TOO, MARY, the machine assured them cheerfully. "ON THE BOTTOM IN SIXTEEN FATHOM O' GREEN WATER"; "LOST OFF TORTUGA IN THE SEVENTY-EIGHT."

"I drowned?" Roger croaked. "Why didn't you *do* something?"

IT WAS OF COURSE NECESSARY FOR ME TO BE SELECTIVE, UKR replied calmly. I MADE A POINT OF RESCUING YOU FROM THE MORE AGONIZING FORMS OF EXPIRATION. BURNING ALIVE, SLOW SUFFOCATION, THAT SORT OF THING: AND NATURALLY, ALL FATAL THREATS IN THIS, THE CORE LINE.

"Name *one*!" Roger demanded. "Tell me *one* time you rescued me!"

WHEN YOU WERE THREE LOCAL CYCLES OF AGE, the voice supplied. ON A PICNIC, YOU ATTEMPTED TO PICK UP A PRETTY CORAL SNAKE. I SNATCHED YOU AWAY. YOU YELLED ALL THE WAY HOME. THAT SORT OF MEDDLING IS OF COURSE QUITE CONTRARY TO REGS, BUT I SUPPOSE I HAVE EXCESSIVE SYMPATHY FOR YOUR UNFORTUNATE KIND; ENDOWED AS IT IS WITH THE CAPACITY TO PERCEIVE A HINT OF THE MAJESTY OF FIRST-ORDER EXISTENCE, BUT FOREVER CONDEMNED TO STRUGGLE IN VAIN TO ATTAIN THAT EXALTED STATE. INSTEAD YOU DISSIPATE YOUR FINEST ENERGIES IN USELESS ATTEMPTS TO PEER ROUND THE CORNERS OF TIME AND TO PENETRATE THE VEILS OF VUG. IT IS FOR THAT REASON THAT I HAVE REPEATEDLY INTERVENED TO PRESERVE YOUR BRAVE BUT FUTILE LIFE AS A VIABLE STRAND IN THE FABRIC.

"Oh, you've saved my life a lot, have you?" Roger retorted in a tone which doubted it.

DO YOU RECALL A TIME, ROGER, UKR resumed,

WHEN YOU TOOK A SHORTCUT ACROSS AN
UNTILLED FIELD OF TALL, DRY VEGETATION
AND WERE SO CLEVER AS TO GET YOUR
MACHINE STUCK IN A HIDDEN, WEED-CHOKED
GULLY? YOU SOON NOTED DENSE SMOKE
GUSTING FROM THE REGISTERS OF YOUR
WHISPER-AIRE COOLING SYSTEM AND SAW
FLAMES BESIDE YOUR WINDOW?

"Sure, I remember that," Roger agreed, "but I got out
of there in a hurry—"

HAVE YOU EVER WONDERED HOW YOU
WERE ABLE TO PASS THROUGH A WALL OF
FIRE SIX FEET IN HEIGHT? UKR inquired blandly.

"I *did*, as a matter of fact," Roger conceded. "I remember
seeing the flames, and the next thing I remember was
walking away from the car, listening to the tires go *plop!*
one by one. That was about the closest call I ever had,
I guess," he added soberly.

NOT QUITE, UKR corrected. ONCE, AT AGE SIX,
YOU NEARLY DROWNED, WHEN THE RAFT YOU
WERE PLAYING ON WAS CAUGHT IN AN OFF-
SHORE CURRENT, AND HAD DRIFTED NEARLY
OUT OF SIGHT OF THE SHORE BEFORE YOUR
MOTHER NOTICED AND SENT A SWIMMER OUT
TO PUSH THE RAFT BACK TO SHORE. THAT
SWIMMER WAS MYSELF, OF COURSE.

"It was *not*," Roger contradicted. "It was my big third
cousin or something, Johnny!"

ARE YOU QUITE CERTAIN OF THAT? UKR per-
sisted. OR DID HE PERHAPS MERELY RESEMBLE
JOHNNY? AS YOU'LL RECALL I CAN APPEAR
BEFORE YOU IN ANY CORPORAL GUISE I WISH.

"Wow!" Roger breathed. "Thanks a lot, UKR. I remember
how scared I was. I learned to swim the next summer."

DO YOU RECALL, UKR queried, AN OCCASION
WHEN YOU PURCHASED TWO ONE-BY-TEN
PLANKS TO REPAIR THE PORCH FLOOR, AND
HAVING NO OTHER SPACE, LOADED THEM IN
YOUR CAR (THE BACK WINDOWS BEING OPEN)

BY PLACING THEM TRANSVERSELY ACROSS BOTH WINDOWSILLS, WITH THE ENDS PROTRUDING?

"Oh, yeah," Roger agreed. "Kind of sloppy-looking, but it was the only way I could get 'em in."

YOU IMAGINED THE UPPER PLANK, RESTING FLAT ON THE LOWER, WAS RESTRAINED BY THE VERTICAL C-PILLAR; ACTUALLY, IT WAS SHORT, AND ITS OPPOSITE END PROJECTED EIGHTEEN INCHES OUT THE RIGHT SIDE. AS A VELOCITY OF FORTY MILES PER "HOUR," YOU PASSED A ROW OF MAILBOXES—

"Right; a rock truck damn near ran me off the road."

HAD YOU SWERVED ANOTHER SIX INCHES, UKR continued implacably, THE PROJECTING END OF THE PLANK WOULD HAVE STRUCK THE MAIL-BOX, AND THE LEFT END WOULD HAVE PIVOTED FORWARD AND DECAPITATED YOU IN A SPECTACULARLY UNTIDY FASHION; I NUDGED YOU AWAY FROM THE MAILBOXES.

"Stop!" Roger croaked. "You're making me feel sick!" He paused to retch experimentally. "I never knew I'd been in danger of being killed so many times."

THAT CIRCUMSTANCE, UKR intoned, PALES TO INSIGNIFICANCE IN COMPARISON WITH THE UNLIKELINESS OF YOUR EXISTENCE IN THE FIRST PLACE.

CHAPTER TWENTY-FOUR

"Huh?" Roger grunted.

CONSIDER; FIRST IT WAS NECESSARY FOR A LIVING-SURFACE—YOUR PLANET—TO COME INTO EXISTENCE UNDER THE PRECISE CONDITIONS THAT WOULD MAKE THE APPEARANCE OF LIFE POSSIBLE. A FEW PERCENTAGE POINTS LARGER, OR SMALLER, OR CLOSER TO OR FARTHER FROM A SUN OF EXACTLY THE PROPER CHARACTERISTICS, AND THAT FIRST LIVING-SURFACE WOULD HAVE LINGERED IN THE REALM OF THE UNREALIZED. THEN, YOUR PERSONAL GENE-LINE WAS REQUIRED TO SURVIVE OVER THREE BILLION TEARS OF COMPETITIVE EVOLUTION, AND AT LAST, AFTER THOUSANDS OF GENERATIONS OF HUMAN PROPAGATION, THE ONLY TWO INDIVIDUALS WHOSE GENETIC ENDOWMENTS COULD HAVE PRODUCED PRECISELY YOU, HAD TO FIND EACH OTHER, SURMOUNT FORMIDABLE SOCIAL ATTITUDES, AND INDEED CONCEIVE AND BEAR YOU. THE ODDS AGAINST IT ARE RIDICULOUS. IN ANY MEANINGFUL SENSE, THE THING IS IMPOSSIBLE.

"Then . . . how . . . ? Roger stuttered.

THE BUILDER INTERVENEND AT MANY POINTS, UKR told him. YOU DIDN'T IMAGINE, ALONG WITH CERTAIN FELLOWS WHO CALL THEM-SELVES "SCIENTISTS," THAT IT WAS ALL COIN-CIDENCE, SURELY?

"Well, I never really thought about it," Roger con-ceded. "I always thought talking about how perfectly we, or any organism fits the environment was like saying 'it's lucky my legs are the exact length they are, or my feet wouldn't reach the ground.'"

I AM FOREVER AMAZED AT THE GULLIBILITY OF THOSE OF YOUR KIND WHO EXPLAIN ALL THE MULTITUDINOUS MANIFESTATIONS OF THE BUILDER'S ACUMEN AS ACCIDENTAL, UKR con-tributed. YOU LOOK FOR EXPLANATIONS ACCES-SIBLE TO YOUR RELATIVELY MINUTE HUMAN INTELLECT. FAILING TO FIND THESE, YOU DIS-MISS THE MATTER AS INEXPLICABLE, PER-VERSE, OR MEANINGLESS.

"Wait a minute," Roger put in. "Are you saying all this confusion poor Mary and I are mixed up in—and Bob and Rusty and the others, too—actually is part of some grand scheme? I don't believe it!"

CONSIDER, UKR directed, THE TIME YOU TOOK A SHORTCUT DOWN AN UNPAVED FARM ROAD, AND ENCOUNTERED A LARGE AND AGGRES-SIVE DOG, WHICH CHARGED YOU, BARKING FURIOUSLY, UNTIL ITS TWENTY-FOOT CHAIN BROUGHT IT UP SHORT BARELY A FOOT FROM YOUR SHIN?

"Sure," Roger agreed. "The old dame that owned it called it back and apologized: said he didn't mean any harm."

HAD THE CREATURE STRUCK YOU, WEIGHING NINETY POUNDS AS IT DID, YOU WOULD HAVE BEEN KNOCKED DOWN, UKR told Roger. INSTINCT WOULD HAVE CAUSED THE DOG TO GO FOR YOUR THROAT: A SUPINE VICTIM IS IRRESISTIBLY

STIMULATING TO THE CANINE KILLER INSTINCT. MRS. GROGGIT WOULD HAVE BEEN MOST UPSET WHEN SHE PHONED THE SHERIFF TO REPORT THE DEAD BURGLAR. IT WAS I WHO SHORTENED THE CHAIN, OF COURSE.

"H-how many times?" Roger croaked, "have I nearly been killed?"

INNUMERABLE, UKR answered shortly. LIVING IS AN EXCEEDINGLY DANGEROUS ENTERPRISE. I, MYSELF, THOUGH A MECHANICAL CONTRIVANCE, HAVE HAD A NUMBER OF CLOSE CALLS.

"What about me?" Mary put in. "Have I been in danger of death?"

EVERY TIME YOU DROVE A CAR OR FLEW IN A COMMERCIAL AIRLINER, UKR confirmed crisply. INDEED, EVERY TIME YOU CROSSED A STREET, OR EVEN WENT INTO YOUR KITCHEN. EXPLODING PRESSURE COOKERS ALONE—

"I see," Mary said, with a little shudder. "And I have you to thank for my survival?"

I, OR ANOTHER AGENCY OF THE BUILDER.

"You mean—the Builder is God?" Roger gasped.

NOT PRECISELY, UKR corrected. NOT AS YOU EMPLOY THE NAME. YOUR CONCEPTION OF GOD IS SERIOUSLY FLAWED, he went on, BUT IT IS NOT TO BE EXPECTED THAT YOUR PETTY MIND COULD CONCEPTUALIZE THE INFINITE.

"This is all getting too serious for me," Roger contributed. "I started to tune the TV, and end up deep in a theological puzzle."

DON'T BE UPSET, ROGER, UKR directed. YOU WILL UNDERSTAND AS MUCH AS IS NECESSARY—

"Necessary for what?" Roger yelled.

TO DO WHAT YOU MUST DO, UKR told him.

"Yeah? And just what might that be?" Roger demanded.

I SHOULD THINK THAT WOULD BE APPARENT BY NOW, the disembodied voice reprimanded sharply.

Mary spoke up timidly. "Couldn't you just let us see you?" she appealed. "You voice without a body is quite unnerving."

YOU PEOPLE HAVE CONCEIVED SECOND-ORDER ENTITIES IN MANY FORMS, UKR pointed out.

"Oh, you mean like the benign old gentleman with a big white beard, sitting on a cloud, rescuing fainting robins and all that," Mary supplied.

NO, UKR corrected. I WAS THINKING OF UK-HOR-ROZ, AND DAGON, AND SIVA—ALL THAT LOT. ONE HARDLY KNOWS WHICH YOU WOULD PREFER.

"Whatever do those ugly idols have in common?" Mary asked, then shied as a fanged, six-armed being appeared, squatting a few feet away. It had a sagging, elephantine hide of a particularly offensive shade of green. It leered at the professor with a giant blood-red eye sat above a noseless nostril, from which it was plucking a curling red hair.

"Not that one," Mary declared.

OH. UKR's voice issued from between the six-inch yellow fangs. SORRY AND ALL THAT. FREDDY'S ONE OF THE MORE BENIGN OF YOUR HUMAN DEITIES; SELDOM EATS HUMAN FLESH.

Freddy winked out of existence, to be replaced by a cow-sized toad of dull slime-yellow, with a yard-wide mouth that opened in a yawn like the entrance to Mammoth Cave.

"No!" Mary spoke up sharply, just in time, she realized, as the cave walls that had begun to coalesce around her position faded back into potentiality.

"Don't you have any nice ones?" Mary appealed.

PERHAPS ONE OF THE ASVINS, UKR's voice, once again disembodied, suggested. There was a *plop!* of displaced air and a slim, girlish figure stood before them, scantily clad in a wisp of chiffon. She turned to look directly at Mary. Her eyes, Mary saw, were like glowing coals. Her delicately formed lips parted in a smile, revealing stainless-steel fangs.

Mary said "Ulp!" and moved closer to Roger.

I SHALL BE GLAD TO ASSIST YOU, MY DEAR, the demon told Mary in UKR's voice. JUST AS SOON AS YOU DEMONSTRATE YOUR REVERENCE FOR ME BY KILLING AND EATING THAT INSIGNIFI-CANT-LOOKING CHAP BESIDE YOU.

"You mean ... Roger?" Mary wailed, then, "Never! Mr. Ucker, stop it! Can't you just look normal?"

The slim demon grew blurry and winked out, leaving in her place a three-hundred-pound nude male ogre with a shaven skull, who grinned at her through broken teeth.

"I said 'normal'!" Mary cried indignantly.

BOB'S AS NORMAL AS CAN BE. UKR paused, to allow Bob to spit, then explained. BOB'S BILLED AS THE DEATH-GOD IN VEGAS. DOING A TWO-WEEK GIG AT THE CHATEAU JUST NOW. WHAT IS IT YOU DON'T LIKE ABOUT HIM? Bob sat smiling gently at Mary, awaiting her reply.

"Why, actually," Mary gobbled, "it's merely that you're so naked. Couldn't you put some clothes on?"

SURE THING, KID, UKR replied. Bob rose, while Mary averted her eyes; he stepped behind a bush, to emerge a moment later wearing a pale pink tutu. He did a clumsy plié and looked at Mary, as if awaiting praise.

"But there's supposed to be more to it than just a tutu," Mary objected. Bob nodded, visited his dressing-bush again, and came out wearing cowboy chaps below the tutu. STILL NO GO, HUH? he said gloomily, observing Mary's expression.

He returned modestly to his bush and added a vest to his ensemble, then went back for a pair of hip boots.

"Look here, Bob," Roger spoke up. "Can't you put some pants on?"

SURE THING, PAL, UKR's voice agreed readily. Bob stepped from view and reappeared in a set of lumpy long-johns, worn over the rest of his costume.

"The flap's supposed to be in the back," Roger said shortly. "And button it," he added. Bob complied.

NOW, YOU WERE SAYING, UKR prompted.

"I was saying a lot of things!" Roger came back hotly. "But it all boils down to 'Get us out of this and back home, safe and sound!'"

YOU MEAN RIGHT NOW? Bob's expression reflected UKR's amazement. JUST AS IT IS? I HAVEN'T YET FINISHED TIDYING UP, YOU KNOW.

"Right now," Roger confirmed crisply.

Mary objected, "Roger, perhaps we ought to think about it, if Mr. UKR isn't ready!"

"What do I care?" Roger dismissed the complaint. "Let's go, UKR, hurry up!"

YOUR ORIGINAL LOCUS HAS BEEN CON-SIGNED TO THE REALM OF THE PARADOXIAL-AND-THUS-NEVER-TO-BE-REALIZED, Bob told him apologetically. STILL, I SHALL DO THE NEXT BEST: I'LL SHUNT YOU TO THE STATE WHICH WOULD HAVE EVENTUATED HAD YOUR MED-DLING NOT ABORTED ITS DEVELOPMENT.

"*My* meddling?" Roger yelled. "Back to that again, eh? You know damn well, UKR, all I've done is try to get out of this mess you've gotten me into and get back to poor Q'nell!"

AT THE MOMENT, UKR stated dispiritedly, POOR Q'NELL IS, AH, NOT AT LIBERTY—"

"Stop that!" Roger commanded. "Get me to her, *now*!"

"Roger," Mary spoke up anxiously. "Shouldn't you know a little more before—"

"Now, I said!" Roger yelled.

The light failed. Mary clutched Roger's arm. The darkness was not complete; there was a feeble glow from a melted-down candle guttering in a chipped saucer on a table at the center of the cell. It provided just enough illumination to reveal Q'nell, still dressed in the negligee in which Roger had last seen her, lying asleep on a rude bench bolted to the stone wall of the ten-by-ten dungeon.

"Q'nell!" Roger croaked and made a move toward her, to be brought up short by a rusty chain attached to his ankle, which was rubbed raw and bleeding by the corroded metal gyves. He got to his feet, assisted by Mary, likewise chained to the wall. He thrust her aside.

"Better act a little more aloof, professor," he suggested. "Q'nell's not good about 'other women.'"

"Why, the very idea," Mary said calmly. "I *happen* to be a happily married woman."

"Are you *really*?" Roger challenged. "This Fred of yours; is he dashing, handsome, passionate, talented, considerate, or smart?"

"Of course not," Mary replied fondly. "He's quite normal. By the way," she wandered from the subject, "you *could* have provided a more comfortable setting for us to spend the next couple of eternities in."

"It just so happened this is where Q'nell is," Roger told her.

"Of course," Mary replied mildly. "And now what will you do?"

"It amazes me," Roger snapped, "how you can jump from the sublime to the trivial without batting an eyelash. Still, I suppose you're right: we might as well be more comfortable. How about the Presidential penthouse suite atop the Chateau, in Vegas?" *Quiver.*

"I detest gambling," Mary sniffed. "It's all so foolish."

"Life's a gamble," Roger said mindlessly.

"Everyone knows all those casinos are businesses which exist to make a profit," Mary persisted. "The percentage of payoff is set well in advance. The customers exist only to supply the cash flow."

"I guess that's about right," Roger conceded. "Still, instead of spending big money on ad campaigns, they arrange for big payoffs at regular intervals; no telling when you might luck into one of those."

DON'T BE SILLY, ROGER, UKR spoke up, startling Roger just as he was drawing the drapes back from the incredible view of desert from the tower windows. He shied and knocked over a side table. At once there was a peremptory hammering at the door. He waded across the ankle-deep carpet and opened the door to admit a grizzled old fellow with the battered features of a former contender.

"Aw right," the ex-pug growled as he hitched up his pants with his thumbs. "No vandalism will not be-alloweded inna room."

"Suits me, pal," Roger replied breezily. "Anything else?" The security guard brushed past him without replying. He took two strides and stopped flat-footed, staring at Mary who was just opening one of the suitcases on the luggage stand. She held up a wispy nightie and turned in surprise to see the stranger eyeing her.

"Par' me, lady," he growled. "Name's Pete." He offered a well-manicured paw, which Mary touched lightly. Pete turned to Roger.

"No dames inna room, Bud," he muttered. Just then Q'nell stirred and sat up in the big brocaded chair where she had been slumped. "Especially not *two* dames," Pete added.

"These ladies are not 'dames,'" Roger snorted.

"Yeah?" Pete muttered, eyeing Q'nell's fine and lightly clad figure. "Then I guess I got ahold of some wrong ideas about anatomy!"

"How dare you ogle my wife?" Roger demanded.

"Wife, huh?" Pete mused. "Then who's the other dame?"

"I told you, Professor Tomkins is no 'dame,'" Roger huffed.

"Well, I like *that*," Mary snorted in a ladylike way.

"No, bub, I di'n't mean—" Pete started.

"Out," Roger ordered tersely, then muttered to the A/C outlet overhead, "Take care of this, UKR, if you have any sense of responsibility at all."

Mary had turned her back and was rummaging through the suitcase. Pete reached for Roger, but was blocked off by a bandy-legged, huge-paunched goblin with a warty purple hide and four three-inch fangs, which he showed Pete in a scowl that drove the bouncer back like a straight right to the midriff.

"Hey!" Pete objected. "Who's this guy? I ain't even *seen* him!"

"I'm the guy who'd just as soon toss you out the window as the door, Sucker," UKR growled in a low tone. "Get lost. Tell the boss. Tyson is indisposed to be harassed just now; and the professor requires separate quarters."

"Right troo duh door, Fats," Pete retorted gamely. "Say," he went on, "where you *come* from? I di'n't see you at first, and then there you were! I don't see you around and about before, neither. Where's yer pants, Fats?"

Fats felled Sucker with a sweep of his overlong arm.

"Dear me," the demonic creature remarked mildly. "Poor Sucker was overzealous, and I fear I've knocked out a number of his teeth. I'll just take a moment to replace them with something better." Roger stared in fascination at the unconscious bouncer's slackly open mouth as snow-white points poked up through the bloody sockets so recently vacated by his upper and lower left canines. The points rose, burgeoning into three-inch tusks of a dazzling sharpness and whiteness.

"There, he'll appreciate that," UKR commented in a self-satisfied tone. "Now to whisk him back to his spartan quarters." He frowned and Sucker was gone.

"How in the world did you *do* that?" Mary gasped. "That violates basic laws of physics!"

"Petty local regulations hardly apply in an entropic vacuole," UKR dismissed the plaint. "What matters here is that I've restored the local integrity of the Fabric to the extent possible. Even so trivial an event as the return of an enraged Sucker to wreak vengeance on the upstart who humiliated him in performance of his duties could provide major consequences Matrix-wise if allowed to stand, in contravention of the natural flow of events."

"What do you think he'll say when he comes to and finds out he's got fangs like a walrus?" Roger inquired.

"He'll be so delighted with his new adornments that

he'll quite forget to report the incident to Mr. Lepke, the Big Boss," UKR replied smugly.

Before Roger could point out the possible flaws in the machine's reasoning, the door exploding inward. Sucker stood there, his expression of fury in no way alleviated by the six—no, seven-inch tusks that curled his lips into a snarl of unparalleled ferocity.

"That's the guy!" He pointed at Roger. The two husky fellows behind him craned for a better look.

"Who, *me*?" Roger demanded incredulously. "It was UKR!" He pointed to the squat, purple demon-shape.

"Don't let him kid you, boys," Sucker yelled. "Nobody here but the wiseguy and the bim! He's tricky, I tol' youse!"

"Don't you dare call Professor Tomkins a 'bim'!" Roger commanded, and in a stage whisper, "UKR, deal with this!"

CHAPTER TWENTY-FIVE

"My idea precisely," UKR replied, stepping forward. "The matter must be handled diplomatically." He confronted Sucker as the big fellows stepped past the ruined door. "Just what is your complaint, Mr. Sucker?" he inquired urbanely.

Pete halted, staring wildly over the demon-shape's lumpy head. "Wheresa voice comin' from? See, boys, he's one o' them ventrikist or whatever, like Charlie McCarthy. Well, not Charlie, but the other guy, you know what I mean.

"What's my beef, you wanna know?" he addressed UKR, "Well, take a look at these two fangs-like I got growing outa my mouf! I never was what you'd call a pretty boy," he conceded, "but what dame's gonna wanna swap spit with *this* puss?"

"You refer, I suppose," UKR replied mildly, "to the handsome tushes, a bit lopsidedly located, I agree, on the left sector of your dental arch, not unlike my own handsome and utilitarian dentition? Don't question your good fortune, Sucker, just enjoy it."

"Yeah?" Sucker came back hoarsely. "What'm I s'pose to do now, join the zoo?"

"Not a bad notion," UKR pontificated, "but I think a carnival would be more appropriate."

"Swell," Sucker mumbled. "Now I'm s'pose to get a job in between the fat lady and Dog-face Boy. A sad end to a big career with the Lepke organization!"

"Don't fret," UKR advised. "Mr. Lepke's organization is about to revert to an unrealized state, since it's necessary to reverse his bout of amnesia in Chicago some 'years' back, so that he can complete his truce talks with Sweet Manny O'Rourke, thus aborting the gang war which would otherwise have eventuated on the Main Tendril, a conflict in which such luminaries as Frankie Rosenfeld, the strong right arm of the U.S. Communist Party, and Albert Capone—"

"You mean *the* Franklin Roosevelt?" Roger butted in. "Why do you pronounce his name 'Rosenfeld'?"

"For historical continuity," UKR explained. "His first ancestor in the new land was one Nicholas Rosenfeld, the father of Isaac Rosenfeld. The change in spelling is one which is due to the inaccuracy of English-speaking colonial typesetters when presented with a difficult Dutch name."

"How about 'Hoover,' " Roger pursued the topic. "He had another of those jaw-breaker Dutch names: " 'Hoevenrucker,' or something! Do you change *him* back, too?"

"No need," UKR pointed out. "Pray overlook my momentary over-zealousness. I shall adhere to familiar designations hereafter, to the extent possible."

"The world is coming to an end, and we're gabbing about spelling," Roger carped. "FDR was a Chicago hood, you say?"

"A fast-rising mobster," UKR confirmed. "But his Communist rantings alienated his patriotic associates. He was disposed of."

"Just like that, huh?" Roger jeered. "A rich New York politician rubbed out by cheap hoods in Chi? It doesn't figure."

"He had close ties to Mayor Cermak," UKR supplied,

"who in turn had necessarily come to terms with certain Syndicate leaders. Luckily, as it eventuated, his early demise aborted a major conflict which would have been called World War Two—on most planes of realization at least. Otherwise, Frankie would have goaded the Japanese into attacking, so as to bring the U.S. into the fray, to save Stalin. This war, in turn, where it occurred, spurred development of rocket engines suitable for space exploration, with attendant—"

"Stop!" Roger urged. "I get the idea: some punk in Chi misses a meeting, so the whole world ends up in WW Two. Goofy!"

"While 'goofy' is perhaps a term of insufficient gravity adequately to characterize the complex maze of consequences arising from each trival incident in the Fabric," UKR pontificated, "it is undoubtedly true that ordinary concepts of logic are in abeyance in the larger context of the Matrix."

"Sure, skip that part," Roger dismissed the profundity. "Let's get back to what we're going to do to save the world. I know we've got our work cut out for us, because even in my own hometown things were going to pot faster than anybody could keep track of, and most people didn't even know it! And the things some people with good intentions *were* doing were just making it worse!"

" 'World War Two,' did you say, Roger?" Mary inquired. "Do you really mean that in your STV the Great War wasn't really the War to End Wars?"

"Ye gods!" Roger blurted. "If things are so different so close to home that you don't even know about Hitler and Churchill and the Cold War, the whole Matrix must be coming apart!"

"Certainly I know about Hitler," Mary objected. "Adolf Hitler, you mean, the silly Austrian painter, who got the critics all upset back in the thirties, with his 'Art Uprising,' they called it, when his mobs, called 'the Nasties' descended on art galleries and burned all the paintings done since the Impressionists. What does *he* have to do with anything? Especially since he married Barbara

S. Funderbloose, the heir to the Spink fortunes, and went in for abstract expressionism?"

"No, no; he was the German dictator, and would have conquered all of Europe if—"

"Then it's already been done!" Mary exulted. "Saving the world, I mean! Apparently that extra war you mentioned turned out to be just what the world needed, probably because Mr. Ucker here interfered with matters."

"I shouldn't have," UKR acknowledged in a feeble tone, as if too depressed to bother with his gigantic disembodied voice. "But when that Franklin fellow started out singlehandedly to give all the fruits of the allied victory to Stalin on a silver platter, candidly, it shorted my circuits, so I—"

"You killed him!" Roger burst out.

"By no means, Roger," UKR huffed. "I merely discontinued the containment of the embolism which would otherwise have felled him in 1933 local. (I had preserved him so as to serve to correct the temporary condition of financial instability which plagued the local Fabric.) His usefulness was over, so, you see, it was my interference in the first place—"

"Did you ever save *my* life?" Mary asked timidly.

"Many times," UKR replied promptly. "Do you recall an occasion when a bus was struck by a fast freight, at the Greenville junction, only a mile from your house? Back in '72—1972, I mean—"

"Of course," Mary acknowledged. "My *grand*mother hadn't been born in 1872!"

"You would have been a passenger on that bus," UKR droned on, "had I not arranged for a young fellow named Fred Tomkins to offer you a lift."

"But what about the rest of the passengers?" Mary protested. "Why save me, and let nineteen others die horribly?"

"As it happened," UKR told her, unperturbed, "you had played—or *would* play—a vital role in the course of human development. It was quite essential that your filament should not be aborted."

"Does that have anything to do with how I got all mixed up in all this in the first place?" Mary demanded heatedly. "And what . . .?"

"Everything," UKR acknowledged. "You see, there was a Matrical flaw at the precise STV locus where your house was built in 1953 (*sic*) and with the entropic charge you had accumulated by your interference with the orderly unfoldment of the cultural progress of Man, it was inevitable that sooner or later you would penetrate the embolism in the Meniscus, as you did."

"I can't see why that's anything for you to sound so self-satisfied about," Mary rebuked the machine sharply. "And what are you talking about, interfered with the progress of man?"

"The tribe with which you lived for some years was a band of late *Homo erectus*, as you doubtless are aware; by showing them techniques that they would not ordinarily have discovered for many millennia, you of course altered the pattern of unfoldment. This little group went on to invent boats, harpoons, and other cultural embellishments, which permitted them to cross, via a last surviving ice bridge, from Greenland to North America. Alas, you archaelogists, having found no evidence of their early migration, save a few questionable spear-points and the like predating the advent of the Na Dene by half a million years, have ignored their role in human unfoldment."

Mary looked shocked. "The cave in Chile, dated at 250,000 B.P.—is that—?"

"Of course." UKR nodded the bald, pointy big-eared head he was wearing. "But be not alarmed; in time the ice-transfer program to alleviate drought in the Sahara and other arid regions will uncover the full story, and careful search in eastern Canada will complete the record."

"I heard about a *Homo erectus* find in Florida," Roger contributed. "Made me wonder why the early humans stuck to the cold climate way up north when they could have been living easy in the sunshine."

"The vegetation line followed the retreating ice," Mary told him. "The large herbivora followed their accustomed fodder, and the hunters followed the herds."

"Sure," Roger agreed readily. "I guess without motels and air conditioning Florida wouldn't be an easy place for a hunter to make a living. And anyway, they probably *liked* miserable weather, like the British."

"I'm devastated," Mary stated, "to think that I actually interfered with human cultural evolution. At the time it just seemed natural to try to help."

"No real harm done," UKR soothed. "Their progress was merely accelerated; the same developments would have come along in any event."

"But what about that fellow, that 'Lump,' as he called himself? He was a modern man—didn't he contribute to the interference?"

"Alas, there were no Harleys available in Pleistocene Greenland," UKR reminded her. "He sickened and passed away soon after your own disappearance."

"Poor man," Mary mourned. "He was only a boy. He never really had a chance . . ."

"Certainly he did," UKR corrected. "He chose his course; he rejected education and social restraint in order to indulge his inherent preference for anarchy. What you and other compassionate persons fail to take into account is that there are people who genuinely *prefer* chaos to order, enjoy destruction, and derive contentment from the suffering of others. Now, that fellow Lump is an excellent example. The moment he treasured most is the one in which he sloshed gasoline inside an unattended seventy-five-thousand-dollar Mercedes and lit it off. It made him feel cheerful for a week to remember watching the leather blacken and burn, to see the paint bubble and char, to hear the tires explode one by one. Had he not gotten himself involved in the present untenable situation by attempting to harass an inoffensive citizen, he'd have met disaster in some other way. His tendencies, happily, go against the texture of the Matrix itself, and are doomed to failure.

"Such deviant and destructive genes survive in the human population in your home era because of misguided forbearance and irresponsible encouragement (don't warp Junior's little psyche) on the part of do-gooders do-gooding (not to be confused with 'doing good') who have ensured these deviants' survival in spite of society's natural instinct to eliminate them, just as the individual's antibodies destroy invading pathogens. Surviving thus unnaturally, these pernicious genes are passed on to yet another generation and survive to this day in the gene pool. Pity. Human progress has been grievously retarded by the load of self-destructive tendencies it has obligated itself to drag along."

"You're advocating eugenics?" Roger gasped.

"Not precisely," UKR objected. "But, clearly, it is prudent to discourage the grossly deformed, and mentally deficient sociopaths, from producing similarly flawed offspring, which would in any case lead miserable lives; instead they are actually encouraged to perpetuate their defective genes by a society perversely intent on assuaging feelings of guilt by performing egregiously self-destructive acts."

"So much for humanitarianism, eh?" Roger grated.

"By no means," UKR contradicted sharply. "Again you seek simple answers to questions of infinite complexity."

"So what's the answer?" Roger demanded grumpily.

"You assume that there is always an uncomplicated answer," UKR pointed out. "But such is not the nature of the Matrix. But be not discouraged. Leave a margin for humanity. After all, you people have only been working on the problem of structuring a society for some fifty thousand years, and have in fact made some progress, remember. Why expect to perfect that structure in one stroke?"

"Well, I guess it *is* asking a lot," Roger mumbled.

"I think," Mary contributed, "that we have to face up to the fact that all people are *not* equal; some are actually endowed with more talent than others; we have to develop a method of identifying and recognizing such talents early, and encouraging them, by rewarding successful effort, instead of confiscating the fruits of one person's efforts in order to confer largess on one who is unable to make a contribution, or who refuses to try."

"Swell," Roger grunted. "But right now, let's get the world back on track *now* away from self-destruction, and get ourselves back home. By the way, UKR," he went on, thinking aloud, "why is it so many of us refugees come from Brantville?"

"A statistical oddity," the squat gnome-form replied. "The intolerable entropic stresses had to be relieved somehow; it happened that the force-lines intersected at the site of Brantville, creating a zone of instability."

"*I* don't come from Brantville," Mary pointed out. "That's over twenty miles from Oxford, where I live."

"The fault-line runs south-south-west for nearly one hundred miles and two thousand 'years,'" UKR told her. "Oxford falls squarely on a side-rift."

"Then why am I the only one . . . ?" Mary wondered aloud.

"Oh, Mary!" a male voice called. "*There* you are. I was about to become alarmed!" Roger whirled to see a tall, athletic-looking bald fellow in a tan cardigan coming toward him with an unmistakably hostile look on his face. "Say," the newcomer barked, "who're *you*, fella? What are you doing with my wife?"

"Don't make a fool of yourself, Freddy," Mary interceded, going quickly to the man. "This is Roger; he's as helpless and bewildered as I am. We were just planning how to escape from this, ah, time trap. How did you—?"

"Went in the pantry," Fred grunted. "Saw a can of stuffed peppers on the floor; figured you'd been there. I got to poking around, and came out in a spooky sort of cave with a skeleton on the floor. *Homo erectus*, perfectly preserved, under a layer of deposited limestone with stalagmites six inches high on it. The way out was

blocked, but I found a rift in the ceiling and got clear.
Boy, was I glad to be back out in the sunlight. So I
started looking around, figured you'd gone the same way,
and here you are! With this—!"

"But it's been twelve years," Mary protested. "Or so
Roger said, but those stalagmites sound as if—" She
looked at Fred reproachfully, then, "What do you mean,
'with this!'?"

"I was just estimating," Roger said hurriedly. "Don't
blame me! Be glad it's only been—ah—how long *has* it
been, Fred?"

"Oh, a couple hours, I guess," Fred replied offhandedly.

"But . . . that's impossible!" Mary objected. "We haven't
just been standing here, after all, we've been to London
and we saw Dr. Johnson, and—"

"Hold on, dear," Fred cut in. "No need for hysteria.
I'm sorry if I sounded a bit surly. After all, I hardly
expected to find you—scantily clad at that—with another
man."

"What do you mean, 'scantily clad'?" Mary demanded.
"And Roger's not 'another man.'"

"Oh, then what is he?" Fred inquired slyly, giving
Roger a look at once contemptuous and challenging.

"I'll show you, you nitwit," Roger supplied, and stepping between Mary and Fred, felled the latter with a
serviceable right hand. "There was a time," he told Mary
apologetically, "when I would have endured this dumb
ape's innuendos docilely, but I've been through too much
to sit around and endure unwarranted insults to both
myself and a swell girl like you."

CHAPTER TWENTY-SIX

"The big dope had it coming," Mary brushed aside Roger's apology. She went to Fred and looking down at him scornfully, said, "If you think you can behave yourself now, Dr. Tomkins, you may get up."

Fred was rubbing his jaw and staring past Mary at Roger, who was nonchalantly rubbing his fist. "All I said—" he started, but Mary cut him off.

"For Heaven's sake, don't repeat it, Fred," she scolded. "Next time Roger might really get angry!"

Fred mumbled and got to his feet. He went over to Roger and thrust out his hand. "Put her there, pal," he blurted. "And thanks for looking out for the little woman."

"Stick it, Freddy," Roger returned curtly. "The less I notice you, the better," he added, turning his back on the big fellow, wondering as he did so why he was refusing the easy out of a potentially painful and humiliating situation.

"Oh, please," Mary spoke up tearfully. "Won't you two make up and be friends? For my sake?"

Tell her to keep her nose out, a seemingly disembodied voice spoke clearly and peremptorily inside Roger's skull. He blundered past Mary, ignoring her outstretched hand.

"Hey, you!" Fred barked behind him. "If you're supposed to know something about all this nonsense, you'd better stick around until you've helped us out of it; *then* you can get lost!"

Roger shied slightly as a blue-black beetle the size of a box turtle scuttled aside from his path. He made a halfhearted attempt to stamp on it, even as he was aware that he had halted abruptly and was turning back to face Fred, to whom Mary now clung anxiously.

"Fred Tomkins!" she was chiding. "Why in the world do you talk so rudely to Roger? If he can help us, I'm sure he will, with no silly threats from you."

"Right!" Roger seconded. "And I'm not waiting around here for your permission to go. As it happens, I've decided to stick around a while. What are *you* going to do about it?" he heard himself add.

"Roger!" Mary rebuked. "I appreciate your willingness to help, in spite of Fred's foolish attitude—but do you *have* to goad him with your own schoolyard taunts?"

"Well, I was just . . ." Roger replied, feeling disproportionately resentful of the professor's severe tone.

"You're a fine one to come carping at me," he felt his mouth say calmly. "After all the times I've . . ."

"Yeah?" Fred put it, blocking Roger off. "All the times you *what*?" He tried to stare Roger down, gave it up and awkwardly extended his hand again to be shaken. "Look, buddy," he muttered, "we're all in this together, and while maybe I don't—"

He cut himself off abruptly. "Dammit, man," he said in a determined tone. "I don't want to fight with you. Let's work together and get Mary out of this, OK?"

Roger almost seized the hand and babbled his heartfelt agreement, but instead he brushed aside the peace offer and heard himself mumble something that included the word "hypocrite." At once he turned again to Fred and took the proffered hand, and heard the voice in his head speak up again.

Tell him to go jump in the nearest body of water. Tell him—

Fred stamped hard at the ground, narrowly missing Roger's foot.

"Suits me!" Roger blurted and pumped Fred's slack hand. "Don't even know what we were arguing about."

"You two should be friends," Mary put in eagerly. "After all, both of you—"

"Both of us *what*?" Fred demanded, dropping Roger's hand like a dirty rag. He stared challengingly at his petite wife.

"What do you think, you ninny?" Mary responded spiritedly. "That you both spent nights of passion with me under a tropic moon? Both of you want to protect me," she added almost parenthetically.

"Say!" Roger contributed. "Do you mean this big ape thought that I—that you and I— With my own wife right here?" Roger turned indignantly to indicate Q'nell in the chair, only then noticing that she was gone. "Oh, no!" he groaned.

"It'll be all right, Roger," Mary consoled. "You'll find her again."

"That's enough, mister!" Fred snapped. "I guess," he continued without conviction, "I owe you thanks for helping my wife out."

Roger almost said, "Aw, shucks, Fred, glad to do it." Instead, on an impulse he made no great effort to stifle, he snarled, "Forget it, jerk! I'd do the same for any lady. And if I'd known she was married to a sap like you, I probably would have let her stay in the clutches of those yahoos!"

"Look, boy," Fred raged. "I'm trying to be nice, OK? So why don't you—"

Don't bother planning my life for me, the voice of recklessness dictated. Roger repeated the words aloud, feeling like Charlie McCarthy. "Hold on!" he added. "I didn't mean— I mean, I only meant—"

"Now, stop it, right now!" Mary ordered. Roger felt his lips forming a snarly reply, but when he looked at her pretty, distressed face, he mumbled, "Sorry, Mary. I just get this impulse some times, and—damn! I remember once when Q'nell accidentally fixed eggplant for dinner, forgot I don't like it, she was almost in tears, and I meant to comfort her, so I took a bite and was going to tell her it was as good as eggplant could be, and instead I told her to put it in the garbage where it belonged. She bawled for half an hour, and I wanted to apologize, but instead I kept making cracks about people who only thought about themselves, and how slimy the stuff is, and—"

"I know just what you mean," Mary interrupted. "Just now, I was considering saying, 'Who cares about you and your eggplant? My marriage, and the whole world is in danger!' But I didn't say it!"

"I just didn't say, 'Sure you did'!" Roger gobbled. "I had the damnedest impulse to stir up trouble, and right now, I'm looking at Fred and thinking, *What are you staring at, you big dope?* Only, I didn't—or did I?"

"Doesn't count," Fred mumbled. "I started to say 'Doesn't matter what you were thinking, stupid!' Only I caught myself and said, 'Doesn't matter' instead! You see, it's easy. All you have to do is remember not to stir up the flames by adding fuel! If you see what I mean," he added doubtfully.

"Of course we do, dear!" Mary said before Roger could say, *"Let's stick to the subject!"*

Fred took a sudden step and stamped down hard on something unseen in the grass. Grass . . .? Roger looked around. Yep, grass.

"Damn bug!" Fred muttered. "I've been seeing them everywhere lately. New species. Never saw one before maybe a couple days ago, but now—" He broke off to stamp again.

"Hold it!" Roger yelled, too late. The nearest hedge bulged and collapsed under the advance of a steer-sized Vrint. It stalked directly toward Fred, whose back was turned.

HOLD IT RIGHT THERE, VRINT! UKR's big voice boomed out. Fred wheeled to see the giant insect's paired chelae snapping a foot from his face.

"My God!" he yelled. "Look at the size of *this* sucker!"

"Yeah," Roger agreed. "This one's almost as big as the first one I saw back in Brantville."

Sure, Roger heard absently, as Fred was yelling, "Let's get out of here!" *You've seen it all, uh, wise guy? Well, what are you going to DO about it?*

"Say, Mary!" Roger said urgently to the lady professor, "Did you hear that? About me being a wiseguy, I mean."

"Certainly," she snapped. "It's just the kind of thing I'd expect Fred to say, just when being diplomatic was important!"

"But—he *didn't* say it!" Roger expostulated. "It was more like a voice inside my head!"

Don't be a bigger jerk than you have to, Roger, the tiny voice ordered. Roger recoiled. Mary's lips hadn't moved.

Who're you calling a jerk, you female? Roger didn't say, almost biting his tongue in the effort to shut off the ill-considered retort. "Say!" he managed. "It's something putting words in our mouths! I'll bet that big Vrint has something to do with it!"

Mary caught Roger's arm. "I can't trust myself to speak, Roger," she blurted. "I have the most powerful impulse to say terrible things . . .?"

"I know, you damn fool—don't count that one," Roger gobbled. "All my life I've been putting my foot in it, when a soft word would have turned away wrath—but all of a sudden, I realize—it's not *me*! It's the Vrint interfering!"

While Roger was experiencing enlightment, Fred had been belaboring the immense blue-black beetle with a club improvised from a length of heart pine, as heavy as iron and studded with natural spikes. The big bug was now attempting to retreat, even as chips of chiton were flying under Fred's furious assault.

"Nice going, Freddy!" Roger yelled, and catching up a bludgeon of his own, he joined in the fray. The giant Vrint, its antennae broken and dangling, a number of its

externally-jointed limbs fractured and scrabbling use-
lessly, was backing away as rapidly as it could.

"Hold it!" Roger shouted at Fred, who continued with
unabated enthusiasm to belabor the stricken creature.
Roger caught his arm and hauled him back.

"It's retreating, dammit!" he told the taller man.
"That's all we want!"

"Sure, I'm sorry," Fred said meekly, and withdrew,
tossing his club aside.

GO IN PEACE, VRINT! UKR's voice rang out. LET
THIS BE A LESSON TO YOU!

Very well, came the chastened reply. *Since the Roger-
entity acted to end the brutality, I shall confer upon him
a special status, as "Exalted of Vrint."*

Roger felt a vague impulse to spurn the gesture, but
his eye fell on the injured limbs, (or were they only
damaged?—since, Roger reminded himself, it was only a
machine). The stubs of its antennae were waggling
frantically.

"None of that!" he barked and stepped in to adminis-
ter the *coup de grace* to the stricken Vrint. He spun to
look around accusingly. "That's what I call 'straight
arrow'!" he yelled to the unseen presence. "You call me
the 'Exalted of Vrint' and at the same time one of your
boys is trying to stick my foot in my mouth!"

CALMLY, ROGER, UKR interceded, then, more quietly: "The Batchmaster was a rogue unit; having rejected
the Vrint's control, it was functioning, and badly, on its
own initiative. Vrint is not responsible!"

"Whose side are you on?" Roger came back hotly.

THE SIDE THAT IS BENIGN AND CONSTRUC-
TIVE! UKR rebuked. AS YOU SHOULD BE, ROGER!
NOW STOP THIS NONSENSE AND BEHAVE
RATIONALLY! WE'RE ALL DEPENDING ON YOU.

"Who, me?" Roger inquired in a tone of astonishment.
You're depending on *me?* That's ridiculous! I'm an innocent victim, and you're a superhuman machine!"

YET YOU, ROGER, came the relentless reply, AS A
LIVING REPRESENTATIVE OF YOUR STRANGE

SPECIES, ARE ENDOWED WITH POWERS—I HESI-TATE TO SAY "TALENTS"—FAR MORE POTENT THAN ANY POSSESSED BY A MERE AGGREGATION OF INANIMATE MATTER, SUCH AS MYSELF.

"Whattaya mean, 'strange'?" Roger yelled. "And I'm not a representative of anything, I'm just me, Roger Tyson, an individual!"

THEREIN LIES THE GREAT PARODOX, UKR intoned solemnly. YOU PETTY CREATURES, ONLY LATELY, BY YOUR OWN CURIOUS CONCEPTS OF SERIAL TIME, EVOLVED FROM A STATE OF RAN-DOM MINDLESSNESS, PRESUME TO ORDER THE MANIFOLD. NOW THE BASIC PROFUNDI-TIES OF THE UNIVERSE ARE OPEN TO YOUR SEARCHING CURIOSITY, A CONCEPT PECULIAR TO YOURSELVES. THE MATRIX ITSELF AWAITS YOUR ENTERPRISE. A HUMAN WHIM CAN DIVERT THE COURSE OF UNFOLDMENT. THE BUILDER, OF COURSE, RECOGNIZES THE RESPONSIBILITY TO CURB YOUR PROBING IMPULSE; THAT IS WHY I WAS CONSTRUCTED, AS A NON-LIVING ENTITY, TO MONITOR THE CHAOS INDUCED BY YOUR ACTIVITIES IN THE ORDERLY FABRIC OF ALL-THAT-IS.

"Does that mean you're not going to help us?" Roger demanded. "I guess I really need to talk to the Builder in person!"

THAT IS NOT PRACTICAL, UKR replied coolly. BUT I SHALL LIMIT MY INTERFERENCE TO ASSISTING YOU IN ATTAINING WHAT YOU YOURSELVES THINK YOU DESIRE, THUS AVOIDING THE INTRUSION OF YET ANOTHER UNCOORDINATED FILAMENT INTO THE FAB-RIC. ERGO, WHAT DO YOU DESIRE?

"That's simple enough!" Roger retorted. "It's not only obvious, but I've told you a dozen times already! I want—"

WHAT ABOUT FRED? UKR cut in.

"Fred? What do I care about Fred?" Roger yelled. "He can fend for himself. Now, as to Mary, she wants what I want: to get back home, safe and sound and not needing to worry about where she'll come out every time she makes a move . . ." Roger hesitated. ". . . And I guess that includes having old Fred right there with her."

ARE YOU TRULY CERTAIN, ROGER? UKR persisted, THAT YOU REALLY DESIRE TO RETURN, IGNORANT, TO THE SITUATION AS IT APPEARED TO BE AT THE MOMENT YOU EMBARKED UPON THIS EXTENDED INVASION OF ASPECTS OF THE COSMIC ALL FOREIGN TO YOUR NATURAL FILAMENT?

"I 'embarked'?" Roger yelled. "I was just minding my own business, when all of a sudden this Vrint—the first one I really saw—came waltzing around the corner, and nothing's been the same since. 'Invasion'—that's another tricky word! You talk as if it was all my idea! And what do you mean, 'ignorant'?"

CHAPTER TWENTY-SEVEN

AS INDEED WE ARE ALL, ROGER, boomed the voice which seemed to emanate from the green-skinned ogre sitting on a rock a few feet away, though the creature's wide mouth was set in a glum expression, and its eyes were idly following the progress of a Vrint-beetle as it crept up a grass stem directly above Mary's head. IT IS FOR THAT REASON THAT YOU HAVE BLUNDERED REPEATEDLY, PRECIPITATING THE DISASTERS THAT HAVE OVERWHELMED THE FINAL CULTURE AFTER FIFTY-TWO THOUSAND YEARS (SIC) OF PROGRESS.

"That's crazy!" Roger pronounced flatly. "I never 'precipitated' anything: I never heard of most of what's been going on! At first there was the Final Culture, and of course Oob, but it's all gotten beyond that now! I'm as much at sea as anybody else caught in this mess!"

"It seems to me, Roger," Mary spoke up gently, "that all this is in some ways a microcosm of life: we find ourselves in an objectionable situation over which we have no control, though we imagine we can influence events; we encounter unpleasant phenomena, and develop a complex system of absolute convictions in an attempt to rationalize, and thus control, our fates. We mess up our human relationships, and we try to explain, and then we have to explain the explanations, and it all just gets too complicated to follow anymore . . .!" She burst into tears.

"But, Mary," Roger objected, patting her shoulder. "I thought you had it all together: you're young and pretty, and already a full professor, and you have a secure home, and Fred, such as he is, and you have your work, and—" He interrupted himself to cast a glance at the green kobold, which was now looking curiously at him.

"Well," Roger demanded, "What are *you* looking at?"

"Not much," the demon replied in UKR's conversational tone. "Considering . . ."

"Considering what?" Roger challenged.

"Considering you're the key element in this entire disaster," was the casual reply.

"If I've said it once, I've said it a hundred times," Roger complained. "I'm an innocent victim; I was dragged into this by you and Oob! Where *is* that rascal, by the way?"

"Tsk," UKR chided. "You've repeatedly complicated matters by your irresponsible efforts to restore a vanished status quo. As for Oob, he's trapped inside a box in an attic. He crept into an open trunk which was being rummaged through by a child; when the tot's father approached, the lad slammed the lid. Oob, a wily being capable of eluding the subtlest of snares, was caught off-guard by the simplest of circumstances. It's just as well. He'll be at hand when we need him."

"How heartless," Mary commented. "If you're talking about Catkin. Won't he suffocate?"

"No danger, worse luck," UKR dismissed the idea. "He's an impudent upstart who has repeatedly violated the integrity of the Bore, exacerbating the problem at hand. As Roger pointed out, it was Oob who was responsible for dragging him into this—and you as well, my dear." The demon smiled, a ghastly rictus.

"Who dragged whom into this?" Roger demanded. "Do you mean *I* dragged Oob in, or that *he* dragged *me* in?"

"A little of both," UKR explained quietly. "Had you not interfered, he'd soon have overtaken the fair Q'nell as she fled on her stolen Honda; Oob had a Harley, you'll recall. She'd have been neutralized and released, mindless, to Culture One, and you'd have gone your way, ignorant of much you now imagine you know. Poor Oob would have received a promotion to Controller of Apex First Class, and—"

"That's enough!" Roger cut him off. "You mean that wasn't really Oob's Control Apex he was so proud of?"

"Certainly not," UKR rejected the idea. "It is the project of the Vorplischers, who built it, and—"

"That alien, Blemp!" Roger burst out. "He's the one causing the trouble!"

"He has indeed contributed his share," UKR acknowledged. "Pity he's outside my jurisdiction."

"Damn your jurisdiction! DO something! Who's jurisdiction *is* he in?"

"That of the Vrint. But Vrint interests lie elsewhere."

"Speaking of elsewhere," Roger persisted, "where *is* that Blemp fellow, anyway?"

"In hot pursuit of Oob, of course."

Mary shuddered. "I hadn't realized my funny little familiar, Catkin, was so important," she said. "Roger told me he was really named 'Oob, the Rhox,' but I still had no idea he was actually some sort of otherworldly being. I do hope he won't suffer too much, locked in a trunk. Does anyone know he's in there? And how did *he* get *me* into this? Actually, I was in my pantry, and all of a sudden I was in a cave, and then later Roger came, and . . ."

"Surely, surely," UKR soothed. "I'm well aware of all that. But, you see, Oob still had strong entropic ties to you, and when he traced you to Brantville, he hurried there, and insinuated himself into a cozy nook in your basement, and carelessly left his unauthorized Aperture deployed there, as a quick line of retreat in case of need. You surprised him when you switched on the pantry light, and he fled, leaving his Aperture open. You stumbled through."

"Heavens!" Mary gasped. "It almost sounds as if poor Catkin can be in two places at once!"

The squat ogre nodded casually. "Of course. That's how he's able to stir up so much trouble."

"Why doesn't Catkin just whisk himself out of that trunk?" Mary demanded.

UKR shook his bald, green head. "He can't; the available space is too confining to permit him to deploy his vram membrane in Zurch mode. Still, he's able to evoke a cozy pseudo-environment surrounding his person, so I imagine he's quite comfortable, though frustrated."

"That's a comfort," Mary sighed. "I was really quite fond of Catkin; an ideal pet, you know. Clean, quiet, and playful, and full of stories he told me by the hearth on long winter evenings, there in Faggotsby. The name means 'firewood market,' you know. A terrible place; I don't recall how I came to be living there."

"After the Tribe had dispersed," UKR supplied, "you, assisted by Lump, who had become your devoted servant, made your way across the ice to Britain. In time (so to speak) the early Celts came along and built their dismal village; you were able to convince them of your value as a shaman, so they didn't kill and eat you. Eventually, the Middle Ages ensued."

"You make it sound as if I'd lived for thousands of years," Mary complained. "And I was mourning about being forty in a few years."

"Ordinary temporal conventions do not apply in the context of an entropic vacuole," UKR clarified. "Your conscious STV sensors were not engaged, so you didn't actually *experience* all that time, and thus did not age accordingly. You're still only thirty-six Basic."

"No *gentle*man would discuss a lady's *age!*" Mary objected. "Actually, I'm still nineteen, subjectively."

"But so much more sophisticated, and thus more appealing," UKR pointed out.

"I'm not trying to be appealing, as you call it," Mary

grumped. "Especially not if you refer to sex appeal."
She looked at the squat, warty, green-hided troll and
shuddered.

"Of course," the monster agreed complacently. "Still,"
he went on, "no human being, however old, young, happily wed, 'morally' strait-laced, or contemptuous of the
idea can suppress the natural imperative to present himself as a candidate for parenthood."

"That's the most ridiculous thesis I ever heard of,"
Mary dismissed the charge. She turned to Roger, looking
indignant. "If all your 'friend' Mr. Ucker is good for is
insulting a lady, I'd as soon we managed without him!"

"Oh, UKR's basically a benign fellow," Roger
defended the potent being. "It's just that being a
machine, he doesn't quite grasp the finer points of
human psychology. Like women who wear corsets and
brassieres to make their secondary sexual characteristics
more prominent, and paint their faces, and expose half
their chest in low-cut gowns and wear uncomfortable
high heels to emphasize their calves and thighs and then
indignantly deny they're trying to bait the males. To us,
that's reasonable enough, but to a mere machine, it
seems a little inconsistent."

"Why," Mary demurred, "you're as bad as he is! I'm
surprised at you, Roger!"

THANK YOU, ROGER, UKR spoke up, FOR YOUR
SPIRITED DEFENSE OF MY GOOD INTENTIONS.

"If you have good intentions," Mary snapped, "let's
see you do something dramatic to demonstrate them!"

"Mary! Don't—" Roger began, but darkness closed down
like a collapsing big top. "Hey!" he objected. "Just a minute! She didn't mean— I mean, she only meant—!"

NEVER MIND, ROGER, UKR returned blandly. IT'S
ONLY A TEMPORARY EFFECT, DUE TO THE NOR-
MAL FRICTIONAL ENERGY-LOSS ATTENDANT
UPON A MAJOR REVERSAL OF ENTROPIC FLOW.

"She didn't say anything about a 'major reversal of
entropic flow'!" Roger complained.

TO BE SURE, UKR agreed. THE REQUEST WAS,

HOWEVER, FOR A "DRAMATIC" DEMONSTRA-
TION, YOU'LL RECALL. WHAT MORE DRAMATIC
THAN A REGRESSION DOWN THE ENTROPIC
TENDRIL TO A PREVIOUSLY EXPERIENCED SIT-
UATION? YOUR PRESENCE, OF COURSE, WILL
BE VIRTUAL, RATHER THAN ACTUAL, DUE TO
THE INVIOLABLE LAW OF CONSERVATION OF
ENTROPY. STILL, YOU CAN OBSERVE.

"I bet you made that up!" Roger charged. "About the
'conservation of entropy,' I mean. I never heard of *that*!"

THERE ARE A NUMBER OF ITEMS, ROGER,
UKR reproved mildly, WHICH HAVE ESCAPED
YOUR ATTENTION, AND INDEED THAT OF YOUR
ENTIRE SCIENTIFIC COMMUNITY. BE NOT
ALARMED.

"'Be not alarmed,' eh? You big gas-bag!" Roger yelled.
Then, "Oops, there must still be a few Vrint around."

NO, UKR contradicted. THAT UTTERANCE WAS
ENTIRELY YOUR OWN.

"Oh, Roger," Mary commiserated, taking his arm.
"Couldn't you just . . . well, sort of keep your mouth shut
for a while, and let Mr. Ucker work this out?"

"A minute ago," Roger snarled, "everybody was
demanding that *I* solve everything! Now, it's 'shut up and
let UKR do his stuff'! Well, his stuff seems to consist of
marooning us in pitch darkness! What do we do now?"

EVOKE, UKR supplied. YOU REMEMBER, ROGER;
JUST CALM YOUR MIND AND BRING INTO REAL-
IZATION WHATEVER YOU FEEL YOU NEED.

"Roger!" Mary gasped. "Can you really do that?"

"Dunno," Roger muttered. "It's been a long time. I'll
try." He closed his eyes, which made no difference whatever in the vista. He groped, found Mary's arm. "We'd
better stick close together," he told her. "If we get separated in this murk we'll never find each other."

"Don't even think of it!" Mary cautioned.

"Sorry," Roger replied. "A fellow can't be too careful,
I guess."

"But what do you intend to 'bring into realization'?"

she queried urgently. "Do be careful; Mr. Ucker seems to be *very* literal."

"I want," Roger stated clearly, "for Mary and me to get out of this ridiculous pattern and back into the real world—I mean the STV locus we were born into—and for everything to be cozy and nice; no big surprises, you understand."

"That ought to be all right," Mary remarked, sounding anxious. "What do you do next, Roger?"

"Nothing," he told her. "Just hang on and watch it happen."

The darkness seemed to brighten slightly; a hint of a dim glow appeared to emanate from all around them. A wall became visible a few feet away. It was of cut stone, Roger noted at once. He took a step toward it, tugging Mary along.

A man stepped into view. It was S'lunt, looking harassed. He halted at the sight of Roger and exclaimed. "You! I might have known! Whenever disorder threatens to overwhelm the Pattern, *you* pop up! What is it you're up to this time?"

"Take it easy, Inspector," Roger replied easily. "I certainly didn't mean to include *you* in a nice, cozy situation."

"Do you realize," the official yelled, "that I was in the midst of a most delicate finesse? All of Culture One is depending on me to restore the Prime Line to viability!"

"Go ahead," Roger urged. Then, "Mary," he said quietly to the professor, "this fellow is a petty official of an outfit that calls itself the Final Authority. He has a tendency to get excited when surprised. S'lunt, Professor Tomkins."

"Delighted, I'm sure," S'lunt muttered, " 'Professor,' did you say? Then perhaps she can contribute some of her primitive lore to the resolution of the present problem."

"Pay no attention to his crack about 'primitive lore,' Mary," Roger cautioned. "Poor S'lunt doesn't know how to open his mouth without being insulting."

"Perhaps," Mary offered breathlessly, "if Mister S'lunt is a representative of a high culture, he can answer some of the burning questions that have puzzled our science for some time."

"I doubt that he'd bother," Roger grumped.

"Tut-tut, Roger," S'lunt chided. "Yours is a jaundiced view of our philosophy: it is that we merely tend to ignore the insignificant. Not that you, as I now perceive, fall into that broad category; your individual life-line has intertwined itself in both warp and woof (in itself a gross anomaly) to an extent undreamed of. You are, in fact, almost singlehandedly responsible for the situation that now obtains." He waved a hand, indicating the broad plaza, strewn with rubbish, broken marble slabs fallen from the deteriorating facades, barely recognizable, its tiles chipped, with a generous distribution of blowing papers, empty containers, defunct appliances, and the bones of small vertebrates; dead, brown plants filled the former garden patches.

"What, *me* again, cast as the villain?" Roger looked disapprovingly at S'lunt. "You people ought to be ashamed of yourselves," he carped. "Dumping your garbage in the plaza like this. Used to be a pretty nice place," he told Mary. "Clean, you understand, with all kinds of flowers and handsome buildings all around. It's gone to pot badly."

Two men emerged from the ground floor level of an adjacent tower of rusting steelwork, with broken chunks of concrete adhering.

"Hey, is that you, Roger?" one yelled. "Where'd the pretty lady come from? I thought you *had* a wife."

"I *have!*" Roger shouted back. "This lady just happened along, and naturally I'm trying to help her. But it looks like I blew it again! Is that you, Rusty? You look older."

"I am," Rusty confirmed. "Do you have any idea how long it's been since you took off so abruptly?"

"Not the faintest," Roger stated flatly. "Time is only relative, you know, so what seems like a few hours to me could seem like a year to you."

"A year?" Rusty jeered. "It's more like a century. I

spent most of the time in a stasis-tank," he explained. "Bob here wouldn't do it, at first, so he's put in some hard time, tracking with the Main Sequence." Rusty turned to take the arm of the old fellow doddering along in his wake.

"Never mind, Rusty," Bob quavered. "I had some high times, watching the world go to hell in a handbasket!"

"You think *you* had it bad," Rusty returned. "You should have been with *me*! I was in an earthquake, and another time a tsunami! Talk about scared! I thought the whole planet was pulling apart! How about you, Roger?" he changed targets. "You been having any tough times, meeting fine-looking gals and all . . .?"

"I met an alien with three eyes and nine fingers," Roger confided. "Called himself a Vorplisher. Also, I came close to getting lost in the Cave of the Great Evil, and another time a bunch of *Homo erectus* wanted to eat me."

"Yeah, you got to look out for them gangs," Rusty agreed. "Look, it sounds nutty, but for a while I was a hoodlum named Lepke. Funny: I was minding my own business, see, and all of a sudden people started calling me 'Mr. Lepke,' and getting out of my way. Later, I think, I was a little kid in a candy store with a movie-star—Katharine Hepburn, it was, waiting on me. Then that Oob guy showed up. He trailed me home to the attic and disappeared."

"He climbed in the trunk to hide," Roger told him, "and you slammed a lid on him. But that won't really slow him down very long," he added. "He can jump around the E-lines like a jackrabbit."

"Not in *total* darkness," S'lunt contributed. "The entire vram-cortex goes into collapse when deprived of a photon flux. He's probably still entrapped there. Pity we don't know where the trunk is to be found."

"Right there in the attic," Rusty supplied. "It was half full of junk that belonged to my great-grandpa or something, and nobody'll ever mess with it except a nosy kid."

"And where, precisely, was the attic to be found?" S'lunt persisted.

"Four-oh-Nine West Third Street," Rusty said promptly. "Little town called Partridge in Vermont."

"That leaves only the STV coordinates to be determined," S'lunt carped. "One petty, undistinguished line of potential from among the infinite strands of the Web! Ridiculous!"

"Not so silly," Roger objected. "That's *our* vram-line, too, remember. UKR found it, and Oob, too; and I think you've been popping in and out of it at will. The trail ought to be pretty plain by now."

"There *is* the possibility of tracing the planes of instability in the Web, induced by the repeated entropic violations," S'lunt mused. "I shall try."

"You sure as hell will!" Roger yelled. "Otherwise how can you get Mary and me back where we belong—and Rusty and Bob, too?"

"I trust," Julian spoke up, "that I shall be included, though I'm not from Brantville." No one had seen him appear. "Odd thing, though, my parents came from there."

"Oh?" Roger said, interestedly. "What was their name? The family name, I mean. You've only mentioned your first name."

"I never use my surname," Julian replied. "It's an honorable enough name, going back to a fourteenth-century ceramicist. Made pots, you know. That's the name: 'Potts.' Not a very glamorous name for an artist, eh?"

"We *met* them!" Bob exclaimed. "Horace and Dellie, they were. Nice folks. I hope they got back all right."

"Must have," Rusty interrupted. "They didn't have Julian, here, when we saw them."

"But that was only a few hours ago," Bob objected. "Or months, or something. "I'm afraid I've lost all track of time."

CHAPTER TWENTY-EIGHT

"Time is only an idea we've got in our minds," Mary contributed. "I spent years being a village wise woman, or witch, and yet—"

"I know what you mean!" Rusty cut it. "Like when I was a couple of other people for a while—then I wasn't! And come to think of it, you look sort of familiar, only younger!"

"Andy Scute!" Mary blurted. "You were *there!*"

Rusty nodded. "It's like remembering a dream," he said. "I remember the town dump, where I lived off scraps."

"How strange that we should meet again," Mary sighed.

"It's an unfortunate snarling of the Strands of the Skein," S'lunt spoke up. "The sort of thing that can impede the normal entropic flow, due to the formation of scar tissue in the Meniscus; pressure builds up. At last it's released explosively, and tends further to snarl the texture of the Fabric—like a rubber band breaking and snapping back, it produces all sorts of flaws in the Matrix, and requires extensive reweaving, itself a gross violation of entropy, to correct."

"You sound cheerful enough about it," Roger

complained. "But at least you're not blaming this one on me."

"Thanks for reminding me," the inspector said. He took out his hand-calculator-cum-TV remote tuner and poked its buttons. "The equations, you know," he drawled, "won't scan unless *all* factors are duly considered."

"Oh," Roger remarked, "now we're scanning equations."

"To be sure," S'lunt agreed. "And let me tell you, Roger, they're in a parlous state. For example, as matters stand now, I could easily produce an algebraic proof that one equals two."

"That's nothing!" Roger snorted. "According to what Bob and Rusty say, the Pottses had Julian when they were about in their sixties, I'd say!"

"Not impossible," S'lunt commented. "Though of course they may well have already had a son of whom they didn't happen to speak in your presence."

"I had the distinct feeling," Rusty countered, "that Horace Potts had no heir. How about it, Julian," he addressed the dapper young fellow, "Your parents a little older than average?"

"They died young," Julian said sadly. "My dad, I'm told by Uncle Trevor, had an old car he kept for years because he'd had it on his honeymoon. Drove it like it was brand new; a wheel came off on a mountain road and they went over. I was only an infant; I don't remember them."

"Madness!" Roger blurted. "As I said, we met them in their middle-aged years, sixty or so!"

"Another badly twisted strand," S'lunt commented. "But, happily, one easy to correct, in this instance, since it's a simple linear flaw, not a case of widely variant lines snarled together." He studied the gadget in his hand and pressed the white bar at the top. The twilight across the plaza flickered; the sound of an auto engine came from a side street. A highly polished early Cougar ragtop coasted around the corner and approached the group standing by the ruined fountain.

"Say, fellows," Horace Potts called. "Can you direct us

to the Brantville road? Seem to have lost our way. Started from here a few minutes—"

"That was twenty years ago, Horsey!" Dellie corrected. "You remember—on our trip to Paris just after Julian's fifth birthday!"

"That makes no sense, girl." Horace snorted. His eye fixed on Roger. "Just where *are* we, anyway, fella?" he asked in a complaining tone.

"This is the Grand Plaza, the center of an advanced civilization calling itself Culture One," Roger offered, feeling the inadequacy of his explanation.

"Where are the folks?" Horace persisted. "And why's everything look so run-down?"

"I am a citizen of Culture One," S'lunt volunteered. "As for the disarray which you see about you, there has been a serious entropic deterioration, I fear. When the bulk of our population moved on to another Center, I volunteered to remain behind, in an effort to discover the source of the catastrophic changes that have overwhelmed us. So far," he concluded, "it appears to be a case of negative feedback, arising from a paradoxical configuration of displaced entropic strands."

"What's that mean in plain American?" Horace demanded.

"It means," Roger interjected, "that we're all caught in a mix-up of space/time/vug that has everything warped out of shape."

"What's that 'vug'?" Horace demanded.

Julian approached the car. "Ah, Mr. Potts," he began uncertainly. "You should dispose of that car."

"Who asked *you*?" Horace demanded. "Fine car, maintained to the minute!"

S'lunt shouldered Julian aside. "One mustn't meddle," he told him.

"Fella," Horace addressed Roger, ignoring the by-play, "I asked you a question!"

"Oh, about the vug," Roger gobbled. "It's a third great domain in which change can occur," Roger told him. "It's like time in some ways, like space in others. It flows, like time, but we can move in relation to it, like space. It's the context in which odd things happen. It's the medium in which the laws of chance operate, for example, the problyon flux and all that, you know. But never mind that right now. This fellow S'lunt is a big shot in the Final Authority, or Culture One, as they call themselves, and I'm hoping he—"

"Why 'Final'?" Horace wanted to know.

Roger looked glum. "Look around," he suggested. "You can see the place has fallen into desuetude. It's not going anywhere; thus it's the final result of human progress, unless we can—"

"Yes, unless we can what?" Dellie and Horace prompted as one.

"Do something," Roger supplied resignedly. "But pontificating aside," he switched targets to UKR, "you were going to put Mary and me back in the situation we started from, remember? Instead, you dumped us in this ruin."

"Make no ill-founded charges, Roger," UKR counseled mildly. "Consider: the locus whence you departed has continued to evolve along its self-determined strands. It began as a village abnormally modified by Mary's interference. It became Brantville, but that was not the end; it went on to become Culture One, and due to your meddling—unintended, I grant—the Final Culture collapsed of its internal stresses. Thus, you stand now at the evolved state of your brief slice of STV, just as you demanded."

"I didn't say anything about 'evolved state,'" Roger snarled. "I meant Brantville, USA, just as I left it in December, or was it May, nineteen eighty-something. Odd, I'm a little hazy about the date."

"As well you should be," UKR said sharply. "Considering that the so-called 'date,' was a mere convention arbitrarily imposed upon the seamless garment of the Matrix."

"Still," Roger countered, "it *was* a real place; I *was* there—and Q'nell is *still* there, wondering what happened to me. My cookies are probably still warm. *That*'s the locus I want to get back to."

"Alas, an aborted filament," UKR told him. "You see, Roger, one can't tamper limitlessly with the Fabric without introducing compelling cross-forces in the problyon flux. All the scenes and phenomena so familiar to you were, after all, simply possibilities arbitrarily evolved from the prematerial flux by the force of circumstance. Alter the circumstance—as you've done repeatedly—and of course the end product at any STV locus will be modified as well. To consider a specific example: in Seville, on April 19, 1490 (*sic*) a drunken sailor named Díaz fell to his death when something startled him as he was negotiating the gangplank to his ship, the *Niña*. He was crushed between hull and wharf. Had he lived he'd have signed on with C. Colón for a voyage to India, and en route he would have led a mutiny which would have resulted in the murder of Colón, and the 'discovery' of America would have been delayed for half a century, when it would have been found by an English freebooter named Musto, and you'd have been born in the United States of Mustonia. You can deduce for yourselves the breadth and depth of the repercussions of that seemingly trivial encounter on the gangplank. What startled Díaz was Oob, of course."

"Yes, but—" Roger said before Mary cut him off.

"I understand your point, Mr. Ucker," she said. "The slightest interference with the course of events can result in vast differences in the later state of affairs. But, as Roger said—" She turned to him. "What *did* you say, Roger?"

"I'm not Christopher Columbus," he carped. "I would never have discovered a new world, so what does it matter *what* I do? There'd be no titanic reverberations if I dropped dead right now!"

"You're quite incorrect, Roger," UKR chided. "Aside from the bereavement of those who hold you dear, in about six years, on one potential strand of your destiny, you're going to give a lift to a hitchhiker who is on his way to assassinate a presidential candidate working a whistle–stop in Brantville. You will suffer a blowout, which the would–be killer refuses to help you change, and instead relieves you of your wallet and watch. In a fit of pique, you will stun him with a tire iron, and when a prowl car comes along, you will turn him over to the beadles, who will recognize him as an escaped convict, having seen a flyer only that morning. You will serve only a brief sentence, luckily, for assault, battery, and mayhem."

" 'Mayhem'!" Roger echoed. "You make it sound as if I ran amok with a machete! But at least I'll be back in Brantville! Anyway, I'm not picking up any hitchhikers!"

"When you threatened this criminal," UKR told Roger, "that was assault; when you touched him, that was battery; when you actually hit him, that was mayhem. However, you had popular support during the trial, and were (or will be) held in a minimum-security facility, with TV in your cell, and a seat on your toilet. Quite posh. Except for the cuisine, of course. And there is the added bonus that you saved the life of the president."

"Strange," Roger muttered. "Mary's little tribe of *Homo erectus* went on to develop Western civilization, and I . . ."

"The presence of Lump in the proto-village was of course an unfortunate coincidence," UKR pointed out. "He introduced lying, thieving, treachery and a number of other innovations into the early human culture, all activities which have thrived in civilization, while unknown among the lesser beasts. Of course, beatings, murder, and rape they already had, so we can't credit poor Lump with *all* the evils of society."

"They were good at gluttony and sloth, too," Mary contributed. "What a pity I didn't devote more time to moral instruction."

UKR shook his lumpy green head, "No use," he comforted her. "Lump's contributions were readily accepted because they fell right in line with the tribe's natural tendencies. In any event, I hope I've demonstrated that great events from trifling incidents grow."

"Couldn't you take another shape, Mr. Ucker?" Mary appealed. "Something a little more reassuring."

The ogre flickered and in its place stood a slim young (female) beauty, as naked as the troll had been.

"Please!" Mary cried. "Put some clothes on!"

"If you prefer," the girl agreed sweetly, and was clad in a nun's habit from head to toe.

"Oh, that's too hot for this weather," Mary commiserated. "Just a light frock, perhaps."

The black garments faded to gray and disappeared, leaving only a gauzy set of undergarments; then a light summer dress with yellow polka-dots on white covered the fine figure. The young lady took a compact from her purse and touched up her lips.

"It's not *your* color, dear," Mary pointed out. "A nice blue would be perfect with those eyes." The dress turned pale blue with deep blue dots.

"That's a *lot* better," Mary said. "That ogre was terrible!"

"Oh, he wasn't such a bad fellow," Roger demurred. "After all, he *was* getting ready to get us back home."

"She still is, surely," Mary countered. "Aren't you, dear?"

"If you're still sure that's what you want," the girl-shaped UKR agreed. "Now, remember, all I can do is shift you forward along the line of actualization in which you've embedded yourselves, quite irretrievably, thanks to your frequent meddling with the Fabric. Penetrating and repenetrating the Bore, you've worn an entropic channel from which there is no escape."

"Swell," Roger deemed. "We'll be back in Brantville, but a few days later than we left, eh?"

"Some decades of temporal disparity exist between your present locus and that from which you originated," UKR corrected.

"No good!" Roger burst out. "I don't want to find Q'nell an old woman, for cripesake!"

"One must bow to the realities, such as they are,"
UKR intoned. "Are you ready?"

"I guess so,' Roger offered, and took Mary's hand.
"Don't worry," he urged. "Fix your mind on the STV fix
you left from, and that will tend to steer you there—I
think."

"Dammit!" Mary snapped. "The lights are out again!"
She took a step and stumbled over something—it was
that case of orange squash she'd been meaning to shelve,
she realized, and groped for the wall switch. She found
it and clicked it: nothing.

"No fair, Mr. Ucker!" she called into the darkness.

Roger groped, felt a damp stone surface. He fumbled
out his lighter and snapped it. The feeble glow showed
him that he was in a cave with stalagmites and stalactites,
as usual.

"Mary!" he yelped. "Are you—?"

"I'm right here, Roger," she replied, her voice emanat-
ing from the empty space beside him. He thrust out a
hand, moved it back and forth. Nothing there.

"Don't move!" he ordered, then, "UKR! You turncoat!
You know damn well we don't want to be dumped in
a cave, in the dark! Now do something right! Get us
home!"

Daylight blinded Roger. He blinked, squinted, and
made out the shape of a ruined building before him,
broken two-by-fours and crumbled brick, and beyond,
decayed furniture dumped in a heap on a rotted carpet
the same color—where it wasn't stained or faded—as the
one he and Q'nell had paid too much money for last
month. The battered chassis of a TV rested at an angle
on a broken table. Roger groped toward it: ATWATER
KENT read the square letters above the ON switch. He
whirled, looked around the devastated room. He was
home, all right! There was that damn Sears chair, still
looking new, in spite of being crushed!

"Q'nell!" he called faintly.

"Roger! Is that you?" she replied and appeared from
the kitchen, looking as fresh and lovely as ever. "I was

beginning to wonder—" She broke off, staring around the trashed room.

"Roger! What in the world?" She was in tears now, but Roger stood transfixed. At last he managed to move a foot, then another, picking his way across the buckled oak flooring to take her in his arms. "Q'nell," he murmured. "You're all right! That's the only important thing. What happened to the house?"

"It's the ice," she sobbed. "It just kept coming. Everyone else has evacuated, but I wouldn't go: I was sure you'd return to this STV locus eventually. I didn't expect it to be a whole week!"

"Where's Charlie?" Roger asked. "He was here with you when I stepped out, you recall."

"Of course," Q'nell agreed. "He sent for bulldozers and big Herman-Nelson heaters to try to stop the ice. His company had plenty of them, but it didn't help much. I don't know where he's gotten to. For days he was in and out of here—he used the house as his headquarters; but the last time I saw him, he said, 'This is the big one, girl: if this doesn't work—' and that was all. He got in his Lincoln and drove off down the street his men had cleared."

Roger looked out past the collapsed walls of his house, and realized that except for the relatively clear area around the house, there were jumbled ice-blocks everywhere.

"Ye gods!" he blurted. "I meant to get back home, to our cozy little suburban nest, but instead I land in one of the future states it would have become! UKR! This won't do! Fix it!"

I HAVE COMPLIED WITH YOUR EXPRESS WISHES, ROGER, the now disembodied voice came back crisply.

"Maybe," Roger temporized, "but I meant—"

WHAT YOU "MEANT," ROGER, IS NOT WHAT I AM PROGRAMMED TO RESPOND TO. I MUST FOLLOW YOUR STATED INSTRUCTIONS. I HAVE NO TELEPATHIC SENSORS FITTED.

"Never mind, Roger," Q'nell intereceded. "After all, we're together. And it's just a dumb machine."

"Shhh!" Roger hissed. "Be careful what you say. UKR has been known to take umbrage at harmless remarks, not to mention deliberate insults."

I DO NOT QUAIL FROM THE TRUTH, UKR announced blandly. WHILE NOT "DUMB" IN THE MUTE SENSE, IT IS UNDOUBTEDLY A FACT THAT I HAVE LITTLE DISCRETION IN "INTER-PRETING" OBSCURE DIRECTIONS. IF THERE IS NOTHING FURTHER, I SHALL RETURN TO ATTEND THE PRESSING NEEDS OF PROFESSOR TOMKINS.

"Wait!" Roger yelled. "Where *is* Mary? Is she OK? Why isn't she here?"

IT APPEARS, UKR told Roger sternly, THAT YOUR VISUALIZATION OF THE IDEAL FAILED TO INCLUDE HER AS A PART OF YOUR MENAGE.

"Obviously!" Roger burst out. "I *have* a wife; two women would be a nightmare!"

"Oh, Roger," Q'nell wailed. "Another woman? I thought you loved me!"

Roger embraced her tenderly. As he patted her back, he addressed UKR: "This mess—the ice and all—is the direct outcome of the way things were already going back when I thought everything was practically perfect—is that right?"

PRECISELY, was the unequivocal reply.

"But what about the greenhouse effect?" Roger protested. "The world was supposed to get hot, not cold!"

THE EFFECT, UKR began then modulated his tone to a more conversational one, "has in fact greatly allevi-ated the glaciation. Your shamans had already deduced that the planet was undergoing a series of ice advances, and that the polar caps represented an unusual situation, glaciation-of-the-planetwise. The latest retreat of the ice, which began some twelve thousand of your planetary cycles ago, relative, was after all but another periodic remission, and in due course, starting, actually, in 1940 (sic) had begun to advance once more. It was quite inevitable, my boy, being the result of the coincidence of the cyclic eccentricities of the orbit, the axis of rotation, periodic fluctuation in the solar output, and so on. Luckily, the accumulation of carbon dioxide in the upper atmosphere trapped heat, alleviating the worst of the disaster."

"Say," Roger mused. "We'd better get busy and launch a 'Save Our Greenhouse' movement; otherwise they'll dissipate the CO_2 layer in short order!"

"I suggest you forbear from meddling in the structure of the Cosmic All," UKR scolded.

"But—can't we do *anything* to save the planet, or at least civilization?" Roger appealed. "We can't just let it go on like this! Suppose we got people together here, and started paying attention to the environment and all that?"

"You have seen the results already," UKR intoned. "With its worst societal ills corrected in-house, so to speak, your simple yet chaotic society evolved in a few millennia into the state of affairs called Culture One."

"So, we're on the right trail after all," Roger exulted. "I guess the ice will melt pretty soon, and we'll get back on track, and in a few thousand years we'll have it all together, like the folks in the Final Culture!"

"Roger," Q'nell interjected. "Please don't call it 'The Final Culture.' That sounds so . . . final."

"All right," 'Culture One' it is," Roger acceded. "Seemed like a pretty nice place, what I saw of it: the Plaza, I mean. I figured all the rest was as classy as that—"

"Roger," Q'nell interrupted, "when you came along, I was *so* bored. The Council had been spending all its time and budget investigating the Bore, you know, and things at home were so monotonous you wouldn't believe it. Old S'lunt and R'heet and the other stick-in-the-muds had eliminated everything that was any fun. That's why I leapt at the chance to take on the assignment of investigating the Bore, and met Oob—and you!"

"So it all worked out for the best," Roger soothed her,

noting, as he did, what a perfectly fine young body she was pressing against him.

"But, Roger, Culture One was actually falling apart," Q'nell wailed. "You saw yourself how things were going to end up!"

"Sure, the Plaza needed a good sweeping last time I saw it," Roger agreed. "But it was nothing that seven maids with seven mops couldn't get clear in half a year!"

"It's worse, Roger," Q'nell said in a tone of gentle remonstrance. "Behind that facade, everything was disintegrating. It was all we could do to monitor Oob's Central Apex to try to keep tabs on the little scamp. And even then, he's succeeded in eluding us! It's horrid!"

"She's right, UKR," Roger addressed the unseen entity. "Why didn't you do something? Or will you do something? It's not too late!"

Abruptly, a surge of ice water came sloshing across the jumbled room to wash around Roger's ankles. He stepped up on the intact coffee-table and pulled Q'nell up beside him, as a more imposing ten-foot wave, bearing bits of debris, a dead cat, and clots of rubbish in its foaming crest came crashing against the already cracked and leaning wall, which fell, barely missing the two refugees.

"UKR!" Roger wailed. "This is worse! You can't just melt the ice and let it drown everything!"

I DID NOT MELT THE ICE, UKR protested. I SHIFTED YOU TO ANOTHER LOCUS WHERE IN FACT THE GREENHOUSE EFFECT HAD BEEN MORE EFFECTIVE, AND THE SITE OF BRANTVILLE WAS COVERED BY A NEW ADDITION TO THE GREAT LAKES.

"*That's* no help!" Roger complained. "Try another locus where there's a bit less water!"

Mary appeared at Roger's side. "Roger," she said quietly, "don't you think perhaps you should be more specific? Mr. Ucker is *very* literal-minded."

CHAPTER TWENTY-NINE

But by then a hot, dry wind had blown a choking cloud of dust into their faces and had converted every previously wet surface into a layer of slimy mud. Roger tried to step down from the low table, but he slipped and fell, hitting his head hard. He sat up, rubbing the back of his skull and complaining, "Stop it, you big boob!"

ROGER! UKR protested. DON'T HOLD *ME* RESPONSIBLE FOR THE RESULT OF YOUR OWN CHOICES!

"My own choices, hell!" Roger roared. "Are you really so dumb you can't just do a simple job of putting me back where I belong?"

"Careful, Roger," Q'nell cautioned. Her voice seemed to come from a long distance.

"When I left here, there was no ice age, and no desert dust-storm either!" Roger pointed out impatiently.

"Alas," UKR replied in the low-level tone he had adopted as his usual mode of communication. "When one meddles with the great forces of nature, as you people did, the repercussions are far-reaching and unpredictable. With the abrupt melting of the ice, heat was withdrawn from the circumambient atmosphere, creating

303

an immense high, which engendered winds in the hurricane range across the entire northern hemisphere, thus
drying the land to an unprecedented extent. You can't
have one without the other, you know. The massive influx
of airborne dust particles impinging on melt-water-
soaked soil created great seas of mud, at the edge of one
of which Brantville happened to be situated."

"Edge, hell!" Roger yelled. "We're in the middle of
it!"

"Not so, Roger," UKR corrected. "The modest mud-
layer in which you're standing is merely the product of
incidental dust on the moisture already present."

"Oh," Roger croaked, "I guess that makes it all right."
He turned to Q'nell, who, he noted *en passant,* was
charming even when mud-spattered.

"Roger," she said firmly, "I think it's time to give up
trying to deal with this on our own, and to call in the
Monitor Service."

"What Monitor Service? If you have an ace up your
figurative sleeve, by all means produce it!"

"When I was a field agent of Culture One," Q'nell told
him quietly, "I was issued a number through which I
could contact a relief team of the Monitor Service in case
of dire emergency. I never used it, though when Oob
was pursuing me, I thought seriously of it; in fact, I *tried*
to use it, but got no response—except, of course, that
you happened along, Roger, dear . . ."

Her kiss interfered with his attempt to yell. "You!
That's why my engine quit in a rainstorm on a lonely
road in the middle of the night?"

"The Service uses whatever means are most expeditious, Roger," Q'nell said soothingly. "And if they hadn't,
we'd never have met, so . . ."

"I forgive you!" Roger yelled, returning her embrace.
"But what about now? Can you still use the number?"

"I think so," she replied tentatively. "I never reported I'd
tried to use it, and apparently there was no record, so
it was never revoked. I'll try." She went to the telephone that was perched on a heap of sodden books

spilled from an upended shelf, and dialed briskly. Roger stared at her expectantly. She nodded. "I'm getting a ring," she said excitedly. "If only someone will answer. . . .

"Former Agent Q'nell reporting, Mriz," she spoke suddenly into the phone. "Class three emergency situation. Request immediate grab."

The force that enfolded Roger was as impalpable as smoke, but as unyielding as a concrete overcoat. It closed in on him from head to toe, lifting and rotating him; he was back in utter darkness. His attempt to yell was choked off by the pressure on his face. *Ye gods!* he agonized silently. *I can't breathe! I'm suffocating!*

He seemed to be traveling at high speed in an indeterminate direction, and he hastily squelched thoughts of a crushing impact, even as the obstruction vanished from his face. He took a deep breath and yelled, "UKR! Help! I'm suffocating!" He hung suspended in *some*thing which somehow didn't feel precisely like space, being of infinite density as well as extent. He could breathe now, he discovered. He lunged toward where he had last seen Q'nell, and felt himself expanding at the square of the velocity of propagation of electromagnetic radiation in a vacuum, in all directions.

"Q'nell!" he shouted frantically.

"Oh-oh, a four-oh-eight," an unfamiliar voice said directly into his left ear. He grabbed, encountered nothing. Now he was rotating gently, end over end.

"Stop!" he yelled. "I'll get seasick!" Then, "No, dammit, I won't!" he corrected before the first spasm could strike. "I feel fine, wonderful, in fact, and I'm strolling along under the elm trees on a fine fall day, on my way to a swell party at Marjorie's house!" Marjorie, he recalled vividly, was a rather mature five, and had red hair, in two long plaits. She had personally invited him to her birthday celebration, and he was bringing her a nice big box of candy *and* a game called *Five Significant Figures*, because she was a whiz at math and already knew the multiplication table up through the sevens. She'd be thrilled! Life was good. He started skipping, marveling only a little at his inexhaustible supply of energy. Skipping in great bounds, he felt as if he could fly.

He was cruising comfortably at ten feet, in a horizontal position, small paddling motions of his outstretched arms sufficing to maintain altitude. He was above the smooth green grass of a vast lawn with immense white houses at the far side, he noticed. The sidewalk and elm trees were far off to one side. He looked around for someone to talk to, saw a lone figure, a little girl, resting lazily on the grass under a tree. He angled downward and came in in a long, swooping slide. Up close, she looked like Q'nell, at the age of five. She sure was cute. He dropped in beside her, in the cool shade. "Hello," Roger said in what he thought was an ingratiating tone. "Who're you? Are you going to the party?"

"Cindy," the tot replied. She jumped up. "I have to go home to eat dinner," she said, and fled. Roger stood and watched her go. Then she stopped, turned, and stuck out her tongue.

"This is all *wrong*!" Roger groaned. "I need to talk to that kid, find out where/when I am!" Then he squeezed his eyes shut, staring into the oatmeal-textured blackness, and tried to remember just how he had done it the last time he had succeeded in shifting paradigms. *Just picture things as they ought to be, and could be,* he counseled himself sternly. My old home STV locus, *after* the ice cap and the desert phase. Sunshine and flowers . . .

He stumbled and opened his eyes to find he was in the middle of a wide meadow strewn with poppies. A herd of immense, shaggy mastodons grazed at the far side, up against the forest wall. "No, no, no!" he moaned. "This is the *past*! I wanted just far enough into the future to get safely past the disasters! UKR! Do it *right* this time!"

IT WAS YOU WHO DID THAT, NOT I, UKR's voice replied mildly, from just behind him. Roger jumped and spun around. S'lunt was standing there, immaculate in his white jumper.

"Don't creep up on me!" Roger snarled. "Where do you have your laundry done?" he demanded, and turned away. His eye fell on a low mound a few yards distant. He went to it, and dug a toe into the soft soil, encountering something hard under the surface. He dug harder and exposed a fragment of broken marble. He stooped and picked up a golf-ball-sized chunk. Squatting, he perceived that the mound was one of a row of such heaps which lay in a straight line, stretching off into the lush grass.

"See it better from an airplane," he reflected, and the stream of air against his face took his breath for a moment. He adjusted his goggles, and squinted past the tiny celluloid windshield and over the ring cowl, through the glistening arc of the spinning propellor at the clearly visible rectangle on the ground ahead and below. The roar of the seven-cylinder radial was a deafening bark. "Too damn noisy," he muttered, and the propellor stopped dead.

He was suddenly aware of the whine of air through the rigging wires and over the taut-doped fabric flying surfaces. He settled himself in the hard seat, grabbed the stick, and eased the nose up. He tried a gentle, banked turn to the left, snapped into a tight spin, and froze on the stick, his eyes tight shut.

He pictured the smooth meadow below slowing its rotation and tilting back to the horizontal, the plane floating down, closer, closer, hold it off, hold it off. He stalled her onto the ground in a perfect three-point attitude, and after a short roll-out, came to a halt. The gentle breeze wafted the reek of hot castor oil back from the silent engine. He could also smell dope and high-octane. With a sigh of relief, he clambered out of the cockpit to the wing-walk, and jumped down to the ground.

The linear formation ran off at an angle here, he noted. A human skull lay half-buried in a mound a few feet distant. He went over to it, and not until he had picked it up did he realize that it was a classic *Homo erectus* cranium, with a neat bullet-hole between the orbits. He stood, tossed the fossil aside and saw a man clad in rags approaching from a point near the mastodons. He went forward to meet the old fellow, who reached out toward him and called, "Roger!" in a ratchety voice.

"You *know* me?" Roger gasped and hurried forward to meet the old boy, who seemed distressed by his effort to run. His hand was like a claw, blue-veined and spotted. Roger looked into the aged, seamed face and recognized it.

"Julian!" he burst out. "What in the world . . . ?"

"I'm not sure it *is* in this world! Everything's been so strange, Roger. In fact, if it weren't for the fact that I'm seeing you, now, I'd think it was all some kind of nightmare! I've been marooned on a desert island with a starving polar bear, served aboard a pirate ship commanded by Charles Laughton, been arrested on Sainte-Addresse beach for indecent exposure when I was wearing the latest-style bikini briefs; I was chased by a stabbing cat, had a collision with a 1912 Simplex that almost flattened my Model T, spent a year in a hick jail, and—"

"I get the idea," Roger interrupted the reverie. "I've had some heavy experiences, too! But now—I have a strange feeling this wilderness is all that's left of the Grand Plaza and of Culture One!"

"That's right," Julian nodded. "Most perceptive of you!" There's not a stone left in place. I saw S'lunt a while ago, and he said the retroaltor equipment was intact, and we'd soon see some changes."

"That's probably not a good idea," Roger objected. "There's been too much meddling with the Fabric already."

"How do you propose to stop him?" Julian inquired. "He has an armored car. We're barehanded."

"I'll talk him out of it, with UKR's help," Roger stated grimly. "Where *is* he?"

"He just went to do a recon over where the ceremonial center used to be," Julian told him. "He thinks maybe

some of the field effects may still be intact in spite of
the destruction of the circuitry that gave rise to them."

"Sounds nutty to me," Roger commented shortly. "By
the way, what happened to Bob Armstrong and the other
fellow who was wandering around here?"

"The ape-man and his buddy, Lump, just disappeared one day," Julian told him. "The two-middle-
aged ladies . . . I don't know."

"Who do you think you're calling 'middle-aged,'
already?" a wrathful female voice demanded abruptly,
causing both Roger and Julian to jump and look around
wildly. The two women to whom Julian had so unchival-
rously referred stood a few feet away. One, the blonde,
was holding a plastic grocery-bag bulging with hard-look-
ing rutabagas, swinging it idly by the handles, Roger
noted—thinking, for some reason, of David and his sling,
about to brain Goliath.

"L-ladies," he blurted, "don't do anything hasty. Julian
only meant—that is, he didn't mean—"

"I heard the bum," Dottie cut in unheedingly. "I'll let
it pass this once. OK, Gert?" She glanced at her friend
for approval, still swinging the bag. Roger backed away
hastily.

"Where's S'lunt?" Roger gobbled. "UKR, can't you get
Inspector S'lunt back here?"

"I'm right here," the inspector's unctuous voice
announced. "Been here all along," he added. "My job,
you know is Designated Observance. Largely due to a
lack of observance on your part, with your grasshopper-
style manipulation of the Flux. Your sense of temporal
sequence, my boy, is badly flummoxed."

"Whose wouldn't be?" Roger demanded. "I got rather
accustomed to effect following cause directly, you know,
and since that arrangement seems to have been suspended, I admit I'm disoriented. So what? Get me back
home!" Roger paused for breath and yelled, "UKR! I
need you! Get on the ball!"

"Just what seems to be the problem here?" a gluey

voice interjected. It was Gom Blemp, who had strolled up unnoticed. His three eyes gazed mildly at Roger.

"Oh, you're the fellow who's been causing all the confusion, aren't you?" he said blandly.

"Who, *me*?" Roger was more indignant than ever. "Absolutely not! I'm an innocent victim! All I wanted was to get back where I started from!"

"Uh, yes, the birth noston. But of course," the Vorplisher mused on, "one can hardly do that: thus the life-long search for the security and the perfection from which one was so unjustly evicted. Pity, but there you are!"

"I wasn't yearning for the womb!" Roger objected. "I was yearning for my happy home with Q'nell!"

"And once you recovered it, what did you do?" UKR put in rhetorically. "You demanded changes, which you received. Now you are more discontented than ever!"

"It *wasn't* home!" Roger contradicted. "It was only the ruins of home!" He stared at the spot where the Vorplischer had been standing.

"Surely you didn't expect the temporal flux to jell at some unspecified point, just for your convenience," UKR dismissed the suggestion out-of-hand.

"Not exactly," Roger demurred. "I just want to get back where I *was*, before all this confusion! Where'd Gom Blemp go?"

"Home, one assumes," UKR dismissed the question. "After all, he's dealt with the Vrint, so why should he linger?"

"Where's his rocket ship, then?" Roger demanded.

"Advanced beings don't need them," UKR told him. "Alas," it intoned, returning to the subject at hand, "you can never go back, Roger. Time is a fluid. It's like wishing to return to a point upstream in a river. The precise arrangement of water molecules, plus impurities, which embraced your boat a year ago—or a moment ago—will never be repeated. Thus your melancholic nostalgia for things past is never to be appeased."

"That's not very comforting," Roger carped.

"Do you desire comfort, or truth?" UKR demanded.

"Comfort!" Roger replied without hesitation.

"I feared as much," UKR told him in a tone of resignation. "I have warped and even punctured the Fabric, on your behalf, Roger," he reminded him. "But as for attempting to distort the Matrix itself, I must draw the line there! Resign yourself. Those halcyon days together with your bride and your beloved Sears chair, your familiar telly, and Daphne's unending dilemnae are lost in the expended past."

CHAPTER THIRTY

"No!" Roger yelled. "They're not! I *know* Q'nell is all right: I just talked to her! As for my beloved chair, very well, I shall attempt to resign myself. As for Daphne, she can apply to the FCC for relief!"

"Your harshness ill befits such a victim of circumstance as yourself, Roger," UKR chided.

"Aha!" Roger retorted. "So you admit I'm a victim of circumstance!"

"Indeed," the mechanical entity agreed blandly. "Are not we all? I myself was constructed to serve a simple, straightforward function: to prevent your ingenious species from eliminating itself from the Fabric before it had attained its high destiny; yet I find myself endlessly embroiled in the misadventures of one obscure individual, namely yourself. Roger, dear boy, can you not somehow restrain your personal compulsions long enough to allow me to exercise my greater powers to restore the entropic Flow to a state of tranquillity?"

"If you're talking about my compulsion to escape from this mess and resume a normal life, the answer is a resounding 'NO!'" he declared resoundingly. "It ought to be easy," he went on breathlessly. "Just let me get back to Q'nell and our little unpaid-for love nest, and—"

" 'And' what, Roger?" UKR demanded, even as Roger saw the gray oatmeal surrounding him stiffen and coalesce into a shabby living room, showing signs of extensive but imcompetent repair, where a middle-aged woman in a dowdy housecoat was listlessly dusting a mud-caked coffee table. Roger took a step toward her and croaked. "Daphne!"

Daphne turned. The poor kid was showing signs of her ordeals, Roger noted, as she cried "Wilberforce! It's you! I hoped, but—" The enthusiasm faded from her voice. "Poor Willie; you've changed. Do you still . . . *can* you still . . . ?"

"Beats me, Daph," Roger gobbled. "I haven't had a chance to try lately."

" 'Love me?,' I was about to say," Daphne cut in. "And, Willie, I must insist: don't be gross!"

"Who, me?" Roger yelped. "My name's not 'Willie'!" he added.

"I know, dear, I know," Daphne cooed. "Do forgive me, Wilberforce. It's just that 'Wilberforce' is well, not exactly silly, I suppose, but unwieldy."

"Hey!" Roger burst out, "You're not Daphne, either! You're Q'nell—only she's not an old bag in a shabby housecoat with her hair not even combed!"

"Roger," Q'nell countered. "Do be kind. The years have taken their toll. Still, I always knew you'd come back someday, and here you are!"

"UKR!" Roger groaned. He sat on the edge of a hard chair which promptly collapsed under him. "This is all wrong!" he yelled. In the process of getting to his feet, his eyes fell on his clawlike, liver-spotted hand. "I have a right to get old the usual way!" he declared emphatically. "You've jumped me right over my entire late youth into advanced middle age! I demand you straighten this out right now!"

"Roger," Q'nell cautioned, "don't demand. I'm sure Mr. Ucker will do the right thing."

IT IS NOT A SIMPLE TASK, UKR boomed out in his old way. AFTER YOU'VE SO GRIEVOUSLY SNARLED YOUR LIFELINES, YOU CAN'T EXPECT THE FABRIC SIMPLY TO RETURN TO SOME CHOSEN STATE. YOU PEOPLE HAD EVERY OPPORTUNITY TO MAKE USE OF THE GIFTS OF NATURE TO MAKE YOUR LIVES HARMONIOUS; YOU CHOSE INSTEAD TO STRAIN AGAINST THE WEAVE OF THE FABRIC AND TO TWIST THE STRANDS. DID YOU REALLY EXPECT TO CUT YOUR WAY ACROSS THE HARMONIOUSLY DESIGNED PATTERN OF THE COSMIC ALL AND NOT PAY THE PRICE? THE PRINCIPLE OF CON- SERVATION OF ENTROPY WILL NOT BE DENIED. RESIGN YOURSELF, ROGER!

"What about poor Q'nell?" he came back sharply. "She's an innocent bystander. All the while I was being tossed hither and thither, she was right here, carrying on the charade, under difficult circumstances!"

"When she first set out to traverse the Bore," UKR replied quietly, "she, all unknowing, detached her vital filament from the warp and woof of the Fabric."

" 'All unknowing'; you said it yourself!" Roger charged. "She was innocent! Put her back where she was, even if I'm doomed to wander around alone in this disaster area!"

YOUR SELFLESSNESS DOES YOU CREDIT, ROGER, the great voice boomed. I SHALL TRY AGAIN.

Instantly, Roger found himself clamped rigidly in place by a form-fitting, bitterly cold mass—ice, he realized as soon as he was able to blink his eyes and see the pellucid blue-green depths encompassing him. There was a vacant space before his face, apparently melted by his breath, that permitted him to continue that function—for as long at least, he realized in panic, as the supply of air in the space lasted. He tried a deep breath, found he could breathe easily, the air-space apparently communicating with the atmosphere via the spongy ice-mass.

He tried a yell; that didn't work. but UKR's voice spoke up calmly:

"I shifted you, quite at random, Roger, to the locus you would now occupy had events proceeded in a very slightly different direction, due to the interference by your compatriot, Lump, who decided to take over the tribe from Yug, the hereditary king thereof. As a result, the migrating group found itself trapped by ice in an isolated valley in Greenland, just prior to the most recent advance of the glacier."

"What's that got to do with *me?*" Roger managed to gasp out.

"You are, of course, a direct descendant of every member of the tribe; when your ancestors found themselves limited to the resources of a ten-square-mile area, they were called upon to exercise all their ingenuity to survive. There in their isolated stronghold, spurred by necessity, they soon developed a rude technology which enabled their descendants to proceed, via skin-boat, to the mainland of Canada, after an interruption of three centuries. They went on to mingle and interbreed with the oriental newcomers arriving via the Bering Strait, and in time to produce the individual known as Roger Tyson. The surname dervies from your hundred-and-tenth-generation-back grandfather, one Tuh the Terrible, who was first to breach the ice-wall to the west."

"What's that got to do with me being buried in ice?" Roger demanded.

"Had the tribe not succeeded in their risky voyage, they'd have remained in Greenland, a temperate and fruitful territory before the ice, and you'd have been born there one hundred and ten generations later. Had the plankton not proliferated, due to iron-rich conditions caused by meteorite impacts in Antarctica, thus producing a plankton bloom and increasing CO_2 production, the ice would have formed even earlier and thicker. The juxtaposition of yourself with the glaciation produced your present situation."

"That's ridiculous!" Roger pointed out. "I *didn't* grow

up in Greenland, and I *didn't* fall into an ice crevasse or
whatever!"

"But indeed you—or your alternate in a variant line—
did, indeed, do just that. I shifted your primary consciousness to a line chosen at random, and it happened
to be the one you are now experiencing."

"How long do you think I'll live, encased in ice?"
Roger yelled.

"Twenty-two minutes and four seconds, according to
your personal—and arbitrary—ordering of entropic flow,"
UKR informed him promptly. "I perceive that this is an
inadequate period in which to experience your full quota
of pain, discomfort, boredom, and frustration, and the
other concomitants of organic existence," UKR conceded. "Accordingly, I shall shift you along a few parameters, and perhaps you'll find yourself in an STV niche
more conducive to the unfoldment of your destiny."

"Why not pick the best spot available?" Roger
demanded. "There must be some possible futures—or
past—where I had better luck!"

"To attempt purposefully to counter the Grand Design
of the Cosmic All," the disembodied voice of UKR informed Roger, "would be to seriously distort the Fabric;
a random modification produces no such stress in the
Matrix. That's why your frequent overt attempts to modify the progress of affairs have not yet precipitated total
doom. Your efforts, unencumbered as they are by any
rational pattern of activity, were able to be rejected as
negligible by the inherent cohesiveness of the entropic
Meniscus."

CHAPTER THIRTY-ONE

"Swell," Roger retorted sarcastically. "I'm doomed to bounce around at random forever—and what do you mean, no rational pattern of activity? You talk as if I were an imbecile just floundering around, striking out at random!"

"Succinctly put," UKR approved. "But just now I'm gathering my vram-energies to attempt, one final time, to restore your personal filament to its *ub initio* state, as developed in the absence of intrusive factors. A complex computation indeed, I assure you."

"No doubt," Roger mumbled. "But let's get on with it, eh? Where'd Julian go? And S'lunt? I was just talking to them." *What I really need to do,* he informed himself, *is to talk to the Builder. He'll fix things!*

"I fear your paradigm has slipped a few million frames of reference," UKR dismissed the query. "They were here over a hundred thousand years (sic) ago."

"No, about five minutes," Roger corrected, a bit impatiently. "You don't quite have the hang of it yet. And what happened to Culture One?" he asked next, while a hundred other pressing questions clamored for relief, as the ice swiftly melted away, leaving him standing on a

317

bleak tundra, soaked and shaking, but with his curiosity unimpaired. *Quiver.*

"Complacency," UKR told him. "They thought they'd solved all the problems that plague mankind, and so became casual in their surveillance of the Bore. It's still an open wound in Matrical STV, you know."

"I didn't realize," Roger gasped. "I thought those boys had all the answers, but look what they came to . . ." He gazed along the line of ruined foundations, remembering the majestic beauty of the former Grand Plaza, palace-lined, with its fountains and flower beds.

"Too bad," he muttered. "Couldn't you . . . ?"

"Tsk," UKR chided mildly. "There you go again, Roger, once more, in spite of all, irresponsibly proposing yet further meddling with the Fabric. It won't do, my boy! You must learn to be content with the natural harmonies, forget about self-conceived Utopias, and accept reality without carping."

"Rats," Roger replied coolly. "Even an amoeba tries to keep eating while avoiding being eaten. I imagine the amoebic dream of Utopia isn't far different from my own."

"The real problem," UKR confided, "is that we must contend with a basic instability in the Web, engendered by an intrusive force."

"The Monitor Service!" Roger blurted. "Q'nell told me they were responsible for getting me into all this in the first place! It wasn't my fault!"

"A fitting epitaph for practically everyone," UKR stated. "As for the Monitor Service, it has long since been reduced to a mere surveillance agency. You were not the only individual unceremoniously snatched from his paradigm and tossed into another, to the detriment of order."

"Well," Roger offered, trying to sound reasonable, "since you admit I was a victim, not a criminal, I should think you'd do the right thing now, and undo what the grab-team did to me. Speaking of which, it was another grab-team that dumped me *here!*"

"'The right thing,' you say, Roger," was the reply. "A highly subjective expression, that. One hardly knows how to define its denotation in this pseudo-context."

"Get me home with Q'nell, safe and sound, with the grass needing mowing, and the mortgage payment due, and the car not starting! That's what!" Roger yelled in spite of himself. Just then, he noticed a shoe-sized Vrint scuttling across the jagged surface of a shattered marble block.

"It's the Vrint!" he yelled. "Step on it! They've been causing trouble, putting words in people's mouths! And I though you said that Blemp fellow had 'dealt with' it!"

I suggest you consider well before initiating any aggressive action, directed toward great Vrint! the silent Vrint voice snapped. *As for Gom Blemp, we have come to an accommodation.*

"Oh, the fix is in, eh?" Roger yelled. "It figures! What did he do? Swap you Earth for immunity back home?"

That would hardly constitute an equitable arrangement, the Vrint sneered. *Actually—*

"UKR!" Roger blurted. "You don't have to take any lip from a damn bug! Show it where the power is!"

"No need, Roger," UKR said, as the Vrint spread wings and buzzed away. "The Vrint and I have come to an understanding, as well. He meant no insolence to me, only to you."

"Oh, I suppose that's all right!" Roger snorted. "I've stepped on plenty of these fellows, and—" He jumped up on the slab, took a quick step after a rat-sized Vrint unit, and stamped down hard on it. It crunched with a satisfying sound, though its legs continued to thresh helplessly. Roger looked up: a Vrint the size of a Sherman tank was advancing toward him from the woods.

"UKR!" he squeaked. "Help! No more of your ineffective waffling around, either! Get rid of this Vrint—or these Vrint—right now!"

"I didn't think it possible, Roger," UKr replied coldly, "but you have succeeded in annoying me, mere mechanical device though I am. As a result, I feel disinclined to

intrude. You may deal with the Vrint Batchmaster as you
wish. I shall observe for the record."

"But I—" Roger picked up a broken brick from what
had once been a petunia bed. He took aim at the yard-
wide compound eye, and threw with deadly accuracy.
Moist matter splattered as the missile impacted dead
center and clung there, embedded in the ruined ocular.
The Vrint came to a shuddery halt, its antennae and
mouth parts vibrating furiously. Its armored legs scrabbled against the macadam, scoring black streaks; then it
flipped over on its back and lay feebly waving its limbs.
All around, Roger noted peripherally, black beetles of all
sizes lay similarly incapacitated.

"Well done, lad!" UKR boomed out. "I knew you
could do it! I realized your intemperate speech was due
to the malign interference of the Vrint, but I thought it
would be salutary for you to deal with the threat yourself.
I congratulate you! You see now you're not quite the
ineffectual nonentity you thought you were."

"I did not!" Roger yelled. "Think I was a nincompoop,
I mean!"

"Still, you prevailed, unassisted," UKR insisted.

"Swell!" Roger snorted. "What if I hadn't?"

"Yet another viable strand in the Fabric would have
been aborted" UKR scolded. "So it's well you succeeded.
I shall make specific mention of that in my report to the
Builder."

"By the way," Roger demanded, "where *is* this Builder
of yours? Where does he stay? I'd like to meet him and
give him a piece of my mind!" *Quiver.*

The sun was warm on the beach. Roger looked along
the deserted strand stretching where the ruined Plaza
had been a moment before. It was deserted except for a
small child earnestly patting a mound of sand into a
roughly conical shape. She looked up at Roger and said.
"Hi, Mister. My name is Cindy. I'm making a castle.
What's your name?"

"I see it has a moat," Roger replied. "I'm Roger."

"It wouldn't be much of a castle without a moat,"

Cindy rebuked him sharply. "Can *you* make a castle, Wodger?" she went on to inquire. "We could have a war."

"I'd rather be friends, Cindy," Roger replied, but he squatted beside her and began to dig.

"Not right there!" his putative foe complained. "That's part of *my* demesne! Anyway, my cannon could blow you up in a minute at that range!"

"Sorry." Roger gulped, and backed off six feet. "This OK?" he inquired hopefully.

"I see you don't know much about tactics," Cindy rebuked.

"It was more the logistics I was concerned about," Roger explained. His fingers encountered something smooth and hard, like a buried bone, he thought: he probed and pulled a human mandible, complete with fillings, from the soil. He dropped it and scrambled hastily to his feet.

"That's probably old Red," Cindy remarked. She squinted along the beach and nodded. "Keep digging," she commanded. "Just ignore Red. The chest is under him."

"Wha-what chest?" Roger gasped. "Don't look, Cindy, there's more bones here."

"Sure," the tot responded. "You think he didn't have a full set?"

"What chest?" Roger hastily pushed the cranium down out of sight.

"The one Walter buried," Cindy explained, not entirely patiently. "You better dig it up, Roger. I don't think I ought to mess with the continua any more right now."

"'Mess with the continua'?" Roger gulped. "You talk as if *you* were Builder!"

"Sure, that's my nickname," she confirmed. "But right now I'm tired of building. It's a lousy castle anyway." With a kick, she returned her construction to the elemental sand from which she evoked it. She turned and ran off along the shore.

"Bye, Woger," floated back over her shoulder.

"Hey, wait!" Roger choked as he got to his feet to give chase, but the kid was remarkably fast, he acknowledged; the little girl was nowhere to be seen.

"Hey, Roger!" a breathless voice called from the direction of the jungle-like vegetation above the tidal zone. Roger put a foot in Cindy's excavation and fell heavily. A firm grip on his elbow enabled him to regain his feet. He spat sand and looked into the youthful face of Rusty Naill.

"How . . . ?" he choked. "Rusty, the last time I saw you . . . !"

" 'The next time,' you mean," Rusty corrected cheerfully. "Say, this is strange. The first time I was here—"

"you mean you've been here before?" Roger gasped.

"Or will be," Rusty continued patiently. "It's all an illusion, this before-and-after stuff," Naill went on. "Anyway, my boat swamped, and I met a couple of Culture One folks, and—" He broke off to look down along the waterline.

"There were some men," he muttered. "They buried a chest, right about here." His eye fell on the bones at Roger's feet. "This is the spot," he said. "They shot one fellow and dumped him in on top of the chest." His eyes went to Roger's shallow excavation. "Did you find—?"

"Just the bones, so far," Roger replied. Both men went to their knees and began digging, sending the dry sand flying.

In a moment they had exposed the top of an old-fashioned steamer trunk, with hardwood battens. The latch was open. Roger lifted the lid, even as Rusty yelled, "Wait!" The explosion threw both men backward in a cloud of sand.

"Say," Roger yelled to Rusty, who was brushing sand from his face. "Did you see her? The little girl, I mean."

Rusty shook his head. "Here, you mean?" he inquired. "No, I was riding along State Street in a gray 1937 Cadillac 75; then all of a sudden the driver hung a left and stopped. I got out, and that Oob character popped out of an alley and got in. Then I was here. I saw you come over. And I've got a hot appointment in ten minutes!" He pulled back a French cuff and glanced at a diamond-studded watch, brushed sand from his knees, and said, "Wait a minute; I want to check the bushes." He walked off toward the wall of Sabal palms.

Roger stared after him, then jumped up. "Hey!" he yelled. "We have to talk!" But Rusty was already lost to sight in the dense vegetation. Roger advanced to the barrier and heard the sounds of someone approaching from the direction in which Rusty had disappeared. A moment later Bob Armstrong burst from a patch of wild bananas to confront Roger.

"Roger!" he blurted, putting out a hand as if to restrain him. "Don't run off! I just saw Rusty, but he pushed me aside as if I weren't there—well, if I wasn't there, he wouldn't be pushing me aside, but you know what I mean. Anyway—"

"What are you babbling about, Bob?" Roger cut him off. "Look, we're in this together, and we have to stick together. So just go tell Rusty to come on back and we'll have a council of war or something and figure out what to do. By the way, I just met the Builder."

"Who's that?" Bob demanded. "*I'm* in charge of the New Visions promotion! When I got back to the office, Mr. Kumchett was just leaving as I came into Design Section. He was upset about the site plan for New Visions here. I grabbed a pencil and showed him how we could dig a lagoon and—well, like I said, he put me in charge on the spot." Bob paused to stare out to sea. "Great location, eh? Buy land on the other side of the highway, Roger. We're due for a boom!"

"I told you about the Builder," Roger groaned. "You remember—"

"Sure, I remember." Bob waved aside the explanation, "Something about the whole human race evolving into a single super-being that includes the essence of everyone who ever lived, which makes you—and me, too—*part* of the Builder, so he's concerned with our welfare, and tries to help us."

" 'She,' " Roger corrected. "A little girl about six years old, she looks like, and she builds things and then gets bored with them and knocks them apart."

"Swell," Bob remarked. "That explains why life has been such a mess! Where's this kid?"

"Beats me," Roger soothed. "We've all had our lives messed up by this thing. But as soon as I catch up with the Builder, she'll get busy putting things back as they should be."

"Yeah, but—" Rusty started.

TUT-TUT, ROGER, UKR came in severely. YOU PROPOSE TO REPAIR PAST MEDDLING WITH YET MORE MEDDLING.

"I do not!" Roger countered hotly. "Fixing what other people have screwed up isn't meddling! Now, do what you were built to do! Get me home and I mean *really* home, and Bob and Rusty, too! Hurry up!"

"That disembodied voice is spooky," Rusty commented. "Maybe you ought to try being polite, Roger."

"Doesn't work. UKR does as it likes. It doesn't really care about us! And the Builder has it outranked. As soon as I find her—"

"Where is she, Roger?" Julian spoke up from behind him.

Roger jumped and spun to address the hapless fellow. "Beats me!" he said once again. Then,

"Don't DO that!" he yelled. "People are always creeping up behind me! I don't like it! OK?"

"Look over there, Roger," Julian suggested mildly. "It's another of those nasty beetles. I thought they were all gone. Didn't that Blemp fellow take care of them?"

"I thought he did," Roger agreed. "But he seems to have missed this fellow. Big one, too."

"Not as big as that one the size of a rhino we saw in the jungle," Rusty remarked.

"I don't remember that," Roger grunted. "This one's big enough."

IT IS A FULL BATCHMASTER, UKR contributed. PITY GOM BLEMP FAILED TO INCLUDE IT IN

HIS MASS TRANSFER. IT SEEMS TO BE COMPLI-CATING MATTERS. SUPPOSE I DEAL WITH IT. ANY OBJECTIONS TO THAT, ROGER?

"Not unless I find it in my living room when I get home!" Roger snorted. "Get rid of it *permanently*!"

THIS WILL REQUIRE A MAJOR DIVERSION OF STV ENERGIES FROM THE IMMEDIATE ENVI-RONMENTAL STRUCTURE, UKR announced. SO BE PATIENT, FELLOWS.

As UKR's booming voice fell silent, Roger felt a sudden chill in the air. He smelled a rank odor of rotting seaweed, or something that seemed to him to smell like rotting seaweed would smell if he'd ever smelled any. The light dimmed to a watery gray, while illuminated a vista of lichen-scabbed rock, black soil, and a patch of snow, stretching to a distant jagged mountain range.

Quiver.

"Hey, UKR!" Roger yelled. "I'll freeze to death—or *we'll* freeze to death," he amended generously, remembering the other fellows. He turned to address them, and saw that he was alone. "What's *this* place? It sure isn't Brantville!"

"This is the region of Greenland known as Ungotarök," UKR told him, "relieved of its ice burden. In a few thousand years, vegetation will have gained a foothold, and the area will be well on its way to becoming arable land."

"Great!" Roger complained. "And what am I supposed to do for the next few millennia, while I'm waiting for a chance to plow solid rock to put in a crop of sugar beets?"

"I suggest you meditate on one of the Cosmic Mysteries," UKR offered. "By the time you solve them, the top few inches of rock will have become friable soil."

"I have no intention of frying any soil!" Roger barked. "Get me out of here!"

"Whither?" UKR's conversational tone inquired.

"Couldn't you assume human form?" Roger pled. "Talking to the atmosphere still give me the willies!"

A coal-black, seven-foot Zulu with a broad-headed spear cleared his throat, causing Roger to jump. "I *told* you—or someone—not to sneak up on me!" he complained, then to the newcomer, "Hi, I'm Tyson, Roger Tyson." He offered a hand, which the warrior inspected carefully from a distance.

"Thank you, no, old chap," he said. "I've already lunched, you see."

"I just meant to shake hands," Roger hastened to explain. "I didn't expect you to eat it!"

"I'm Cetaslopaas," the African offered. "I've heard the palm of the hand is the best part, but of course I'm not an anthropophagist, myself."

He looked around. "I think perhaps old Opener-of-Roads was right about this valley being taboo," he commented. "Too damn cold by half, and no vegetation. What're *you* doing there, stranger?"

"You mean 'a cannibal,'" Roger interpreted.

Cetaslopaas nodded. "Prefer rat, personally," he commented. "Easier to get, too: village is full of the beggars."

"Which way is the nearest police station, or hospital, or nut-house?" Roger asked humbly. "Any kind of official installation, you know, where I can register a complaint. OK if I call you 'Setty'?"

The latter shook his head. "'Sloppy' is my informal sobriquet," he corrected. "Ever since I was a nipper."

"Okay, Sloppy," Roger conceded. "You live around here?"

"My word, no," Sloppy disdained. "I was taking my constitutional, postprandial stroll—you know, do it every day, good for ails one and all that—and I had a minor impulse to defy the taboo—and all of a sudden—"

"I know." Roger nodded. "You were someplace else." He looked at the bleak landscape and at Sloppy's scant costume of beads and feathers.

"UKR will *have* to get us out of here quick," he said reassuringly, "or you'll freeze."

Sloppy nodded, "I offered a jungle-fowl only last

evening," he remarked. "I'm in good grace with old Snaky-bones."

"Who's 'Snaky-bones'?" Roger gulped.

"A snake, of course," Sloppy explained. "Bloody immense beggar; we feed him a goat every week. Built a special sanctuary for him, very big juju. Anyone who even looks hard at it falls dead. Gets him in out of the hot sun—can't stand too much, you know, and we have fellows on the job twenty-four hours a day, praying to him. My jungle-fowl was an extra, you see, thus doubly appreciated. What was that you called him, 'Ucker'?"

"That's right." Roger looked around nervously. "Where does this 'Snaky-bones' stay?"

"Oh." Sloppy waved the spear carelessly, missing Roger narrowly. "Over that way, when he's not in his sanctuary. Ate one of his prayer-slaves only yesterday, so he won't be likely to snack on us."

"That's comforting," Roger sighed. "Is the bite poisonous?"

"Oh, my word, yes," Roger's new friend assured him. "Once we did a bit of an experiment: milked him for a drop of venom and put it on a spear, and pricked twenty-five goats. Every last one dropped dead."

"Impressive," Roger commented with a shudder, eyeing the tarry-coated spear-point. "Could you just point that some other way?"

"Oh, got the wind up, eh, old chap?" Sloppy murmured and shifted the weapon, being careful not to poke himself in the process. "Now, old boy," he continued briskly, "you'd better invoke this 'Ucker' avatar of yours against the new plague. My invocations have availed naught. *Very* unresponsive today, old Snaky is."

"UKR!" Roger yelped. "*Do* something!"

Sloppy jumped and mumbled under his breath as UKR, back in his green-demon guise, emerged from the underbrush. He waved away Sloppy's magical passes.

"Kindly don't DO that, sir," he carped. "Tends to make my bones itch."

"Most dreadfully sorry," Sloppy apologized quickly.

"Perhaps you could suggest a more pleasing incantation . . ."

"Perhaps the Potent Puce," UKR suggested.

"Could you refresh my memory?" Sloppy begged hopefully.

"Glad to," UKR replied. "Hold your nose, as if you smelled a cop, say, and shift your weight quickly from one foot to the other, to the rhythm of *'Casey Jones.'* "

Sloppy complied, bouncing from foot to foot with commendable agility, and peeking cross-eyed past his nose-holding hand with an anxious expression.

"A little slower," UKR specified. "And you might flex your elbows just a bit, for dynamic balance, you know."

"Great Heavens!" Sloppy blurted. "That's almost—no it *is*, the traditional Thunder Dance! I'd better—"

"Keep going!" UKR decreed. "It feels *so* good, especially in that hard-to-reach area between the shoulder blades, you know."

"But," the bouncing warrior objected, "we'd better get to high ground! When one invokes Umble-Doob, one gets prompt results!"

"Yummy retired years ago," UKR dismissed the plaint. "Get those knees up! Pick up the beat: *'Two locomotives are a-goin to bump!'* There, that's better! Excuse me, Roger, it's been a long time." With that, the squat ogre winked out like a switched-off light.

"My word!" Sloppy breathed, panting from his exertion as he slowed his prance and let his arms fall to his sides, the spear-point poking the ground, where it acquired a coating of leaf litter adhering to the sticky venom. He wiped it absently. "That Ucker of yours is an ugly beggar," he remarked. "And fancy his knowing Yumble-Doob, after all these years. We gave up his cult when he failed us in the Year of the Beetles," he explained. "Look! There's one now!" He ducked behind a tree and urged Roger to do the same. "Filthy creatures have the power to swell up suddenly to the size of a rhino," Sloppy explained.

"Say," he went on, "the reason I was out here, actually,

was that I heard that gang of degenerates in the next hollow over were holding some palefellas like you prisoner; plan to eat them, one supposes. Thought it would wipe their eye for fair if I could manage to set the blighters loose. At first, I thought you were one of them, escaped on your own, but then I realized . . ."

" 'Palefellas' like me?" Roger squeaked. "In the hands of cannibals?"

"Oh, they're quite all right, so far," Roger's new acquaintance reassured him. "They're in the 'fattening-up' stage. Resting and eating, you know."

"We have to do something," Roger moaned. "You lead the way, and I'll think up a plan as soon as I see the situation."

"No 'plan' needed, old chap," Sloppy told him. "It's clear enough: we need to release them before they get to the awkward part—when the priests come along to strangle them, as a humane gesture, you know."

"Sure, but—" Roger offered, just as, with a crunching sound, an oversized Vrint burst from the surrounding jungle. Sloppy yelped and dodged behind Roger, his spear in working position.

"Don't bother poking it with that," Roger suggested. "It's a machine; poison won't hurt it."

"Poissibly," Sloppy returned, "but I'll wager a good jab in the junction box, just there . . ." He indicated the spot by thrusting the broad spear-point into the area between the Vrint's foremost pair of mandibuloids, at which the massive thing came to an abrupt halt, said *"skirt-chuff-zing,"* and went limp. Sloppy twisted the spear and thrust it deeper. Suddenly Roger noticed other, smaller Vrint which had been creeping unobtrusively closer, all flipping onto their backs, moving their limbs feebly.

"Just as I thought," Sloppy commented with satisfaction. "The beggars are slaved to the master unit." He withdrew his weapon, sniffed the point, frowned, and went forward to study the broken apparatus. He picked up a foot-long slave unit, sniffed again, and turned to Roger. "These damn things are *tunt*." He cast the dead

Vrintlet aside and wiped his hand on some convenient leaves. "All we need to do—"

"Watch it!" Roger cut in, as he noticed the sounds of something approaching from the left. Then Oob appeared, his color faded to a lifeless pale violet.

"Roger," he called in his glutinous voice, sounding out of breath, "I appeal to you as a fellow sentient being—help me! I'm being pursued by—"

Before Oob could explain further, a slim young brunette came into view, modishly dressed, but looking exhausted and out of patience. Her eye fell on Roger.

"You, there!" she yelled. "Don't go away. I got a bone to pick with you!"

"Who, me?" Roger gasped. "Don't blame *me* for your problems, Madame, whatever they are! I'm as much at sea as you!"

A second stylish young matron, this one blonde, followed the first. "Dottie!" she called. "You—I—what?"

Dottie had halted and stood, her fists planted firmly on her shapely hips, staring from Sloppy to the dead Vrint, then to Oob.

"Looky here, Dot," Gert snapped. "It's the monster! The same one we was after seeing in the market! *It's* responsible for all the craziness! Hey, you!" she barked at Oob, who tried unsuccessfully to hide behind Roger. "What's after going on here, entirely?"

"Have I not enough misery?" the Rhox inquired of an indifferent universe. "Madame," he said sternly to Dottie Gelbfleisch, "I should think you'd appreciate the great benefit you've derived from your passage across the loci: you're young again, slim and pretty, just as you were before you met Irving! Appreciate! Enjoy!"

Dottie whirled to confront Gert, froze, then blurted: "It's right, Gertrude! The rutabaga's right! You're not a day over twenty-five!"

"Twenty-three next March," Gert corrected. She was staring, transfixed, at Dottie. "Oh, Dorothy," she gushed, "I never realized you were so good-looking! You're like when we first met, in the war, remember?"

"Certainly I remember," Dot came back. "All that rationing! Still, we met in the meat line, so some good came of it."

The two pretty young ladies fell into an exchange of mutual reminiscences, punctuated by comments on their changed appearance.

CHAPTER THIRTY-TWO

"Dot! Is my complexion as smooth as yours?" Gert touched her cheek and smiled contentedly. "And my bazooms! Are they back—?"

"All the way, Gert!" Dot congratulated. "Those hips!" She held out her hand and stroked the back of it. "Poifect!" she judged. "And Gert, I *feel* good!"

"Sure!" Gert agreed. "You know, Dot, feeling good isn't just the absence of feeling *bad*. It's—I don't know: it's like life is s'pose to be! Like when I was a little kid!" She broke off to study Oob carefully.

"Is this *your* doing, you big ugly darling, you?"

Oob hung his tentacles modestly. "In a sense," he conceded. "You see, when you passed the Portal, a great deal of accumulated entropic detritus was stripped away—"

"Skip all that," Gert cut in. "Just show us how to get home, and we'll take it from there! Dot, can you imagine the look on Irving's face when you—"

"And that Patrick Moynihan, too!" Dot reminded her friend. "The two of 'em, they'll reform right on the spot, the . . . the . . ."

" 'Spalpeens,' " Gert supplied. "Come on, Dot, let's go find 'em."

"Roger!" Oob persisted, "I've had a ghastly time of it!

332

I was locked in a truck by someone disguised as a child, and was only released when you broke the mantra by disturbing poor old Red's bones! Difficult spell, that one!"

"Where's your Portal?" Roger demanded. "I want to use it, and so does Cetaslopsomething here. He likes to be called 'Sloppy.'"

"Spare me, Roger," Oob groaned. "My vram energies are depleted. My Portal . . ."

"Don't tell me you've *lost* it!" Roger commanded.

"Not at all," Oob protested. "After all, one hardly 'loses' equipment lent one by the Authority."

"That's a new one," Roger carped. "Who's this Authority with a capital 'A'?"

"The Authority," Oob replied stiffly, "administers the potency of the Builder during her minority."

"Well, that's a help," Roger conceded. "I thought we were all at the mercy of the whim of a baby."

"Not precisely a baby." UKR came in, startling Roger. "As the embodiment of the entire genus Homo, the Builder, of course, can be manifested as an individual of either sex, and of any age. Why assume a middle-aged male?"

"No reason, I guess," Roger mumbled. "I guess six-year-olds do have a better deal."

"In any event, the Builder at any stage of maturation is not lightly to be dismissed!" Oob reprimanded Roger sharply.

"Of course not," Roger agreed fervently. "She can fix everything, if I just have a chance to talk to her."

"Here," Rusty put in. "What—or maybe who—is this talking vegetable? Who were the chicks?"

"Pray forgive me," Roger replied hastily. "Clarence, this is Oob, a Rhox who conceives it as his duty to interfere with my life at critical moments. He's on Culture One's Most Wanted List. On the other hand, he *can* be helpful at times."

"Then by all means, let this be one of the times," Rusty urged. "Where'd Bob go?" he demanded inconsequentially.

"Over there." Roger waved toward the palm trees. "But what I'm wondering is how Oob got free from that attic onto a ship, and why they buried him here."

"Oh, the trunk was sold for junk when the old man fell dead," Rusty informed Roger. "I'm still sort of in touch with young Bobby; he went on, met Mel Lepke, and eventually became an international scrap dealer. He was the one who ran down the trunk through channels and was smuggling it into the U.S.A. Lepke thought it was full of dope. His boys found out about it and mutinied, then had the bright idea they'd kill old Bobby and retail the horse themselves. They planned to come back after dark and get it. Then old Red made a mistake: he told them he was a narc, and Itchy shot him. That's him back in the hole."

"How about it, Oob?" Roger demanded. "Why'd you stay in the trunk all that time? By the way, how long *were* you in there?"

"Sixteen years, local," Oob replied grumpily. "I had no room in which to deploy my bope nodes," he added. "Most frustrating."

"So you get your bope nodes going and get us out of here!" Roger demanded.

"Hey!" Rusty interrupted. "There's *another* of those damn bugs!" Roger turned impatiently to shush the nervous fellow, but instead froze, with his mouth open, staring at the moving-van-sized beetle, which stood poised on six shiny blue-black beetle-legs that seemed to bow under the apparatus's immense weight. Its antennae were moving in a hypnotic pattern.

"Get back, Roger," Rusty cautioned. "It's going to charge!"

"Oob!" Roger choked. "*Do* something! You can't squat there and let this alien squash humans in their own world!"

"I don't quite see the relevance of planetary origin to the issue," Oob carped. "It would willingly squash anyone who got in its way. It's a full-fledged Swarm

Master, possessed of potencies unknown to lesser Vrint."

"So, do you plan to let it squash you?" Roger demanded.

"By no means," Oob said coolly. "Stand back, fellows, this is a matter for serious incantation."

"'Incantation'?" Rusty echoed. "You mean you're going to try to use magic on this monster?"

"Precisely," Oob confirmed smugly. "A Swarm Master is capable, quite easily, of negating any overtly physical measures I might take. There's an old juju, however, which will fix its wagon!" The rutabaga-shaped being, now a deep purple, turned to Sloppy. "Would you care to assist, Chief?"

"Say," Roger spoke up, "you didn't tell me you were the chief of that tribe of yours!"

"There was no occasion for an exchange of credentials, Roger," the tall spearman replied. "One hardly desires to appear boastful. As for the juju, Mister Oob, it will be my pleasure. Suppose I handle the *zang* ritual behind you, whilst you make the big juju in front."

"My idea exactly!" Oob agreed as he bustled past his assistant to take up a position before the immobile Vrint. He said, "Huh! Vrint!" in a hoarse croak; then he began to wave his multiple limbs in counterpoint to the superbug's antennae-waving. Sloppy took up a stance with his arms spread, while wiggling his fingers and waving his rear from side to side. He glanced over his shoulder at Rusty.

"Sorry, chaps," he said in an undertone. "Quite undignified, but in such a situation, dignity must go by the board. Huh!" he snarled, and advanced a step, wriggling, toward the object of his efforts. Oob waved him back.

"Kindly don't get ahead of my vram-line," he admonished. "Messes up the vibrations, you know. Otherwise, you're doing fine. I can feel the glimigton line rising to operational level. Keep it up!" As he spoke, Oob advanced until he was almost under the bug's mouthparts, which were working nervously now.

"Look out!" Roger yelped. "He might bite!"

"No fear," Oob replied urbanely. "A Vrint Swarm Master requires no food; only a supply of vram energies, drawn from the cosmos, the access to which Sloppy and I are now depriving it of."

The huge Vrint attempted a lunge past Oob, but collapsed instead and lay motionless, emitting a faint buzzing sound. Oob turned to congratulate his colleague in necromancy, and Roger grabbed Rusty's arm and led him off, protesting, along the beach. Rusty looked around suddenly and halted.

"Hey," he exclaimed. "How'd I get *here*? I was in Chicago—"

"You came out of the bushes," Roger explained mildly.

"Where are you—what—?" Rusty expostulated. "That Oob-thing knocked out the Vrint-thing, and now we can—"

"We can get back up into that bunch of palm trees and out of sight, before Oob decides to start playing more tricks," Roger countered. "He's an impulsive fellow—and the impulse is usually to do mischief."

"Oh. I was wondering . . ." Rusty's voice trailed off as he saw Oob, now glowing a vivid blue-violet, squat over the fallen Vrint and deftly open a panel and grope inside. He withdrew his grasping member holding a small disk, which he tucked away even as he turned his attention to Roger.

"Oh, there you are!" he caroled as well as one can with a voice like a bowl of gruel.

"Don't hurry away, Roger my boy," Oob went on. "I have it! The Prime program; and we can discover all the Vrint secrets!"

"I'm not interested in any secrets," Roger grated, but Rusty demurred, pulling free of Roger's grasp on his sleeve.

"*I* am!" he announced, and went back to confer with the Rhox.

"Look here, Roger," Oob called. "You'd better explain

matters to this fellow: his demands are even more unreasonable than yours are!"

"What's to explain?" Rusty grumbled. "I was minding my own business, just out taking a few mackerel on the hook, and all of a sudden my boat was swamped by a wave that came from nowhere, and . . . after that it got ridiculous."

"As to the wave," Oob spoke up, "I must admit it was careless of me. In my struggle to get my bope nodes aligned in the confines of that confounded trunk, I incidentally allowed a vram charge to build up in my framistron membranes. Naturally, I had to dump it before—but never mind—that particular ordeal is past. So I shifted it above the vram spectrum to the matter-energy band, and expelled it along a line of eiss. Failed to realize the effect it would have on a fluid mass, plus, of course, I didn't know you were nearby."

"What were you—or your trunk—doing aboard a square-rigged brig in the first place?" Rusty demanded.

"Oh, that was far from the first place," Oob corrected. "I—and 'my trunk' as you call it—had lain, ignored, in a junk yard in Duluth, then in a bazaar in Algeria, and finally in a warehouse in Hong Kong. Dreary years, those. Every so often some nosy parker would attempt to open the trunk—would have triggered an abrupt equalization of accumulated E-charge, you know. But I managed at last to shift the energies to a distantly related but nonmentational biomass—the rutabaga crop in Idaho—"

"I heard about the blight," Roger put in.

Oob waggled the upper portion of his lumpy anatomy in an approximation of a nod. "Pity and all that," he conceded. "But there was nothing for it, you see, or I'd have undergone yazz-transformation right there in the trunk." His shudder, though repressed, was unmistakable. "It was fortunate you dug up Red just then, shattering the yazz-paradigm."

"You're talking jargon again!" Roger charged.

"The technical terminology of Zarz-science is hardly

jargon, Roger," Oob reprimanded. "And when speaking of concepts unknown to your vocabulary, one has little choice but to employ the established terms."

"Swell," Rusty was muttering. "I lost my tackle and my catch because you had to molt or something. Not to mention the rutabagas. Never liked 'em myself, but I guess the farmers are hurting."

"Never mind," Oob counseled. "I've provided pots of Spanish gold which the affected agriculturists can dig up in their fields, and anyway, most of them shipped their produce in spite of the disease. Doesn't show, you know. And hardly affects your sort of folk at all."

"That's supposed to make it OK to dump me in the drink?" Rusty demanded.

"Clarence, Clarence," Oob gurgled in his lowest vocal register. "You've become tiresome. Go away. Go fishing." On the last word, Rusty was gone. Roger made an abortive lunge toward the spot where he'd been standing, but checked himself.

"Dammit, Oob, you can't just go around banishing people like that! Where'd you send Rusty? Get him back here right now, or I'll tell the Builder!"

"Don't care," Oob replied saucily. "He's aboard his Mako, as happy as a clam."

"That's fine, for Rusty, but what about *me*? I *have* to talk to the Builder!"

"Here she comes now," Oob pointed out.

Roger spun to see the six-year-old skipping along the beach, sending up puffs of dry sand with each bound. She came up to him, halted and stared at Oob.

"Who's *that*?" she exclaimed. "I don't remember building *that*!"

"You didn't, Cindy," Roger told the confused superbeing. "He's a Rhox—came from another Galaxy."

She looked at him. "What's *your* name?" she demanded.

"Hannibal," Roger replied promptly. "Hannibal Missouri."

"Its is *not*!" she stated indignantly. "It's 'Wodger'!"

"Yes, yes, I was only playing, dear," Roger assured the

tot. She took his hand. "Come on, Wodger," she urged. "Let's go play."

"Good idea," Roger agreed heartily. "But what about . . . ?"

"Never mind," the Builder dismissed the matter. "*That's* no fun!"

FALLEN ANGELS

Two refugees from one of the last remaining orbital space stations are trapped on the North American icecap, and only science fiction fans can rescue them! Here's an excerpt from *Fallen Angels*, the bestselling new novel by Larry Niven, Jerry Pournelle, and Michael Flynn.

* * *

She opened the door on the first knock and stood out of the way. The wind was whipping the ground snow in swirling circles. Some of it blew in the door as Bob entered. She slammed the door behind him. The snow on the floor decided to wait a while before melting. "Okay. You're here," she snapped. "There's no fire and no place to sit. The bed's the only warm place and you know it. I didn't know you were this hard up. And, by the way, I don't have any company, thanks for asking." If Bob couldn't figure out from that speech that she was pissed, he'd never win the prize as Mr. Perception.

"I am that hard up," he said, moving closer. "Let's get it on."

"Say what?" Bob had never been one for subtle technique, but this was pushing it. She tried to step back but his hands gripped her arms. They were cold as ice, even through the housecoat. "Bob!" He pulled her to him and buried his face in her hair.

"It's not what you think," he whispered. "We don't have time for this, worse luck."

"Bob!"

"No, just bear with me. Let's go to your bedroom. I don't want you to freeze."

He led her to the back of the house and she slid under the covers without inviting him in. He lay on top, still wearing his thick leather coat. Whatever he had in mind, she realized, it wasn't sex. Not with her housecoat, the comforter and his greatcoat playing chaperone.

He kissed her hard and was whispering hoarsely in her ear before she had a chance to react. "Angels down. A scoopship. It crashed."

"Angels?" Was he crazy?

He kissed her neck. "Not so loud. I don't think the 'danes are listening, but why take chances? Angels. Spacemen. *Peace* and *Freedom*."

She'd been away too long. She'd never heard spacemen called *Angels*. And— "Crashed?" She kept it to a whisper. "Where?"

"Just over the border in North Dakota. Near Mapleton."

"Great Ghu, Bob. That's on the Ice!"

He whispered, "Yeah. But they're not too far in."

"How do you know about it?"

He snuggled closer and kissed her on the neck again. Maybe sex made a great cover for his visit, but she didn't think he had to lay it on so thick. "We know."

"We?"

"The Worldcon's in Minneapolis-St. Paul this year—"

The World Science Fiction Convention. "I got the invitation, but I didn't dare go. If anyone saw me—"

"—And it was just getting started when the call came down from *Freedom*. Sherrine, they couldn't have picked a better time or place to crash their scoopship. That's why I came to you. Your grandparents live near the crash site."

She wondered if there was a good time for crashing scoopships. "So?"

"We're going to rescue them."

"We? Who's we?"

"The Con Committee, some of the fans—"

"But why tell me, Bob? I'm fafiated. It's been years since I've dared associate with fen."

Too many years, she thought. She had discovered science fiction in childhood, at her neighborhood branch library. She still remembered that first book: *Star Man's Son*, by Andre Norton. Fors had been persecuted because he was different; but he nurtured a secret, a mutant power. Just the sort of hero to appeal to an ugly-duckling little girl who would not act like other little girls.

SF had opened a whole new world to her. A galaxy, a

universe of new worlds. While the other little girls had played with Barbie dolls, Sherrine played with Lummox and Poddy and Arkady and Susan Calvin. While they went to the malls, she went to Trantor and the Witch World. While they wondered what Look was In, she wondered about resource depletion and nuclear war and genetic engineering. Escape literature, they called it. She missed it terribly.

"There is always one moment in childhood," Graham Greene had written in *The Power and the Glory*, "when the door opens and lets the future in." For some people, that door never closed. She thought that Peter Pan had had the right idea all along.

"Why tell *you*? Sherrine, we want you with us. Your grandparents live near the crash site. They've got all sorts of gear we can borrow for the rescue."

"Me?" A tiny trickle of electric current ran up her spine. But . . . *Nah.* "Bob, I don't dare. If my bosses thought I was associating with fen, I'd lose my job."

He grinned. "Yeah. Me, too." And she saw that he had never considered that she might not go.

'Tis a Proud and Lonely Thing to Be a Fan, they used to say, laughing. It had become a *very* lonely thing. The Establishment had always been hard on science fiction. The government-funded Arts Councils would pass out tax money to write obscure poetry for "little" magazines, but not to write speculative fiction. "Sci-fi isn't literature." *That* wasn't censorship.

Perversely, people went on buying science fiction without grants. Writers even got rich without government funding. *They couldn't kill us that way!*

Then the Luddites and the Greens had come to power. She had watched science fiction books slowly disappear from the library shelves, beginning with the children's departments. (That wasn't censorship either. Libraries couldn't buy *every* book, now could they? So they bought "realistic" children's books funded by the National Endowment for the Arts, books about death and divorce, and really important things like being overweight or fitting in with the right school crowd.)

Then came paper shortages, and paper allocations. The science fiction sections in the chain stores grew smaller. ("You can't expect us to stock books that aren't selling." And they can't sell if you don't stock them.)

Fantasy wasn't hurt so bad. Fantasy was about wizards

and elves, and being kind to the Earth, and harmony with nature, all things the Greens loved. But science fiction was about science.

Science fiction wasn't exactly outlawed. There was still Freedom of Speech; still a Bill of Rights, even if it wasn't taught much in the schools—even if most kids graduated unable to read well enough to understand it. But a person could get into a lot of unofficial trouble for reading SF or for associating with known fen. She could lose her job, say. Not through government persecution—of course not—but because of "reduction in work force" or "poor job performance" or "uncooperative attitude" or "politically incorrect" or a hundred other phrases. And if the neighbors shunned her, and tradesmen wouldn't deal with her, and stores wouldn't give her credit, who could blame them? Science fiction involved science; and science was a conspiracy to pollute the environment, "to bring back technology."

Damn right! she thought savagely. We do conspire to bring back technology. Some of us are crazy enough to think that there are alternatives to freezing in the dark. *And some of us are even crazy enough to try to rescue marooned spacemen before they freeze, or disappear into protective custody.*

Which could be dangerous. The government might declare you mentally ill, and help you.

She shuddered at that thought. She pushed and rolled Bob aside. She sat up and pulled the comforter up tight around herself. "Do you know what it was that attracted me to science fiction?"

He raised himself on one elbow, blinked at her change of subject, and looked quickly around the room, as if suspecting bugs. "No, what?"

"Not Fandom. I was reading the true quill long before I knew about Fandom and cons and such. No, it was the feeling of hope."

"Hope?"

"Even in the most depressing dystopia, there's still the notion that the future is something we build. It doesn't just happen. You can't predict the future, but you can invent it. Build it. That is a hopeful idea, even when the building collapses."

Bob was silent for a moment. Then he nodded. "Yeah. Nobody's building the future anymore. 'We live in an Age of Limited Choices.' " He quoted the government line without cracking a smile. "Hell, you don't *take* choices off a list. You *make* choices and *add* them to the list. Speaking of which, have you made your choice?"

That electric tickle . . . "Are they even alive?"

"So far. I understand it was some kind of miracle that they landed at all. They're unconscious, but not hurt bad. They're hooked up to some sort of magical medical widgets and the Angels overhead are monitoring. But if we don't get them out soon, they'll freeze to death."

She bit her lip. "And you think we can reach them in time?"

Bob shrugged.

"You want me to risk my life on the Ice, defy the government and probably lose my job in a crazy, amateur effort to rescue two spacemen who might easily be dead by the time we reach them."

He scratched his beard. "Is that quixotic, or what?"

"Quixotic. Give me four minutes."

POUL ANDERSON

Poul Anderson is one of the most honored authors of our time. He has won seven Hugo Awards, three Nebula Awards, and the Gandalf Award for Achievement in Fantasy, among others. His most popular series include the Polesotechnic League/Terran Empire tales and the Time Patrol series. Here are fine books by Poul Anderson available through Baen Books:

THE GAME OF EMPIRE

A *new* novel in Anderson's Polesotechnic League/Terran Empire series! Diana Crowfeather, daughter of Dominic Flandry, proves well capable of following in his adventurous footsteps.

FIRE TIME

Once every thousand years the Deathstar orbits close enough to burn the surface of the planet Ishtar. This is known as the Fire Time, and it is then that the barbarians flee the scorched lands, bringing havoc to the civilized South.

AFTER DOOMSDAY

Earth has been destroyed, and the handful of surviving humans must discover which of three alien races is guilty before it's too late.

THE BROKEN SWORD

It is a time when Christos is new to the land, and the Elder Gods and the Elven Folk still hold sway. In 11th-century Scandinavia Christianity is beginning to replace the old religion, but the Old Gods still have power, and men are still oppressed by the folk of the Faerie. "Pure gold!"—Anthony Boucher.

THE DEVIL'S GAME

Seven people gather on a remote island, each competing for a share in a tax-free fortune. The "contest" is ostensibly sponsored by an eccentric billionaire—but the rich man is in league with an alien masquerading as a demon . . . or is it the other way around?

THE ENEMY STARS

Includes for the first time the sequel to "The Enemy Stars"; "The Ways of Love." Fast-paced adventure science fiction from a master.

SEVEN CONQUESTS

Seven brilliant tales examine the many ways human beings—most dangerous and violent of all species—react under the stress of conflict and high technology.

STRANGERS FROM EARTH

Classic Anderson: A stranded alien spends his life masquerading as a human, hoping to contact his own world. He succeeds, but the result is a bigger problem than before . . . What if our reality is a fiction? Nothing more than a book written by a very powerful Author? Two philosophers stumble on the truth and try to puzzle out the Ending . . .

ROBERT A. HEINLEIN

"Heinlein knows more about blending provocative scientific thinking with strong human stories than any dozen other contemporary science fiction writers."
—*Chicago Sun-Times*

"Robert A. Heinlein wears imagination as though it were his private suit of clothes. What makes his work so rich is that he combines his lively, creative sense with an approach that is at once literate, informed, and exciting."
—*New York Times*

Seven of Robert A. Heinlein's best-loved titles are now available in superbly packaged new Baen editions, with series-look covers by artist John Melo. Collect them all by sending in the order form below: